THE GATES OF HELL

THE GATES OF HELL

A Mystery of Alexander the Great

PAUL DOHERTY

CARROLL & GRAF PUBLISHERS
New York

Carroll & Graf Publishers
An imprint of Avalon Publishing Group, Inc.
161 William Street
16th Floor
NY 10038–2607
www.carrollandgraf.com

First published in the UK by Constable,
an imprint of Constable & Robinson Ltd 2003

First Carroll & Graf edition 2003

ISBN 0–7867–1157–4

Printed and bound in the EU

This book is dedicated to Sarah and Laura Murray, beloved students of Trinity Catholic High School, Woodford Green, Essex

"Μετα δε ταυτα του Αλεξανδρου φιλοτιμουμενου τω την ιδιαν."

"Then Alexander set his heart on showing his father his prowess."

Diodorus Siculus, *Library of History*,
Book 16, Chapter 86

THE GREEK WORLD, 334 BC

BLACK SEA

ILLYRIA

MACEDONIA

THRACE

Pella

THASOS

SAMOTHRACE

SEA OF MARMARA

Sestos Lampascus

Elaeus   Zeleia Granicus Dascylium

Troy Abydos

HELLESPONTINE

THESSALY   TROAD   PHRYGIA

AEGEAN SEA

ASIA MINOR

Chaeronea   EUBOEA

LESBOS

Delphi

Thebes   CHIOS

Sardis

Olympia   Corinth   Athens

Argos   SAMOS   Ephesus

Sparta   Miletus

Halicarnassus

MEDITERRANEAN

RHODES

CRETE

SEA

N

Historical Personages Mentioned in the Text

The House of Macedon

PHILIP   King of Macedon until his assassination in 336 BC. Father of Alexander.

OLYMPIAS OF MOLOSSUS   (Born Myrtale): Philip's queen, Alexander's mother. Co-Regent of Macedon during Alexander's conquest of Persia.

ALEXANDER   Son of Philip and Olympias.

EURYDICE   Philip's wife after he divorced Olympias: she was niece of Philip's favourite general, Attalus. Eurydice, her baby son and Attalus were all executed after Philip's death.

ARRIDHAEUS   Philip's son by one of his concubines, poisoned by Olympias. He survived but remained brain-damaged for the rest of his life.

The Court of Macedon

BLACK CLEITUS   Brother to Alexander's nurse: Alexander's personal bodyguard.

HEPHAESTION   Alexander's boon companion.

ARISTANDER   Court necromancer, adviser to Alexander.

ARISTOTLE   Alexander's tutor in the Groves of Mieza: Greek Philosopher.

PAUSANIAS   Philip of Macedon's assassin.

DEMADES   Engineer and creator of Macedon's siege equipment.

Alexander's Generals and Admirals

PARMENIO, PTOLEMY, SELEUCUS, AMYNTAS, ANTIPATER   (left as Co-Regent in Macedon), NEARCHUS, NICANOR.

The Court of Persia

DARIUS III   King of Kings.

MEMNON OF RHODES   A Greek mercenary in the pay of Persia, one of the few generals to defeat Macedonian troops.

ORONTOBATES   Governor of Halicarnassus.

EPHIALTES   Greek renegade: a general of mercenaries in the pay of Persia.

CYRUS AND XERXES   Former great emperors of Persia.

The Writers

AESCHYLUS, ARISTOPHANES, EURIPIDES, SOPHOCLES: Greek playwrights.

HOMER Reputed author of the two great poems the *Iliad* and the *Odyssey*.

DEMOSTHENES Athenian demagogue, ardent opponent of Alexander.

HIPPOCRATES OF COS Greek physician and writer, regarded as the father of medicine.

The Mythology of Greece

ZEUS Father god.

HERA His wife.

APOLLO God of light.

ARTEMIS Goddess of the hunt.

ATHENA Goddess of war.

HERCULES Greek man-god. One of Alexander's reputed ancestors.

AESCULAPIUS Man-god, a great healer.

OEDIPUS Tragic hero, King of Thebes.

DIONYSIUS God of wine.

EYNALIUS Ancient Macedonian god of war.

The Trojan War

PRIAM King of Troy.

HECTOR Priam's son and Troy's great general.

PARIS Hector's brother, whose abduction of the fair-faced Helen led to the Trojan War.

AGAMEMNON Leader of the Greeks in the Trojan War.

ACHILLES Greek hero and warrior in the Trojan War, the slayer of Hector. He was eventually killed by an arrow fired by Paris. Alexander regarded him as a direct ancestor.

PATROCLUS Achilles' lover: his death in the Trojan War led to Achilles' homicidal rage.

The Court of Halicarnassus

MAUSOLUS Former ruler of Halicarnassus.

PIXADORUS Former Prince of Halicarnassus.

ADA Rightful Queen of Halicarnassus, driven into exile by Pixadorus.

Preface

I n 336 BC, Philip of Macedon died swiftly at his moment of
supreme glory, assassinated by a former lover Pausanias as he
was about to receive the plaudits of his client states. All of Greece
and Persia quietly rejoiced – the growing supremacy of Macedon
was to be curbed. The finger of suspicion for Philip's murder was
pointed directly at his scheming wife, the witch-queen Olympias,
and their only son, the young Alexander. Macedon's enemies
quietly relished the prospect of a civil war which would destroy
Alexander and his mother and end any threat to the Greek states as
well as the sprawling Persian empire of Darius III. Alexander soon
proved them wrong. A consummate actor, a sly politician, a
ruthless fighter and a brilliant general, in two years Alexander
crushed all opposition at home, won over the wild tribes to the
north and had himself proclaimed Captain-General of Greece. He
was to be the leader of a fresh crusade against Persia, fitting
punishment for the attacks on Greece by Cyrus the Great and
his successors a century earlier.

Alexander proved, by the total destruction of the great city of
Thebes, the home of Oedipus, that he would brook no opposition.
He then turned east. He proclaimed himself a Greek ready to
avenge Greek wrongs. Secretly, Alexander wished to satisfy his lust
for conquest, to march to the edge of the world, to prove he was a
better man than Philip, to win the vindication of the gods as well as
to confirm the whisperings of his mother – that his conception was
due to divine intervention.

In the spring of 334 BC, Alexander gathered his army at Sestos
while, across the straits, Darius III, his sinister spymaster the Lord
Mithra and his generals plotted the utter destruction of this

Macedonian upstart. Alexander, however, was committed to total war. He crossed to Asia and shattered the Persian army at the battle of the Granicus. He then marched south, capturing vital cities such as Ephesus, but the great prize was Halicarnassus (modern Bodrum), the sprawling city with its deep harbour on the Aegean.

Alexander wanted to take Halicarnassus, not only because of its strategic importance or to demonstrate his skill as the "Great Besieger of Cities": Halicarnassus also had a link with his own dark past, in particular his entangled relationship with his dead father Philip. Alexander's enemies knew Halicarassus would attract the Macedonian, and hoped that he would shatter his armies against its formidable fortifications. The three commanders there, Alexander's old enemy Memnon of Rhodes together with the Persian Orontobates and the Greek renegade Ephialtes, believed that this time they would be able to trap the "Macedonian Wolf" and bring his dreams of conquest to nothing. Halicarnassus was fortified, the trap prepared, and Alexander brought his troops up for one of the most dramatic confrontations in ancient history . . .

Please note The secret code used here is that of Polybius as described in Chapter X of his *Histories* (see the author's note at the end).

Prologue

"Memnon had already been appointed by Darius, Controller of Lower Asia and Commander of the whole fleet."

Arrian, *The Campaigns of Alexander*,
Book I, Chapter 20

The road from Mylasa to Halicarnassus had been cleared for the passage of the Great One, the personal emissary of Darius, King of Kings. The Lord Mithra, the Keeper of the King's Secrets, a man who worked in the shadows, had been despatched by Darius from Persepolis on a matter of great importance. Lord Mithra, hooded and cloaked in black, his face covered by a red–gold mask, hastened to do his master's business. Surrounded by the Cowled Ones, his personal guard, he thundered along the road towards the Triple Gate, the yawning, cavernous entrance to the sprawling sea port of Halicarnassus. Outriders had gone before him: these were dressed in black robes, purple sashes round their waists, their faces half hidden by silver–white masks pulled up as much to protect their mouths from the dust as to conceal their identities. Each carried Darius's cartouche, his personal seal, on a leather strap round his wrist. They swept along the highway like the Angels of Death. They did not have to shout or argue: their very presence cleared the road. Travellers, fearful of these grim fighters on their dark horses with black and silver saddlecloths and harness of the same colour, leapt quickly aside. Some even prostrated themselves, pressing their foreheads against the ground and keeping their thoughts to themselves. No one dared raise a protest, not in these dangerous times. The Macedonian Wolf, Alexander, had shattered

1

the Great King's army at the Granicus in a welter of blood, and marched south-west, capturing the great cities of Ephesus and Miletus.

The travellers, naturally, talked among themselves in the post houses, taverns and resting-places set up at the many oases along the King's highway. They talked of the Persian Lion having to challenge the Macedonian Wolf, but such speech was more the result of heavy wine than military strategy. Alexander's armies were on the march, sweeping along the coastline of the Aegean Sea, capturing one port after another with the ease of a young maid plucking ripe apples in a richly packed orchard. Everyone suspected what Alexander would do next: the merchants were men of peace and money, but they kept a sharp eye on the men of war.

Alexander, so gossip had it, was in the mountains to the north-west: he was being entertained by the plump, white-skinned Ada, she with henna-dyed hair, who had been Queen of Caria and ruler of its greatest city Halicarnassus. She had, however, been driven out by her own kinsmen, Pixadorus and the Persian satrap Oronto-bates, and forced to skulk in a mountainous, owl-haunted place, in a mere shadow of her former glory. Alexander, that cunning wolf, had gone a-courting, or so the merchants said. He'd presented himself at Queen Ada's petty court, kissed her bejewelled fingers and promised to restore her to her rightful throne. Ada had blinked black-kohled eyes, fingers fluttering, glancing coyly at this golden-haired conqueror, not yet in his twenty-fifth year, who was striking like a fiery arrow at the heart of Darius's empire.

Oh yes, the merchants knew the story well. Ada had cooed and simpered before making the most surprising announcement: Alex-ander was her adopted son. He would seek vengeance for her and the removal of her enemies from the ancient kingdom of Caria. Alexander, of course, had accepted this. The news had spread. Ada might look plump and vapid but her fat, heavily painted face was only a mask for a brain as sharp and agile as a flesher's knife. She and Alexander exchanged loving messages in their new-found relation-ship. Queen Ada sent the Macedonian meats and delicacies every day, even offering him cooks and bakers, masters of their craft. Alexander may have been laughing at her, but he kept this well hidden. He refused the delicacies and sent the cooks home, adding politely: "He needed none of them, for the best preparation for breakfast was a night march and for his lunch a sparing breakfast." The reply had delighted Ada, and Alexander was true to his word. He struck immediately south, aiming like Zeus's thunderbolt for the great fortress of Halicarnassus. No wonder Darius was disturbed and the Lord Mithra and his cortège thundered under sun-filled blue skies towards the soaring walls and fortified battlements of Halicarnassus. The merchants made their own decisions. They would sell their produce and leave as quickly as they could, before the Macedonian arrived and ringed Halicarnassus in a band of steel.

Lord Mithra, as he passed these merchants, stared malevolently through the slits of his mask. His bald head and cheeks were drenched in sweat: his thighs and legs ached from the impetuous ride but, even on his headlong journey, he had recognized the signs. People were fleeing, leaving their farms and villages, going up into the mountains to wait until the men of war had had their day. Merchants were loading their carts, muttering excuses and going further inland. To a certain extent Lord Mithra was pleased by this: some apparently mistrusted the Macedonian and were waiting to see the outcome of this bloody business before they decided which side to support. Lord Mithra raised his fly whisk, flailing it gently around, driving away the myriad flies which had bedevilled his journey. The captain of his escort slowed down. Outriders came galloping back: all was safe while the road ahead was clear. They had watered their horses scarcely an hour ago, and Lord Mithra hoped to be in the shade of Halicarnassus before the full brunt of the midday heat made itself felt. He would have loved to push back his hood, pull down the mask and wet his face, yet his sombre disguise was worth more than a hundred Scythian mercenaries.

"Lead men by love," he had whispered to his master Darius, "if you can, and if not, by terror. It is unfortunate, my lord, that most of them must be ruled by terror."

Mithra smiled wryly at his own motto. Terror would not defeat Alexander of Macedon, nor his phalanx men with their long sarissas, iron discipline and brilliant war stratagems. For that Darius and Lord Mithra needed someone else.

3

"My lord." The captain of his guard edged his horse forward, pulling down his mask. "The horses are strong enough. Halicarnassus is only two miles more."

Lord Mithra raised his fly whisk. The captain shouted an order: the escort broke into a canter and then into a furious gallop. The black-garbed riders pounded along the great white dusty road. On either side, the lush countryside with its well-watered copses, fields, meadows and carpet of multicoloured wild flowers gave way to harsher, drier terrain. Lord Mithra noticed this, and smiled his thanks. This was where Alexander would have to set his camp, bring up his siege weapons. And what shade was here? What trees, springs and wells? Let him camp here, Mithra thought, burn under the strengthening sun. He heard further shouts and glanced up. The walls of Halicarnassus came into sight: its soaring citadels, narrow windows, crenellated battlements and, dominating them all, the huge fortified tower which commanded the approach to the Triple Gate. This was now thrown open, its Greek mercenary guards flat against the wall, spears brought up in salute. Lord Mithra and his escort thundered into the great fortified enclosure beyond the walls, where the garrison had its barracks and supply houses. Here the outriders paused. Lord Mithra made his way to the front: a further iron-studded gate was opened and they entered the city proper.

Officers went ahead to escort them to the Governor's palace. Mithra gazed around. Memnon, Darius's Commander-in-Chief, had been busy. Already certain houses were razed, cleared away, while the thoroughfares were packed with carts bringing up munitions, catapults, mangonels and siege towers: these would be taken onto the fighting ground and quickly assembled. Soldiers were being drilled, fresh latrines dug, old springs opened. Lord Mithra nodded appreciatively. Memnon knew his trade, fighting and killing. If Alexander came here he might well be lured into the trap. Mithra's black-garbed escort attracted many glances, but everyone had been warned beforehand and no one stopped to stare. They lowered their heads or turned their backs. The King of Kings' emissary, his Master of Secrets, was not to be gazed at like some travelling fair or troupe of actors.

4

They crossed the suburbs of the city, into its heart, with broad avenues lined by cypress and plane trees, narrow lanes running between white-painted houses. They passed small temples with their porticoed and pillared entrances, across busy, noisy market-places. The air was bitter-sweet with the smell of fruit and meat, perfume and the pervasive odour of olive oil. Mithra studied all this most carefully. Marketplaces were the lifeblood of any city, and it seemed to be business as usual in Halicarnassus. He sensed no panic or hysteria; was this good or bad? Were the citizens of Halicarnassus confident that, whatever happened, they would survive? Since he had landed at Abydos some five months earlier, Alexander had not sacked one city. Instead he had restored Greek rule, allowing the Democrats to take power. Mithra ground his teeth. Did the wine-sellers and tent-makers, the leather merchants and perfume-sellers of Halicarnassus, realize this? That whatever happened, if Alexander were defeated, then it was life as normal, and if he won, life might get even better? Mithra tugged savagely at his reins, and his horse whinnied, throwing its head back.

"The city is prosperous," his captain whispered. "No shortage of food or water."

Mithra ignored him. They were now climbing a small hill towards the palace: Mithra's attention was drawn by the great Mausoleum, the funeral monument of Mausolus, once ruler of this city, brother of the exiled Queen Ada. Mithra was fascinated by the awesome splendour of this gorgeous homage to the dead. It soared at least four hundred feet into the sky, a craftsman's delight of marble, gold and silver. On the top of the pillar was a temple-like structure, nine pillars on each side, a perfect square and, rising from that, a twenty-four-step pyramid surmounted by a huge marble carving of a chariot and four horses.

"A great wonder," the captain whispered.

This time Mithra nodded. Halicarnassus had once been the capital of the independent kingdom of Caria: Mausolus was its last great ruler. Darius would have loved to have torn such a monument down as an affront to his own majesty, but Mithra and the other magi had urged caution. The Master of the King's Secrets narrowed his eyes. Perhaps, if a miracle occurred and Alexander did break into the city, secret orders should be left for the Mausoleum's destruction. But there again, how could you burn marble and gold?

"My lord, we are nearly there."

The broad avenue was now quieter. Before them gleamed the white walls of the Governor's palace, its gates thrown open. A mixed guard of hoplites, in full dress armour, mingled with the gorgeous apparel of the Persian Immortals, the backbone of Darius's army. These soldiers now formed a guard of honour. The Persians went down on one knee, the Greeks removed their plumed helmets and stood heads bowed. Mithra, staring ahead of him, entered the green, pleasant coolness of the palace gardens, up pebbled paths into a small courtyard. Grooms came running out. One fell to his hands and knees beside Mithra's horse. The Master of the King's Secrets used him to dismount. Other servants came up bearing goblets of wine chilled with sherbet, small clusters of flowers and bowls of fruits. Mithra ignored the flowers: he removed his mask, then grasped and pressed the chilled cup against his cheek. He poured a small libation into the dust and thrust it at his captain, who tasted it and handed it back. Only then did Mithra drink slowly, wetting his lips, cleansing his mouth and throat. He peered into the shadows thrown by the columns of the portico: a man, dressed in a white tunic, hands hanging at his sides, was standing in the doorway. Mithra pushed his way through, only now pulling back his cowl. His bald-headed, craggy-faced host came forward, one hand extended. Mithra grabbed this.

"Memnon of Rhodes," Mithra whispered. "Our master, the King of Kings, sends his greetings and a mark of great honour."

The dark, hard eyes of the Greek mercenary betrayed no emotion. "How is my wife Barsine and our children?"

"They are close to the great king's heart. He treats them as he does his own family."

Memnon allowed a slight smile. "My lord, the others are waiting."

"The prisoner?" Mithra demanded. "The spy?"

"He is dying."

"Then we must see him first."

Memnon shrugged and walked along the portico. Mithra and

two of his escort followed. They crossed a cobbled yard into an outhouse where wine and oil was stored. The air was sweet, though Mithra detected something else: fire, blood and burning flesh. Memnon went down steps at the far side of the room and hammered on the heavy oaken door, which swung open. Guards in leather armour stood along the weakly lit passageway which ran past storerooms. They went deeper into the darkness. The air grew cold and stale. They passed cells, dungeons: eyes peered out from small grilles high in the doors. They turned a corner, and Mithra covered his mouth and nose at the offensive stench. The passageway debouched into a small circular chamber with a vaulted stone roof. The walls were wet and mildewed; they gleamed in the light of oil lamps set in niches as well as the glow of the great brazier in the centre. Figures, dark as shadows, moved around, men dressed in leather caps and aprons. To one side was a table, on which lay the cruel instruments of torture: pincers and branding irons in pools of blood. A man, fastened with chains, hung in a small enclave, his naked body slack, head down: black hair, matted with sweat and blood, covered his face. Memnon, gently as a mother would with a child, went across and tipped the man's head back. The prisoner's face was stained with dried blood. One eye was missing, nothing left but a glaring socket; the other eye was half closed; his nose had been broken and pushed back, no more than a bloody pulp. Dry blood streaked his moustache and beard.

"Bring a torch, Cerberus!"

The leather-garbed master gaoler plucked a cresset torch from the wall and came over.

"Cerberus?" Mithra queried.

"Master gaoler of Halicarnassus," Memnon explained. "Skilled in torture."

"How skilled?" Mithra demanded. "Has the prisoner talked?" He stared at the gaoler, a small, squat man with the face of an ugly mastiff, his head bald, apart from tufts of hair just above each ear.

"He can talk no longer," the gaoler replied, staring insolently back.

Mithra would have liked to strike him across his fat, sweaty cheeks with his fly whisk, but bit back his anger. "He is dying?"

7

Cerberus refused to be overawed. "I had my orders, sir: to make the man talk, and talk he did, for a while."

"And what did he say?" Mithra demanded. "What's his name? What did he say?"

"He gave no name, but described himself as the songster from Ephesus."

"And what songs did he sing?"

"That he's not a songster from Ephesus," the gaoler replied cheekily.

Mithra raised his fly whisk and tapped the man gently on the side of his neck. Cerberus's eyes, almost hidden in rolls of fat, shifted towards Memnon. "I have done good service, my lord."

"He has. He has," Memnon agreed. "The man's no songster from Ephesus," Memnon continued, "but one of Alexander's companions: a courier, a spy."

"And what did he tell us?"

"That Alexander is marching."

"I know that."

"That he's bringing his siege machinery in by sea."

"I know that."

"That he needs to find a port close to Halicarnassus." Memnon's voice grated.

"I know that too." Mithra held the gaoler's gaze and pressed the fly whisk a little harder.

"Tell him!" Memnon ordered. "Tell him what you learnt!"

Cerberus took a step back. "The Macedonian has the Pythian Manuscript."

Mithra lowered the fly whisk. "And what else?" He glared at Memnon.

"The Macedonian has a legion of spies in the city!" Memnon paused as the prisoner groaned.

"Did he give names?" Mithra demanded.

"A few," Cerberus replied. "Democrats, artisans, merchants. They have all been rounded up, or most of them."

"They'll be killed?" Mithra demanded.

"They have been," Memnon assured him.

Mithra felt the rage boil inside him. "He has no eye and he's lost his tongue." He stepped closer. Throwing the fly whisk at the gaoler, Mithra withdrew the dagger from beneath his cloak, lifted the head of the songster of Ephesus, and neatly slit his throat from ear to ear. The prisoner gasped and gurgled, body shuddering in a clank of chains. Mithra stepped back and, wiping the blood on Cerberus's apron, re-sheathed his knife and snatched back the fly whisk: spinning on his heel, he left the chamber.

Outside in the courtyard Mithra paced up and down, beating the whisk against his riding boot. Memnon stood, arms crossed.

"So, they have it!" Mithra cursed. He stared full at Memnon. The Greek mercenary studied the cadaverous, skeleton-like face of this most sinister of courtiers. Hooded eyes glittered in a narrow, furrowed face, thin-nosed with a mere slit for a mouth. Mithra's head and face were closely shaved and oiled, his rage apparent by the red spots of anger high on his sunken cheeks.

"They may have it," Memnon assured him, "but can they understand it?"

Mithra sighed. He stared up at one of the cornices of the building. The sculptor had carved the emblem of the Persian court, the insignia of their god Ahura-Mazda, the All-Seeing Eye borne aloft on the feathery wings of a golden eagle. Darius wondered if their god was with them, or had he withdrawn his protection from Persia? Had he retreated into the high courts of heaven and allowed the God of Darkness, the Accuser, the Assassin, Ahirman, to prowl his empire and do his worst? Mithra chewed on his lip. In truth, Mithra didn't believe in any gods, be it the gaggle of Greek deities and their sexual exploits or the hidden splendour of the Divine Flame burning before Ahura-Mazda's shrine in Persepolis. Alexander would be defeated, not by the intervention of the gods, but by ruthless cunning and blood-soaked ferocity.

"Our master sends his greetings, Memnon of Rhodes!"

The mercenary bowed imperceptibly. Mithra fished into his wallet and took out a scroll. He tossed it to Memnon, who caught it deftly.

"You are now Governor of Lower Asia," Mithra murmured. "Commander-in-Chief of all Persian forces on land and sea."

Memnon unrolled the parchment and glanced up, eyes glowing with pride.

"The King of Kings has great confidence in you," Mithra continued. "If your advice had been followed, the battle of Granicus would not have been fought. Alexander would not have achieved his victory. The King of Kings has confirmed your execution of the satrap who led his forces into such disgraceful defeat. There must be no repetition . . ."

"There will be no repetition, but Alexander has the Pythian Manuscript." Memnon rolled up the parchment and tucked it into the cord round his waist. "The others are waiting," he declared. "We have business to discuss."

"And the other matter?"

"In the second hour after noon," Memnon replied. "I will meet him by myself."

They went into the palace, along silent corridors lined with guards, the polished cedarwood floor gleaming bright, the air fragrant with the heavy scent from the flower baskets. They reached the far end of the palace, facing east. Mithra's escort, already guarding the cedarwood doors, swung them open, and Mithra swept into the andron, the men's room, a long, low-ceilinged chamber with couches and tables, its walls bare of any ornaments except for a frieze depicting Apollo in his chariot.

The two men already there rose as they made their entrance. The first was Orontobates, Governor of Halicarnassus. He was dressed in a gorgeous cloak of glory over a white tunic pushed into purple, gold-edged pantaloons, soft buskins on his feet: his oily ringed hair hung down to his shoulders. He had taken off his round, cylindrical cap with its tassels of office, which lay on a small table before him. A small, thickset man with the olive skin and dark soulful eyes of a Mede, Orontobates had a passing resemblance to his distant kinsman Darius, King of Kings: a likeness he enhanced by constantly stroking his luxuriant moustache and beard drenched in a costly perfume. Mithra showed Darius's cartouche; Orontobates knelt and kissed it, murmuring a quiet prayer that his master would always be protected by the Sacred Flame. He rose and gestured forward his companion, the blond-haired, ruddy-faced

10

Ephialtes of Thebes. Again the introductions were made. Mithra was fascinated by Ephialtes, a tall, gangly man with piercing blue eyes, strange colouring and a warrior's face. At first Mithra thought the red flush was due to wine, but Ephialtes was steady on his feet, clear-eyed, his voice clipped. Like all Greeks he gave the most perfunctory bow, but when Memnon coughed noisily, he knelt down and kissed the royal seal. Pleasantries were exchanged, then Memnon guided each to a couch. Servants brought in dark Carian wine, baskets of fruit, freshly baked bread and cheese. Scented water was poured for Mithra to wash his hands and face. He flung the napkin at a page, took off his black robe and threw it on the floor, then made himself comfortable on the couch. Memnon was whispering to Ephialtes. He broke off, lifted his goblet and toasted Mithra.

"So, the Macedonian comes on." Mithra drank deeply. "When will he arrive here?"

"He's been visiting that fat bitch Ada in her mountain fortress," Memnon replied. "He'll come through the passes and advance along the coastline to Halicarnassus."

"What are your preparations?"

Mamnon gestured at the maps piled next to his table. "To take this city, Alexander will need siege equipment. He will have to bring this by sea."

"But he has no ports," Orontobates declared.

"Precisely." Memnon grinned. "He has a choice of fighting for Myndus to the west or this harbour. Both are protected by the Persian fleet, so he'll have to land his siege machines somewhere and bring them along by cart. That's going to take time and be expensive."

Memnon swung his legs off the couch. He cleared his table and, using pieces of bread, made a makeshift map. "Halicarnassus is a city and a port. On the south side it is protected by the Aegean, controlled by the Persian navy. Alexander has dismissed his fleet, only a few squadrons remain. The rest of the city –" Memnon shrugged "– is protected by soaring fortifications and rocky ground. In turn, the walls are defended by towers and small castles."

"Are they impregnable?" Mithra demanded.

11

"They're thick enough to withstand the most violent assault."

"And what else?" Mithra asked, his words cutting through the scented air like the lash of a whip.

"Our engineers are already digging a great ditch around the walls, some twenty feet wide and ten feet deep."

"Good! Good!" Mithra murmured. "And what else?"

"You've seen the land around the city," Memnon explained. "Harsh and dry. Very little grass, almost no shade. No springs or wells. Now this stretches for about five miles on every side. Alexander's front line will be a mile from the city walls, his camp behind that." Memnon shrugged. "The further you travel, of course, the more fertile and arable it becomes. A number of farmhouses and wealthy mansions lie to the east. Alexander will take one of these over as his headquarters."

"So." Mithra sipped at his wine. "The Macedonian will come here. He can't attack by sea. The ditch, not to mention the terrain, will prevent his engineers from mining the walls. He'll have difficulty bringing his siege machinery up. If he does, the Macedonian will have few supplies. His camp will be exposed to the elements and the sun is getting hotter."

"Yes, you are well prepared."

"If Alexander appeared now," Memnon assured him, "we would be able to lock the gates and let him starve."

"If that could only happen!" Ephialtes pulled himself up on his couch, blue eyes sparkling with excitement.

"If that could only happen," Mithra mimicked. "General Ephialtes, do you think you will win a victory?"

"I know we will." The Theban found it difficult to keep still. He sat on the edge of his couch and leaned forward, pushing a lock of blond hair from his forehead. "Tell the King of Kings we will fight to the death."

"You have no choice," Mithra smiled. "You are from Thebes, General Ephialtes. Alexander wants your life. He has vowed that if you fall into his hands, you'll hang for days on a cross."

"And if I take him," Ephialtes retorted, "the same fate awaits! I have a blood feud with Alexander of Macedon. Thebes was utterly destroyed." His voice became thick with emotion. "My wife, family, kinsmen, all put to the sword." His glance never wavered. "Do not doubt me, Lord Mithra. I have fled my country. I have eaten your bread and salt and taken your gold. I dress in your silks, wear armour from your stores. Nevertheless, if you turned me out into the road in my loincloth, I would still fight Alexander of Macedon!"

"I can vouch for that." Orontobates spoke up, his voice rich and cultured.

Mithra shifted his gaze. Orontobates was not what he looked. He acted the role of a plump, luxury-loving courtier but he had seen good service against the Scythians; a superb general, a wily tactician, Orontobates would not give up his city lightly. Mithra turned to Memnon and smiled thinly.

"I am pleased," he whispered. "You three are as one. The Lord Darius was anxious about this."

"We are as one," Memnon agreed: he had been lounging on his couch staring moodily into his wine cup as the others spoke.

"You seem worried." Mithra pressed his point. "Anxious?"

Memnon stared up at the dark, rich Lebanese rafters. "I have sent my beloved wife and children to the King of Kings' court. Like Ephialtes, I am in this to the death. I am Memnon of Rhodes. Alexander calls me a renegade, a traitor to the Greek cause. If I fall into his hands I will ask for no mercy because none will be shown. Halicarnassus is well fortified. I have the best mercenaries and some of the most elite brigades of Persia."

"And yet?" Mithra added testily.

"Alexander has a genius. He seems to have been touched by fortune. Nothing he puts his hand to ever fails."

"He has been lucky," Orontobates scoffed.

"Can you think of a better virtue for a general?" Memnon retorted. "He'll come padding here with his other wolves to sniff out our weaknesses."

"What weaknesses?" Orontobates demanded.

"He has the Pythian Manuscript!"

Orontobates nearly dropped his goblet: Ephialtes looked puzzled.

"Tell him." Mithra gestured at Memnon. "Tell Ephialtes what this is."

"Years ago –" Memnon sipped from the goblet "– Halicarnassus was the principal city of the kingdom of Caria, ruled by Mausolus whose tomb you can see outside. One of the great wonders of the world," he added sarcastically. "Mausolus died and went to his glory. A civil war broke out. Queen Ada, Mausolus's sister, was later driven from Halicarnassus and took refuge in her mountain fortress of Alinde. Now Mausolus was a great builder. He and his successor, Pixadorus, fortified the city as you see it now: strong walls, fortified gates, citadels, battlements: the man responsible for this was an architect, Pythias. Pythias was a genius, a brilliant mathematician but a sour, embittered man. He claimed Pixadorus, Mausolus's successor, had cheated him out of certain treasure. The king, of course, dismissed these accusations as nonsense. Pythias was a miser. Pixadorus became angry at the constant allegations and threatened to seize Pythias's wealth so the architect hid it some-where, probably in the city, and fled. Before he did, he wrote a secret cipher."

"The Pythian Manuscript?"

"The same one," Memnon agreed. "It's written in a code no one understands. According to legend, in this secret cipher Pythias revealed where he had hidden his treasure." He gestured at Orontobates. "You know this story?"

"True." The Persian Governor nodded mournfully. "We have had our fair share of treasure hunters digging here and there."

"More importantly," Memnon continued, "Pythias revealed a great secret. He claimed one section of the city wall was weaker than the rest. An intrinisic flaw, a terrible weakness any besieger of Halicarnassus could exploit."

"What sort of weakness?" Ephialtes demanded. "Surely it could be detected?"

"When I assumed the governership," Orontobates spoke up, "I took the legend seriously. I hired the best engineers. They could find no flaws. However, in their report, they intimated what the weakness could be." He picked up two incense sticks from the table and held them parallel. "Ephialtes, you're a general. You've besieged cities and supervised the construction of fortified walls?"

The Theban nodded.

"Now think," Orontobates continued. "When a wall is built, you first dig deep into the ground and sink foundations." He brought the two incense sticks closer together. "These foundations, with the ground on either side, form a strong vice on which the wall can be built. Yes?"

"Ah!" Ephialtes breathed out. "And you suspect . . . ?"

"In one section of the walls," Memnon continued, "the foundations may be weak, the ground flawed, the vice which holds the stone not so secure."

Mithra listened intently. The great king's scribes had studied this manuscript with little success. Darius had dismissed it as childish nonsense; Mithra disagreed. The Pythian Manuscript was the reason for his visit here.

"Continue!" Mithra refilled his cup.

"Pythias wrote his message in a cipher." Orontobates spread his hands. "On a sheet of pure vellum parchment, no more than a foot long, and sent it to Queen Ada. According to rumour, Ada hired the sharpest minds, the keenest mathematicians, to see if the cipher could be broken; it proved futile." Orontobates leaned over and picked up his own goblet. "The manuscript was dismissed, and no one paid much more attention to it. Queen Ada hid in her mountain fortress, muttering threats and complaints. The years passed. The Pythian Manuscript posed no danger until now. Alexander of Macedon has come snuggling up to Queen Ada, calling her 'Sweet Mother', and she responds by proclaiming him to be her darling adopted son."

"And the Pythian Manuscript has been given to him?"

"Yes," Memnon agreed. "Ada, our plump bitch, has proclaimed Alexander to be her son and heir. She has given him the Pythian Manuscript and the secret it contains."

"It does exist?" Ephialtes insisted.

"It does exist," Memnon nodded. "Orontobates, show him!"

The Persian rose and walked across to a side table. He undid the ivory-inlaid coffer on the top, and plucked out two rolls of parchment. He gave one to Ephialtes and the other to Mithra. The Master of the King's Secrets opened his.

"It's a fair copy?" he demanded.

15

"We paid good gold and silver," Orontobates replied. "We have spies at Queen Ada's court as they have spies in Halicarnassus. The copy was made two months ago and brought here."

Mithra held his hand up for silence: he stared down at the manuscript, a copy of whch was also lodged in the archives at Persepolis. The writing was clear and distinct: all he could see were numbers including the shape of a square. The first line ran:

45 : 64 : 54 : 33 : 34 : 11 : 53 : 11 : 52 : 23 : 33 : 34 : 54 : □ : 23
: 54 : 54 : 44

"My scribes have been very busy," Orontobates continued. "They have tried time and again to break the code. I have offered them wealth beyond their imagining, but they cannot translate it."

Mithra's scribes in Persepolis had been just as unsuccessful: he rolled the scroll up and pushed it into the pouch of his belt. "But if we can't break it," he asked, "why should the Macedonian? Our scribes are skilled. What does Alexander possess that we don't?"

"Luck!" Memnon rasped. "Good fortune."

"Nonsense!" Mithra drained his goblet and banged it down on the table. He leaned back on the couch. The wine was now making itself felt: his leg muscles were no longer cramped, he felt sleepy, heavy-eyed. Mithra's hand fell to the dagger at his belt, a common gesture when he felt worried or anxious.

"And the songster of Ephesus?" he whispered. "Did he know anything about the contents of the Pythian Manuscript?"

"No," Memnon replied. "Only of its existence and that Alexander holds it."

"So." Mithra gathered his thoughts. "Alexander will find the walls are hard enough to crack. He has the Pythian Manuscript, which might give him an advantage. What else?"

"He has sympathizers in the city."

"And what else?"

"His siege machinery and the officers who man them."

Mithra pulled himself up on the couch. "The spies in the city we can take care of. What secret advantages do you have?"

"We have a copy of the Pythian Manuscript," Memnon

16

declared. "And an offer of help." He got to his feet and walked over to the water clock in the far corner. He stared down: the water had fallen below the middle ring.

"And you are going to meet this traitor?" Mithra demanded. "You know who he is?"

"My lord," Memnon laughed and shook his head, "outside this palace are men who would take our heads for a purse of gold. In Alexander's camp there are men who would take his for even less. We have spies and traitors, they have spies and traitors. It's all a matter of who strikes first and fastest."

"And you've been approached?" Mithra demanded.

"Oh yes, we've been approached."

"Why not arrest him? Bring him in here? Torture him?"

"And frighten every other man who offers his help?" Memnon smiled. "My Lord Mithra, I expected better of you."

"Where will we meet him?"

Memnon stared out of the window down at the vine trellises which lay on the other side of the fragrant flowerbeds. Despite the power of this city, Memnon felt vulnerable, anxious, not just for himself but for his lovely wife Barsine and his children. Sometimes, as he lay on his cot bed in his stark chamber deep in the palace, Memnon would wonder if he had made the right choice. The demons hovered, the temptation was almost tangible. Should he stay in the service of Persia? Why not slip away, offer his sword to Alexander of Macedon? Make his peace? Was that why the Lord Mithra was here? Were his doubts becoming obvious? Was that why the King of Kings had, ever so sweetly, ever so gently, demanded Memnon's wife and family be sent to the Persian court? And this spy he was supposed to meet in the wine shop in the tent-makers' quarter? Was he genuine? Or a secret assassin?

"My lord!"

Mithra's harsh voice shook Memnon from his reverie. The Rhodian came back.

"We will not meet him," he declared.

"What?" Mithra scowled.

"We will not meet him," Memnon repeated. "I have given my word. I shall go by myself, armed only with a sword." He gestured

17

at Orontobates. "None of your Secret Ones, no guards, no soldiers."

"How do you know he's genuine?" Mithra was now sitting on the edge of the couch.

"Because he talked of the Pythian Manuscript: because he said Memnon of Rhodes's word could be trusted." Memnon walked to the door. "My lords, I shall not be long, and I must not be followed!"

Memnon slipped out of the chamber and walked back to his own quarters. He picked up his military cloak and put it round his shoulders. He was at the door when he remembered and, coming back, took the sword belt from the peg on the wall and wrapped it round his waist. He took a small dagger from a coffer and pushed this into a pocket inside the cloak. He then removed the rings from his fingers and the bracelet from his left wrist, pulled up the hood of the cloak and slipped out of the palace grounds. He went through the gates, having shown his pass and paused, momentarily, at the bottom of crumbling steps leading up to a temple of the sea god Poseidon. He turned and glimpsed the beggar, shambling behind him, covered in a dirty cloak, a stout ash pole in one hand, a small leather bag in the other. Memnon smiled and walked on. He would not leave everything to chance: the beggar was really one of his lieutenants, who would stay some distance away.

"In this life," the Rhodian whispered to himself, "no man's word can be trusted."

Once he was away from the palace, Memnon quickened his pace, shoving and pushing his way through the crowd. After the subtle intrigue of the palace, the sunlight and noisy tumult of the marketplace was refreshing. The cookshops were doing a thriving trade, the air was sweet with gazelle meat and fish being grilled over portable ovens. Now and again Memnon would pause and stare round. The beggar was still in sight. He was there to protect Memnon's back as well as to make sure his master wasn't followed. Memnon had walked too fast so he dallied, as if listening to a storyteller who claimed he had visited the great snows to the north: how he had been captured by golden-haired tribesmen with eyes as green as emeralds who rode winged horses and hunted griffins and

18

huge dragons. Memnon stared at the cunning man's face and idly wondered if he was a spy, one of the many whom Alexander must have sent into the city to foment dissent. The Rhodian walked on. He could detect nothing wrong: no panic buying, muted hysteria or that hideous fear which spreads through a city preparing to be besieged.

Memnon idly wondered if he and Alexander were not like actors on a stage, and these people didn't really care who came and went. He paused and stared up at the great Mausoleum. He smiled grimly. What everyone else, including Orontobates, didn't know was that in the commission brought by Lord Mithra, Darius had decreed that if the city fell and Memnon had to retreat, everything was to be put to the torch. A young dancing girl, small bells stitched into her clothing, came up to him, clicking her castanets, moving sinuously to attract his attention. Memnon pushed her aside and walked on. He reached the tent-makers' quarter and found Little Peg Street, a needle-thin alleyway with shabby shops and houses on either side, the offal piled in heaps. He entered the gloomy wine shop.

"Is the visitor from Corinth here?" he asked, giving the pre-arranged password.

"He is, and waits upstairs," the fat-faced wine-server replied.

Memnon crossed the room, went up the shabby staircase and pushed open the door at the top. The room inside was dark and musty, empty of all furniture: an oil lamp glowed in the middle of the floor. A glimmer of light in the far corner showed there must be a door leading to outside steps.

"Close the door."

The voice echoed throatily through the darkness. Memnon narrowed his eyes. He could make out a shape against the far wall. He jumped as something hard smashed into the plaster beside him, and his hand went to the hilt of his sword.

"Don't do that, Memnon of Rhodes! I wish you no ill, but I must be careful. Your eyes are now accustomed to the dark. We will speak and I shall go. Close the door! Sit down!"

Memnon did so. He stared across the dark chamber; the small window was completely covered and the oil lamp was placed to create as many shadows as it did light.

"Am I wasting my time?" Memnon asked harshly.

"You know you are not." The voice was now high. Was it a woman? Memnon wondered. "You know you are not."

The tone changed again: this time it had a harsh Greek accent as if the man were speaking the Koine, the commercial Greek of the ports, and then, as if to mock Memnon, lapsed into Attic.

"Is my Lord Mithra in good humour? I saw him arrive." The speaker didn't wait for a reply, his voice now became cultured. "Words are physic to the distempered mind, Memnon."

"My mind is not distempered," Memnon replied quickly, recognizing the quotation from Aeschylus. "Even though —" he now quoted from the same playwright, citing a line from *Agamemnon* " ' — Zeus has ordained that wisdom comes through suffering.' "

His reply was greeted by a chuckle of laughter. "What is the matter?" Memnon demanded. "I will have nothing to do with one who blows hot and cold in the same breath."

"Ah, that quotation!" the shadow replied. "From Aesop's *Fables*, isn't it, 'The Man and the Satyr'? Well, I'll give you one from the same author, his marvellous tale about Hercules and the Waggoner: 'The gods help those who help themselves.' Are you going to help yourself, Memnon of Rhodes?" Again the change of tone.

Memnon wondered whether he was dealing with an actor. He peered across the room: he could make out more details. Wasn't that a dwarf's mask his mysterious visitor was wearing? One of those used by travelling troupes of players?

"It's just a mask," the voice answered his thought. "Anyone can buy them."

"What do you offer?" Memnon asked quietly.

"The Macedonian is coming," came the reply. "He is to march on Halicarnassus and besiege it. He has the Pythian Manuscript."

"What do you offer?"

"Confusion and chaos. I shall strike and strike again, against Alexander and his might."

"You'll try to kill the Macedonian?"

"If I can, but his life is sacred. I will smite those who do his bloody work for him. I will give you information. I will translate the Pythian Manuscript."

Again the chuckle at Memnon's sharp intake of breath. "Oh yes, Memnon of Rhodes, I can do all this and more."

"How will you get messages to us?"

"Lift your eyes to the skies," came the whispered reply. "When the siege begins I shall make my presence known." The shadow moved; a rounded pole, about a yard long, clattered across the room. "Take that, General! Read your Herodotus, find out about scytale."

"I know it — so, what do you want?"

"In return, Lord Memnon, when I've proved my word, half a talent of gold, the personal protection of the great king . . ."

"And?"

"And the Pythian Manuscript."

"For what? To discover the secrets of the city?"

"No, my Lord Memnon, for the treasure it contains. Give me your word."

Memnon paused.

"Give me your oath!" came the sharp demand. "On the lives of your wife Barsine and your children!"

"I give it."

"Good!" The shadow moved towards the door. "We shall talk again. Farewell!"

The door opened quickly: Memnon glimpsed a black shape then the door slammed shut, and a bolt was pushed across. Memnon stared into the darkness. He didn't doubt what his visitor had said. Whoever had planned this meeting so carefully was confident and cunning — Memnon leaned forward and grasped the pole — but would he be successful?

Chapter 1

"The whole of Caria had now submitted except Hali-carnassus, which was defended by a numerous garrison of Persians and Greek mercenaries."

Quintus Curtius Rufus: *The History of Alexander the Great*, Book II, Chapter IX

"Blood and flowers don't mix." Telamon dipped the small sponge into the wine and bathed the cuts on the man's hands.

If that were only true, he reflected. He paused and stared around. On a day as beautiful as this, he could half imagine that he was back in one of the temple gardens of Egypt, he and his lost love Anuala lying in the long grass beneath a terebinth tree. The sun was strong, but the many trees of this garden provided cool shade, heightened by the bubbling of a fountain and the small fishpond rippling with light.

"Flowers and blood don't mix," Cassandra, Telamon's helper, repeated as she prepared the linen bandages and a pot of acacia gum. The light-blue eyes of the injured man crinkled in amusement. The physician looked at his patient curiously. Sarpedon was a Spartan, a mercenary: of medium height with the body of an athlete, he looked like a soldier with his furrowed, sunburnt face and cropped hair, though his face was clean-shaven.

"You don't grow a beard and moustache?"

Sarpedon smiled. Telamon noticed how some of the gleaming white teeth were neatly filed.

"I am a Spartan, physician. When I left my country I decided to leave everything behind." His smile widened. "That included my moustache and beard."

23

"Where have you been?" Cassandra asked.

The soldier stared hard at this white-faced, green-eyed woman with a shock of red hair, like a burst of fire round her head. "Certainly no place you've been. I'd remember hair like yours. Are you a Celt?"

Cassandra shook her head. "Of Celtic descent. I was a temple handmaid in Thebes before the Great Killer —" she ignored Telamon's sharp intake of breath "— before Alexander, King of Macedon," she added wryly, "levelled the city, not leaving one stone upon another."

"You are a slave?" Sarpedon asked.

"Free born, but I was taken prisoner. Until my master," Cassandra gently touched Telamon's shoulder, "freed me to become his helper."

"I am not her master," Telamon replied. "If I was, Sarpedon, I would try and do something about her clacking tongue and hot temper which" – he glared at Cassandra – "will one day get her into serious trouble. Now spread your hands out, fingers splayed."

Sarpedon did so. Telamon looked at the deep cuts and gashes on the palms and between the fingers.

"Right, hold them out!"

Sarpedon pushed back the stool as Telamon began to pour a wine, so thick it was almost purple, over his hands. Telamon took a napkin, cleaned and dried the mercenary's hands, then dabbed each cut with a mixture of honey and salt.

"I have never seen this before," Sarpedon declared.

"I learnt it in Egypt," Telamon replied.

The Spartan glanced up. Telamon was tall and dark-faced, his hair and beard neatly clipped, with high cheekbones and deep-set eyes: Sarpedon couldn't decide whether they were dark blue or violet. A careful, precise man, Sarpedon studied him carefully as he cleaned the cuts and prepared the bandages: a keen-eyed, sharp-witted physician, Sarpedon would remember that.

"I have never seen cuts treated before like this," he repeated.

"The Egyptians have been practising it for centuries," Telamon murmured. "They insist that all wounds be cleaned. In fact, their word SEREF, which stands for infection, is represented in their hieroglyphics by a hot bowl. If the pus remains in the skin," the physician explained, "the flesh becomes infected, hot and swollen. I have seen men die from a simple cut on the leg." He grasped Sarpedon's calloused hand and peered at one cut. "I wonder whether to stitch that?"

"What?" Sarpedon exclaimed.

"I'll use a thorn," Telamon explained. "Bring together the folds of flesh and let them knit carefully. How long have you been a soldier, Sarpedon?"

"I have wandered the Middle Sea like a croaking frog," Sarpedon joked, quoting a famous line of Socrates.

"You have a hero's name."

"Ah yes. The great hero who fought at Troy." Sarpedon shrugged. "But I wouldn't know about that. I have little book knowledge: sometimes I take pride in having the name of a man conceived by Hera. I served in Egypt," he continued. "I was with a garrison outside Memphis."

"I was there." Telamon picked up one of the bandages and began to tie it round Sarpedon's hand. "I won't tie it too tight: I'll keep the folds fast with gum. Cassandra here will give you fresh bandages. You should change them at least twice a day."

"Twice?" Sarpedon queried.

Telamon stared up in amusement. "Don't believe the old wives' tales! Twice a day, morning and night. Wash your hands in hot water, bathe them in a heavy wine. Use honey and salt to cleanse each wound. Keep your nails pared." He peered closer at Sarpedon. "And, by the way, your right eye is infected. Bathe it with cold water and wear some kohl, it will protect the eye against dust."

"You learnt all this in Egypt?" Sarpedon asked.

"I learnt some of it in Egypt," Telamon agreed. "A beautiful place."

"He was in love," Cassandra broke in. "But a Persian killed his woman so Telamon killed the Persian and had to flee. Alexander's mother, Olympias, seized him. He had nowhere to go," she added mischievously, "except to join her son's army."

Telamon ignored her as he fastened the bandages. "Keep these loose!" he warned. "Not too tight or you'll keep the infection in. The flesh must breathe. There." Telamon turned to bandage the man's right hand.

"Did you kill a man?" Sarpedon asked.

Telamon paused: he was back in that wine shop in Thebes. The Persian officer who had raped and killed Anuala was grinning, bleary-eyed, stroking his oil-soaked moustache as if preening himself on a great achievement. Telamon remembered the blood beating hard in his head. The knife in his hand. The quick thrust. The satisfaction of seeing that stupid, arrogant smile fade.

"I killed a man," he confessed. "I have no regrets."

Telamon pressed his lips together. No regrets, he reflected, except that I will never again see Anuala's lovely eyes, press my lips against hers, feel her body close to mine, hear her laugh merrily when I don't know whether she's teasing me or not. He glanced up quickly; Cassandra was staring at him, her eyes hard, no mockery, no smile, as if she was trying to see into his very soul.

"And you, Sarpedon? What on earth is a soldier, a captain of Queen Ada's guard, doing gardening?"

Sarpedon held his hand steady. He was dressed in a simple leather vest over a white kilt, marching sandals on his feet. Telamon had already noticed the scars on the sinewy brown arms, the spear wound just beneath the collarbone. "You're a warrior, Sarpedon, not a gardener!"

"I served out in the Red Lands in Egypt. I was with other mercenaries: Kushites, Greeks, Cretans; all the rogues and villains who sell their sword for a bag of silver. We were attacked by Libyans and became lost in a sandstorm. Most of us died from lack of water. I vowed, in that sea of hot sand, that I would never ignore a cool place or garden again." He paused. "Later I wandered the Persian empire from Troy to Persepolis. I heard about Queen Ada." He shrugged. "I became captain of her guard. You have seen her fortress?"

Telamon raised his eyes heavenwards.

"I have never been so bored in my life!" Sarpedon continued. "No fighting, no marching, very little drilling."

"So you turned to gardening?"

"I turned to gardening. This morning I went out to prune the roses, a wild rambling bush." Sarpedon pointed to the red-tiled roof of the villa which peeped above the trees. "It's beyond that. Someone must have brought the rose here. Anyway, I was digging around it . . ."

"You should have worn gloves," Cassandra declared.

"Do so from now on." Telamon finished the bandaging. "You've worn leather gauntlets?"

Sarpedon nodded.

"Find a pair, two sizes too big for you. Wear them over the bandages. Your hands will become sweaty: oh, and be careful about those roses."

Sarpedon got to his feet, both hands swathed in bandages.

"And see Cassandra later about changing them."

"I'd love to." Sarpedon winked at Cassandra who glowered back.

"I am not what you think!"

"What am I thinking, Red Hair?" Sarpedon leaned down.

Cassandra wrinkled her nose at the smell of sweat and leather. Somewhere in the trees a bird chattered noisily. Telamon looked up: there was a flurry of leaves, and a soft-feathered wood pigeon burst out into the sunlight.

"This is a lovely place, isn't it, Sarpedon?"

"Apart from the snakes." The Spartan straightened up. "The garden teems with them."

"Snakes or not," Telamon replied, "it's certainly a change from Alinde. What do you know about those whom you guard?"

Sarpedon spread his bandaged hands. "That you are Telamon, personal physician to Alexander of Macedon, a trusted counsellor. When the king visited Queen Ada you sat close to him at the banquet."

"The king can drink too much," Telamon replied. "I am there to add as much water as I can to his wine."

"You've been sent here to the Villa of Cybele —" Sarpedon stared round " — to keep an eye on the scribes working on the Pythian Manuscript."

Telamon squinted up at him. "Do you know much about that?"

Sarpedon shook his head. "One of my duties was to guard the muniment room near Queen Ada's quarters, where she kept books and manuscripts. When the news of Alexander's victory reached us, the Pythian Manuscript was taken out. She ordered her scribes and archivists to recommence trying to decipher it, but they're a bloody useless lot; they made no progress."

"Do you know what it is?" Telamon asked.

Sarpedon made a face. "Solan the chief scribe is an acquaintance, we sometimes shared a cup of wine. He says the Pythian's a puzzle which can't be solved. Bessus the junior scribe believes it can. Cherolos the priest wishes to win great fame and favour by doing so."

"And Pamenes?"

"He's a strange one." Sarpedon pulled a face. "No one knows where he came from – some say Athens, others Corinth. He's a clever scribe. He claims to know ciphers, secret signs. I think he even worked in Egypt."

Telamon leaned back on the wooden seat and stared up at the vines which laced the matted roof of this garden alcove.

"And our other guests?" Sarpedon asked. "Why has the king sent them here?"

"Gentius," Telamon explained, "is considered to be one of the finest actors in all of Greece. His rendition of Sophocles's Theban trilogy –" he ignored Cassandra's sharp burst of laughter "– is considered a masterpiece. He and his wife Demerata move from court to court. Now Alexander is victorious, Gentius has travelled to Asia."

"The king considers himself an artist," Cassandra broke in. "He claims to know all the great plays but," she added contemptuously, "Alexander knows nothing except Homer's *Iliad*, which he can recite line for line and bore everyone to sleep."

Sarpedon leaned down, his face very close to Cassandra's. He smiled and winked quickly at Telamon as a sign that he meant no ill. "Are you as passionate as you are fiery, Theban?"

"You'll have more than cuts on your hands if you're not careful!" Cassandra snapped.

"So, the king will come here?" Sarpedon straightened up.

28

"The king will be here tonight," Telamon agreed. "If you ride out, Sarpedon, you'll find his troops. Look for the great cloud of dust."

"I'll be looking for more than that."

"What do you mean?"

"I am here to guard the Villa of Cybele," Sarpedon explained. "In the countryside beyond they know war is coming. Halicarnassus, only a few miles away, is to be besieged; the roads are emptying. I'm sure Memnon's spies are watching the villa."

"You're sure?"

"As I am that roses smell sweet. Anyway –" the Spartan stretched out his hand "– I thank you for the treatment. Now I'll find a pair of gauntlets. How much do I owe you, physician?"

Telamon pushed away the small table. "Two cups of wine and a conversation about Egypt." He saw the surprise on Sarpedon's face. "You are here to guard us, Spartan, or at least Queen Ada's scribes and clerks. Fetch a rose for Cassandra," he added mischievously.

"She'll have one every day." Sarpedon sauntered off, whistling softly under his breath.

"A strange one!" Cassandra exclaimed.

"Everyone's strange." Telamon gestured at the pots. "Cassandra, will you return these to our medicine chest?"

Cassandra put her hands together and bowed. "Yes, oh Great Majesty, oh Pharaoh of my heart!"

"There's no cure for impudence."

Cassandra was about to reply when a deep voice cut through the air.

"After I got back to the place,
With all your threats and curses ringing in my ears.
You swept up all the soil which covered the body
And once again exposed it as a sodden, naked corpse."

"Gentius!" Telamon murmured.

The actor peered round a bush and came striding towards them. A tall, gangly man with thin legs and a broad chest, Gentius had a scrawny neck, his head pushed slightly forward like a bird's, an impression heightened by his beaked nose, small mouth and ever-darting eyes under a shock of black hair. He was dressed in a simple green tunic. Telamon was fascinated by the camel skin Gentius draped over his shoulders, the hooves still attached. He strode up to the vine arbour, his dark-haired, petite wife Demerata trotting behind. She was dressed in a dark-blue tunic under a blood-red mantle, with copper bracelets on each wrist and a ring of small bells on her right ankle. Demerata apparently adored her husband, and followed him everywhere like a veritable shadow. Cassandra joined Telamon on the garden seat and stared at this curious pair. The physician quietly wondered if Gentius had been born deformed – his shoulders were slightly hunched – yet his great gifts were his art of mimicry and that powerful rich voice which could conjure up the magic of the plays.

"Are you ill?" Telamon asked.

Gentius stood, legs apart, hands hanging down by his sides, staring fixedly at the physician. Demerata hid partly behind him, her kohl-ringed eyes full of wonderment.

"I am not ill though my throat needs goat's milk, rich and creamy," Gentius barked. "Anyway, don't you recognize the lines?"

Telamon bit back his impatience. "Sophocles: *The Theban Plays*."

"Everyone knows that!"

"Which one?"

"*Antigone*." Telamon pursed his lips. "The sentry's speech to Creon."

Demerata clapped her hands and jumped up and down like a child. Gentius pushed one foot forward, hand going to his chest.

"We are busy." Telamon rose. "I would love to hear you . . ."

"I am rehearsing for tonight," Gentius declared pompously. "I understand the king will dine here. I must not disappoint him. Come, Demerata." And, spinning on his heel, he walked away.

"Astonishing," Telamon whispered, "that such an ugly man can create such beauty."

"Is he good?"

"I saw him in Corinth," Telamon declared. "He insisted on playing the part of Medea in Euripides's play *The Bacchae*."

"He played the part of a woman?"

"He wore a mask. Everyone was preparing to jeer but Gentius surpassed himself. I saw men cry. Oh yes, don't look surprised, Gentius is a great actor. Alexander always hires the best!"

Across the garden drifted further quotations from the play. Telamon began to laugh. At first quietly. He tried to stifle it, but then sat down, tears running down his cheeks, shoulders shaking. Cassandra stared open-mouthed: this was not Telamon the solemn physician, the quiet, reserved man.

"What's the matter?"

Telamon paused. He was about to answer but the laughter came bubbling up again. He put his face in his hands.

"Thank the gods Aristander's not here!" he managed at last.

"Why?"

Telamon looked at Cassandra's angry face and burst out laughing again.

"He doesn't know." Telamon paused to take a breath. "Gentius doesn't know who the Chorus is going to be."

"Oh no?" Cassandra turned away and glanced across the garden. "Not Aristander's lovely boys?"

"Aristander's lovely boys." Telamon stopped laughing.

Aristander, Keeper of the King's Secrets, warlock, necromancer, astrologer, confidant of the king, and his "lovely boys", his bodyguards, whom he called the "Chorus". Cassandra laughed and walked away to the edge of the pool, staring down at the lotus flowers fully open to the sun. Telamon came up behind her.

"Why does Aristander have his Chorus?" she asked.

Telamon linked his arm through hers. "Aristander was told by a witch he'd die a violent death brought about by treachery and betrayal. So he hired his own bodyguard, a dozen great Celts. Aristander calls them his 'lovely boys' or the Chorus. He taught them Greek and all the heart-throbbing speeches from the plays of Sophocles, Euripides and Aristophanes. I am not too sure if Aristander is trying to educate them or quietly poking fun at the poets."

31

"And when will the Great Killer arrive?" Cassandra demanded.

Telamon placed his hands on either side of her face and squeezed gently. "Cassandra, I regard you as my friend, my helpmate."

"But not your bed companion."

"Not my bed companion. Alexander of Macedon is also my friend."

"He has no friends."

"Alexander of Macedon is my friend," Telamon continued evenly. "He is kind, generous, and . . ."

"And a great killer."

"He is kind, generous, open-handed, brave . . ."

"And the other side?" Cassandra asked softly.

"He can be a great killer," Telamon conceded. "Savage as a panther, sly as a mongoose. In his cups he will take no insult. Cassandra, you must keep your mouth shut! Promise me that."

Her green eyes glittered with anger, her full lips curled.

"Promise me, or I'll send you away!"

Cassandra broke free. "I promise by the gods!"

"You don't believe in them."

"Neither do you."

"Promise by the friendship we have?"

Cassandra nodded. "By the friendship we have." She sighed and folded her arms. "Why are we really here, Telamon? We arrived five days ago. Tell me why we are really here. What is our noble mongoose plotting?"

"To take Halicarnassus," Telamon replied. He grasped Cassandra's hands, leading her out away from the trees and bushes where eavesdroppers could lurk, opened his wallet and brought out a map sketched on a piece of paper. "Look, Cassandra, this is the coastline of southern Asia, the Aegean, and here's Halicarnassus." He handed her the crudely drawn map.

"Did you draw this?"

"No, one of Alexander's scribes: it shows the problem. Notice how Halicarnassus is ringed by walls. Here on the east is the Mylasa Gate, on the west the Myndus Gate and to the north the Triple Gate. The city is well fortified with towers, walls and citadels. Its southern line is protected by the sea and the Persian navy.

According to our spies the moat round the city has been completed, twenty-five feet broad and very deep."

Cassandra whistled under her breath.

"You can see the problem," Telamon continued. "Alexander has to cross that moat before he can attack the walls, while he'll find it almost impossible to mine underneath. However, Halicarnassus does have one Achilles' heel."

Telamon wafted away a bee which came up from the flower beds around them. He smelt the fragrance of hyacinths: such a strange contrast to the death and destruction he was about to describe.

"Storming those defences will be a bloody business," he observed. "We will be very busy in the hospital tents."

"You mentioned an Achilles' heel?"

Telamon was about to reply when they heard the discordant clashing of cymbals in the house; above it, Gentius's voice bellowing a line from Sophocles's play: "Dark day, how long since you were night to me?"

"Must they do that?" he demanded. Telamon stared across the garden to where Sarpedon was lifting one of the long poles used to construct a vine trellis. The Spartan was now wearing thick heavy gloves. He waved at them and disappeared into the trees.

"That's Demerata," Cassandra replied. "Apparently the cymbals are to give more dramatic effect to her husband's words."

"They are giving everyone a headache!" Telamon snapped. "But to go back to Halicarnassus, I've told you the story. Pythias the architect claimed there was a weakness in the walls of Halicarnassus. He kept it secret but wrote it down in a manuscript no one can decipher: in the same manuscript he revealed where he had hidden his considerable treasure. For years the manuscript lay in Queen Ada's archives; now everybody wants it. If Alexander discovers where this weakness is, that's where he'll attack."

"And there's no other way of finding that?"

"None whatsoever." Telamon moved to the side of the carp pond and stared down: the reeds and leaves were lush and green, the water swirlng around. Now and again the glint of gold appeared as a fish surfaced to snout at the flies which buzzed on the surface.

"And why are we here?" Cassandra repeated.

"Queen Ada's scribes, the archivist Solan, Bessus the clerk, Cherolos the priest and Pamenes have, for months, been working on the cipher. Alexander and Queen Ada decided that they should be brought here, and I am to keep an eye on them."

"Why you?"

Telamon noticed the flecks of blood on his green tunic from dressing Sarpedon's hands. "I have some knowledge of ciphers, of secret writing. The king believes I can help."

"And can you?"

Telamon shook his head. "I have studied the Pythian Manuscript time and time again. What we must find is the key, but that's impossible. If I could only discover a pattern, a key, I'd have some chance of breaking the cipher." He pulled a face. "But there's little I can do."

"The Kill . . ." Cassandra corrected herself. "The king will be here tonight demanding what progress has been made."

"Well, he'll receive a short answer, won't he? None!"

The scribe Bessus appeared, gesturing at them to come. A hand bell sounded from the house. Sarpedon walked out of the trees, plucking at his gloves. Telamon and Cassandra made their way out of the garden, through the main gateway and across the great cobbled yard. Servants thronged around the well, carrying jugs. On each side of the courtyard were long, low-storeyed buildings with dark tiled roofs. At the far end, its stones painted white, stood a two-storeyed building, its roof of bright red tiles gleaming in the sun.

"Oh, not another meeting," Cassandra groaned.

"Yes, another meeting."

They crossed the courtyard, went through the main door and along a paved passageway into what must have been the spinning room. The floor was of black and white pebbled mosaic; loom weights and spindle staffs were packed in a corner. The room had been chosen because of its windows high in the wall. It was also tastefully decorated, with coloured cloths on the walls. The comfortable, circular-backed chairs the women used in their spinning were already arranged in a horseshoe shape. Cassandra and Telamon sat down at one end while the rest of the scribes filed in. Solan, busy as ever, short-sighted, dry lips constantly moving: the archivist reminded Telamon of an old vulture with his hunched shoulders, screwed-up eyes, long thin nose and receding chin, an impression heightened by his balding head and the hair straggling down each cheek.

"Does he ever change?" Cassandra whispered.

Solan, carrying a writing pallet, threw himself into the centre chair and started dabbing at ink stains on his dirty grey tunic. Bessus was younger, a small barrel of a man who had the nut-brown face of a wizened monkey, with sparkling eyes and an ever-grinning mouth. He was elegantly dressed in tunic and mantle, a cornelian necklace round his plump neck, while his fingers constantly shimmered from the cheap jewellery he wore. A short while later, after servants were heard shouting his name, Cherolos the priest processed in as if he was entering the Holy of Holies. Cherolos imitated the Egyptian fashion; his head and face, closely shaved, gleamed with oil. He was dressed in a linen robe from head to toe, decorated sandals slapping on his feet and, over one arm, a mantle, under the other a mask: Cherolos always carried this and put it on when he prayed to whatever strange god he worshipped. Around his neck hung a medallion depicting a snake, and a similar insignia was emblazoned on the large ring on his left hand.

Telamon turned round at a disturbance at the door, Gentius and Demerata were trying to come in, but Sarpedon was gently shooing them away.

"We could help!" Gentius bellowed. "We might be of use!"

Bessus winked at Telamon. Sarpedon, successful, closed the door and leaned against it.

"I am not having those two in here!" Solan barked, head forward, eyes full of anger. "I have had enough of his speeches. I have had enough of those bloody cymbals! Oh, by the way, where's Pamenes?"

"I think he'll be down soon enough," Bessus murmured. "He's still in his room, what they call the Ghost Chamber."

Solan drew his eyebrows together.

"There's no ghost," Bessus explained. "I've told you before, the floorboards creak. Anyway, Pamenes has been pacing up and down."

"But we can't wait! We can't wait!" Solan declared. "We have business in hand."

"What business?" Cherolos simpered, lifting the mask to his face. Telamon studied this and couldn't decide whether it was that of a goat or a demon.

"If you studied more and prayed less," Solan retorted, "perhaps we'd make progress." He handed out scraps of parchment. "This is what I found. Can anyone add to it?"

Telamon moved his chair to use the full light from the window: he felt a deep sense of despair. They had been in the house for five days and had decided to concentrate on the first line of the Pythian Manuscript. Now he looked at Solan's findings, he realized they had made very little progress – in fact, none at all. The room fell silent. Sarpedon now lounged in a chair, gloves off, more interested in the bandages round his hands. Bessus noticed these and began to ask questions. Sarpedon replied, Solan told him to shut up.

"The king arrives tonight," he declared, face all peevish. "Can't we give him anything except gossip about ourselves?"

Telamon stared down at the first line of numbers.

45 : 64 : 54 : 33 : 34 : 11 : 53 : 11 : 52 : 23 : 33 : 34 : 54 : □ : 23 : 54 : 54 : 44

"I don't know what the small square denotes," Bessus declared, "but what if each number stood for a letter of the alphabet?"

"That's impossible!" Solan retorted. "I would accept it if no number was greater than 26, the sum of letters in the alphabet." He shook his head. "I have tried every way . . ."

"What happens," Cherolos now placed his mask on the floor, "if there is no solution? Perhaps Pythias set a riddle which no one can solve?"

"Pamenes thinks he can," Bessus spoke up.

"Where is he?" Solan glared at Sarpedon. "The king said we had to concentrate on this. Queen Ada expects great things." He tapped the arm of the chair, arms moving like the wings of a pinioned bird. "Sarpedon, go upstairs and tell Pamenes we are waiting!"

The Spartan shrugged and left. Telamon stared down at the scrap of parchment. He understood ciphers and had seen them in Egypt and elsewhere. Physicians often kept their observations hidden in a formula only known to them, but usually they were easy to break. Solan was correct: Pythias had used a key, but what was it? He heard shouts, running footsteps. Sarpedon burst into the chamber.

"Pamenes's chamber is bolted! I have knocked and shouted!"

"Ah!" Cherolos declared. "I thought I heard someone yelling."

Telamon sprang to his feet. Pamenes was a young but very skilled clerk: his air of studious quiet had impressed him from the start, and he was never late for a meeting. Telamon followed Sarpedon out and along the passageway. A servant carrying a pot of water hurriedly stood aside. They went up onto the second gallery, turned a corner and down past other chambers to the one at the far end. Telamon banged on the door with his fist: the others came up, thronging close about him.

"Something's wrong!"

Sarpedon hurried away and came back with an iron bar. "I found this in the porter's lodge." He wedged it between the door and lintel.

"Can't we smash it down?" Solan queried.

Sarpedon, straining on the bar, shook his head. "The leather hinges are close set. There are four of them."

He wedged the bar deeper into the gap, pushing the door back. The wood cracked with a snap. A gap appeared though the inside bolts, at top and bottom, still held fast. Sarpedon kept the iron bar wedged. A bench was brought and, with everyone helping, they drove this against the door like a battering ram. There was a satisfying crack as the top bolt gave, followed by the second, and the door swung open.

"Empty!" Telamon exclaimed.

He stared around. There was a desk and a writing stool. Pieces of parchment littered the floor; a small cot bed stood in the far corner, its linen hangings pulled back. On the table was a goblet, a platter with a piece of cheese and scraps of bread. The great window at the

37

far end was open, its shutters pulled back. Telamon went across and stared out. He noticed the ledge running underneath, the bushes below him, then he saw Pamenes sprawled on the paving stones, the blood forming a pool round his head, like dark wine from a spilt cask. Telamon stepped away, and his sandals crunched on something. He crouched and picked up the bird seed.

"What is it?" Solan quavered.

Telamon brushed past him. Others now looked out and glimpsed the corpse with cries and exclamations. Telamon, followed by Sarpedon and Cassandra, hurried down and outside, back across the courtyard and out to the back of the house. The garden here was thick and overgrown with bushes, tangled weeds and long grass. Pamenes had fallen onto the narrow, red-bricked path which protected the wall of the house against damp. He lay sprawled, one sandal loose, mouth gaping, eyes staring. Telamon felt his cheek. It was cold. He turned the corpse over. The left side of the head was smashed in, and purple bruising marked the top of the ear, down the neck, shoulder and arm where his body had smashed onto the hard stone. Telamon felt the cracked skull and, gently using his fingers, moved aside the dark-brown hair.

"A deep gash," he murmured. "Blood, bone, even brain. He fell with some force, and he's been dead for some time."

Telamon looked up at the window and reckoned it must be a fall of about fifteen feet. Solan still stood peeping out; with his gaping mouth he looked even more vulture-like. The others came down, gathering round, asking questions. Telamon turned the corpse on its back.

"What's that?" Cassandra asked.

Telamon picked up the dead man's right hand. Small seeds still clung to his sweaty cold palm, others lay about the corpse. A pigeon burst out of the trees above him.

"Oh no!" Bessus whispered.

"Oh no what?" Telamon demanded.

"Pamenes loved birds and animals," the scribe replied. "He was forever feeding the pigeons."

Telamon examined the corpse carefully. He noticed the loose sandal, the short, knee-length tunic. He pulled this up to expose more bruising on the left side, though no other wound. He then examined the back of the man's head: again no contusion or cut. He got to his feet and stepped back onto the grass, treading carefully to avoid the blood over which the flies now buzzed.

"An accident?" Cassandra demanded.

"Possibly," the physician replied. "But I want to make sure. Would everyone please stand back."

"Shall I come down?" Solan, in any other circumstances, would have been comic.

"No!" Telamon shouted back. "Remain where you are. Touch nothing in the chamber. Cassandra," he urged, "go and make sure he does what I say."

She hastened off. Gentius and Demerata now appeared with a gaggle of servants. Gentius gazed soulfully at the corpse. Demerata gave a scream and went into the bushes to retch.

"Stand back!" Telamon warned. "Sarpedon, help me!"

They knelt by the corpse. Telamon rearranged it as he had found it, on its left side, legs twisted, arms flailed out.

"I want you to remember this, Spartan," Telamon declared. "The corpse lay on its left side. I can detect no other wound or blow to the head or body except those which can be explained by a fall. One of his sandals was loose. Notice its thongs are not fully tied."

"Could he have slipped?" the Spartan asked.

"It's possible. If Pamenes was leaning out with bird seed, he may have simply lost his balance, tried to regain it, the loose sandal wouldn't help and he fell. Notice how he tumbled onto the brick paving, which is logical. Pamenes missed his footing, tripped over the sill and fell headlong onto the stone: his head hit the ground first, his body would bounce. This explains the smashed skull and the bruising along the left side. There's a fresh cut on his left knee where his leg probably grazed the wall as he fell. Death would have been immediate."

"How long ago?" Sarpedon asked.

Telamon squinted up at the sun. "Soon it will be noon. I would . . ." He ran his hand over the man's tunic: the flesh was cold and clammy. He dug his finger into a thigh and felt the hardness of the muscle. "Perhaps an hour? The sudden loss of blood and shock would chill the body."

"But that's impossible." Bessus crouched down beside him. "I heard him walking up and down his chamber shortly before we met in the loom room."

"You're sure of that?" Telamon asked.

"For the love of Apollo!" Bessus replied. "Can't you remember when you entered the room?"

In his haste at what he had seen, Telamon had forgotten how the floorboards creaked.

"I heard him," Bessus insisted, "walking up and down as if he was lost in thought."

"But that can't be," the Spartan declared. "You heard the physician! Pamenes has been dead for at least an hour."

"Did anyone enter that room?" Telamon got to his feet, staring up at the window where he could glimpse Cassandra's red hair.

"The door was bolted, we had to break it down," Sarpedon declared.

"And there are no other entrances?"

"Only the window."

"Someone could have climbed up?" Gentius decided to join the conversation.

"No, they couldn't." A broad-shouldered, pot-bellied man pushed his way through, his fat face stained with smoke and ash: a blood-stained apron was lashed round his plump waist, and his hands and arms gleamed with fat.

"Who are you?" Telamon demanded.

"I am the Mageros."

The fellow turned and pulled a thin-faced, shifty-eyed girl, with more than a passing resemblance to himself, up beside him. She, too, was dressed in kitchen attire, a spoon pushed through the cord which kept her apron in place.

"I am the Mageros," the man repeated. "Steward and cook."

"Who hired you?"

"He did." The Mageros pointed up at the window. "The thin-faced busybody Solan. I have made an inventory of the house and garden," he continued, fat lower lip jutting out.

"Would you please tell me what you want to say," Telamon demanded.

"Well, you've seen how high the window is. We've no ladders to reach there."

"You're sure?"

"No one's laying siege to this place," the Mageros declared amidst chuckles of laughter from his companions. "You won't find a ladder that long, not in this villa. I know. Look! If you want to get up there from outside, you'd have to go along the ledge from another window."

Telamon peered at the broad ledge which ran beneath the window on the second storey. "I'd like to study that,' he murmured. "But let me have another look at poor Pamenes."

Telamon pulled up the tunic and examined the chest, feeling the clammy skin, the thin ribs. He picked at the tunic, studying its neckline, but could detect no rip or tear as if someone had clutched at it.

"It was an accident," Cherolos drawled. "Nobody visited him."

"Oh, someone did," Bessus retorted.

"Who?"

Bessus shrugged his shoulders. "Pamenes rose early: he went down to the kitchens then returned. I heard him walking about. I also heard someone go past my door, I'm sure of it, but I don't know who."

"Going to Pamenes's room or leaving it?" Telamon asked.

"I'm not sure!"

Telamon nodded: to all intents and purposes, he thought, an unfortunate accident. Yet he felt a chill of apprehension, for he suspected it was murder.

Chapter 2

"Ada presented a petition to recover the position of her ancestors and requested Alexander's assistance."

Didorus Siculus: *Library of History*, Book XVII, Chapter 24

O rontobates leaned back on his couch and gracefully accepted the compliments of his colleagues.

"Rock eel with mulberry sauce," the Persian Governor declared proudly, "is one of the many delicacies my cooks serve up. I must give you the recipe: red and white wine, oregano and fish sauce . . ."

"An excellent meal," Memnon broke in sharply.

He was sitting on the edge of his couch, wine cup in his hand, staring across at the oil lanterns hanging from the trees. They had dined in the Governor's private pleasaunce, a roofed enclosure overlooking the garden with its soaring fountain in the shape of a leaping dolphin. In the fading light it looked as if the dolphin was carved out of pure silver. The night sky had turned a purple hue, slashed with slivers of red–gold as the sun finally set.

"It's hard to imagine war," Orontobates murmured.

Memnon watched the fireflies dance above the fountain. Some-where beyond the enclosure musicians played softly: Memnon recognized the lilting tune, a love song about a young soldier far from home. The air was warm and sweet. The baskets of flowers heaped round the enclosure had been freshly cut, and slightly squeezed, so their sweetness would not be lost. The tables in front of each couch were piled high with silver dishes and platters, the remains of Orontobates's feast. The Governor had drunk deep, a look of sly pleasure on his face as if he was savouring a very pleasant secret.

43

"My Lord Mithra is back in Persepolis." Orontobates leaned over and grasped the wine jug.

"May the Lord of the Hidden Flame be thanked!" Ephialtes murmured. Orontobates lifted his cup and toasted the Theban. "It is good to see him come and it is good to see him go," he agreed. "He returned well pleased by what he saw and heard . . ."

Orontobates paused as a Syrian dancing girl, naked except for a silver loincloth, appeared in the entrance. She leaned archly and posed, the little silver bells on her bracelets tinkling softly. She had a soft, babyish face, sloe eyes, a pert nose and pretty mouth, all framed by an oil-drenched wig kept in place by a gold fillet. She moved sinuously: Orontobates toasted her with his cup then fluttered his fingers. He could tell from Memnon's face that the Rhodian was not in the mood for dancing; he wished to speak. Orontobates dismissed the girl.

"You are deep in thought, Memnon."

"Are they ready?" Memnon replied harshly.

"They slipped out of the city some time ago." Orontobates smiled. He looked up at the stars glittering like tiny silver jewels on purple cushions. "They will be in position and welcome my Macedonian visitor. How did you know?" He glanced across at the Rhodian. "How did you know Alexander would be staying at the Villa of Cybele this evening?"

Memnon shrugged. He refilled his goblet but added as much water as he poured wine. "What do you think, Orontobates? I wager five gold darics that Alexander will emerge unscathed."

Orontobates moved his head from side to side, assessing the wager. "I'll accept it," he replied. "My men are skilled fighters. They have fought in the deserts, in mountain passes . . ."

"Won't Alexander be well guarded?" Ephialtes queried.

"He'll be well guarded," Memnon agreed. "But he is also impetuous, as we will probably see tomorrow morning. He believes he is protected by the gods. He regards himself as the new Achilles, though without any vulnerable heel. It will be good to remind him that he is mortal like the rest of us."

"How did you know?" Ephialtes repeated Orontobates's un-answered question.

Memnon gestured at the orchard beyond the small pavilion. "Do you hear the nightingales, Ephialtes? When I was in Rhodes I had a pet nightingale and it always began to sing when darkness fell. But, to answer your question, the birds told me." He scratched at the sweat at his neck. "It's best if I say no more."

Ephialtes glanced away to hide his annoyance. Earlier that evening, Memnon had summoned both him and Orontobates to a meeting. Memnon, for once, was agitated with excitement, unable to contain himself. Lord Mithra had left some days previously, and Memnon had thrown himself into preparing the city defences. He'd made the occasional reference to a spy, to "valuable information" but, when they'd met, the Rhodian had been elated.

"I first thought the man was a trickster, a fraudster," Memnon had confessed. He then told his fellow commanders what he'd learnt: how Alexander was about to arrive at the Villa of Cybele protected by only a light skirmishing force. Orontobates had been elated until Memnon shared further news: the scribe Pamenes had been killed. Memnon's spy had confided how the dead scribe's corpse was now lying in an outhouse at the villa; in its shroud could be found Pamenes's secret journal. The smile had faded from the Persian Governor's face. In his excitement, Memnon ignored all this.

"My spy has insisted that both corpse and journal be moved. We must send a skilled attacking force."

"Yes, yes," Orontobates had agreed quickly. "Both corpse and journal!" The Persian Governor had become agitated, scratching at his cheek, plucking at his beard. At length Memnon had asked him why.

"Pamenes," the Persian Governor sighed, "was Lord Mithra's spy at Queen Ada's court."

"What?" Memnon had snarled.

"I don't know who your source is, my Lord Memnon," Orontobates had declared, "but he seems to know a great deal. As I said, both corpse and journal have to be removed. I will see to it!"

Orontobates's usual good humour had returned. Ephialtes was aware that the Persian Governor's agents in the city had brought him good news. Orontobates had decided on a celebration and arranged a small banquet where his cooks had surpassed themselves. During the feasting Ephialtes and Memnon were bemused at how Orontobates kept preening himself, lips moving soundlessly as if savouring a joke. The Persian Governor refilled his goblet, and grasped the two silver handles on either side.

"I have a gift for you, Memnon." He lifted the cup and sipped. "You are not the only one with secrets."

"Not another dancing girl?" Memnon snorted. "If I've told you once, I've told you a thousand times, Orontobates, there's only one woman in my life!"

"I know," Orontobates intervened. "The beautiful Barsine. No, this is not a girl." He flicked the side of his goblet with his fingernails. 'Or treasure, or a sword, but a eunuch. In fact, *the* Eunuch!"

Orontobates laughed at their surprise. He put the cup back on the ground, leaned back and clapped his hands: his captain of the guard appeared in the doorway.

"Bring in the prisoner!"

The captain left and returned with one of the most curious individuals Memnon had ever seen: at first he thought it was due to the poor light.

"Bring him closer!" Orontobates ordered.

The man, dressed in a dirty smock from head to toe, was pushed closer in a jangle of chains and manacles round his wrists and ankles. He was very tall, at least six foot, and thin as a needle: a strange face, balding head, and the way his lower lip jutted reminded Memnon of a carp cold on the slab. He did not stare at Orontobates but straight ahead of him. The captain of the guard squeezed his shoulder and forced him to kneel. The eunuch glanced over his shoulder at his tormentor, malice glittering in his eyes. He moaned and groaned as if his knees were bruised and, without being asked, sat back on his heels. He lifted his hands and brushed the scar which covered the place where his right ear should be.

"Not much of a present," Ephialtes murmured.

Memnon studied the eunuch's slit eyes, protuberant nose, that lower lip jutting, ready to protest. The prisoner still refused to look at the Governor or his companions: he seemed fascinated by a tapestry hanging behind Orontobates.

"Are you going to gloat?" The eunuch's voice was harsh. "Is that why I have been brought here? For you to gloat? Or would you have me dance? Am I to be crucified? Or shall I just lose my head?"

"Gentlemen, gentlemen!" Orontobates spread his hands. "Look on this creature and wonder. He calls himself the Eunuch, an accident at birth I believe. What most men have between their legs, he lacks."

"And what I have between my ears, most men lack!" the Eunuch retorted.

Memnon studied him more closely. The Eunuch's gown was dirty, there was unsightly stubble on the chin and, when the prisoner moved, his sour smell cut through the fragrant perfumes of the Governor's pavilion. The right side of his face was scarred where his ear had been removed, but it was the Eunuch's hands which fascinated Memnon: his fingers were long and slender, slightly curled like the talons of some great bird, nails clean and neatly pared.

"Shall I introduce you to my guest?" Orontobates murmured. "I am so pleased I caught you. You are not for the execution ground, Eunuch. Oh no!"

The change in the man's face was startling: his eyes seemed to enlarge, mouth not so jutting, lips parted in a display of fine white teeth. He would have lurched forward, but the captain of the guard, a Greek mercenary, grasped him by the nape of the neck and pulled him back.

"As I said," Orontobates continued, 'we don't know this man's name, he calls himself the Eunuch and makes no secret of his deformity. Some people claim he's an Ammonite, others that he was born in Canaan, the offspring of a witch."

"Oh, not black magic and necromancy!" Memoon intervened.

The Eunuch turned, a supercilious look on his face.

"No, not that," Orontobates countered. "Our friend the Eunuch has wandered the face of the earth. Hold up your hands, Eunuch!"

The prisoner obeyed.

"Notice those hands, those fine fluted fingers, Lord Memnon. My musicians, particularly my harpists, would regard such hands as a gift from the gods."

"Even though he has only one ear?" Memnon intervened.

"Oh, that's the result of a rather dissatisfied customer some years ago. The Eunuch is the most skilled of scribes, be it with a wax tablet, a piece of papyrus or parchment. He's a master forger – from the little bag he carries come warrants and letters, passes and licences, all sealed by this Governor or that Governor. He has even forged the King of Kings' own seal! Anyone who wants to cross the frontiers, produce a false bill of sale or a licence to trade, seeks out the Eunuch. He very rarely fails them. Only once, eh?" Orontobates leaned forward. "A merchant from Damascus? The Eunuch made a mistake, a very simple one. He drew up a document in the name of a border official but a sharp-eyed scribe, who was a member of that official's family, realized the date was wrong . . ."

"By only a few days," the Eunuch moaned.

"Anyway," Orontobates sighed, "the merchant's goods were impounded. He and his associates went looking for the Eunuch. I must say he was very lucky to escape with only the loss of one ear. A wealthy man, our Eunuch likes to gamble. He also likes young women, don't you? They may not be able to do much for him, but he can certainly do something for them: our Eunuch is a man of secrets!"

Memnon abruptly realized where Orontobates was leading. "The Pythian Manuscript?"

"Correct!" Orontobates grinned. "Eunuch, you have heard of the Pythian Manuscript, the cipher of the architect who built this city's walls?"

"I thought it was a fable."

"Do you understand ciphers?" Memnon demanded.

The Eunuch held his gaze, his eyes black and obsidian, their pupils so enlarged the whites could hardly be seen.

"Are you treacherous?" Memon asked.

"Can a fish swim?" Orontobates joked.

"Yes, I think you are treacherous." Memnon stretched his hand out and cupped the Eunuch's chin. "But you do have knowledge of ciphers, secret writing? Could you solve the Pythian cipher?"

"Tell him! Tell him!" Orontobates was rubbing his hands together.

"What His Excellency the Governor has said is true," the Eunuch confessed. "I have wandered the face of the earth, master."

Memnon withdrew his hand. The Eunuch, getting up, moved forward on his knees until only the table separated them.

"I have studied the temple manuscripts of Memphis in Egypt as well as those in Babylon. I even worked for a while in the city of Delphi."

"Oh yes, the place of oracles." Memnon nodded. "The secret writing of the priests."

"I can vouch for that." Orontobates spoke up. "Our friend has even intercepted royal messengers, borrowed the missives they carried and translated them for those whose eyes should never really have looked upon them: that's why we have been hunting for him here, there and everywhere."

"How did you catch him?" Memnon demanded.

"With bait," Orontobates answered. "A merchant prince, an acquaintance of mine, began to whisper that he needed certain passes and licences. A heavy price was offered and our friend couldn't resist. We caught him in the Tanners' Quarter. He tried to escape by pretending to be a beggar. What a triumph, eh?"

"Will you translate the Pythian Manuscript?" Memnon demanded.

"I could try."

"You certainly will," Orontobates threatened. "Have you been out to the Place of the Skull?"

The smile faded from the Eunuch's face.

"Have you seen the gibbets? We crucify men there. Some have taken days to die, haven't they, Captain?"

"In one case, weeks, Your Excellency."

"A hideous death, crucifixion," Orontobates continued, leaning back on the couch. "We keep you alive with water so the sun doesn't roast you, but eventually, your legs grow weak. You've got long legs, Eunuch, strong limbs. You keep pushing yourself up as

49

you slip from consciousness only to faint again, feel your body sag, your ribcage close like a band of iron round your chest. You begin to choke, so you push yourself up and the dance begins again. I think you could survive, oh," – Orontobates narrowed his eyes, lips pursed – "four, even five days."

"What do you want?" the Eunuch asked.

"The Pythian Manuscript translated," Memnon demanded.

"And if I do?"

Memnon scratched his chin. "A full pardon for all crimes and offences. Two purses of gold darics, a licence and pass to travel anywhere in the empire."

"And the treasure?" The Eunuch's head came up.

"Ah, so you do know about the Pythian Manuscript?"

"The treasure?" the Eunuch repeated. "They say the architect revealed where he had hidden it. I want half."

Memnon cocked his head to one side, studying the Eunuch carefully. "Do you know Alexander of Macedon?"

"In my travels I have seen his army."

Memnon's hand went beneath the cushion. The Eunuch swallowed hard. "Have you been in his camp?" Memnon continued.

Ephialtes swung his legs off the couch. Orontobates was no longer smiling.

"Where were you before you arrived in Halicarnassus?" Memnon demanded.

"I, er . . ."

Somewhere a harpist strummed strings, soft, melodious, like running water, a lilting tune. Memnon pushed the table aside, brought his hand from beneath the cushion and laid the razor-sharp edge of his dagger against the Eunuch's left ear.

"You might be crucified," he murmured, "and, if you are, I assure you you will hang from that cross with both ears gone."

"What is this?" Orontobates rasped.

"I am wondering about our friend here," Memnon continued. "How long have you been in Halicarnassus?"

The Eunuch licked his lips. "Three days."

Memnon didn't move the dagger but leaned across to Orontobates.

50

"How long was your merchant friend whispering how much he needed those passes?"

"At least seven days."

"So, why didn't you rise to the bait sooner?" Memnon pressed on the dagger so hard the Eunuch's face contorted in pain. "Shall I tell you where you've been? You are a forger and a trickster," Memnon continued. "A man who takes to mischief like a bird does to flight: there's no better place for mischief than a marching army. Have you been busy among the Macedonians, Eunuch? Let me see. Forging letters and licences to collect provisions, eh? My Lord Governor, you mentioned a little bag this creature carried?"

"We never found it," Orontobates replied. "The Eunuch visited a wine shop on the edge of the Tanners' Quarter. He became suspicious and fled: his bag could be down some well or thrown on a rubbish heap."

"It would have been interesting to look through that," Memnon smiled. "I watch your eyes, Eunuch; you are wondering whether to tell the truth or a lie. You like gambling, games of hazard? Gamble now. If you lose, I'll take your ear and His Excellency will take your life."

"It's true."

The Eunuch was trembling. He'd intended to lie, but the hooded eyes of this Greek mercenary seemed to read his innermost thoughts. "When the Macedonian army came down from the passes I became a camp follower. As you say, I was looking for possibilities and there were many. Any stranger who appears in a village or city is taken to be a friend of the Macedonian . . ."

"And treated with great honour," Memnon intervened. "I am sure you carried forged letters which proclaimed you as a friend of the King of Macedon. Correct? That's why you threw your little bag away. Why you are now so nervous. But, do continue."

"I heard about the Pythian Manuscript." The Eunuch swallowed hard; his throat was so dry he felt he'd swallowed dust. Memnon offered his wine goblet, and the prisoner drank greedily.

"Everyone knows Alexander is marching on Halicarnassus. There was gossip among the camp followers. How Alexander

51

had taken scribes from Queen Ada in order that the Pythian Manuscript could be translated."

"And?"

"I went and offered my services."

The Eunuch moaned as Memnon's knife went a little deeper, a trickle of blood ran down his cheek. "But something went wrong," he yelped. "Alexander's creature, the warlock . . ."

"Aristander?"

"The same."

"I suppose he began to ask questions?"

"Yes, yes. So I fled. I was carrying Macedonian letters: that's why Aristander and his brutes were interested in . . ."

"Do you think you can translate this cipher?" Memnon took the dagger away.

"For the reward?" The Eunuch nursed his left ear. "And for revenge. Master, I can solve the cipher, and more swiftly than any of Alexander's scribes!"

"Was it an accident or was it murder?"

Alexander of Macedon pulled himself further up on the couch, his strange-coloured eyes red-rimmed with tiredness: his hair was sweat-soaked, lines of exhaustion furrowed his cheeks. The wine cup he held contained more water than it did the juice of Lesbos. He had hardly tasted the dishes of lampreys, shellfish and chicken stuffed with olives, nothing but a few pancakes of honey and sesame seed.

Telamon gazed round the dining chamber. He wanted to make sure no one was listening. Hephaestion, Alexander's boon companion, was fast asleep on the couch to the left of the king, as was General Ptolemy, who had drunk two cups of wine and immediately fallen into a deep slumber, a piece of pancake still clutched between his fingers. The rest of the guests, including Solan and the scribes, were chattering among themselves. The Mageros stood in the doorway staring mournfully at the king. Alexander turned and saw this.

"What's wrong with the fellow?" he whispered.

"You've hardly touched the food," Telamon murmured.

"You've hurt his feelings. He was going to prepare a dish of rock eels."

"My stomach's bubbling like a pot over a fire. But, I suppose –" Alexander lifted his wine cup in the direction of the Mageros. "A fine meal, sir!" he shouted, drowning all conversation. "I did not do it justice, but that's my fault, not yours. You may have this cup as a token of appreciation."

The Mageros bowed and withdrew. An officer of the Silver Shield-Bearers, an elite infantry unit, closed the doors behind the cook and returned to his guard post in the shadows. He and other officers circled the dining couches, silent as statues, hands on the hilts of their swords, eyes on their master. Other members of the unit patrolled the galleries and corridors or squatted out in the garden under the acacia, sycamore and palm trees. The musicians had now left, given up in despair. The king had hardly noticed them: he'd whispered to Sarpedon, who sprawled on a couch opposite, that he wanted peace and quiet as much as anything else.

"Accident or murder?" Alexander repeated.

"I'll tell you in a while," Telamon teased.

The king drew his brows together, a sign of mounting anger. Telamon quietly promised himself to be wary. He thanked the gods Cassandra had not been invited. Sometimes Alexander found her sardonic comments difficult to take.

"What I want to know," Telamon insisted, "is, why the hurry? How many men have you brought with you?"

"Not many."

"You could have been ambushed."

"I won't be."

"Why are you so sure?"

"My mother told me that I'd be the world's great conqueror." Alexander smiled. "I will march to the rim of the eastern shore while my life is in the hands of the gods."

"Do you believe Olympias?"

"I fear her." Alexander sipped at the cup.

"She won't be pleased to know that you've adopted another mother."

Alexander now threw his head back and laughed. "You mean

53

Queen Ada? A master stroke, wasn't it? I am now her rightful heir! Cities and villages loyal to her have welcomed me with gold crowns and garlands of flowers. Mother will know what I'm up to. She knows there is only one Olympias." The king lowered his voice. "May the gods be thanked!"

"And you still insist on leaving early tomorrow?"

"At dawn," Alexander replied. "I want to view the defences of Halicarnassus for myself."

"That, too, is dangerous."

"Life is dangerous!" Alexander snapped, pointing to the dishes. "They could be poisoned, a fish bone could have stuck in my throat."

"And the rest of the army?"

"About half a day's march behind us." Alexander closed his eyes. "I've left Parmenio in charge; the old bear will be driving his troops with the lash of his tongue."

Telamon glanced away. He could just imagine Parmenio, with his sunburnt face and grey-white hair, riding up and down the ranks of sweaty men, urging them forward. Clouds of dust would shroud the different units bawling bawdy songs. Officers would be shouting orders amidst the bray of trumpets. The clatter of carts and the thunderous hooves of the cavalry would echo as the army, like a horde of locusts, ate up the produce of the countryside and drank dry its streams and wells.

"Memnon will be waiting for you."

"And I'll be waiting for Memnon. I have him trapped this time."

"He thinks he's trapped you."

"True." Alexander picked up an olive and bit at it carefully. "I've seen all the maps. My siege machinery is still at sea."

"So what will you do? Leap the walls of Halicarnassus? Grow wings like Icarus and fly to the sun?"

Alexander leaned over the head of the couch, face only inches away from Telamon: his breath smelt of wine, but even the dust and sweat couldn't hide the strange fragrance Alexander's skin exuded. He was unshaven, red and gold stubble gleaming in the light of the oil lamps, and his hair was swept back untended and unoiled. Telamon pointed to the king's wine cup.

"You're not going to drink too much, are you?"

"You're not going to drink too much, are you?" Alexander mimicked. "I worry about you, Telamon. Or I wonder about you," he added. "You don't believe me, do you? You think we are just marching backwards and forwards. Look at your maps!" the king hissed. "When Halicarnassus falls, every sea port on the Aegean will be mine. The Persians can float about like dust on the pond while I strike at the heart."

"Why don't you do it now?" Telamon retorted.

The king sighed and eased himself down on the couch.

"You could avoid the city," Telamon continued. "Or is it something else, Alexander? You've won your great battle at the Granicus. Are you trying to emulate your father, Philip, the great besieger of cities? Do you want to show the world that no place, however great its fortifications, can withstand Alexander?"

The king spat the olive out on to the palm of his hand and wiped it on a napkin. "You seem intent on debate. I ask you questions, Telamon, and you don't reply."

"I just want to know the reason why," the physician declared, "you're going to sit down in front of Halicarnassus?"

"I need the port."

"No, you don't. Even if you take the city, Memnon can retreat to one of those citadels and the Persian fleet could remain there. I just wonder . . . ?"

Alexander glared at him and winked. "Halicarnassus . . ." he declared. "Oh, by the way, why is Sarpedon wearing gloves?"

Telamon told him.

"Just like your father, eh, physician?" Alexander teased. "He left my father's army to become a gardener, a farmer."

"He grew tired of the killing, the bloodshed."

"Many soldiers do." Alexander lifted his wine cup and toasted Sarpedon, who then rose to his feet and walked to the door.

"You were saying?" Telamon insisted.

"Halicarnassus is a great city. Beyond its walls lies the magnificent Mausoloeum. Halicarnassus represents the best defences in the western part of the Persian empire. You are correct, physician. If I take that, against all odds, it's better than any great victory on land or sea. I shall be proclaiming to the world that no fortress can withstand me."

"And your father?"

"Philip sleeps in Hades," Alexander muttered. "I want him to stay there, not plague my dreams!"

"You still have nightmares?"

Alexander nodded. "Outside the gateway, Telamon, Philip is going into the amphitheatre: all the delegates of Greece are waiting to salute him. Pausanias the assassin is running forward, dagger in his hand. I see him strike. I don't know whether to warn my father or urge the assassin on."

"Do you talk about this to Hephaestion?"

"No." Alexander seemed lost in his own thoughts. "But I talk about it to myself. Did I kill my father?" He tapped the side of his head. "Remember, when we were boys in the Groves of Mieza, Aristotle's academy? Our great philosopher, when he wasn't painting his nails, would talk about the soul and will. He claimed we human beings moved and acted on different levels. We are what we think we are. We are what we want other people to think we are. Finally, we are what we really are. Did I really want Philip's death? Did I secretly applaud the assassin? Was Philip my father? Or is Olympias correct, was I conceived by a god?"

"You are Philip's son, Alexander. You are innocent of his murder, though your mother isn't. Philip begot you. You have his genius."

Alexander's eyes narrowed.

"You may even be greater," Telamon continued. "But greater at what, I am not too sure."

Alexander laughed, and gestured to where Gentius and Demerata were kissing each other. "I look forward to hearing him – but not tonight," he added wearily.

"Where are Aristander and his lovely boys, the Chorus?"

"Oh, I have news for you." Alexander began to laugh. "We had to leave Aristander behind. He is not well."

"Nothing superficial, I hope?"

"Aristander wants to see you. He is suffering from catarrh. He trusts only you and sent the other physicians, Cleon, Perdicles and

Nicias, packing. He said he won't have their fingers anywhere near his nose or ears! Now, Telamon, Pamenes's death: murder or accident?"

"It could be murder. Pamenes was in his chamber by himself."

"This so-called ghost chamber?"

"Yes, the floorboards creak, like a ship becalmed. Pamenes rose early this morning: he came down to the kitchens where he ate some bread, cheese and grapes. He then returned to his studies. The rest of the household went about their duties. The Mageros and his scullions were busy in the kitchens. They knew you were coming, which means any Persian spy did as well."

Alexander waved his hand, dismissing this.

"I was out in the garden with Cassandra . . ."

"How is she?"

"As loving and adoring as ever."

Alexander smiled.

"Sarpedon was tending his flowers. He only returned to the house once, to drink some watered wine. We then gathered in the loom room to discuss progress. The discussion was very short," Telamon added drily. "Now, according to Bessus, Pamenes was still pacing up and down when he left his chamber to join our meeting."

"But you claim Pamenes had been dead for at least an hour?"

"I could be wrong," Telamon confessed. "Sudden death brings its own chill."

"And if it was an accident?" Alexander demanded.

"Pamenes apparently liked animals and birds. He kept a basket of seed in his chamber and used to lean out of the window to feed the different birds, particularly the pigeons who roosted along the ledge. I've been in his chamber. I picked up some bird seed and leaned out of the window. It's quite possible that Pamenes leaned forward, missed his footing, overbalanced and fell. It's a common enough accident. He fell down the side of the house, his left knee was slightly grazed." Telamon clapped his hands together. "His head hit the pavement, a red-brick path built around the walls to keep the damp out. Death must have been instantaneous – his skull was crushed."

"Would such a fall kill a man?"

57

"Yes. Do you remember Aristotle's lectures on motion? For a few seconds Pamenes may have fought to regain his balance, and that would give greater weight and speed to his fall. He tumbled out, turning at least once or twice, and his head smacked into the hard ground."

"But wouldn't he cry out? Surely someone would have heard?"

"Pamenes's room is separated from Bessus's on the outside by a small buttress about a foot deep. He may have fallen silently, or the scream was inaudible." Telamon pointed at Gentius and Demerata, still gazing adoringly at each other. "Our master actor, of course, and his wife were preparing their play to the clash of cymbals, which was driving everyone to distraction."

"Could someone have come into the room and thrown Pamenes out?"

"The doors were locked, there was no sign of a struggle. No other bruise or mark was found on Pamenes's corpse which can't be explained by a sudden fall."

"Could someone have come in and bolted the door, persuaded Pamenes to come to the window, thrown him out and left by the ledge?"

"I thought the same myself," Telamon agreed. "But Pamenes would still have had time to struggle, yet there was no disturbance in the chamber. I've examined the ledge: it's covered with dirt and bird droppings. I assure you no one walked along it."

"Could they have climbed up?" Alexander was now enjoying this question and answer.

"Not unless they were a monkey or a fly. I have had the villa searched. There are no ladders to scale such a height."

Alexander leaned his head against the arm of the couch. Telamon couldn't decide whether he was going to sleep or thinking.

"Did Pamenes have enemies? Look around you, Telamon: that priest with the strange mask? He didn't like Pamenes."

"There was bad blood between them," Telamon agreed, "over some lady-in-waiting at Queen Ada's court. Bessus was friendly enough to Pamenes: he had great admiration for his skill. Solan was jealous: apparently Queen Ada was showing Pamenes more attention than she should have."

Both stared down at the senior scribe, his lank hair hanging down his face. Despite his emaciated appearance, he was picking as avidly at his food as a vulture would at a corpse.

"If I remember correctly," Alexander drawled, "Solan was the one who chose the Villa of Cybele. Well, he and Sarpedon, but it was Solan who made the final decision. He also hired the Mageros. Didn't our cook once work in the Governor's kitchens at Halicarnassus until an investigation arose over certain missing dishes? The fellow promptly decided to join Queen Ada's court."

"Are you saying they could be assassins, spies?" Telamon pulled a face. "That's possible: Darius and Memnon, not to mention Lord Mithra, would pay a king's ransom to have your head." He gestured at the platters. "Sarpedon himself tasted your food."

"What about him?" Alexander pulled himself up. "Oh, by the way, where's he gone?"

"Sarpedon's a good soldier," Telamon replied. "Conscientious in his duties, not very learned. From what I understand he liked Pamenes. He and Bessus often shared a goblet of wine with him."

Telamon stared at the oil lamps guttering low in their bowls. "Remember what Aristotle said? Look at the evidence!" he murmured. "What is possible must be probable. All the evidence surrounding Pamenes's death points to an unfortunate accident."

"I know you, Telamon, perhaps better than you know me," the king whispered.

Telamon gazed quickly around. The scribes, other guests and officers had drunk deeply. Cups and dishes banged. The noise of the conversation had risen. Some were shouting for an oil lamp to be relit. Ptolemy was snoring his head off, Hephaestion struggling awake.

"There are coincidences and there are coincidences. Pamenes's death," Telamon explained, "looks like an unfortunate accident."

"Or was made to look like an unfortunate accident?"

"Precisely. He was working on the Pythian Manuscript."

"So is Aristander." Alexander laughed. "Except when he is complaining about his nose. He was offered help by a villain called the Eunuch who'd been busy forging passes and licences. However, before Aristander's lovely boys could get their tender hands on him, he fled the camp. He is now probably working for Memnon in Halicarnassus."

"Is he good?" Telamon asked.

"The more I have learnt about him, the more I wish Aristander hadn't been so impetuous. A very clever forger. It takes a cunning man to catch a cunning man – that's why I need you, Telamon." Alexander paused to sip at his goblet. "Was Pamenes close to deciphering the cipher?"

"Sarpedon had a great respect for him, so did Bessus," Telamon answered. "I have sifted among Pamenes's manuscripts. There was something peculiar about that chamber." Telamon chewed on his lip. "But I can't place it. Everything was in order. Anyway, I came across a wax tablet in its wooden case. I recalled a story from Herodotus, about how the Spartans were warned about Xerxes's imminent invasion: the message wasn't written on the wax but carved on the wooden case beneath."

"So you found something?"

"Yes I did. 'Epsilon' and 'Pente'."

"Greek for the letter 'E' and the number '5'!" Alexander exclaimed.

"And something else: a line from Sophocles's *Antigone*. 'Let no touchstone'–" Telamon paused. "Yes, that's right, 'Let no touchstone test the hearts of men'."

"'As the fabric of their minds and spirits'." Alexander finished the quotation. "'So they be tried in the practice of authority and rule'. I couldn't think of better lines to describe myself."

"I found the quotation on a scrap of parchment," Telamon explained. "Pamenes had ringed the letter 'E' in every word." He shrugged. "More than that I cannot say. I also found a pole, a few scraps of parchment, but nothing else."

"Did I hear you quote Sophocles?" Gentius shouted.

Telamon glanced up. He would remember that! Gentius was of sharper hearing than he thought. Or could he lip-read? Telamon had met actors who possessed that skill. Had Gentius been following their conversation?

60

Meanwhile, Alexander had plucked at a bunch of grapes and was throwing them into Ptolemy's open mouth. There was a disturbance at the door, and Sarpedon came hurrying up.

"I have alerted the captain of the guard," he murmured to Telamon.

"What's this?" Alexander turned round.

"My lord, you had best stay where you are," Sarpedon whispered. "I may have it wrong. I do not want to be laughed at like a child who complains of noises in the night."

Telamon rose from the couch and followed Sarpedon out. The passageway was cold; doors had been opened. Soldiers were arming themselves in their muscle-shaped cuirasses and silver shields. Grey leather kilts were strapped on with the purple sash, the insignia of their unit, Boetian helmets which protected their ears and the nape of their neck. An officer was checking swords and belts.

The door to the outside yard was flung open. A burly man strode in, hair, moustache and beard closely cropped, his head square-shaped, his face like a twisted quince. The great scar across his face just missed his right eye, curving down beneath the ear. He was dressed in a leather cuirass and kilt, marching boots on his feet: his thick black cloak, lined with bear fur, proclaimed him to be "Black" Cleitus, Alexander's personal bodyguard. Cleitus's ugly face was full of sleep; in one hand he held a wine jug, in the other a half-gnawed chicken leg. He glared around, and his good eye squinted at Telamon.

"What's the matter, physician? Has the banquet begun?"

"It's finished," Telamon retorted. "You arrived, threw your reins to an ostler, then took that jug and meat from the kitchen. The next minute you were snoring on your back in one of the stables."

"What's all the fuss?" Cleitus placed the jug and chicken bone down on a table. Sarpedon approached; Cleitus recognized him and clasped his hand. "Would you keep quiet!" he bellowed at the soldiers still preparing.

The group fell as quiet as mice before a cat. A page boy came running in with Cleitus's war belt: he strapped this on. Sarpedon gestured at both Cleitus and Telamon to follow him outside into the moon-washed courtyard. Telamon peered across. The gates at the far end hung open; beyond lay the gardens, dark and silent. Sarpedon stood, moving from foot to foot, peering into the night as if he could see something. From the house came the sound of running footsteps, shouted orders.

"What's the matter?" Cleitus demanded, swaying dangerously on his feet.

"I'm not too sure," Sarpedon replied. "But I think we are under attack."

"What?" Cleitus roared.

"I don't wish to be dismissed as a nervous girl," Sarpedon half-joked. He gestured at the gate. "I was standing there with a kitchen wench taking the cool of the evening. I am sure I heard the scrape of steel, a faint cry. I recalled that a servant and his girl had gone out a little time before." He sighed. "Someone's out there who's not been invited to the king's banquet!"

Chapter 3

———————◦∞∞◦———————

"The Macedonians, . . . reinforced, at length repelled their desperate assailants without suffering much loss in the affair."

Quintus Curtius Rufus: *The History of*
Alexander the Great, Book II, Chapter IX

C leitus and Telamon hurried back into the house. The bodyguard went to warn Alexander. Telamon picked up a sword belt, strapped it on and joined Sarpedon at the courtyard gate. The night was beautiful, the stars like fairy lights in a cloud-free sky. A full moon rode as majestic as a ship at anchor. The breeze wafted in the fragrance of the flowerbeds and herb plots. Now and again the croaking of a frog, interspersed with the chirping of a cricket and the muffled call of some night bird, disturbed the silence. Sarpedon had drawn his sword: he stood listening, like a cat ready to spring.

"I'm sure," he murmured, "the sound came from over there."

They crossed the grass, already wet from the first dew. Telamon recalled his nights out in the Groves of Mieza when Cleitus would drill them in night attack; how to move, what dangers to look for. A bird on a branch above them broke free in a flutter of wings and sailed out like a silent ghost. Telamon's heart beat faster. He could hear his own breathing, Sarpedon's quick intake of breath. The muscles in his legs hardened: he felt as if he were going to take root on the spot. The bushes and trees assumed a threatening shape. Was that foliage? Was that a shrub or some secret assassin skulking silently, dagger drawn, ready to strike? He was glad when Sarpedon urged him forward, taking relief in the movement. They went deeper into the clump of trees.

Telamon's foot struck something. He crouched down, and his hand felt clammy flesh, a sticky substance already cold. He held his fingers to his face, then felt again. He made out the long hair, the breasts of a girl, and the dagger wounds, one to her throat, the other to her belly. Sarpedon was already crouching by the corpse of the man sprawled next to her.

"We've got to go back!" Telamon hissed.

As he turned, black shapes seemed to rise from the ground. Telamon caught the whiff of sweat. He moved sideways even as the assassin struck, and lashed out with his sword. Behind him the screeching clash of steel as Sarpedon knocked aside a second opponent, then they were running fleet as deer, across the grass into the pool of light around the entrance to the courtyard.

Telamon was aware of a cry behind him. Other shapes were appearing, dark and sinister, threatening to cut off his escape. He thought of Sarpedon, and turned. The Spartan, close behind him, pushed him on. As he turned Telamon glimpsed a terrifying sight: the whole orchard seemed to have come alive with men. In the poor light, black-garbed figures streaked like wolves towards the villa. Sarpedon pushed him on. Telamon dropped his sword but, at last, slipping and slithering on the cobbles, they reached the gateway. Ahead of them lights glowed through windows. Already Cleitus was ordering out a detachment of Shield-Bearers, helmeted and armed, spears out, shields up. They formed a defensive line stretching from one wing of the villa to the other, at least three men deep. One young shield-bearer ran forward.

"You stupid idiot!" Sarpedon cursed. "Friend, not foe!"

The man faltered. Telamon was allowed through the lines of men in full armour, eyes peering out from beneath their helmets. They were pushed through the doors. Alexander stood there, arming. Ptolemy, heavy-eyed, found it difficult to fasten on his sword belt. Telamon went back and stood in the doorway, climbing onto the small Hermes shaped in the head of Apollo. He glanced over the helmets of the Shield-Bearers now massing in the yard. Torches had been lit and placed in niches. At first Telamon thought he had imagined the attackers: the courtyard stretching to the gate lay silent. He was about to step down when suddenly the gateway was thronged, the attackers appearing like a sinister, racing wave. They burst in, well organized, and the first line knelt down, bows pulled back, a second line behind, arrows notched. Torches were lit and thrown to provide more light. A voice shouted. The arrows were loosed in a twang of cord and a whoosh of air. The Macedonian Shield-Bearers, however, brought their shields up to form a bronze wall, into which the arrows thudded. Here and there a man screamed, dropping shield and spear, clutching at the cruel barb piercing face or neck. A second volley was loosed. Telamon was pulled down. Cleitus dragged him away, slamming the door shut even as more arrow shafts pounded into it and the wooden shutters. Around the house rose screams and yells, the clash of weapons. Alexander sat on a stool, sword across his lap, talking quickly to two officers. Ptolemy had gone back to sleep in a corner.

"Cleitus!" Alexander called out. "Sarpedon! What's the situation?"

"They're attacking at every point," Cleitus snapped. "Archers, swordsmen, they've also brought bowls of pitch: one of the barns is fired."

From outside came yells and screams, the crash of armour as the Shield-Bearers were given the order to advance. One of the royal pages burst into the kitchen, his face bloody, tunic torn.

"They're upstairs!" he screamed. "They've climbed the walls!"

Telamon felt his stomach lurch, the wine he had just drunk curdled, a bitter acrid taste at the back of his throat. Cleitus rapped out an order. Sarpedon and some of the Shield-Bearers left the kitchens heading for the stairs. Somewhere a woman was scream-ing. Alexander got to his feet: he held the sword up as he laced his arm through a shield.

"I wonder what they want? Telamon, you stay here!"

Underneath the Boetian helmet, Alexander no longer looked tired or frayed, his face as boyish as if the years had fallen away, and they were back in the woods in Macedon, eager to participate in some military game.

"You should stay here," Telamon warned, then he recalled Cassandra. "My helpmate . . . !"

"She'll be all right." Alexander moved to the door. "My guards defend the first gallery." He looked over his shoulder. "There's no real danger, Telamon. This is not an army but a horde of assassins. They'll soon realize they'll be trapped between the villa and my troops beyond it. Calm yourself, physician!"

Alexander left. Telamon sat down on the stool. He was trembling, sweat-soaked. The night air was riven with the clash of metal, screams, yells, the sound of running footsteps. He left the kitchen and went out into the passage. Sarpedon and others were already dragging corpses out. They stood aside as Cassandra, a blanket around her, red hair flying, almost threw herself down the stairs. She was wide-eyed, pale-faced: as soon as she reached Telamon she started patting his chest and stomach. One of Sarpedon's helpers cracked a joke, and the men laughed. Telamon pulled her into the kitchen.

"Calm yourself!" he urged. "Get some wine. Better still, I'll fetch it myself!"

He found a jug in the far corner and, with a ladle, half-filled two bowls and added some water. The sound of fighting began to die. Soldiers with cuts and bruises came into the kitchen. Cassandra stood clutching the wine cup, staring wild-eyed around her. Telamon sent a guard to bring down his medicine chest and, helped by Cassandra, cleaned wounds and bandaged cuts. The kitchen became crowded. Cleitus returned, his sword bloody from tip to hilt. He soon imposed some order. He moved Telamon and Cassandra to the loom room to tend the wounded: most of the injuries were superficial cuts and bruises.

"I gather we lost about twelve men."

Telamon turned. Sarpedon stood behind him, face soaked in sweat. Telamon grinned and pointed to the bandaged hands protected by the heavy leather gloves. "They must have come in useful."

"Good to grip a sword, at least it didn't slip from my hands." Sarpedon took a cloth from the table and wiped his face and neck. A loud cheer echoed from further down in the house, followed by bellows of laughter.

"The king has returned." Cleitus came striding in, with what passed for a smile on his ugly face.

"Now, there's a man who likes killing," Cassandra whispered.

"Why the laughter?" Sarpedon asked.

"They found Ptolemy still asleep behind the kitchen table. Someone thought he was dead. He's now woken up and realized he's missed all the excitement. Physician, Sarpedon, the king wishes to see you. Leave the red-haired wench to tend the wounds."

"I'm not a wench!" Cassandra spat out.

"You are to me," Cleitus taunted and, spinning on his heel, left the chamber.

Alexander had returned to the dining chamber – one of the few rooms, he declared merrily, the attackers had not infiltrated. He had now taken off his armour and was examining a slight scratch on his forearm. Telamon went to help, but the king waved him away and threw himself down on a couch, legs splayed, hands out. For a moment he just lay mouthing silently at the ceiling, then he pulled himself up, gesturing at Sarpedon, Telamon and Cleitus to sit wherever they wanted. A harassed-looking servant brought in wine. Solan and the other scribes returned, but Cleitus waved them away, kicking the door shut.

"What does it say in Homer, Telamon?" Alexander asked. "I have a copy under my pillow. About 'sudden bloody attacks in the dead of night'?"

"That was no attack." Cleitus broke in. "It was an ambush. They knew we were here." Cleitus crouched like a great bear, hands hanging between his legs. He drained his wine cup and ran a finger along the scar on his face. 'Do you agree, Hephaestion?'

"I do," Hephaestion replied. "They were all dressed in black; desert fighters, veterans from Persia's wars against the Sand Wanderers in Egypt. They must have come in small groups and, when darkness fell, slipped through our meagre picket line, climbed the walls and hid in the garden." He nodded at Sarpedon. "If you hadn't gone to investigate, they'd have been in the villa itself before the alarm was raised."

"And their task?" Alexander asked.

"Why, sire," Cleitus growled, "to kill you!"

Alexander glanced at Telamon. The physician still felt rather

67

nauseous, yet any show of weakness among these killers would only provoke laughter, not sympathy. They knew his past, his father's revulsion of blood, his own abrupt departure from the academy and studies abroad.

"Well, physician? You've seen the symptoms. What do you think is the cause?"

Telamon recalled those dark shapes, his mad race across the grass. "I agree," he replied slowly. "If Aristander was here, perhaps he would be able to analyse it more coolly."

"He'll be here in the morning," Alexander murmured. "Continue."

"We should have had a better guard," Ptolemy declared, his brown, monkey-like face still flushed with anger, his speech thick and slurred. "I've told you before, Alexander, you are always in front and always have to be. What do we have here? A few hundred men at the most? The villa is large. I wager most of our sentries and pickets were fast asleep . . ."

"Following your example?" Cleitus taunted. Ptolemy glowered back.

"Everyone in this farmhouse knew you were coming," Telamon continued, "so the news could have been passed to Memnon and his commanders in Halicarnassus. Only one puzzling question remains, though it should be easily checked." Telamon paused.

"Come on, Aristotle!" Ptolemy taunted. "The suspense is killing me."

"We knew this morning Alexander was arriving here. But no one left this villa for Halicarnassus. No servants, none of the scribes. Memnon must have been well advised. The attackers, surely, had a plan of the villa: which chambers were important, the garden, the entrances?"

"Someone could have shot an arrow with a message attached?" Hephaestion spoke up.

"It must have been a heavy arrow," Sarpedon retorted. "Telamon is correct. The attackers were given a richness of information. They knew the place, the time. It's almost —" he pulled a face "— as if someone wrote out every detail."

"Are you sure no one left?" Alexander demanded.

"My lord," Sarpedon replied, "my orders are very strict. This farm lies at least four miles from Halicarnassus, a good hour's walk."

"They could have taken a horse from the stable?"

Sarpedon shook his head. "That would be missed. Halicarnassus is now an enemy city. They would find entry difficult, even if they were a spy. They would have to meet Memnon or one of his captains, then return here. No one was missing for so long."

"Do we have prisoners?"

"Three," Hephaestion declared. "One had a stomach wound, so I slit his throat."

"Bring in the other two!" Alexander ordered.

Ptolemy was about to rise when there was a pounding on the door. Solan, followed by Bessus, was admitted. They both immediately sank to their knees. Cherolos the priest came in behind them, still carrying his mask. All three looked agitated, especially the priest, who had lost his air of haughty arrogance.

"What is it?" Alexander demanded.

"My lord, Pamenes's corpse has been taken!"

"What!" Telamon sprang to his feet. The cadaver had been removed to an outhouse. Because of the heat, the funeral pyre had already been prepared for the following morning.

"We went there," Solan gabbled on. "They have taken the corpse!"

Alexander and his companions fell silent. Telamon closed his eyes. He thought of Pamenes lying in that dark pool of blood, the corpse being lifted and taken to the outhouse. He and Cassandra had prepared it: stripping it completely, wrapping it in linen bands soaked in perfumed oil to ward off the stench of corruption.

"Telamon?"

He opened his eyes. Alexander was looking at him curiously. "Is that why they came? To take the corpse of a man who had suffered an accident?"

"Was it an accident?" Telamon whispered. "Was poor Pamenes killed? Did the assassin leave some information hidden on the corpse?" He shook his head. "It proves one important fact: someone here at the villa, in a very short period of time, managed to convey vital information to Memnon, though I don't know how.

First, that Alexander was coming here. Secondly, that his protective force was paltry. Finally," Telamon sighed, "that Pamenes was dead and that his corpse held a secret Memnon wanted."

"But what?" Alexander demanded.

"I don't know. Solan?"

The chief archivist shook his head.

"And you are sure the corpse has gone?" Alexander beat his fist against the table.

Solan remained as mournful as ever. "We have searched, my lord."

"Search again!" the king snapped. "Cleitus, bring in the two prisoners!"

The scribes left. A short while later Cleitus led in the prisoners, hands tied behind their backs, the ropes round their throats held tight by two Shield-Bearers. They were forced to their knees in the ring of couches. Cleitus pulled down their dark hoods, ripping the jerkins so they were naked from the chest upwards. Alexander took a stool and sat almost between them, head going to one side, a gesture he always made when studying someone closely. He stared at one then the other.

"Are you Persian?" He spoke in the Greek Koine, the lingua franca of the provinces.

The two men stared back. Telamon, sitting behind Alexander, watched carefully. Both men had their hair shaven, no moustache or beard: their bodies were soaked in oil. Telamon recalled this was to help them in hand-to-hand fighting. Dressed in those black linen robes, their bodies greased, it would be hard for the enemy to clutch and hold them. They wore no rings or ornamentation. Men of middle age with the dark, weathered features of veterans, skin burnt and coarsened by the sun and desert wind. They were of medium height and looked like twins with their thin features, sharp noses and dark, liquid eyes. One of them replied in his own tongue. Telamon caught the word "Alexandros".

"I am Alexander, the Horned One," came the soft answer. "I am of Macedon."

One of the men brought his head back and spat. Alexander

70

waved Cleitus away and, clutching the man's tattered robe, wiped the phlegm from his cheek.

"Why did you come tonight?"

The man brought his head back again to spit. Alexander punched him in the mouth, splitting the lip and drawing blood.

"Why did you come tonight?" he repeated.

Again no reply.

"Were you to kill me?"

The Persian with the split lip smiled.

"Who sent you here?"

"Memnon, Ephialtes." The reply came in a sing-song voice.

"So, you understand my tongue?" Alexander continued the Koine. "Why did you take the corpse?"

Again the smile.

"Are you going to talk to me?"

One of the men sat back on his heels, head down; the other began to sing softly beneath his breath. Telamon recognized a hymn to the God of Light.

"Ask them?" Alexander looked at Cleitus.

The bodyguard, smiling, came forward. He looped a circle of coarse rope round one of the men's foreheads and turned it slowly. The rope tightened like a vice but the Persian still kept singing. Cleitus turned again. The man coughed and spluttered as blood burst from his nose and mouth, his eyes popped: his companion kept his head down.

"Tighter!" Alexander ordered.

Again the rope was turned: the man's screams rent the air.

"Release it!"

Cleitus let the rope loosen, and the man fell forward on his face. Cleitus pointed to the second one. Alexander shook his head.

"They are professional assassins. They won't tell us anything." He crouched down before the second Persian, who had now taken up the hymn. "You've fought in the desert, haven't you?" Alexander's voice was kindly. "I could take the skin from your flesh and still you wouldn't tell me. Ah well, you are not soldiers taken in battle." He got to his feet. "Cleitus, have them removed!

Take them outside the gate. When I leave at dawn tomorrow, I want to see them crucified!"

The guards came forward. The unconscious Persian, moaning and groaning in his own blood, and his companion were hustled out. Alexander returned to his couch and picked up the wine cup, his hand trembling. He drained the cup, glared round at his companions, flung the cup into the corner, sprang to his feet and left, Hephaestion hurrying behind him. The dining chamber fell silent.

"They came to kill him," Ptolemy murmured. "If it hadn't been for you, Telamon, perhaps they would have done. Our noble king must realize he is not Achilles. He bleeds the same as we all do, drunk or sober."

And, staggering to his feet, Ptolemy lurched over to a corner to be sick.

Sarpedon caught Telamon's eye and gestured him outside. The galleries were still busy with soldiers: corpses were being removed to a makeshift pyre which had been erected outside the main gate. Sarpedon led Telamon out into the courtyard. This was still littered with the detritus of the short, sharp battle: arrows embedded deep in doors and shutters, broken spears and discarded shields. Figures moved about. A hideous scream rent the night air.

"Another enemy wounded," Sarpedon whispered. "Some of them crawled away to die."

An officer came out of the gloom: he recognized Telamon and let them through. They stopped at the gateway where the alarm had first been raised.

"You could have been killed," Telamon murmured. "How did it happen, Sarpedon? You're a soldier."

"I suspect small groups of Persian night fighters met in the countryside, taking shelter in the copses, clumps of trees, using the rise and fall of the land." The Spartan paused. "Then they would move in. Our picket line is thin, the men exhausted. It would be easy for such skilled fighters to prowl through the dark and cross the wall in a black, silent wave: those poor kitchen servants probably disturbed them."

"And they came to kill the king?" Telamon asked.

"Possibly. They certainly removed Pamenes's corpse."

"Why?"

Sarpedon glanced up, eyes red-rimmed with tiredness. "We are not what we appear to be, physician. Queen Ada's court is a dream world, full of refugees from Halicarnassus, embittered men and women. Everyone carries their own bundles of grievances and frustrations. However, that's for you to find out, not me!"

"They were almost successful, weren't they?"

"It was well executed," Sarpedon agreed. "They knew Alexander had a paltry force. The real danger for such attackers was being pinned between troops garrisoning the villa and those outside."

An owl hooted in the trees.

"Athena's bird," Sarpedon whispered. "But the warning comes too late."

"Why did you bring me here?" Telamon felt the cold night air dry the sweat on his skin.

Sarpedon turned him round and gestured at the second storey of the villa. "What do you see?"

"Why windows, most of them shuttered, chinks of light."

"Stay there!" Sarpedon ordered.

He went back, not towards the main door, but the side entrance which led into the kitchen. He returned with a girl whom he introduced as the Mageros's daughter. She was unwilling, but Sarpedon gripped her by the arm, her sulky face heavy with sleep.

"I'm tired," she moaned. "I want my bed."

"Aye, and whoever occupies it with you. Now, do you remember?" Sarpedon continued. "Early in the evening I came out here with you. You were a little more merry, your mouth full of the cheese you love, the wine warming your belly. You said you wanted a kiss?"

"You offered me a coin," the girl pouted.

"And what did we see?"

"We looked back at the house and saw the lantern light swinging."

"You're sure of that?" Sarpedon demanded.

73

"Yes, it was there." She pointed to a window, its shutter ringed with faint lights. "Why?"

"Tell the physician what you actually saw."

"It was like a lantern being swung backwards and forwards, then it disappeared."

Sarpedon shoved her away. "That's what really raised the alarm," he murmured as he watched the girl trail back across the cobbles. "I came out with her looking for a tumble. She told me that we had to be careful because a scullion and his maid had gone out into the dark: she was frightened they might tell her father. She turned back and saw the lamp hanging in that window. I glimpsed it too. I told her to go back and went up the stairs – the feasting was still going on."

"Whose chamber was it?"

"Solan's: the door was open. I went in but no one was there, no sign of any lantern or light. I came back downstairs and returned here: I sensed something was wrong and raised the alarm."

"You mean the lantern was a beacon light? A message to the Persians?"

"I think so. Some pre-arranged signal."

"Could it have been Solan?"

Sarpedon shrugged and pulled his cloak round his shoulders. "As I said, physician, we are all carrying bundles on our backs. Solan is an embittered man. He resented Pamenes because he had won Queen Ada's favour."

"And the real reason?"

"Solan doesn't like women: his relationships have always been with men. I think he fancied Pamenes. He also lusts for young Bessus."

"And Cherolos?"

"He's a priest who worships some mysterious serpent god. Cherolos doesn't like anyone. He had to leave Halicarnassus in a hurry. As I said, he quarrelled with Pamenes over a woman."

"So any of them could be in the pay of Persia?"

"They could all be in the pay of Persia, Athens, Alexander." Sarpedon shrugged. "Our scribes are learned men, desperate to gain a high ranking post or office at anyone's court."

Telamon chewed on his lip: the lamp had been displayed in Solan's chamber, but anyone could have done that.

"Who stands there in the dark?"

Telamon whirled round. "Oh no!"

Gentius and Demerata walked across the cobbles. The actor was wearing that curious camel skin; Demerata was swathed in a robe like a doll.

" 'Horror beyond all bearing!' " Gentius's voice carried.

" 'Foulest disfigurement
That I ever saw! Oh cruel,
Insensate agony!
What demon of destiny with swift attack launching
Has ridden you down?'

"You recognize the lines, physician?" Gentius swaggered closer.

"How could I forget? I saw you recite the same lines at Corinth." Telamon replied. "I stood and cheered with the rest."

Gentius sketched a bow.

"Where were you when the attack took place?" Telamon continued.

"Why, my boy," Gentius waved a hand, "I am not one for swords or shields. I will not stand in the battle line. I am not swift Achilles."

"So you're preparing to recite Homer as well?"

Gentius took a step closer, his perfume billowing out like a cloud. He stood, one hand on his wife's shoulder.

"Where were you?" Telamon insisted.

"In the cellars, shivering with the rest."

"And why are you here?"

The actor's horse-like face crumpled into a grin. "Because I am here, the king has asked me to recite."

"And when were you last in Halicarnassus?"

Demerata stepped back. Gentius, alarmed, raised his hand, fingers fluttering as if ready to launch into some agonizing speech about Oedipus.

"Just tell me when you were last there." Telamon ignored Sarpedon's chuckle.

"Two months ago, just as summer, in all its beauty, carpeted the grass with flowers."

"And did you recite for Memnon and Ephialtes?"

"Of course."

"And did they reward you?"

"That's my business. I tried to write a play," Gentius continued in a rush, "about the ancient king of Halicarnassus, but the Persians didn't like it so I left in a hurry, didn't I, Demerata? I went through the Triple Gate and shook the dust from my feet." Gentius brought his finger up against his lips. "I shall not return there. Halicarnassus will never witness my artistry or my genius."

"But Queen Ada did?"

Gentius stretched his chicken-like throat. "I performed speeches from Euripides. I took the part of Medea. I brought tears to the queen's eyes."

"I am sure you did," Telamon declared drily. "And you met our scribes?"

A change in the actor's eyes, the sucking on the lips, the way his wife no longer stood beside him but almost crept behind her husband, showed something was wrong. Sarpedon stood beside Telamon, head down, shoulders shaking with laughter.

"I met the scribes, including the dead one, Pamenes. Sarpedon knows the truth. Pamenes tried to seduce my Demerata."

"And did he?"

"Can a worm fly?" Gentius snapped. "I am not here to discuss my . . ." He waved a hand. "The night is still yet young. I have seen the king, the soldiers." Gentius's nose wrinkled. "They sleep in their sweaty blankets, but we shall have a party and you are invited. There's food still left, wine undrunk."

And, not waiting for an answer, Gentius left the yard as dramatically as he would any stage.

"Did Pamenes try to seduce Demerata?" Telamon asked.

"So the gossips say," the Spartan replied. "That's what I find so funny: Gentius's fury over his little wife who fusses him but still has eyes for others. More than that −" he shrugged "− I cannot say."

Telamon bade him good night.

76

"Are you not coming to the party?" Sarpedon imitated Gentius's drawl.

"Perhaps, perhaps not," Telamon replied.

They entered the villa. The soldiers were now settling down for the night, the signs of the recent conflict all about them. Telamon stood and stared at a bloodstain, a dark-red splash against the white-painted wall. In many ways the attack had been Alexander's fault: his well-known impetuosity, his total disregard for his own safety, left him exposed. His enemies, like Memnon, had studied him well. They must have half guessed that the man who charged the Persian cavalry single-handedly at the battle of Granicus was in a hurry to see the fortifications of Halicarnassus.

Somewhere down a passageway a soldier began to sing. "Noble and beautiful was she on whom there rained the silver shower!" A voice bawled demanding silence, and the song faded away.

"Are you ever going to sleep?"

Telamon looked up. Cassandra stood halfway down the stairs, a cloak still clutched round her shoulders.

"Where are the killers?" she asked. "I thought we'd all be turned out of our chambers to accommodate them."

"Out in the orchard." Telamon grinned. "Alexander likes to sleep under the stars."

"To prove he's tough?"

"No. First, it's more comfortable. Secondly, he likes to show his men he asks no favours for himself."

"Where are the rest of our companions?"

"With Gentius," Telamon replied. "At his famous party. Gentius is a creature of the night: he was well known in Corinth for his speeches at midnight."

He walked up the stairs. Cassandra blocked his way. He glanced up; her face was rather pallid, and the lamp she carried shook slightly in her hand.

"Why, Cassandra!" He pressed her fingers, which were cold. "You are still anxious, fearful?"

"Why, master?" She mockingly pushed her face forward. "Why must you fight?" she hissed. "You are a physician, a healer! You're useless with a sword! Black Cleitus says you close your eyes when

77

you strike. What are you trying to prove, Telamon? That you are as brave and ruthless as the other panthers?"

"Perhaps." Telamon smiled back. He kissed her on the tip of her nose. "Perhaps I am a coward and I am trying to prove I am wrong?" He laughed abruptly. "Oh Cassandra, you should have seen me run! Well, come on, I am too agitated to sleep."

They reached the top of the gallery. Telamon started as a black shape shot across their path, a loud miaow echoing through the darkness.

"The villa cat," Cassandra explained. "It's half wild, poor thing. The only person it trusted was Pamenes, he gave it milk."

"It's his chamber I want to investigate." Telamon walked ahead. The passage was long, with rooms on either side. Pamenes's stood by itself in a small recess at the end, looking out over the garden. The door hung open, though someone had closed the shutters. Cassandra fumbled about and lit two oil lamps and, going back to her own chamber, brought some more. Telamon pushed past the heavy door and sat on the edge of the bed.

"Is the master going to give a speech?" Cassandra asked, sitting cross-legged on the floor.

"Your master is going to give you a slap if you're not careful!" Telamon retorted, gazing round.

"Why didn't the king and his bully boys take this?" Cassandra asked.

"I've told you why. To put it bluntly, they all have their fears, Cassandra. In a chamber you are caught, confined. Alexander, Ptolemy, Hephaestion, they don't like walls and ceilings. You called them panthers – they like the open air and the thin walls of a tent: it's a legacy of their childhood. When we were scholars in the Groves of Mieza, we always slept out in the open. Soldiers are also superstitious. I wager if we put Ptolemy into a corner, and pummelled him with questions, he's frightened that Pamenes's ghost still lurks here."

"Do you believe in ghosts, master?"

Telamon tapped the side of his head. "Up here yes: that's where Pamenes's ghost hovers."

"You think he was murdered?"

Telamon got to his feet and scratched his head. "I suspect he was murdered. But how? I don't know." He led Cassandra across to the small acacia-wood writing table, now cleared of its manuscripts.

"We know –" Telamon made Cassandra sit on the strange, circular-backed chair which had been brought up from the loom room "– that Pamenes sat here. He was not an Egyptian scribe who'd squat cross-legged with a writing tray on his lap. He sat at the desk to support his weight so he could concentrate more easily." Telamon, standing behind Cassandra, pointed to the window. "That is open. The sunlight pours through, the birds come and perch on the ledge or windowsill."

Telamon walked across to the far corner and picked up the basket of seed. He dug his hand in, carried a handful back and pushed open the shutters. The cold night air gushed in.

"Now it's possible that Pamenes leaned forward – for what?"

"Wild birds wouldn't take seed from his hand."

"Clever girl!" Telamon murmured. "So what?"

"He'd lean down," Cassandra replied, "and sprinkle the seed either on the sill or the ledge beneath."

Telamon did so. In the poor light he could just make out the ledge, and leaning down he realized how precarious his hold was. He straightened up.

"I . . . !"

A hideous scream rent the night air, followed by shouts, the faint noise of knocking. Again the scream.

"By Athena's light!" Cassandra whispered.

Again the scream, hideous, a man's soul being torn from his body. All the other, faint sounds of the villa died. A night bird screeched back. Telamon looked out into the darkness. More screams, a man shouting, then he remembered the Persians.

"They are crucifying the prisoners."

Cassandra shook her head, fingers going to her cheeks as she clawed her skin, a gesture she always made when nervous. "Telamon!" she hissed. "At night I lie in my cot bed and look across at you. I think, why can't we take ship, go somewhere else? This was a pleasant villa with cherry orchards, berries on the branch, flowers in the garden, some chickens still running around." Her voice dropped to a whisper. "They say the melons are rich and thick. The King of Killers then arrives, and he brings the stench of death with him. I wonder, why am I here? Why are you here?"

Telamon couldn't reply. Cassandra came closer, her red hair flaring out, green eyes glittering.

"You look like Medea."

"I wish I was the Gorgon Medusa! I'd turn all these fighting men to stone. I saw them in Thebes, when the smoke plumed up and the blood gushed ankle-deep."

Telamon put an arm round her shoulders to comfort her, pressing his lips against her hair. He pressed again as another scream rent the night air.

"I don't know why we are here, except that I am," he murmured. "I have no place to go. I live in my own world, Cassandra, and you live with me. I cannot explain the deaths of thousands. I can only concentrate on the task in hand. It keeps me sane."

Cassandra pulled away.

"When I was at Queen Ada's court," Telamon continued, "I tended a sick infant. Do you remember? She had been attacked by a dog, a lump taken out of her little arm. All I concentrated on was healing the wound and soothing the pain. If I started asking myself why, I wouldn't be able to concentrate. I wouldn't be able to do any good at all. I'd end up wandering the roads like a madman baying at the moon. This is our task, Cassandra. Pamenes's ghost cries for vengeance, but as for saving the world –" Telamon walked back to the window. "I am a nomad," he murmured. "No." He shook his head. "There's more to it than that. Once, out in the Red Lands of Egypt, I watched a gold-maned lion, magnificent in its terrible beauty, stalk its prey. I stood transfixed." He glanced over his shoulder. "Alexander has the same fascination for me."

"He is, was, your friend?"

"True, but that makes him all the more fascinating." Telamon forced a smile. "Perhaps I can do some good here, as anywhere else. The priests of Isis claim a man's fate is written on his forehead, there is no escape. So." He leaned against the wall. "I am here, listening to men die while I investigate the death of another."

Cassandra came across and grasped his hand. "You think Pamenes was pushed?"

Telamon nodded. "Someone came into this chamber, bolted the door, killed him and somehow escaped."

"But that's impossible!" Cassandra flounced her red hair back. "I talked to Bessus, who sleeps in the adjoining chamber. He repeated his earlier story: his door was slightly open, he heard some footsteps, but nothing else."

"Are you sure?" Telamon turned.

"Yes. Moreover Solan maintains he kept going in and out of his own chamber. He saw nothing untoward. How could someone come through a bolted door, take Pamenes to the window and throw him out?"

"The assassin could have climbed up?" Telamon suggested weakly.

"Physician! Physician!" Cassandra teased. "The walls are sheer. There is no ladder, no one stood on the ledge. Your own sharp eyes," she mocked, "noticed that."

Telamon stamped his foot and walked away. As he did so the floorboards creaked, just slightly, like the sound of a ship riding at anchor.

"Pamenes was murdered!" he exclaimed. "I know that. But Cassandra . . ." He walked back to the desk and pulled across a small casket of styli: all their ends were blunted. "Pamenes was a scribe," Telamon declared. "He would use quills like an archer does arrows, yet I cannot find one sharpened. Now, isn't that strange? He didn't even have one in his hand when his corpse was found. So, where is that stylus?"

81

Chapter 4

"Alexander encamped near Halicarnassus and set in
motion an active and formidable siege."
Diodorus Siculus: *Library of History*, Book XVII, Chapter 24

T he Dolphin Chamber in the Governor's palace at Halicarnassus was described by visitors as exquisite. Its walls were a
light glazed blue: the chamber earned its name from the painted
silver dolphins with golden fins that leapt and sported on a brilliant
sea without ripples or waves. The columns of this small audience
hall were painted in the Egyptian fashion: dark blue with blood-red
capitals and bases. The floor was of marble, so visitors thought they
were walking on water as it shimmered in the light of a myriad of
oil lamps placed in niches and on great bronze stands or small
wooden tables around the chamber. The room was dominated by a
raised enclave containing couches, covered in gorgeous cloths
emblazoned with brilliantly coloured peacocks, as well as small
dining tables. Because of the night air, servants had brought in
dishes of charcoal sprinkled with perfume.

Ephialtes and Memnon, when they joined Orontobates in the
enclave, took little heed of their surroundings. They, like the
Governor, had been roused from sleep, slipping on tunics and
cloaks, tight-fitting sandals on their bare feet, to hear the news. The
leader of the assault force against the villa knelt on a cushion before
the enclave, his face all stained and dirty. Around him his lieutenants crouched like statues, listening intently as their leader, in a
soft but carrying voice, reported what had happened.

"We broke up and gathered in small groups." The officer looked
thirstily at the goblets of chilled sherbet on the tables.

Orontobates picked up a cup and thrust it into the man's hand. The commander closed his eyes and murmured a prayer of quiet thanks. Orontobates was pleased: they might not have killed the Horned One, the Wolf of Macedon, but they had returned with the spoils of war.

"Continue," Memnon grated.

"The Macedonian had brought few soldiers. The villa was only protected by units gathered round their camp fires. Most of the Macedonians were exhausted, fast asleep. We encountered little opposition, cut the throats of a number, slipped by the rest and reached the villa. The guards were lax and few. We scaled the wall and, as instructed, gathered in the orchard in the far corner. The original occupiers of the villa had fled and, may the Lord of Fire be thanked, taken their dogs with them!"

"We should have launched an all-out attack!" Orontobates leaned forward, tapping his foot on the floor. "We should have attacked, you could have killed them all."

"Hush!" Memnon raised a hand. "How many of them were there?"

"A few hundred, all told." The officer cleared his throat.

"And how many did you lose?"

"Thirty: we brought five wounded back, but they were beyond help so we cut their throats." The commander raised a hand, fingers splayed. "Their souls are now with the Lord of Light."

"They are now part of the living flame," Memnon agreed. "You found the messages left by our spy?" he added.

"As promised, in the outhouse. We discovered the corpse naked, covered by a sheet and a linen cloth. The journal was placed beneath him. We removed the corpse immediately."

"Good! Good!" Memnon murmured.

"We gathered," the officer continued. "I saw a light being shone from an upstairs window, the pre-arranged signal that the feasting had begun. Alexander and his captains were in their cups."

"But they weren't?" Memnon smiled.

The commander of the attacking force shrugged and sipped from the goblet. "I gave orders to approach the villa, but the alarm was raised."

"Who by?"

"I think it was Sarpedon, the captain of Queen Ada's guard. One of my men recognized him from the trees. He was with another, the physician Telamon: I learnt this from their conversation."

"Telamon?" Memnon broke in. He leaned forward. "I have heard the rumours."

"Who is he?" Orontobates snapped.

"A reputable physician, a boyhood friend of Alexander. He was raised in the Groves of Mieza at Aristotle's academy but his father withdrew him. He became a physician and wandered the Middle Sea like a lost soul."

"Have you met him?"

"On a number of occasions." Memnon grimaced. "If Alexander has the likes of Telamon about him he has good advice, keen wits and sharp eyes."

Orontobates banged a silver plate against the table. "Commander, I would have rewarded you if you had taken Sarpedon and cut his throat. He has been a thorn in our side."

"They had the advantage. They escaped us and reached the villa. The alarm was raised so I launched the attack. We tried to penetrate the villa but we did not know where the king was lodging and, although the soldiers outside were lax, a squadron of Shield-Bearers guarded the king's quarters. We reached the upper chambers – that's where we lost most of our men, they were trapped in a passageway. By then the alarm had been raised in the camp beyond the walls. I was wary of being cut off, so I gave the order to withdraw. We took our wounded and fled. No pursuit was ordered."

"And you have read the journal?" Orontobates snapped.

The commander shrugged. "I brought the corpse of the scribe Pamenes and his journal with us. Once we were out of danger, I ordered torches to be lit. I wanted to make sure we had brought everything."

"And the corpse?"

"Excellency, you can see it for yourself. The man has been dead for at least a day: a savage blow to the left side of his head, wounds down his side."

"An accident?" Ephialtes's voice was harsh. Memnon stared curiously at him. Ephialtes was brave and a resourceful general, a brave fighter, yet, in the last few days, he had been nervous, agitated, his hatred for Alexander and the Macedonian's destruction of Thebes more and more apparent.

"An accident?" Ephialtes repeated his question.

"Lord, I am not a physician."

"Tell me." Memnon kept his voice calm. "In the attack on the villa did the spy who was helping us show his or her hand?"

The commander shook his head.

"Were any of your men taken prisoner?" Orontobates asked.

"Eight are unaccounted for, possibly more." The commander spread his hands. "But, if they are captured, they will not talk."

Again Memnon gestured at the man to drink, which he did greedily before passing the cup to his companions behind him.

"You may go." Orontobates rose to his feet. He plucked a leather pouch and moved among the men, giving each a gold daric. "You have done well."

The desert fighters rose, bowed towards the dais and slipped out into the night.

"We could have killed him." Ephialtes spoke as if to himself. "We could have trapped him like a rat in a gully."

"Ephialtes! Ephialtes!" Memnon soothed. "We sent a small force through the night: any more and the Macedonians would have known we were coming." He lifted his cup towards Orontobates. "Your men did well. They brought back the corpse – but why did you agree to it?"

"My lord," the Persian smiled back, "I can be as mysterious as you. Have you ever considered that your spy may have murdered Pamenes? This is where it all gets very interesting. Come, I will show you."

They left the Dolphin Chamber, along moonlit galleries and down to the dungeons beneath the palace. The guards and turn-keys looked nothing more than huddled bundles. Cerberus was in his small chamber halfway down the passage, his fat, sooty face wine-flushed, lips slobbery and wet. He gave the most ingratiating bow.

"You wish to see the Eunuch?"

Orontobates shook his head. "No, the corpse!"

Cerberus led them along the passageway, past the comfortable room where the Eunuch was lodged, but its lamps were extinguished, the cell in darkness. They reached a chamber at the far end. Cerberus opened the door and ushered them in. Pamenes's corpse, circled with oil lamps, lay sprawled on a table. The stench of corruption, despite the small blocks of perfume placed round it, was offensive. Pamenes's face looked livid, a dirty white, eyes half-closed, his head disfigured by the dried blood from the hideous wound. The legs, arms and torso were still coated in dust and dirt from its hurried journey through the night: the head had been closely shaved, its hair littering the table and floor around.

"By Athena's eye!" Orontobates muttered. "What is this?" He picked up an oil lamp and held it close to the dead man's scalp. Memnon made out the tattoo printed just beyond the hairline: the all-seeing eye of Ahura-Mazda borne between eagle wings.

"That's the emblem of a magus!" he exclaimed. "A Persian priest, a keeper of the hidden flame!"

"And so it is," Orontobates agreed. "This young man is a Mede by birth, a priest of Persepolis, one with the gift of tongues. When Queen Ada fled Halicarnassus, Lord Mithra and I decided it was essential we had spies at her court. We wanted a man skilled in letters who could speak the Greek tongue and ape their customs. Pamenes was chosen: his devotion to the Divine House is unquestionable. He grew his hair, dressed in Greek clothes, acted the part of a learned scribe and won a place at Queen Ada's court. The information he sent was always valuable."

"So?" Memnon pinched his nostrils.

"His death could be an accident," Orontobates continued. "But that would seem such a strange coincidence."

"Which leaves us with two conclusions," Memnon whispered. "Either he was killed by someone who knows he was a spy . . . ?"

"Or he was killed by your spy," Orontobates declared. "Only the God of Light knows the truth."

"Is there any way of finding out?" Ephialtes asked.

87

Memnon retreated to the doorway, still pinching his nostrils, staring back at the corpse.

"If he is guilty of this priest's death —" Orontobates caressed Pamenes's head like a mother would a child — "then, my lord . . ." the Persian glanced up, his eyes fierce ". . . I will have a blood feud with him. Pamenes was a magus, a faithful servant of the King of Kings."

"We do not know," Ephialtes offered. "If Pamenes was killed by Memnon's spy, his death may be the work of Alexander's agents."

"My spy," Memnon added, "may have even been Pamenes's ally. When the magus was killed, he simply hid the journal beneath his corpse: he must have known we would remove both."

Orontobates gazed suspiciously back.

"The journal?" Memnon demanded harshly, changing the topic.

"Ah yes, the journal." Orontobates led them out of the cell, walking quickly up the steps and along the passageway back into the Dolphin Chamber. On his way he paused and had a word with a guard, who hurried off. They made themselves comfortable. Ephialtes plucked up a cluster of grapes, recalled how late the hour was, and placed them back on the dish.

"You are agitated, my lord, you should rest." Orontobates broke up a sweetened pastry, popping pieces into his mouth. "You should be sleeping."

"I'll rest when Alexander's dead!" Ephialtes spat out.

"If Pamenes was murdered," Orontobates ignored the outburst and returned to his original question, "I wonder if it was your spy, Memnon?"

"It's possible," the Rhodian agreed. "He may not have known Pamenes's true identity. Remember, this spy has no loyalty to anyone except himself, or he may have regarded Pamenes as a threat . . ."

He paused at the sound of slippered feet: a shaven-headed scribe, a linen gauze robe about his bony shoulders, came in and knelt on a cushion before the dais. He carried a writing tray about two feet long, which he placed on the ground. On one side was a battered collection of leaves of vellum, crudely sewn together, on the other a smooth fresh piece of papyrus on which the scribe had been writing.

"What have you discovered?" Orontobates asked.

"Pamenes," the scribe replied, "was most faithful and erudite. His journal provided gossip about the court of Queen Ada."

"We know that." Orontobates waved his fingers.

"He talks of the special relationship between the Macedonian and the queen; about the invaders' interest in the fortifications of the city and the Pythian Manuscript. The Macedonian faces one great difficulty." The scribe allowed himself a smile. "Alexander disbanded most of his fleet, but his siege machinery is still on his ships, which are sailing for a port."

"What?" Memnon exclaimed.

"According to Pamenes, Alexander hopes to seize the port of Myndus to the west of Halicarnassus, and so bring his siege equipment in. He claims to have spies in that port who will deliver the harbour to him."

"Well, he's in for a surprise, isn't he?" Memnon chuckled, clapping his hands.

"Continue!" Orontobates ordered.

"Queen Ada has given Alexander the best scribes from her court to translate the Pythian code. They are accompanied by the Greek physician Telamon. Pamenes did not trust him. 'Too sharp for his own good'–" the scribe tapped the battered piece of parchment "– is how Telamon is described. They are protected by Sarpedon, captain of Queen Ada's guard, a Spartan mercenary, an illiterate boor who is devoted to the queen and may have been her lover."

"Queen Ada has shared a couch with half of Greece! She has little or no fortifications!" Orontobates laughed at his own jest.

"Solan," the scribe continued, "is arrogant and peevish: an old man, he still desires honours. Pamenes believed he could be turned; he is venal and shallow. Cherolos is sharp, fanatically devoted to his strange god: he was placed among the group as Queen Ada's spy. Bessus, the young scribe, is depicted as the most skilled. Pamenes, however, worked on his own and had his own ideas."

"What do you mean?" Memnon broke in.

The scribe picked up a piece of vellum and handed it across. "Pamenes was working on the Pythian cipher. Yet, for some strange reason, he quoted lines from the Greek playwright Sophocles's *Antigone*. I have copied some of the verses as Pamenes wrote them. He has ringed every 'E' and 'I'. He also drew a sketch, as if the Pythian Manuscript was a shrub with two roots: the first he describe as Pente, which I believe is Greek for five, the second is 'Epsilon', the fifth letter of their alphabet, my Lord Memnon."

Memnon smiled to himself. Even though he had worked for Persia and defeated the King of Kings' enemies, the Persians did not regard him as one of them. He stared down at the manuscript. He recognized the lines from *Antigone* and felt a pang of homesickness. When he had last visited Athens he had watched this play being enacted by his own countrymen.

"My lord, if you look further down," the scribe persisted. Memnon obeyed.

"You see the numbers and the letters?"

Ephialtes came over and sat beside Memnon.

"The letters of your alphabet are arranged in five rows and five columns. Each is numbered."

Memnon traced it with his fingers.

	1	2	3	4	5
1	A	B	C	D	E
2	F	G	H	I/J	K
3	L	M	N	O	P
4	Q	R	S	T	U
5	V	W	X	Y	Z

"You see, my lord, five rows, five columns: each is numbered one to five."

"Is it possible?" Memnon asked, "that this is the code for the Pythian Manuscript? That's written in numbers. Couldn't each number stand for a letter?"

"I thought of that, my lord," the scribe replied. "I took the letter 'E' and wondered if it was 15 and the letter 'B' 12." He shook his head. "But it doesn't work; something else is missing."

"What else did Pamenes record in his journal?"

The scribe spread his hands. "My lord, you now know as much as Pamenes wrote."

Memnon passed the sheet of parchment back. "If you break the cipher?"

"My lord, I could boast, but I would fail."

"In which case –" Memnon glanced at Orontobates "– what Pamenes has discovered must be given to the Eunuch. Let's see if he can earn his bread and save his life."

The scribe was dismissed. Orontobates, pleased with himself, murmured something about visiting the women's quarters and, clutching his wine cup, waddled out of the chamber. Ephialtes refilled their goblets.

"Ciphers and secrets," he murmured. "The Macedonian should be killed!"

"He may yet smash his skull against the walls of Halicarnassus." Memnon moved on the couch, his eyes heavy. "I wonder?" He paused. "Ephialtes, I want our best squadron of cavalry ready, early tomorrow morning."

"You will go out to meet the Macedonian?"

"Well," Memnon threw his head back and laughed, "I have studied Alexander since he was a boy. My brother and I spent time at his father's court. Alexander may come and see us tomorrow, so I wish to be prepared."

Ephialtes's eyes gleamed. Memnon leaned over and grasped his wrist. "You are my blood brother, Ephialtes. I trust you with my life. You, I and Orontobates can hold Halicarnassus, but what is wrong? You snap and start like a fresh recruit."

"We have spies in Alexander's camp," Ephialtes replied slowly. "And they have spies in ours."

"Of course!" Memnon scoffed. "That's the way of the world, Ephialtes. Apart from the chosen few, who can resist the lure of gold, silver, precious jewels, preferment? This is different, isn't it?"

Ephialtes nodded. "I come from Thebes. Before Alexander stormed that city, he demanded that I be handed over to him. Thebes refused. You know its fate." Ephialtes smoothed out the folds of his cloak. "My Lord Memnon, I lost everyone; mother, father, brothers, sisters and, the apple of my eye, my sixteen-year-old daughter. I have searched throughout Greece and beyond. None of my kin were taken into slavery. I broke my heart, I have no tears left." He sighed. "Life sweeps forward. You put a brave mask on, like an actor playing a part."

"Someone has been baiting you, haven't they?" Memnon asked. Ephialtes drew out a piece of parchment. "Tumult reigns throughout the town," he read. "Against it advances a towering net of rumours. Man encounters man and is laid low by the spear." Ephialtes glanced up. "You recognize the line?"

"Aeschylus's play *Seven Against Thebes*," Memnon replied. "It's from the chorus of Theban women."

Ephialtes tossed the parchment over. Memnon studied the crude writing: there were also quotations from Homer and Euripides's play *Hecuba*, one constant theme throughout: the sack of cities, the capture and violation of women. Memnon weighed the parchment in his hand. Whoever had sent this to Ephialtes had studied his quarry most closely. Ephialtes thirsted for vengeance: his soul was consumed by a blood feud with the Macedonians. Memnon recalled the phrase from another play: "Such actions can tip a man's fevered brain into madness."

"You don't know who the writer is?" he asked.

"If I did, I'd have his heart on the tip of my spear. It was pushed under my chamber door. A similar parchment was given to one of my grooms, slipped into a basket of fruit as he came in from the city."

"You are being baited," Memnon said. "Macedonian sympathizers prowl this city. Men who would love to open the gates to Alexander. They mean to sap your courage, weaken your will, invoke memories of the past."

"I have thought of that," Ephialtes retorted. "But there is something else. My lord, have you been down to the city recently? Walked among its artisans, the sellers of pots and skins, the petty merchants, the loafers and the idlers around the wine-shop doors?"

Memnon stared bleakly back.

"There's a change of mood," Ephialtes continued. "An ugliness."

"But that is true of any city about to go under siege." Memnon kept his face impassive.

"No, this is different. I did not wish to alarm Orontobates. Three nights ago one of my captains, a Theban like myself, went into the rope-makers' quarter."

"A rat-infested place," Memnon agreed.

"The man is hot-tempered. He does not accept surly glances or hot-eyed stares. A quarrel broke out. He and his men pursued their tormentors into a shabby house near the old temple of Apollo: their quarry escaped, so my men decided to help themselves to some wine. They found a bundle of Macedonian swords, lashed with rope, hidden at the bottom of the cellar steps."

"You are sure of this?" Memnon stroked his face and swore silently.

"I have the swords and studied them closely: they're recently forged and of Macedonian origin. I'd know such swords if I felt them in the dark."

"But that's impossible!" Memnon protested. "For the last seven weeks the gates have been closely watched, every cart, every bundle examined. They must have been brought in earlier."

"Months earlier," Ephialtes retorted. "Alexander was fighting for his life at the Granicus: I am sure our great marauder would not have the foresight to think of Halicarnassus."

"So you are saying these swords were recently brought in by some secret entrance?"

"Possibly." Ephialtes came over and sat beside Memnon on the couch. He handed across another piece of parchment, a crude map of Halicarnassus.

"Look at that, my lord. Tell me our weakness."

Memnon studied the parchment. "The walls are high and well fortified, the gates are secure, outside is a broad ditch which will trap the enemy. We have more than enough troops, an elite brigade of the Persian army and some of the best mercenaries Greece can offer. We have control of the harbour, the Persian fleet controls the shoreline . . ."

"What happens?" Ephialtes interrupted, jabbing the centre of the map, the very place where the great monument of Mausolus soared up to the sky. "What happens," he repeated, "if there is a rising in the city? The demagogues inciting and arming the mob?"

93

"We could crush it, especially if they tried to open the gates."

"And what if," Ephialtes insisted, "this rising took place while we were manning the walls? Can't you see, my lord, we would be trapped, between the attackers outside and those within. We would have to fight our way down to the port."

Memnon stared at the map: he groaned quietly as he fully understood the nightmare Ephialtes was so graphically describing.

Telamon and Cassandra had stripped Pamenes's chamber, piling all his possessions in a heap on the floor. Telamon picked up an earthenware bowl, sniffed it, then threw it away. "Sour milk, I hate that smell! By the way, was that cat here the morning we broke down the door?"

"I can't remember."

Telamon sat cross-legged: he closed his ears to the terrible screams from outside. "Not much, is it?" He stared around. "Something's missing."

They'd found pieces of parchment with the words "PENTE" and "EPSILON" scrawled on them, a rounded pole, scraps of parchment with strange symbols, but nothing remarkable or significant. Telamon tried to keep still. The silence was disturbed by sounds from the villa; on one occasion, a burst of laughter from below, where Gentius was entertaining his guests. Telamon closed his eyes and summoned up Pamenes's dark face.

"If you were murdered," he whispered, "why did the killer choose you? Why did the Persian attackers remove your corpse?"

"Madmen talk to themselves," Cassandra remarked.

"We are all mad." Telamon tapped the paltry possessions. "Why was Pamenes's corpse removed? Was there something the killer wanted to hide?"

Cassandra walked to the window, treading gently on the floorboards. She turned and crossed her arms. "Continue, oh master!" Her voice echoed hollow in the darkness.

Telamon smiled to himself and gazed at the cot bed, linen sheets over a straw-filled mattress which rested on thongs of rope stretched over a wooden pole frame. He got up and pushed back the protective linen veil. He shook this, then turned the mattress over, patting it carefully. Cassandra brought across an oil lamp; Telamon could discover no slit or secret pockets. He pulled the mattress onto the floor and examined the rope support: again, nothing. Telamon studied the frame, how its wooden poles slipped into each other.

"I had a lute once." He patted the wood. "It was Corinthian, you had to assemble it piece by piece."

He removed the support ropes and pulled vainly at the wooden poles. "They're fastened with gum from the acacia tree!" Telamon exclaimed.

He moved to the foot of the bed and tried one of the poles there. This came away easily.

"Ah!"

Telamon now pulled the bed apart, tipping it over; from the pole which ran along the base came a clatter. Telamon shook all its contents onto the floor. He gathered these very carefully together. Cassandra crouched beside him, their heads almost touching, as they sifted through these hidden possessions.

"A rich man."

Telamon picked up the clinking gold darics, the finest coins from Darius's treasury, then the small wax seal depicting Ahura-Mazda and a bronze ring with the same insignia. He clapped his hands, all tiredness forgotten.

"Will the master reveal his wisdom?"

"Don't tease!" Telamon picked up the seal. "Pamenes wasn't a Greek. He was a Mede, a highly trusted court official; that's why he carried this seal."

"And the ring?"

"The ring is only worn by priests who tend the Sacred Fire in Persepolis."

"He was a Persian spy?"

"No, my glorious Theban. Pamenes was more than that: a well-trusted priest, beloved of Darius and his Master of Secrets the Lord Mithra. Our friend Pamenes must have been skilled in tongues: he was sent to Queen Ada's court to worm his way into her affections, learn her secrets, then betray her."

"The Pythian Manuscript?" Cassandra asked.

"The Pythian Manuscript among other things. I am sure Lord Mithra, not to mention Orontobates, the Persian Governor of Halicarnassus, now has a copy of it. He would have also betrayed other secrets: Queen Ada's plans, Alexander's meeting with her, anything he could learn. So, it's interesting. Was Pamenes killed because he was a spy? Did someone just arrange his long fall into eternal night as a means of getting rid of a nuisance?"

"That's possible."

"Or was Pamenes killed because he had learnt something about the Pythian Manuscript, and his killer wanted to claim the glory? Or, finally," Telamon scratched his stubbled chin, "was Pamenes killed because he knew how to translate the Pythian Manuscript and his assassins simply didn't want the Persians to acquire such knowledge?"

"You are sure he was murdered?"

"As there are trees outside."

"So why was his corpse taken?"

"Ah, now we come to our killer. Somehow he came into this chamber and pushed or helped Pamenes through that window." Telamon paused and spread his hands. "The assassin then managed to get a message to the city that Alexander was arriving here with a light skirmishing force. Halicarnassus is a few miles away. No one left the villa, so the killer must have some secret way of communicating with his masters."

"Pigeons!" Cassandra spoke up. "There's a dovecote in the villa."

Telamon laughed and shook his head.

"The message must have been given after Pamenes was found, which was around noon yesterday. Memnon received information that Alexander was about to arrive and that Pamenes was dead. Ah, yes." Telamon rubbed his hands together, lost in his own thoughts.

Cassandra hid her smile: unless he had a problem to turn over in his teeming mind, Talamon became bored and restless, whether it be how to treat a certain wound, heal an injury, or some problem at Alexander's court. She half suspected that was the real reason Telamon stayed with Alexander. The physician really couldn't make his mind up who Alexander truly was: the king was a problem which constantly vexed him. She decided to return to her teasing.

"And will the great philosopher share his conclusions?"

"I believe Pamenes was killed because he had made progress with the Pythian Manuscript. His killer, who is also working for the enemy, wanted the glory as well as to remove a rival."

"Would he know Pamenes's true identity?"

"Perhaps. Anyway, the assassin kills Pamenes and, in his hurry to escape from this chamber, gathers up Pamenes's manuscripts and stylus, the one the scribe was using, freshly sharpened. Pamenes's corpse is then found. The killer passes this information on to the Persians and, to show he is as good as his word, also confides that a manuscript, stolen from Pamenes, is hidden beneath the corpse. None of us would dream of looking there."

"So, as I've asked before, why did the attackers take the corpse as well?"

"The Persians," Telamon murmured, "regard their priests with great awe. They would need his body for honourable burial in one of their Towers of Silence. They might also not want Alexander to discover that Pamenes was a Persian spy."

"So the attackers took both corpse and this so-called manuscript?" Cassandra rose and walked away, measuring her steps carefully. "It must have been a very large pigeon," she teased over her shoulder, "to carry so much information."

"What do you mean?"

She turned round. "This man is sending a great deal of information: the plan of the villa, Alexander's whereabouts, the strength of his escort, Pamenes's death, the whereabouts of his corpse . . ."

"Not to mention pre-arranged signals, like a lantern being shone from a window," Telamon added. "I agree, Cassandra: the killer would need a pigeon as big as an eagle."

"Who shone that lantern?" Cassandra asked.

"Sarpedon and a kitchen maid saw it: when he reached the chamber, both the lantern and whoever was holding it were gone."

"Does Alexander know this?"

"No. Sarpedon didn't tell him, he was probably frightened. If men like Cleitus had their way, anyone under suspicion would be tortured."

"So who do you think it could be?" Telamon pointed to a lamp glowing on the table. "Look at that, Cassandra. What do you see dancing around it?"

"Moths and flies."

"That's what we have here," Telamon continued. "Alexander is the flame: all forms of strange creatures are attracted by the glow and heat of his court. A similar light burns at Persepolis, with the same results. Where there's power, like a corpse on a hillside, the vultures and scavengers gather." He walked over to Cassandra. "How many men do you think Darius can really trust? When he seized the throne of the King of Kings, he had the man who helped him, Bagoas, killed, his corpse stuffed with sawdust, transformed into a mummy which Darius always keeps in his Hall of Audience at Persepolis." Telamon paused. "Alexander is no different. He is surrounded by men and women who, if they thought his death would advance them, would strike with all the compassion of a snake. Spies and traitors throng each court. At Halicarnassus, in secret shadowy chambers, men plot against Memnon and, somewhere in this villa, a killer plots against Alexander. We live in a world of shadows, Cassandra. There's no truth or honesty. Alexander could count on the fingers of one hand the number of people he can truly trust."

"Are you one of them?"

"I may be. What worries me is, how long will I remain so?"

They heard the sound of footsteps outside. Telamon hastily put away what they'd found. A rap at the half-open door, and Solan, followed by Bessus and the priest Cherolos, came into the room. All were carrying wine cups. Solan looked much the worse for drink. Cherolos kept putting the mask on and off. Bessus looked slightly embarrassed by his companions' antics.

"We thought you'd come down," Solan slurred. "We know the hour is late, but the wine is good. And tomorrow? Well, tomorrow is another day."

"Did you trust Pamenes?" Telamon asked abruptly, watching their faces carefully.

"Don't be stupid!" Cherolos pouted. He blinked and stared round the chamber. "You certainly didn't. You've been through his possessions."

"Those we've found! Did he ever tell you," Telamon insisted, "about his past?"

"He said he came originally from Sardis," Solan stammered. "But he was secretive."

"Everybody at court is secretive. Did he ever tell you about the Pythian Manuscript?"

"Well, he would have done, wouldn't he?" Solan stumbled across and sat on a stool, the front of his tunic all wine-stained.

"I once found him," Bessus spoke up, eager to divert Telamon's attention, "with a copy of Homer's *Iliad* . . ."

"And?"

"He seemed to be counting the letters."

"Why should he be doing that?" Cassandra asked. "What has the *Iliad* got to do with the Pythian Manuscript?"

"I don't know." Bessus stepped back, as if embarrassed.

"You suspect," Telamon persisted, "Pamenes had discovered more than he ever told you, don't you, Bessus?"

The young scribe nodded.

"What happens if I tell you," Telamon declared, "that Pamenes was a Persian spy?"

His three visitors gazed blankly back.

"How do I know –?" Telamon paused as another blood-chilling scream rent the air.

"Why doesn't he kill them?" Bessus hissed. "Why doesn't he just take them down and cut their heads off?"

"You were saying?" Solan glanced up.

"How do I know that you're all not spies? You were raised and reared, educated, under the rule of Persia. Why didn't you stay in Halicarnassus? Why did you decide to join Queen Ada?"

"She was driven out by her nephew," Solan slurred. "A man who rejoiced in the name of Pixadorus. Pixadorus married a Persian and Darius took over the government of the city."

"Ah yes," Telamon interrupted. "I heard a vague story – didn't

Alexander, while Philip was still alive, offer to marry Pixadorus's kinswoman, only to be rebuffed?"

"Philip was always trying to get his hands on Halicarnassus," Solan retorted. "We would have welcomed that. We may not be Greeks in the true sense –" the old scribe glared at Telamon "– but we have our pride. You are not the only one, physician, who dislikes Persian rule."

"I didn't say I disliked it." Telamon came over and crouched before this old man, whose eyes and wits were dulled by wine. "But why did you go with Queen Ada?"

"I went because I loved her." Solan blinked. "Bessus came – well, why did you come?"

"For the same reason."

"Well, that's what he says." Solan winked conspiratorially at Telamon. "But his family were disliked by the Persians. As for our good priest here, well, go on, Cherolos, tell them who you really are."

The priest just lifted his mask.

"That's right, wear that stupid mask!" Solan jibed. He leaned closer. "Cherolos left Halicarnassus because he had to. He's a heretic. He used to be a Persian priest. You know how they worship Ahura-Mazda! According to Cherolos, the God of Life did not create this world: it was the work of some dark Snake-Lord. The Persian authorities wanted to question Cherolos, so he grew his hair long and fled."

The priest, stung by Solan's remarks, stamped his foot querulously. He was starting to protest when there was a sound of heavy footsteps and Telamon's name being called: Black Cleitus shoved aside the door and strode in. He dismissed the rest, pushing Solan aside and grasping Telamon's arm.

"You've got to come! You've got to come now! It's the king, something's wrong!"

Chapter 5

"On the first day Alexander moved up towards the
fortifications . . . the defenders made a sortie and flung
weapons at long range."

Arrian: The Campaigns of Alexander, Book I, Chapter 20

T elamon followed Black Cleitus down the stairs. The royal
bodyguard wouldn't answer his questions: when the others
tried to follow, he roared at them to mind their own business.
Cleitus was wearing his usual black cloak.

"I never slept," he growled as they crossed the cobbled yard.
"I've told the king it was a mistake, he should have waited for the
rest; all this hurrying and scurrying about!"

They entered the orchard, strode past rows of sleeping men and
out into what must have been a grazing paddock, now ringed and
guarded by silver Shield-Bearers. Groups of men camped round
fires, some sleeping, others talking quietly. Telamon could detect
no upset or alarm. Alexander's pavilion had been set up in the
middle of the paddock. The tent-makers had not done a very good
job; some of the guy-ropes were slack, and half the pavilion hung
like drapes in the night breeze. The guard lifted a flap, and
Telamon followed Cleitus in. There was the usual mess: pieces
of armour lying on the floor, a sword encrusted with blood, articles
of clothing, a parchment scroll. Hephaestion stood crouched at the
entrance to the king's private quarters.

"What's the matter?" Telamon demanded.

Hephaestion lifted the flap and pushed the physician through.
Inside it was gloomy, smelling of spilt wine and cooked meat. A
tray had been upset. Telamon cursed as he slipped on a greasy

platter. The bed was empty, the makeshift netting pulled aside, the bolsters on the ground.

"Alexander!"

"In the corner," Hephaestion whispered.

Telamon looked over his shoulder: Black Cleitus hadn't joined them, but stood on guard outside.

"Is it one of his panic attacks?" Telamon murmured. Alexander could succumb to fits of high anxiety, especially after he had been drinking: these attacks manifested themselves in either frenetic activity or a cold tension which kept him seated in a chair or lying rigid on a bed.

"He was sick," Hephaestion replied. "Some stomach disorder. I was sleeping outside when he began to scream and yell. He's in the far corner."

Telamon went round to the cot bed. Hephaestion followed carrying an oil lamp. Telamon took this, and in the dim pool of light, he caught the glint of metal.

"Alexander! Alexander! What's the matter?"

Telamon paused and crouched down. It was dangerous to approach the king in one of his moods: he often failed to recognize even his closest friends. Telamon held out the oil lamp. Alexander, naked except for a loincloth, crouched holding a dagger, his strange, different-coloured eyes glaring at Telamon.

"Is that you, Father? Have you come for me? I had no part in it! It was Mother. She laid a wreath on your assassin's head and offered sacrifice to his shade. I didn't do anything! I am your loving son."

"Alexander, it's Telamon! You've been dreaming!"

The king's gaze didn't falter. Telamon thought how young he looked, the skin of his face drawn tight, emphasizing his cheek-bones; the muscles of Alexander's neck were rigid, and when he talked, his chin hardly moved.

"What shall we do?" Hephaestion whispered.

"Go back to my quarters," Telamon replied. "Tell Cassandra to fill a goblet of wine and add some poppy juice."

Alexander's arm began to tremble.

"Will he be safe?"

"Just go!" Telamon hissed. Hephaestion left.

102

"I was there." Alexander's eyes blinked. "Outside the amphitheatre. Philip was walking by himself, his mantle over his arm, that stupid laurel wreath on his head, no bodyguard. I don't know why he did that. None of his companions was there. He was strolling, as if through a garden. Pausanias came running forward, a dagger in his hand. Philip turned, smiling; Pausanias struck twice here." Alexander tapped his left side. "The dagger pierced Philip's heart, struck him down in his moment of glory."

"I know," Telamon whispered. "I know."

"Mother buried him in a tomb at Vegina! Marvellous tomb, Telamon! Am I dreaming?"

"You have been dreaming, Alexander. You've ridden far and fast. You're exhausted both in mind and body. You've drunk too much wine and now you are dreaming. Do you remember when you used to dream at Mieza? You'd wake up screaming. Ptolemy used to laugh at you."

"I'll take that upstart's head one day!"

"No you won't." Telamon edged forward.

Alexander's shoulders had drooped; the hand holding the dagger hung slack. Telamon leaned forward, plucked the dagger and threw it over his shoulder. His fingers brushed Alexander's hand; it was clammy and icy.

"Come on now." Telamon picked up a blanket and draped it gently round Alexander's shoulders. "Back to bed."

The king, however, remained in his tense crouch.

"Alexander, you're freezing. You must get warm." Telamon dragged the king to his feet. Alexander swayed drunkenly, pulling away, coughed and retched.

"You must get back to bed." Telamon led him over and gently eased the king down. Turning on his right side, Alexander curled up like a child, hand going beneath his face. Telamon felt for the pulse in his neck, strong but erratic. He picked up every piece of clothing he could and laid it over the king and, sitting by the edge of the bed, began to rub his back. Hephaestion returned carrying the goblet of wine. Alexander refused to drink but Telamon, helped by Hephaestion, made him sit up and forced the cup between his lips. Alexander coughed and tried to draw back but, eventually, he swallowed, drained the cup and lay back on the bed. He lay there for a while, body jerking as the potion took its effect. He muttered something about Olympias: he tried to keep his eyes open but after a while fell into a deep sleep.

"How long has this been happening?"

Hephaestion went across to a chest and pulled out a military cloak, which he laid over the king. "Almost every night: this is the worst attack. Alexander dreams about his father walking into the amphitheatre on the day he was assassinated: he sees Pausanias running towards him."

"But Alexander had nothing to do with his father's murder. I've told him that, you've told him that. Philip had divorced Olympias, married again and begot a son."

"I know." Hephaestion led Telamon away and rubbed the side of his face. "What a night, eh, Telamon, very little sleep! The king insists we rise at dawn and ride to Halicarnassus, he wants to view the fortifications for himself. Telamon –" Hephaestion's long, dark face was heavy with sleep, eyes red–rimmed: he scratched his unshaven cheek and gestured towards the king. "I hear what you say, physician. I tell Alexander the same. However, while riding here, he confessed he was close to Philip when his father was killed but remained rooted to the spot."

"He thinks he could have intervened?"

Hephaestion agreed. "He talks of those few seconds, of watching Pausanias's crazed face, his murderous lunge, the dagger going in and out."

"I wasn't there." Telamon glanced towards the sleeping king. "But you were, Hephaestion. Tell me the truth, did Alexander know his father was going to die?"

"I don't know." Hephaestion's reply was quick, blunt.

"So you have doubts?"

"I have doubts," Hephaestion confessed. "And, I suspect, so does Alexander. He asks himself: did he secretly wish for it? Did he, in his own soul, desire his father's death?"

Telamon sat down on a stool. Hephaestion knelt on the ground before him, picked up a sword belt from the floor and kept moving the dagger in and out of its sheath.

"Olympias was the cause. She drove Pausanias, fanned his grievances, provided him with a dagger. The Witch Queen feels no guilt, but Alexander does. I sometimes wonder if that's why he keeps talking of being begotten by a god."

"So if Philip wasn't his real father," Telamon smiled thinly, "he's not guilty of patricide?"

"Yes, it possesses its own bizarre logic."

Cleitus lifted the tent flap and crawled in. "Is the king safe?"

"He's asleep," Telamon replied. "A mixture of wine and poppy seed." He stared at the ugly, twisted face of the bodyguard. "Aren't you pleased, Cleitus, that I left the Groves of Mieza and trained to be a physician?"

"You were a worthless soldier," Cleitus grated. "You had two left hands, but you were good at running."

Telamon ignored the jibe. "Cleitus, you were with Alexander the day Philip was murdered. You were standing next to him?"

"Yes, I remember when the old goat was struck down: shuffling along, with his battered leg, his one good eye glaring. He looked as ugly as I do!"

"Did you see Pausanias the assassin?"

"For a very brief instant. Ignore all the stories about Pausanias running up, that's just the king's fevered imagination. Pausanias strolled up as if he wanted to present a petition. He caught Philip's left hand then struck with the dagger, all in the blink of an eye."

Telamon took the knife from Hephaestion's hand. He balanced this and tossed it at Cleitus, who caught it deftly.

"That fast?" Telamon asked.

"Even faster," Cleitus grinned, and thrust the dagger into the soil. "A blink of an eye, a few heartbeats."

"Could you have stopped Pausanias?"

"I'm a soldier, not a god," Cleitus joked. "Nobody could have stopped Pausanias. Philip deserved his death, strolling there without any guards, naked to his enemies. But the boy —" Cleitus used his common term for Alexander "— the boy thinks differently, and that's the boy's great fault. He thinks too much, lets his imagination run like an unbridled horse. But now he sleeps. And, talking of horses," Cleitus turned and lifted the tent flap, "I want to make sure those lazy grooms have done their jobs!"

He disappeared into the night. Hephaestion picked up the dagger and resheathed it.

"These dreams are getting worse?" Telamon asked.

"Cleitus doesn't want to discuss them." Hephaestion glanced out of the corner of his eye. "He just hides any weakness in Alexander. The only thing Cleitus is wary of is the soldiers getting to know."

"Is there something about Halicarnassus which has provoked these nightmares?"

Hephaestion nodded. "Possibly, but I don't know what. Whether he wishes to emulate his father, surpass Philip's achievements, win the crown of being the Great Besieger of Cities, show the world that no fortification can withstand him, I am not too sure. Anyway, he will sleep now?"

"Deeply, but I am not too sure for how long." Telamon rose to his feet.

"What shall we do?"

"When I was in Egypt," Telamon replied, "I was hired by a very wealthy merchant's wife: her husband had developed a deep fear of water. They used to cross the Nile to visit their family tomb in the Necropolis on the west bank. The very sight of the river came to terrify him. He'd begin to sweat, scream. He confessed that he had crossed the Nile more times than he could remember without a second thought. Eventually he mentioned one occasion when the crocodiles had attacked a fishing boat and plucked a man straight into the water. Crocodiles turn their prey over and over. The merchant had seen this. I pointed out that he had witnessed other bloody scenes, so why did this in particular provoke such a fear? I visited him for a month before I found the source. When he was a child he had gone swimming in a reed-filled pool beside the Nile. Usually it was safe . . ."

"He had been attacked by a crocodile?"

"Yes, the creature had apparently moved from the river and was lurking among the reeds. He and his companions escaped unscathed, but after he witnessed the attack, all his childhood memories came flooding back."

"And what did you do?"

"I sedated him with wine and an opiate." Telamon smiled. "And I took him for a fishing trip down the Nile. The next day I did the same, and the day after, but each time, I reduced the opiate." Telamon rubbed his eyes. "One of the pleasantest treatments I have ever given. Beautiful! It was just after the Irrigation: the Nile was in full flow, bringing that vivid green freshness back to the land. My beloved, the temple girl Anuala, came with me."

"And the merchant?"

"Oh, he paid me well and had no more trouble in crossing the Nile."

"And can you do the same for the king?"

"Perhaps we can," Telamon shrugged. "Perhaps it will work. You, me, Cleitus, perhaps Ptolemy, will re-enact the scene, let the king experience his own nightmare: let him realize, as Cleitus says, that despite what Alexander felt about his father, he had no part in his assassination."

"And these present troubles?" Hephaestion got to his feet. "The attack, a traitor lurks here?"

"Traitors lurk everywhere," Telamon replied, lifting the tent flap. "The king should be careful. But," he smiled over his shoulder, "I know he'll do the opposite."

Telamon returned to his quarters. Cassandra was already rolled up in a blanket on a cot bed under the window. Telamon decided to shave and did so, sitting in the dark, trimming his moustache and beard. He then stripped and, with the sponge on the end of a stick, washed himself carefully, dried himself off and rubbed in oil.

"Is the Great Killer sleeping sweetly?"

Telamon hurriedly pulled his tunic over his head.

"Don't worry!" Cassandra called out. "I won't even peep. Oh, by the way, I've thrown the chamber pot out. One of those lazy bastards at the feast must have used it: our chamber smelt like a midden heap!"

"Don't worry," Telamon replied. "I'll use the latrine pits, and, yes, the king sleeps sweetly."

Cassandra rolled over, her face hidden in the dark. "I wonder if he does, Telamon? How many ghosts must throng his soul? You've given him poppy seed?"

"Of course!" Telamon pulled back the linen veil around his own bed and lay down, pulling the heavy military cloak around him.

"In which case," Cassandra murmured, "he'll be up fresh with the dawn, proving that there is nothing wrong with the Great Alexander!"

Her words were prophetic. Telamon felt he had hardly been asleep when he heard a pounding on the door and Black Cleitus came in, clapping his hands.

"Stop playing with yourself, Telamon, the king wants you. We are to see Halicarnassus!"

Telamon pulled himself up, heavy-limbed and heavy-eyed. "I want to sleep," he yawned. "I don't give a damn about Halicarnassus!"

Cleitus had moved across to stand over Cassandra. "Don't even think of it!" she shouted, not even moving. "Lay a hand on me, you black, ugly bear!"

Cleitus leaned down, smacked her bottom and strode out of the room bellowing with laughter.

Telamon got up and quickly dressed, pulling on the long leather marching boots, tying the thongs. He went across and poured some water from the jug and splashed this over his face. He took down his cloak and sword belt, hanging on a peg on the wall. He was more aware of the sounds coming from below. Cassandra muttered something but Telamon, still half asleep, staggered out. One of the royal pages thrust a half-eaten piece of bread and a cup of watered wine into his hands. Telamon took one look and handed them back. "I prefer a clean fast," he muttered.

The courtyard below was full of mounted men: members of the Silver Shield Cavalry Squadron, dressed in their muscle-shaped, bronze cuirasses, grey leather war kilts, purple sashes about their waists, cloaks of the same colour clasped around their shoulders. Young men, dandies, they prided themselves on their appearance as well as their fighting ability. They carried button-shaped shields and short lances, sword belts slung over their shoulders. Most of them were not wearing their Boetian helmets, but had these hanging from a strap looped to the harness of their horses, the best mounts from the royal stables. These were caparisoned in purple saddlecloths, the colours of their regiment, and black, gleaming harness, cleaned and polished. Alexander was in the middle of them checking horses, joking and chatting. A groom led across a war horse, a magnificent bay with a leopardskin shabrague which covered it from neck to withers. Alexander took the horse's reins, letting the animal nuzzle his neck and hands before vaulting into the saddle. He glimpsed Telamon.

"Your horse is outside, physician," he grinned. "A good morning's ride will do you the world of good!"

And, turning his horse, Alexander clattered out, the Shield-Bearers jostling behind him like a group of schoolboys preparing for mischief. Cleitus and Hephaestion were waiting beyond the courtyard gate, Telamon's horse between them. After some difficulty Telamon mounted, ignoring Cleitus's jibes. He gathered the reins and patted the horse on its neck.

"The gentlest in the stables," Hephaestion whispered. "I chose it myself. You look as tired as I do."

"The king should be more prudent," Cleitus growled. "We are only taking a light force."

They followed the royal cavalcade down the track, through an avenue of sycamore trees, to the main entrance gate where more soldiers waited. Telamon heard the shouts and neighs of horses, and when he reached there, discovered the cause of excitement: on either side, facing the villa entrance, Alexander's soldiers, using the long poles from a vine trellis, had set up two makeshift crosses to crucify the Persian prisoners. One was already dead, his body hanging slack: the other still squirmed, arms lashed to the wood, feet scrabbling for the wooden plinth, so he could pull himself up and breathe more easily. A little further down, soldiers had erected a funeral pyre for the victims of the previous night's battle. A company of archers stoked a makeshift brazier nearby. Trumpets rang out, and Alexander's escort organized themselves. The king sat on his horse staring at the funeral pyre, eyes half-closed, mouth a tight grimace. The dead lay piled, wrapped in their blood-soaked cloaks, Greeks and Persians together in death. The man on the cross cried out, a heart-rending moan. Alexander glanced at him. He leaned down and whispered something to the captain of archers. The man picked up his bow and pulled an arrow from his quiver. Hardly anyone noticed, and few cared, as the barbed arrow whirred through the air and struck the man full in the heart. The corpse slumped down the cross. Again Alexander whispered and the captain, helped by other archers, took the corpses from the crosses and tossed them like brushwood on top of the funeral pyre. Alexander sprinkled a flask of oil as an act of oblation. His escort fell silent, row upon row of watching horsemen. A cresset torch was fired: Alexander dismounted, approached the funeral pyre and threw the torch. Horses whinnied as the flames leapt up and the smoke curled out. Alexander mounted, turned his horse, and stared along the ranks of cavalrymen.

"No one dies in vain!" he proclaimed. "The Persian dead are a witness to the desperation of the defenders of Halicarnassus! The Macedonians who died prove how fierce our attack will be! Let them all walk in the Fields of Elysium!"

He gestured at the captain of the archers: more firebrands were hurled onto the funeral pyre. The flames roared heavenwards, the grey-black smoke lifting like a cloud. Telamon, who'd ridden ahead, some distance from the escort, gazed up at the sky. The sun had not yet fully risen but a beautiful day was promised: only white wisps of cloud against the pink-blue sky. A breeze wafted the funeral smoke towards him, and Telamon wondered how many more would die before the city fell.

Alexander came galloping up, Hephaestion and Cleitus behind him. He reined in, murmured to his companions, then rode towards Telamon.

"Stay by me," he ordered: his horse skittered and bucked a little. Alexander pressed in his knees and, expertly grasping the reins, calmed it. Behind them, Hephaestion and Cleitus brought up the columns of cavalry. Alexander looked over his shoulder then, leaning across, patted Telamon on the back.

"You did good work last night, physician." He rubbed between his horse's ears. "And how does your patient look this morning?"

"Not as tired as I feel."

Alexander laughed. Telamon studied him closely. The king had prepared himself well, face shaved and oiled, hair washed and dressed. In his gold cuirass and war kilt of the same colour, his purple gold-edged cloak billowing out and plumed Boetian helmet hanging from his war belt, Alexander looked the conquering hero, the young adventurer, the general without a care in the world.

"I don't like it when you look at me too closely," he murmured. "You make me feel as if you are searching for symptoms."

"You shouldn't be having nightmares like that."

"Philip is never far behind me. If it's not him, it's Mother." Alexander leaned over. "Do you like your horse? Chosen especially, physician, for a comfortable ride. Let's hope this day is better than yesterday."

Telamon gazed out over the countryside. In some ways this reminded him of Macedon: a ridge of mountains in the far distance, undulating plains clustered with wild flowers, their colours bright as banners across the grasslands. Copses of holm oak, cypress, willow and sycamore, provided more greenery. Occasionally a plume of smoke stained the sky, but the grasslands either side of the road seemed deserted: a buzzard swooped then rose in alarm at the clatter of hooves and clink of metal as Alexander led his squadrons across the plain to the city of Halicarnassus.

Alexander sniffed the breeze. "I can always smell the sea!"

"Even so far inland?"

Alexander laughed. "Perhaps it's my imagination. Today I hope to surprise the Persians. Nicanor –" he referred to his admiral "– will see to what remains of my fleet. Socrates –" another commander "– is under secret orders to strike south-west and seize the port of Myndus. He has been given guarantees that the port will open its gates. Nicanor will bring in his ships and I shall have my siege equipment."

"That easy?"

"That easy," Alexander mimicked. "Then we'll seize every cart and show Memnon that walls cannot withstand me."

"To emulate your father?"

"Don't start!" Alexander retorted.

"What is it about Halicarnassus?" Telamon persisted. "Its

111

capture will enhance your reputation, but why does it mean so much?"

Alexander peered up at the sky. "Is that a buzzard or an eagle?" he wondered. "If it's an eagle, it's a sign of good fortune."

"At the moment," Telamon replied, "I couldn't care if it was your mother Olympias."

Alexander laughed and patted his horse.

"I asked a question. What's so special about Halicarnassus?"

"It's funny you mention Mother." Alexander grasped the reins in one hand. "I don't dream of her so much, not like I used to, when she used to lie on that bed with snakes coiling all about her. Ever since then snakes always repel me; even the common variety, anything that coils or writhes. Funny, isn't it, how childhood fears can return to haunt you? There's a line about that from the *Iliad* but I can't place it."

"Halicarnassus?" Telamon repeated.

"Oh yes, there's a story. You know Father had two sons?"

"Yourself and Arridhaeus?"

"Poor Arridhaeus, the offspring of one of Father's concubines, a healthy, boisterous boy, so they said, until Olympias gave him some sweetmeats. The boy had a seizure and nearly died. You've seen the effect, nothing more than a shambling, dribbling idiot. Now, as I got older —" Alexander pushed his horse closer to Telamon's. The king had apparently forgotten they were riding into the heart of enemy territory. He was oblivious to the thundering cavalry behind them or the quiet countryside, its grass bending under the morning breeze, the slight mist rising under the strengthening sun. It was always the same when Alexander discussed his parents, as if nothing existed except him and them.

"Matters between Father and me turned sour. I objected to his womanizing and, perhaps to snub me, he opened secret negotiations with a gentleman called Pixadorus, Queen Ada's nephew, who was then ruler of Halicarnassus, before the Persians took over. Philip wanted to marry Arridhaeus to one of Pixadorus's kinswomen. I became alarmed."

"You or Olympias?"

"I became alarmed," Alexander repeated crossly. "So I sent a secret messenger to Pixadorus. I described Arridhaeus as a complete and utter idiot, and offered myself in marriage to this princess. My plot was betrayed; Father was furious and that was the end of the matter."

"So, you see this siege as revenge?"

"No, no." Alexander's voice fell to a whisper. Telamon didn't catch what he said, but he was sure that Alexander referred to a mystery which had to be solved. He went to question him further but Alexander made a cutting movement with his hand.

"I will take Halicarnassus! I will have my own way!"

"And Philip?"

Alexander shrugged. He undid the strap of his helmet, placed it on his head and, guiding his horse with his knees, carefully fastened the strap under his chin. He glanced at Telamon from under its brim.

"Let Philip's ghost wander Hades. Let him witness what I do."

Alexander turned his horse and rode back. Telamon felt rather foolish, alone by himself at the head of the column. A short while later Alexander, Hephaestion and Cleitus joined him. The king's mood had now changed, talking excitedly about the countryside and how, when the war ended, he would settle Macedonian soldiers to farm the land. Telamon became lost in his own reverie. The sun rose and he felt the first real heat of the day. By now his face was coated in a fine white dust, and he noticed the countryside had begun to change. On occasions he could catch the tang of the sea, the smell of the port. Scouts thundered ahead of them to ensure all was safe. Alexander became immersed in the details of the coming siege. The closer they approached Halicarnassus the deeper Telamon's agitation grew. The countryside was quite different, the grasslands and trees disappeared, giving way to harsh, sandy craggy terrain. It reminded Telamon very much of Egypt, when he'd left the lush, green fields which flanked the Nile, and entered the harsh scrubland which separated the fertile black earth of the Nile from the searing heat of the vast, sun-scorched Red Lands. Nothing but rocky escarpments, dotted here and there with bushes and the occasional small oasis where pools of water were fringed by coarse grass and crooked palm trees. In turn this gave way to a flat, bleak landscape of hard rock, where the wind whipped up dust to sting their faces.

"The peninsula of Halicarnassus," Alexander declared. "Sheer hard rock which surrounds the city on all three sides. No one knows the reason for it. My engineers claim it's due to the rivers and streams which separate as they come towards the city and take a different route to the sea. No water, so no grass or trees."

"And you'll camp here?" Telamon asked.

"As close to the grasslands as we can."

They breasted a hill and reined in. Telamon gazed in astonishment. He had never approached Halicarnassus from the landward side. The city seemed to rise out of the very ground: huge, soaring walls, crenellated at the top, interspersed by fortified towers. The cavalcade fell silent. The wind blew the dust away. Telamon glimpsed the lofty gatehouse, a small fortress in itself, which dominated the Triple Gate, the main entrance to this great city and harbour. He felt as if he were dreaming. He was aware of noises behind them and the excited chatter between Alexander and his captains. The view in front of him, however, was of forbidding silence: fearsomely high grey-white walls built on sheer rock, towers stretching up to the skies. Armour glinted along the parapets, between the crenellations. The heavy main gate was protected by iron bars, while along the wall, as far as he could see, a broad trench had been hacked out of the ground. Telamon pushed his horse forward and calculated this must be at least twenty-five yards wide. Yet it was the silence which unnerved him. Three years ago Telamon had joined a military expedition into the Red Lands of Egypt, a chariot squadron despatched to relieve one of the great fortresses built by the pharaohs against Libyan raiders. When they'd reached the place, desolate under the searing sun, every single one of its defenders had simply disappeared. They found nothing except a fortress armed and ready, gates still secure but no one inside. Sometimes the image came back to haunt Telamon's dreams. How he had to pinch himself to make sure he was awake: Halicarnassus was the same. It was a teeming city, one of the busiest ports on the Middle Sea. A cultivated, sophisticated Greek settlement which had grown and prospered and, for a while, been an independent

114

kingdom; now it was like approaching a city of the dead. The windows along the walls had been shuttered, any buildings beyond the walls levelled to the ground, and that great yawning ditch . . .

"Its walls are blind," he murmured.

"What's that? What's that?" Alexander, discussing different points, pushed his horse closer.

"When you aporoach a city," Telamon replied, "be it Corinth or Athens, you gaze on the city and the city gazes back. But Halicarnassus is like staring into the face of a blind man. Only this time you wonder whether he is blind or dead. No life, no movement."

A prickle of fear coursed up his back, and his horse moved restlessly beneath him. "Is this wise, Alexander? Your army hasn't arrived, yet Memnon is acting as if it has."

Telamon gazed along the parapet. The silence was growing oppressive; even Alexander fell quiet. Nudging his horse forward, the king studied the city. Cleitus, too, was unable to hide his unease. A quick murmured conversation between Alexander and Hephaestion and the cavalcade moved forward, fanning out in a long line before the city walls.

"They must have seen us," Telamon declared. He gazed up at the battlements and caught the glitter of spear points. "How far do the walls stretch?"

"We are looking at it from the north," Cleitus retorted. He gestured with his hand. "The Triple Gate. The walls curve either side to the west and east, down to the sea."

"And somewhere there," Hephaestion spoke up, "you will find its weakness."

"Aye, we will."

Telamon gazed to his left and right. The Macedonian cavalry had fanned out, a long curving arc either side of the king. The formation was two men deep. All were armed for battle, helmets on, shields brought up. A trumpeter lifted his salpinx, orders were shouted, the salpinx brayed and the line advanced threateningly to the creak of harness and clatter of weapons. Horses whinnied, moving excitedly as they sensed the growing danger, the prospect of battle. Telamon was now behind the king. Alexander whispered an order which was passed down the ranks. Again the bray of trumpets, the advance halted.

"What's he doing?" Telamon looked to his left and found himself staring at the smiling, friendly face of Sarpedon, his gauntlets still on, head and face almost hidden by the Boetian helmet. He was dressed in a leather cuirass and kilt: he carried no spear or shield, but had drawn his sword from its scabbard.

"I didn't know you were coming!" Telamon exclaimed.

"And nor did anyone else," Sarpedon whispered. "But life at the villa becomes boring for a soldier." He leaned even closer. "Alexander is showing off. He wants to see the fortifications. As a gesture of contempt, he probably intends to ride the entire length of the walls."

Telamon nodded. Alexander would do that. Anything to depict himself as a hero, to emulate his great heroes Agamemnon and Achilles: those Achaean warriors had laid siege to Troy and ridden around its fortified walls as a challenge, a gesture of defiance.

"I wish I had a chariot!" Alexander's voice carried.

"Thank the gods he hasn't!" Hephaestion whispered loudly.

"I wonder if Memnon's awake?" Cleitus bellowed.

As if in answer came a faint whoosh. Glancing up, Telamon saw the fiery missile, a huge arrow soaked in oil, being loosed from beyond the walls.

"They have catapults!" a cavalryman yelled. "They have catapults!"

"Now you tell us!" some wit responded.

The huge bolt, coated in fire, fell like a shooting star: it crashed to the ground about ten yards in front of them, sending up columns of sparks and shards of scalding wood. Telamon gazed fearfully up as he heard more cries and exclamations. Three similar missiles had been launched, streaks of flame, up in a fearsome arc and then down. Two fell short, but one hit the Macedonian cavalry further along the line. The air was rent with chilling cries, the screams of horses. One cavalryman, his cloak and saddlecloth on fire, careered forward, a moving flame of man and beast. The horse charged wildly, recklessly towards the trench: its rider, in his own agony, had lost all control, and both horse and rider tipped into the man-made ravine. Other horses were careering around, some with

116

riders, some without. Telamon saw a cavalryman run forward, his cloak a sheet of fire, as if he could out-race the horrors which had engulfed him. He, too, ran blindly towards the walls. Two of his companions dismounted and desperately tried to follow. Telamon glanced up. The parapets were now busy: archers leaning through the crenellations, arrows notched, bowstrings pulled back. A rain of arrows fell. All three cavalrymen were struck. The man on fire simply collapsed, fire glowing all around him. Of the other two, one was killed instantly, but the other tried to crawl back to his lines until further arrows struck him, and he writhed and lay still. Confusion and chaos reigned. Officers rode along trying to impose order. Alexander had hardly moved. He sat as if carved out of stone, just patting his horse's neck and staring up at the walls.

"They must have been expecting us," Sarpedon murmured. "Machines have to be prepared, greased with oil, braziers lit and brought to the parapets."

Telamon urged his horse forward and stared to his left. Gaps had appeared in the Macedonian lines. Horses lay kicking, cavalrymen sprawled on the rocky ground. Smoke curled towards him, bringing the stench of cooking flesh. Somewhere a man screamed in agony and a horse whinnied, a high-pitched neigh which abruptly fell away as its throat was cut. Black Cleitus was now beside Alexander, pointing to his left. Telamon followed his direction and glimpsed the clouds of dust. He glanced to his right, where similar dust clouds were rising.

"Cavalry!" Cleitus shouted. "They've sent squadrons through postern gates further along the walls! Alexander!" He leaned over and shook the king.

The King remained impassive. He seemed fascinated by the great Triple Gate, as if by very thought he could make that huge cavernous entrance open up to receive them. More firebolts were launched. One, aimed at the centre of the line, fell short. Soon it was the turn of the right flank of the Macedonian line to receive casualties, with the same hideous results, man and beast engulfed in flame. Horses, maddened beyond belief, careered forward, bucking wildly, throwing their riders and, occasionally, killing them with lashing hooves. Alexander broke from his reverie.

117

"Tell the line to advance! Quickly, at a trot!"

Cleitus made to protest.

"Shut up!" Alexander shouted. "Just move forward as far as we can!"

The order was relayed to the right and left flanks. Trumpets brayed, a long single blast, the signal for a general advance. Riders were now breaking through the clouds of dust, Persian cavalry in their soft felt hats, brightly coloured coats, long lances and round shields. The Macedonian line moved forward to meet them. Telamon realized Alexander's tactics. By moving as close as he could to the enemy cavalry, he silenced the catapaults beyond the walls, their engineers fearful of hitting friend as well as foe. The two Persian forces now united, a long line of horsemen with the huge ditch behind them.

Alexander edged his horse forward, Hephaestion and Cleitus on either side. He whispered instructions. The Macedonians had quickly recovered from the attack. Wounded men had already been withdrawn, horses put out of their misery. A series of trumpet blasts echoed as Alexander's orders were relayed down each flank. Cleitus appeared very concerned about fresh clouds of dust which could be seen on the far horizon.

"We have to be careful." Sarpedon wrapped his reins round one gloved hand and brought up his sword.

Telamon's stomach curdled with excitement and tension. He realized how foolhardy Alexander had been. The Persians had come out to confront them, but what if other horsemen had been sent out into the grasslands to cut off their retreat, circle them, drive them back against the walls of Halicarnassus? Alexander was being appraised of the danger. He shook his head and whispered something. Fresh orders were issued. The centre of the Macedonian line surged forward, Alexander leading it, in the form of an arrowhead, he and his commanders at the tip. The Persian line was at least three men deep. Amidst the jostle and bustle, Telamon glimpsed officers dressed in Greek armour in the Persian centre. One stood out, a scarlet plume in his Boetian helmet, the escutcheon on his shield a red griffin.

"Ephialtes!" someone whispered. "Ephialtes of Thebes! I can't see Memnon!"

Alexander rode forward. The battlements and gatehouses of Halicarnassus were now dark and thick with clustering troops. The catapaults and mangonels fell silent. Alexander paused and raised his hand. Again the trumpets emitted a loud blast.

"Ephialtes of Thebes!" the Macedonian trumpeter called out. "Have you come to surrender? Hand yourself over to justice for fighting against fellow Greeks?"

"Murderer of Macedon!" came the bellowed reply. "Have you come to receive your just desserts from the gods?"

Alexander's reply was to draw his sword in a hiss of steel and raise it high. Telamon closed his eyes. They were going to charge. Yet all around him came anxious comments about being trapped and circled, killed on this barren peninsula.

Chapter 6

⇒•◦•⇐

"A counter-attack by Alexander checked them without difficulty and they were driven back within the walls."

Arrian: The Campaigns of Alexander, Book I, Chapter 20

Alexander sat motionless, sword still raised, the sun gleaming on its polished metal. Telamon drew his. He could tell from movements among the Persian centre that Alexander had confounded his enemies. Instead of retreating, he was intent on a full-frontal attack. Yet secret orders were being issued to squadron commanders. Alexander was deliberately using his showmanship to mask his own preparations. The king was now slightly forward, astride his horse, cloak neatly arranged, sword in the air. He looked like a commander taking the salute on a drill ground rather than a man facing the might of his enemies. An arrow, shot from some master bowman on the walls, smacked into the ground about ten paces in front of him.

"Someone's trying their luck," Sarpedon whispered.

"Eynalius! Eynalius for Macedon!"

Alexander's cry was taken up with a roar. The king moved, not at a trot but straight into a full charge, using the flat of his sword to urge his horse forward. The Macedonians behind had no choice but to follow a mad, headlong rush for the centre of the Persian line. The enemy were taken by surprise: swords were drawn, standards lowered, the Persian line starting to move, but the Macedonian cavalry was now in full charge. Men on either side of Telamon urged their horses on, shields up, lances lowered ready for impact. The hot breeze whipped away the roars and cheers, shouts and cries. Some of the archers on the walls loosed arrows;

121

here and there man and horse went down in a crash of colour and dust. Alexander rode like a man possessed, Cleitus and Hephaestion like racers behind him, trying to keep up. The Persian line had hardly moved when the tip of the Macedonian arrow formation hit them full in the centre in a scream of metal and the neighs of horses. The fury of the charge sent men and mounts flying back like skittles hit by a ball. Telamon was fearful of the ditch behind the enemy but Alexander, a superb horseman and cavalry commander, had gauged his distance well.

In the centre of the horsemen, Telamon felt relatively safe: on either side, he glimpsed olive-skinned faces, glaring eyes, the glint of scimitars. Sarpedon, too, was hemmed in. The Macedonians' arrowhead grew thinner. Alexander was coming back, leading the retreat as the Macedonian line turned in on itself. Now the tip of the arrow was moving the other way. Having driven back the Persian centre, Alexander was retreating, leaving his flanks to protect his withdrawal, to batter the Persians, drive them back towards the ditch and reduce their zeal for any pursuit.

Telamon was caught up in the hurly-burly. He glimpsed Alexander's face in the crowd, Cleitus and Hephaestion shouting for the horsemen to pull aside. Soon it was Telamon's turn, and forcing his mount's head round, he, too, joined in the mad gallop away, leaving behind the bloody din of battle. Here and there a horse stumbled, legs buckling, riders being tipped off. Sometimes the horses were fit, pulled up again, the rider vaulting back into the saddle: on other occasions soldiers leaned down, picking up dismounted comrades, joining in the pell-mell chase across the rocky peninsula.

Telamon's world was reduced to the nodding head of his horse, the cries of men, riders either side of him, the hot, dusty breeze and the white rock racing beneath him as if the earth itself was on the move. He dared not look back, but concentrated on keeping upright, reins gripped firmly but not too tightly. His horse's head began to bob up and down, a sign of growing exhaustion. They left the escarpment: clumps of dry grass, bushes and trees appeared, and a trumpet blast shrilled through the din. The riders in front of Telamon were reining in, the pace slowed; he was in a jostle of armoured men, some with their swords still drawn, dyed in blood from tip to hilt, eyes gleaming in white, dusty faces. Telamon's horse, now blown, slowed down. A hand clutched Telamon's shoulder, but he shrugged this off. He looked around. The Macedonian cavalry were a swirl of horsemen in a billowing cloud of dust. Somebody pushed a waterskin into his hand. He pulled back the stopper, lifted it up and let the water rinse his face and mouth. Men were dismounting; someone plucked the waterskin from his hand. Telamon, slumped over the neck of his horse, felt a tug at his arm. Alexander, helmetless, stared up, his face covered in white chalk as if he were wearing an actor's mask.

"I thought we'd lost you, physician. Come on, get down!"

Telamon swung a leg over his horse and almost collapsed into Alexander's arms.

"There, there, physician!" Alexander patted him on the back. "You'll feel rather strange and wobbly, as if you've been on the deck of a storm-driven ship."

Telamon's legs nearly buckled, but Alexander held him up. "He's here!" the king shouted, pushing Telamon through a crowd of cavalrymen, all chattering excitedly. The air stank of sweat and leather, the iron tang of blood. A path was made for the king up to a small hillock where other commanders were waiting. Hephaestion lay sprawled on the grass. He had taken his corselet off, splaying out sweat-soaked legs while Cleitus poured water over his face and neck. Alexander pushed Telamon past these up into the shade of a large holm oak, its outstretched branches affording welcome relief from the sun, and made him sit down.

"Don't waste that water, Cleitus," he shouted. "Hephaestion doesn't deserve it!"

Telamon just wished the trembling would stop, and the strange sounds echoing like waves in his ears. He prayed that he wouldn't be sick. Cleitus would love that. He glanced up: the king was smiling gently down at him.

"I did think I'd lost you, Telamon. I passed you in the charge back: you looked like a man who had lost his wits."

"I'm a physician," Telamon moaned. "Not a cavalryman, a fighter."

"Come on." Alexander patted him on the shoulder. "Think of something else, it will pass."

Telamon stared out across the grasslands. The Macedonian cavalry clustered there. Beyond the white track, further south, clouds of dust still rose like smoke.

"Nothing there to worry about," Alexander commented. "A very clever trick."

"What were they trying to do?"

"Come on." Alexander crouched down. He picked up a twig in the shape of a horseshoe and laid it on the grass. "That's the wall of Halicarnassus. Think of it as a U shape, the two ends stretching down to the sea. We approach the centre where the Triple Gate stands. We can't see the walls on either side or the gates hidden there. Ephialtes is a cunning fighter. I took Thebes because a commander left a gate open. This time Ephilates played the trick back."

"I saw two lines of horsemen," Telamon murmured.

"Good!" Alexander breathed, squinting up. 'We'll make a soldier of you yet, Telamon. They knew we couldn't see them, so they opened the postern gate on their side of the wall, threw a makeshift bridge across their moat and out they came. We were supposed to attack. Cavalry against cavalry. What they had also prepared were squadrons of light horse to ride out onto the grasslands: these were to turn and either attack us in the rear or, if we tried to retreat, force us back. Thank the gods for dust, eh?"

"We could have been trapped and killed," Telamon rasped.

"I doubt it. One Macedonian cavalryman is worth ten Persians, and it was a clumsy, lengthy manoeuvre. The Persians out on the grassland would have found the terrain difficult going. We would still have broken through."

Alexander got to his feet, kicked the twig away and stared down at the mass of milling men and horses.

"That doesn't bother me: what does, is that they knew I was coming. It would have taken time to practise a manoeuvre like that. They had cavalry mounted, makeshift bridges ready, catapults prepared and loaded. In my reckoning that would take at least three or four hours."

"I know what you're saying," Cleitus, sprawled on the grass beside Hephaestion, shouted out. "The bastards were waiting for us."

"We have a traitor in our midst," Alexander smiled at Telamon.

"You always have traitors," Telamon replied. "You know that: Pamenes for one."

"The dead scribe?"

"I discovered that last night before I was summoned to help you." Telamon wiped the white dust off his cheeks. "He was a magus, a Persian priest, and his corpse was taken away. I suspect his killer left documents near the corpse."

"But why should the Persians take his body?"

"Because he was a magus, a priest of the Sacred Flame. He carried a ring and a seal." Telamon pointed in the direction of Halicarnassus. "Now, I have met the Persians again, and had the pleasure of renewing their acquaintance, I suspect he wore the emblem of Ahura-Mazda on his person, probably on the scalp covered by his hair."

"Yes, that's the usual place," Alexander replied. "The Persian magi have their heads and faces shaved so they cannot be polluted. So," he continued, "Pamenes was a Persian spy at the court of Queen Ada?"

"He hid his ring and seal," Telamon replied, getting up to stand next to the king. "Pamenes pretended to be a Greek scribe. He probably kept a record of what he had learnt, but that's only the beginning of the real mystery."

"There's someone else?"

"There has to be." Telamon wiped his lips on the back of his hand. "This killer somehow sent a message to the Persians that you were to arrive at the Villa of Cybele when Pamenes was dead and any secret manuscripts he kept were hidden on his corpse."

"Does this killer know Pamenes was a magus?"

"Possibly, that question still confuses me. Anyway, the Persians came last night. They took Pamenes's corpse. They would regard it as sacred. They also took whatever secret record Pamenes was keeping, as well as information that the Macedonian king might be reckless enough to ride out with a skirmishing force to view the fortifications of Halicarnassus."

125

"Was I foolish, Telamon?"

"Very!" Telamon retorted. "We could have all been killed."

"What do you think of our traitor?" the king murmured.

"He's a man who works for himself and doesn't give a fig for Greek or Persian. Perhaps he killed Pamenes because he saw him as a rival, as well as to get information for his masters. He may have been sending those same masters a message, that he works for himself and by himself. No one else is allowed to compete."

"So who?" Alexander asked.

"Anyone." Telamon pulled a face. "It is interesting that Sarpedon came here this morning: he could have been killed. I know from another witness that he saw a lantern being flashed last night as a signal to the Persian attackers: he seems above suspicion."

"He's also illiterate," Alexander added. "He wouldn't know the value of the Pythian Manuscript. He did raise the alarm last night. More importantly, Queen Ada vouches for him. When she fled from Halicarnassus, Sarpedon was her helper. If he returns to the city, sentence of death will be passed. He's wanted by the Persian authorities dead or alive."

Telamon reflected on what the king had said. Sarpedon had been out in the garden with himself and Cassandra when Pamenes had been killed. Moreover, his bandages and heavily gloved hands would have hampered any attack on a young man like Pamenes.

Alexander sat down and beckoned Telamon to join him.

"Shouldn't we be leaving?" the physician asked.

Alexander shook his head. "The Persians won't follow us now. The grasslands are too open and they fear an ambush. They never know what force will be coming up the road towards them. No, they'll now shelter behind the walls and wait for us to attack. You were talking about your companions at the villa?"

"We have Solan the chief scribe, a man bitter about everything and ambitious for all things. Cherolos the priest may be here to watch the others, but he could have a motive for murder. Finally, there's young Bessus."

"Could any of them have thrown Pamenes from the window?"

"It's possible. All were in the house at the time."

"But I thought the chamber door was bolted?"

"Yes, I wonder about that," Telamon murmured. "We know certain items, including a stylus, must have been removed from Pamenes's chamber. When I found his corpse, the flesh was cold, the blood congealing. I thought he was thrown from his own chamber, but it's possible he might have been killed elsewhere: the corpse was then moved, any blood or gore cleaned up."

"I disagree!" Alexander drove his fist into his hand. "Pamenes's chamber was locked and bolted: he must have been killed there. You are too sharp-eyed, Telamon, you would have noticed if the corpse had been moved."

"In which case," Telamon sighed, "we are talking about someone who was in Pamenes's chamber when he arrived and left by a different route."

The king lifted his head, savouring the breeze on his face and neck.

"But there are no ladders," Telamon added. "We searched that villa from cellar to attic."

"What about a rope?" Alexander asked. "Someone like Sarpedon could have clambered up, entered the window by stealth?"

"And Pamenes just allowed him to come in?" Telamon shook his head. "If Sarpedon had thrown Pamenes from the window and then climbed down the rope, he would have to release it. I can't see how that was done." Telamon narrowed his eyes. "Moreover, if Sarpedon climbed up he might have been seen, either from the garden or from the adjoining chambers. And what did he use? How could he do that with his hands all bandaged and gloved?" Telamon wiped the sweat from his face. "No, Sarpedon was with us. I bandaged his hands. He went to look for some gloves and then became busy doing some gardening, nothing suspicious. What's more probable is that ledge. It's broad enough for the killer to edge along, climb into Pamenes's chamber and wait for him there. Perhaps he skulked stealthily and, when Pamenes came in, waited for him to go to the window with his bird seed. He pushed him over, took what he wanted and clambered back along the ledge to whatever chamber he wanted to go to. However," he conceded, "that either makes Bessus the killer or at least he should know if anyone passed his open window to get into Pamenes's chamber."

127

Alexander plucked at a blade of grass and thrust it between his lips. Telamon recalled the outside wall at the back of the villa: the open windows, Pamenes's at the end, the killer edging along the ledge, which was dirty and covered in bird-droppings.

"I think I'm wrong about that," he sighed. "The ledge is too obvious: the killer could be seen, certainly heard, by Pamenes. Even if the killer did get in, Pamenes would have resisted. Finally," Telamon wetted his lips, "I have examined that ledge, and I've found no trace of anyone using it."

A soldier shouted. Telamon glanced up: the man's voice was carrying, and the physician abruptly realized that he had forgotten about Gentius and Demerata's possible involvement.

"Ah well." Alexander got to his feet. "You don't feel sick any longer?"

Telamon grinned. "No, I don't."

"Good! Let's return to the villa."

They went down the hill. The cavalrymen, now a jostling, noisy circle of colour and chatter, greeted the king by drawing their swords and screaming the Macedonian battle cry. Alexander raised both hands in salute.

"We have seen the fortress of Halicarnassus!" he shouted. "Memnon has seen us. He cannot move, but we shall be back and those walls will not protect him!"

A loud cheer greeted his words. Alexander's horse was brought up. He vaulted onto it as if he hadn't a care in the world, gathering his reins, coaxing his horse to rear on its hind legs, caracolling to the shouts of adoration from his men.

The king's party rode along the grasslands. The rest mounted and, under the shouted orders of their officers, organized themselves into units. The king broke into a canter and, with his horsemen streaming behind him, pounded along the dusty track away from Halicarnassus.

On their return to the villa, Telamon and Cassandra became busy tending wounds and cuts. According to the muster rolls they had lost at least two dozen men and thirty horses. Most of the wounds were sword and dagger slashes, bruises, broken or sprained limbs. Telamon set up a makeshift hospital in the shade of one of the orchards, and organized the few orderlies, who looked after the minor scrapes and bruises while he and Cassandra attended more serious wounds. Telamon, using heavy Chian wine, salt and honey, cleansed wounds. Linen was stripped from beds to fashion bandages, wooden crates broken up and pieces cut in order to serve as splints. Both Telamon and Cassandra had a wide experience of serving in field hospitals. Cassandra indulged Telamon's demands for hygiene by constantly washing her hands in hot water and drying them on clean rags which were then thrown away.

"Why are you doing this?" one soldier asked as Telamon dressed a deep cut just beneath his knee.

"Everybody asks me that," Telamon replied. "I can't really answer it. The Egyptians believe the air causes pollution, and that all dirt and pus must be removed." He poured the heavy wine mixed with salt onto the man's leg. The soldier went taut, biting back his scream as the wine licked the exposed flesh.

"Good," Telamon reassured him. "When a wound is dead, turning slightly green and beginning to smell, that's when you should really scream."

He applied honey around the cut and, using linen strips, fashioned a loose bandage. "Don't undo it," Telamon warned. "And don't tighten it."

Distracted by screams deeper in the trees, he left the soldier to Cassandra and walked further into the cool darkness. Two men lay on sheets, their faces and upper torsos very badly burnt by the firebolts at Halicarnassus. In one case the skin had simply burnt away, exposing raw, seeping flesh. The man had lost an eye: his black socket gazed blankly as flies, despite the attention of the orderlies, buzzed round the exposed wound.

"Is there anything you can do?" The squadron commander sat with his back to a tree.

Telamon crouched down between the two men.

"I have given them wine," the orderly remarked, "mixed with poppy seed and mandrake."

Telamon looked at both faces, and his heart sank. Layers of skin had disappeared; the flesh was shrivelling. One man kept moaning in his drug-induced sleep, chattering in his nightmares, calling for his mother.

"There's nothing I can do." Telamon stared at the officer. "It's not so much the wounds." He gently pressed the brow of one of the wounded men. "It's also a shock to their bodies and minds."

"Is there nothing?" the officer replied. "Is that the best you can offer?"

"It's the best I can offer." Telamon stared steadily back. "I am a physician, not a miracle-worker."

"But I've heard you clamp veins? Stitch flesh, hold back the blood flow?"

"I can tend what is bruised, what is broken, ripped and torn, but these men have had their flesh burnt away. I can't replace that. I can only treat the wounds to keep off infection. You've fought long enough to know which wounds cannot be healed."

The young officer put his face in his hands. Telamon walked over and sat beside him: he stared helplessly across at the black flies hovering above the wounded men.

"When they wake," he murmured, "their agony will be unbelievable. Of all wounds, the most terrible are caused, not by iron or bronze, but by fire."

The officer sighed and took the long, thin dagger which he had thrust into the ground beside him. "What shall I do?"

"You know what you have to," Telamon retorted and, getting to his feet, walked out of the trees. He bit back his anger. He was not responsible, yet he couldn't help. He cleared his mind and returned to those cases he could. He concentrated on the task in hand, talking reassuringly, promising men that they would soon be mended. In his heart he knew those who had suffered broken legs and ribs would not be riding horses for many a month.

"Look on the bright side," he smiled at one cavalryman. "It will be the convalescent carts for you, and the pleasures of some city garrison."

The day drew on, shadows lengthened. Alexander, who had been closeted with his officers, came out and walked among the wounded, distributing coins, small presents, crouching down to talk to this officer or that. He was accompanied by Ptolemy, who

130

had been left to guard the villa: Alexander's commander looked more refreshed and alert than he had the night before. Telamon could tell from his flushed face that he and Alexander had been arguing, probably about the king's rash escapade earlier that day. Telamon began to clear up and, as he did so, he returned to the problem Alexandar had raised about Pamenes's death.

"If I could resolve that," he murmured to Cassandra, "I might discover something."

"I've been to see our worthy scribes," she replied. "They claim to have been working all day, but some of them look as if they have a hangover." She squinted up at Telamon as she knelt on the ground folding some bandages. "The villa was very quiet today. I am glad you returned safely."

"Get Solan and the rest," Telamon ordered. "Ask them to meet me behind the house beneath Pamenes's window."

Cassandra finished what she was doing and hurried off. Telamon went across the cobbled yard, lifted the water bucket from the well and washed his hands and face. He went into the kitchen. The Mageros and his scullions were busy over their portable stoves and ovens baking bread and meats, preparing a grill which would be wheeled outside to roast the strips of meat lying in a bloody mess on the kitchen table. Telamon felt his stomach curdle. The Mageros asked if he wanted something to eat; he shook his head and went outside.

By the time he had walked round the villa, Cassandra had the scribes assembled. They sat on the grass verge, staring up at the window as if, by power of thought, they could recreate Pamenes's dreadful fall. Telamon stood on the red-brick path which ran along the side of the house.

"I'm sorry I'm late." Sarpedon came hurrying across. He carried a wine cup, and the way he walked showed he'd been drinking heavily. "I'm just relieved to be alive." He winked at the physician. "I prayed to the gods that my horse wouldn't stumble."

"That was foolish." Solan spoke up. "The king could have been killed."

"Well, he wasn't," Telamon replied more tersely than he intended. "But Pamenes was."

Sarpedon joined the group, squatting down, cradling the wine cup in his hands. Telamon went and stood over them like a teacher would schoolchildren.

"I shall tell you what I know about Pamenes. He was a Persian spy, probably a magus, a priest from one of their temples. No, no." Telamon quietened their protests. "He was working hard to translate the Pythian Manuscript while keeping an eye on the rest of you to see if he could learn anything."

"And did he?" Cassandra asked.

"What do you mean?" Bessus hotly demanded.

"I know you scribes," Telamon declared. "Every one of you wishes to be the one who breaks the secret cipher. You work together, but each of you dream that it will be your achievement. Did you tell Pamenes anything?"

"We couldn't tell him what we didn't know ourselves," Solan smirked.

"Pamenes certainly didn't tell us anything remarkable," Bessus added.

"Very well. On the morning he died," Telamon continued, "Pamenes was in his chamber. Did anyone visit him there?"

A chorus of denials greeted his words.

"But, Bessus, you claimed someone went down the gallery past your room. You must have heard Pamenes's door open and close. What time was that?"

"I don't know," Bessus stammered. "The sun had risen. I had been down to the kitchen. Sarpedon was already working in the garden, I saw him from my window."

"I never went up there," Sarpedon slurred. He thrust forward his legs, still wearing the mud-covered riding boots. "I was wearing these. I would have left a trail of dirt all over the passageway and chamber."

"Did Pamenes go down?" Telamon asked. "To the kitchen for food or drink, or out in the garden?"

"You've been told that," Solan retorted. "Whatever he did, Pamenes kept to himself. Now we know he was a spy, he probably made his own morning prayers to the rising sun or whatever god he worshipped."

132

"Bessus." Telamon turned to the pale-faced young scribe: he hadn't shaven and his eyes were still red-rimmed. "Your window is around the buttress. You could have gone out on the ledge, walked along and stepped into Pamenes's chamber."

"Just like that." Bessus clicked his fingers. "And not dislodged any of the encrusted dirt? While Sarpedon in the garden wouldn't have seen anything? Of course, Pamenes wouldn't object to me stepping through his window."

Telamon smiled apologetically. "I was just testing a theory."

"What is important," Sarpedon declared, "is this person who went down the passageway to visit Pamenes."

"Well, I was in my chamber," Bessus replied, "so it wasn't me. Sarpedon was in the garden." He gazed accusingly at Cherolos and Solan.

"It must have been you." Solan pointed at the priest. "It must have been. I heard no one pass my chamber, and yours is next door to Bessus."

Telamon hid his surprise at how agile the old scribe's mind really was. He winked at Cassandra: he hadn't thought of that.

"If I didn't hear anyone," Solan continued excitedly, "then that person must have been you, Cherolos. Moreover —" Solan waved his hands " I could prove for most of that morning I was dealing with the Mageros over food and supplies. He kept coming up and down those stairs, a damnable nuisance, bothering me with this question and that!"

"I . . ." Cherolos stammered, "I . . . I . . . admit I did go down on one occasion. I knocked on the door: there was no answer. I tried the latch but the door was bolted."

"That's strange." Bessus spoke up. "I never heard you call out or knock."

"Even stranger," Solan snapped, "Pamenes never bolted his door, or very rarely. I couldn't understand that the morning he was killed."

"I swear I speak the truth." The priest's sallow face was now flushed, his almond-shaped eyes gleaming. "I went to see Pamenes." He took a deep breath. "I'd visited him the night before. The door to his chamber was open so I went in. I would have left

133

immediately but there was a scrap of parchment on the floor. Curious, I picked it up." He undid his wallet and took out a yellowing piece of parchment, its edges all torn, which he handed to Telamon. The priest's hand was trembling.

"You should have told me this before." Telamon looked at the parchment. "It gives the alphabet." He handed it to Cassandra. "Pass it round."

"He's formed the alphabet into a square, five across, five down," Solan murmured. The old scribe was excited at what he had seen. "He was trying to work out a key to the cipher. Look!" He tossed it back.

Telamon studied it more closely. The letters were roughly etched in a square.

	1	2	3	4	5
1	A	B	C	D	E
2	F	G	H	I/J	K
3	L	M	N	O	P
4	Q	R	S	T	U
5	V	W	X	Y	Z

"The Pythian Manuscript is numbered." Solan was so agitated he could hardly keep still. "Perhaps that's the key?"

Telamon folded the piece of parchment up and put it into his own wallet. He squatted down facing Cherolos. "You knew this was important, didn't you?"

The priest nodded.

"Yesterday morning, you went back to ask Pamenes what it meant?"

Cherolos licked dry lips. "I was up most of the night trying to apply that to the Pythian," he whispered, "but it makes no sense. I thought I'd go back and ask. I was curious –" he stared angrily around "– about why Pamenes hadn't informed us about it. I wanted to be quiet. I tapped very gently on his door, that's why no one heard me: I tried the latch. It was locked, yet the floorboards were creaking, Pamenes must have been there, he just wasn't

134

answering the door. I tiptoed back to my own room. Later we all met in the loom room. When Pamenes was found dead, I didn't know what to do. I thought it best to keep silent. I did mean to tell you . . ." His voice trailed away.

"Sarpedon." Telamon turned to where the Spartan sat, eyes half closed, heavy with sleep. "When you were working in the garden that morning, did you ever walk back here?"

"On one occasion, before I got my hands cut in the briar bush. I remember the shutters to Pamenes's chamber were open but I saw nothing. I would have raised the alarm!"

"Did any of you notice anything untoward?"

"Milk." Solan spoke up. "Sour milk." His head came forward, lower lip jutting out. "When I woke that morning, I went out on to the gallery. The place stank of milk, spilt, just at the top of the stairs. I sent for the Mageros to clear it up. He claimed no servant had brought any milk up."

"Of course," Telamon replied. "The cat! Pamenes used to look after it, didn't he? Gave it bowls of milk?"

"It's so strange," Solan declared. "Pamenes was very clean and neat. If he had spilt milk, he'd have washed the floor. Goats' milk turns very rancid."

"And?" Telamon asked.

"I challenged the Mageros. He couldn't remember any of his servants bringing milk up the stairs. In fact, they are specifically instructed to keep away from our chambers."

"Why is that?" Telamon asked.

"Because they are magpies, they'll steal whatever they want! I don't trust them."

"Did any of you bring up that milk?"

The group shook their heads.

"It must have been brought up the night before," Solan trumpeted.

Telamon recalled the bowl he had found in Pamenes's chamber. "He certainly fed the cat, but he never brought it from the kitchen himself?"

Solan shook his head.

"Gentlemen of Thebes. We greet you, my companion and I."

"Oh no!" Bessus groaned.

Gentius and Demerata appeared round the corner of the house. The tall, gaunt actor was dressed in his camel robe and clutched a small vine pole. He had his eyes closed, one hand out.

"Do you recognize the line, ninnies?" The actor opened his eyes and glared at them.

"Tereisias, the blind soothsayer of Thebes," Cassandra retorted.

"I sent for you," Telamon declared. "Why have you taken so long?"

"I visited the king's pavilion," the actor retorted, clutching his staff as if it were a rod of office. "Demerata and I are preparing for our great work."

"Did you see anything untoward the morning Pamenes was killed?"

The actor shook his head.

"Did you visit his chamber at any time?" Telamon asked. Demerate was standing in her husband's shadow: a shift in her eyes, a fleeting expression, intrigued the physician.

"Ah well!" Telamon sighed and got to his feet. "Should you remember anything . . ." He stared up at the window. Behind him the rest of the group got up, chattering among themselves. Telamon looked over his shoulder.

"Oh Gentius, Demerata, perhaps you could stay?"

He waited until the rest had left.

"You wanted a word in private, physician?"

"Yes, I do. You have chambers at the far side of the house?"

"One chamber," Gentius retorted.

"And which of you drinks goats' milk?"

The actor blinked and forced a smile. "Why, I do, for my throat, it's rich and . . ."

"Did you take goats' milk to Pamenes's chamber the night before he was killed?" The actor made as if to turn. "You can walk away, but I'll ask you to come back. You took some goats' milk up, didn't you?"

Demerata slid her arm through her husband's, her fingernails pressed deep into his arm.

"You see," Telamon continued, "the Mageros in the kitchen

136

does not remember any of our scribes coming down for milk, or any of the servants taking some up. However, he might recall you coming in and filling a bowl but you didn't drink it. You took it up to Pamenes's chamber. You were in such a hurry, you spilt some at the top of the stairs. Now, why should you do that for a man you don't like? If gossip is correct, Pamenes had designs on your lovely wife."

Demerata acted all coy, clinging closer to her husband. Gentius's head came back as if he was about to deliver a speech. He sucked in his cheeks.

"You're not on the stage now." Telamon gazed over at Cassandra squatting on the grass, staring curiously at them. "Why should you take milk for Pamenes's cat?"

"It was my fault." Demerata spoke up. "My husband couldn't find me."

"Ah, I see, so Gentius went looking for you? You might have gone to Pamenes's chamber, once darkness had fallen, so your husband thought up an excuse. And what happened?"

"I had gone for a walk," Demerata declared heatedly.

"And you, Gentius?"

"I . . . I . . ." Gentius stammered. "I very rarely forget my lines, physician." He looked down, then his head came up, lower lip trembling, tears in his eyes. "Of all stage roles," he whispered, "none is more ridiculous than the jealous husband. I couldn't find Demerata, she had gone for a walk. So, yes, I took the milk up. I filled the bowl too much. I spilt some but I couldn't stop to clean it up. I knew the other scribes were downstairs taking the cool of the evening."

"And Pamenes?"

"He was in his chamber by himself, seated at his desk, oil lamps burning."

"Did you notice anything untoward?"

"No, he just took the bowl of milk from me and said it was a kindness he would remember. I was hardly in the room. I felt stupid. Pamenes was his usual secretive self. I remember the cat was on the bed." Gentius stepped back. "I left," he mumbled. "Can I leave now?"

137

Telamon was about to reply when loud cheering broke out on the far side of the villa. Sarpedon came hurrying round the corner, slopping the wine in his cup.

"They've been sighted!" he yelled. "The main army is arriving!"

Chapter 7

———————◦◦◦◦———————

"The garrison [of Myndus] made a determined resistance: a reinforcement sent by Memnon from Halicarnassus arrived, and this enterprise of the Macedonians was frustrated."

Quintus Curtius Rufus: *The History of*
Alexander the Great, Book II, Chapter IX

Telamon and Cassandra joined the rest on the track leading up to the villa. Peering down it, they could see great columns of dust. On this warm, late summer afternoon, Telamon found it difficult to imagine what terrors that approaching army brought. The funeral pyres were now nothing more than a heap of charred cinders blown by the breeze, while the makeshift crosses had been taken down. He heard another cheer. Alexander, in full dress armour, came riding out of the villa escorted by his officers.

"He's happy now," Cassandra whispered. "Surrounded by his boys!"

Telamon ignored her sarcasm. The dust cloud drew nearer. He caught the glint of spears, the sound of marching songs and the ominous crash of thousands of marching boots, the rattle of carts, the hollow-sounding hoofbeats of the cavalry. The grey cloud thinned and broke. The Thessalian light horse, Alexander's auxiliaries, came galloping forward, white cloaks flapping, metal cuirasses gleaming in the sun. Most carried lances, and others had drawn their swords. They galloped up as if on the parade ground, lifting their swords in salutation as Alexander, who had positioned himself judiciously, lifted his hand in greeting. Marshals on either side of the track urged the horsemen forward. The

139

Thessalians passed: some of them had the severed, blood-caked heads of their enemies tied by the hair to their horses' harness.

Cassandra hid behind Telamon, fearful of these savage horsemen, who had caused so much destruction in her own city of Thebes. The quiet of the countryside was shattered, as if this great army had risen from the very soil, a mass of armour, gleaming hordes of men, spilling along the trackway and across the grasslands. After the Thessalians came the regular cavalry in their metal helmets and cuirasses, heavy ornamental shoulderpieces and flowing cloaks. They carried lances of cornelian wood with a counterbalancing button and a tip of metal, curved swords strapped to their waists: their mounts were geldings, easily controlled by spiteful bit and spurs. These were the men who would smash an enemy flank, and they rode with all the arrogance they could muster. Interspersed with them were Thracian light horse who served as scouts or lancers: ferocious warriors, helmetless, hair falling down to their shoulders, they prided themselves on their long beards and moustaches. The phalanx men, the infantry, followed; Alexander's shock troops, dressed for battle in helmet, greaves, a small button shield on the left arm, their great sarissas, eighteen-foot lances, expertly held against their shoulders. Telamon had seen the sight many a time, but these marching men, the colours of their banners, the different sashes tied round their waists to indicate their brigades, were a spectacle which always drew him: the rhythmic beat of their march, the lusty battle paeans. Telamon was embarrassed, for he felt more comfortable now they had arrived. He would not forget that ferocious charge earlier in the day, the fire falling from heaven, the frenetic clash of arms, the hacking and hewing, the blood-spouting wounds. He must have stood for about an hour as brigade after brigade, squadrons of cavalry out on their right flank, surged past the villa up towards the edge of the grasslands where they would camp and lay siege to Halicarnassus.

There was a break for a while. Parmenio and other officers who had stayed behind clustered round Alexander, delivering reports. These ended as the Guards regiments of Shield-Bearers, in full battle dress, their brilliant helmet plumes dancing in the breeze, swaggered by. Afterwards came the auxiliaries: Cretan archers with their long, reinforced bows and quivers full of cruel barbed arrows, Agriarian footmen, and Rhodian slingers. The carts brought up the rear, hundreds of them loaded with equipment, tents and supplies.

"Can we go back?" Cassandra whispered. "Now we've seen all the brave boys arrive?"

Telamon clasped her hand. For all her courage, Cassandra always felt nervous on such occasions. In the field tents and hospitals, the soldiers were only patients, victims of war, but the armed might of Macedon in full battle cry evoked nightmares of the same troops who had shattered the sacred town of Thebes. They had stormed through the Electra Gate and left her city a blackened ruin, where the blood flowed ankle-deep and not one stone was left upon another.

"Where will they go?" Cassandra asked as they walked up the track.

"The grasslands stretch like a horseshoe," Telamon replied, "round the city of Halicarnassus. They'll pitch their main camp there, breaking up into different groups. Each camp will be connected by armed lines of soldiers. They'll then move forward and choose which section of the city walls to attack."

"I didn't see any siege equipment."

Telamon let go of her hand. "You have a sharp eye, Cassandra. You're right, neither did I."

"Does the great Alexander hope to vault over the walls?"

Telamon laughed and led her back into the villa. They returned to their own chamber on the east side of the building, a large rectangular room with bare, white walls and polished floorboards.

"Was this just a villa?" Cassandra asked, sitting on her bed.

"There are so many chambers," Telamon replied, "I suspect it also served as a wayside tavern, a hostelry. Its owner was probably a very prosperous man, a merchant farmer."

"He was until Alexander arrived," Cassandra jibed. "Now he's rich no more."

Telamon sat on a stool and took out the scrap of parchment he had taken from Cherolos. "Cassandra," he murmured, "bring me our copy of the Pythian Manuscript."

She went across to a travel bag and undid the straps.

141

"Stop!" Telamon lifted a hand. "Do you remember, Cassandra, when we were collecting Pamenes's possessions? We didn't consider there were many, did we?"

"That's right."

"Did you notice any saddlebags?"

Cassandra shook her head.

"Now, why is that? I thought there was something missing."

Cassandra came over. Telamon absent-mindedly plucked the scroll of parchment from her hand.

"Here we have a Persian spy," he continued. "A man who has joined Queen Ada's court. He rises one morning and returns to his studies. A short while later he's found dead, apparently a fall from a window which smashed his skull. He had bird seed in his hand, some is scattered near the windowsill. It looks as if he suffered an accident, leaned over too far and fell out, but he must have been pushed. We know documents were taken, certainly a stylus. We are not too sure how he fell and, finally, his saddlebags have gone."

"Why do you keep returning to Pamenes?" Cassandra asked.

"Solve that and we solve the mystery," Telamon retorted. "Someone murdered Pamenes. They picked up his saddlebags and hastily collected what they wanted from that chamber and left. We know they can't have climbed out of the window. There were no ladders, no rope. When we sent up to search for him, the door to his chamber was bolted. Inside, no sign of a scuffle or forced entry." Telamon shook his head and smoothed out the Pythian Manuscript on his lap. "Cherolos visited him the night before and discovered this, a mere scrap. Gentius also visited him around the same time but, he claims, Pamenes was alone in his chamber." Telamon winked at Cassandra. "One of them's lying."

"Cherolos also visited Pamenes the morning he died," Cassandra added. "Bessus heard something. Cherolos claims Pamenes's chamber was bolted, though the scribe may have been inside at the time."

"Anyone entering that chamber," Telamon declared, "either from outside or along that gallery, ran the risk of being seen by Sarpedon, Solan, Bessus, not to mention Cherolos, even Gentius and Demerata, who had their own reasons for keeping an eye on

Pamenes. Yet," he concluded, "Pamenes is pushed, his possessions stolen, and his killer mysteriously leaves, like some ghost." Telamon paused. "Right, Cassandra, let's go through this. According to the parchment taken from Cherolos, Pamenes drew up a key: five rows of letters across, five columns down."

They both stared at the ill-written script.

	1	2	3	4	5
1	A	B	C	D	E
2	F	G	H	I/J	K
3	L	M	N	O	P
4	Q	R	S	T	U
5	V	W	X	Y	Z

"Now, take the first numbers in the Pythian Manuscript. 45 : 64 : 54 : 33 : 34 : 11 : 53. Let us say the key is quite simple: the number 15 stands for E, 24 for I."

Telamon rose and walked to his small writing desk. He picked up the stylus, unstoppered an inkwell and tried to translate the numbers: the words he formed were meaningless. Telamon threw the stylus down.

"It doesn't make sense, none whatsoever. I can't see how the number 64 is included. Look, Cassandra, the king and his companions will be returning, they'll plunder the kitchen. Go down and see what food you can find."

"You'll not join the king at his party tonight?"

"It won't be a party," Telamon murmured, "but a drinking contest."

"While the great men boast to each other and do their war dance?"

"Just keep out of their way," Telamon replied.

Cassandra, muttering about Macedonians being murderous lechers, left the chamber, closing the door behind her. Telamon straightened up and stretched. He moved across to the bed, pulled back the protective linen curtain fastened to a hook in the ceiling, and was about to lie down when he froze. The bolster had been moved.

Telamon had worked in many a military camp: he had a strict routine which he always followed. He made up his own bed, brought his own water, fetched his own food or asked Cassandra to do it for him. He had not left his bed like this. He was about to step back when something cold and slimy curled across his bare ankle. Telamon, not daring to breathe, stared down. The light was poor but he glimpsed the gleaming, scaly black and green of a rock adder. The snake had curled across his sandalled foot, brushing his naked ankle. Telamon tensed. He had travelled enough to re-cognize the true danger. This was no accident. He watched the bolster. A slight movement and another snake, roused by the noise, curled out; it looked like a piece of hardened rope, except for its flat head, glassy eyes and that flickering tongue. Telamon dared not move. The snake on the bed posed no danger but how many lay beneath, coiled, ready to strike? He had to keep still. He closed his eyes and quietly prayed Cassandra would not be long.

He remembered the snake cult in that small temple at Karnak. Anuala had taken him there to see the sights. The priest had been most voluble, showing them how to handle snakes properly, not to alarm them. Sudden movement, food, warmth, or the belief they were being attacked made them dangerous. Telamon could hear his own breathing. A cold wisp brushed his ankle. He opened his eyes and resisted the urge to scream or step back. He had already been very fortunate. These snakes had been plucked up and brought here in a basket, placed under the bolster, the rest under the bed and around the chamber. But who had done it? He recalled Cherolos the priest. Didn't he have a snake emblem round his throat? The same insignia on a finger ring? And didn't he worship some Snake Goddess? Telamon kept himself calm.

I must not move, he thought, the snakes must not be agitated. In other circumstances he would have laughed at himself, turning the problem over as if it were some academic puzzle. Snakes were so easy to trap. Basketloads of them were sold in the markets for their meat or skin. Anyone could have done that. He heard a sound in the passageway outside. The door opened. Cassandra entered carrying two bowls.

144

"It's the best I could do! It smells fragrant enough. The Mageros said . . ." Cassandra paused. "Telamon, what's the matter?"

"Snakes," he replied.

"I know. The garden teems with them: the hot weather has brought them . . ."

"They are here!" Telamon snarled.

Cassandra let out a screech.

"There's one on the bed." Telamon moved his hand palm downwards. "For Apollo's sake, Cassandra, keep calm! No, no, don't come over here. I want you to put that food on the floor. It smells, doesn't it?"

"And what else?" Cassandra's face was fearful.

"Run down to the kitchen. Don't tell anyone. Rake some hot coals into a bronze bowl. You'll have to carry it with a cloth. Hurry now, don't tell anyone!"

Cassandra fled. Telamon turned. A dark shape snaked sinuously out from underneath the bed, moving slightly sideways towards the bowls. Another joined it, slithering tail moving, head slightly raised. The snakes had already sensed the food, the same attraction which brought them into many a camp fire. Another appeared.

"How many?" Telamon whispered.

An age seemed to pass before footsteps sounded on the stairs: Cassandra appeared holding the bowl wrapped in a cloth. She leaned against the closed door and gazed fearfully at the thin, dark, slithering shapes of death.

"Put the charcoal down!" Telamon ordered. "Push it towards the bowls and leave it there!" Cassandra obeyed. "Now, stay still!"

Telamon tried to control his breathing. He went both hot and cold. Something brushed his sandalled foot. Other snakes were now curling out from dark recesses.

"Cassandra," he ordered, "I want you to come over here. Do you see that spear lying in the corner?"

She nodded.

"Avoid the bowls. Tread softly."

Cassandra obeyed.

"Now look behind me."

"I can see behind your feet," she whispered. "The light is poor but I'm sure nothing's there."

Telamon stepped quickly back, almost colliding with Cassandra. He felt his legs go weak: a spasm of cramp made him clutch his thigh. He stared towards the door. At least eight snakes curled round the bowls.

"Fine." Telamon pushed Cassandra back. "The snakes were placed on my bed, that's the place they're coming from."

"And how do we get rid of them?" Cassandra asked.

"Go downstairs. The way to the door is safe. All they are interested in is that food and the heat. Go to the storeroom, find a basket, a mattock, a shovel, anything you can lay your hands on."

Cassandra slipped across the room and out of the door. A short while later she came clattering back. Telamon hoped the noise wouldn't rouse the snakes, but they were now concerned with the bowls of food, sliding over them, curling around the bronze dish containing the charcoal. Cassandra had a basket, the type used to hold seed. At his instructions she put on her pair of marching boots, and Telamon did likewise. They wrapped linen cloths round their arms and hands and, using the mattock, hoe and spade, began to lift the snakes into the basket.

"They are warm and have eaten," Telamon whispered, "so they are sluggish."

At last the floor was cleared. Telamon and Cassandra made a scrupulous search of the chamber but could find nothing. Bolsters and blankets were shaken out, beds moved, cots and chests gingerly lifted. At last Telamon pronounced himself satisfied. The charcoal had turned to crumbling grey ash. One of the bowls had tipped over, spilling food onto the floor.

"Thank the gods for the food and the heat!" Telamon wiped the sweat from his brow.

They spent another hour cleaning the mess up. Telamon himself took the basket out of the villa into the trees, and sent it flying with all his might into the darkness. On his way back to his chamber, he brushed by Gentius, who asked if anything was the matter. Telamon just glared at him. He went back and helped Cassandra tidy the room, then poured two large cups of wine.

146

"That was deliberate, wasn't it?" Cassandra asked.

"Of course!" Telamon snapped. "Our would-be assassin took a basket out to the fields, anywhere in this accursed villa, used a rod or spear to fill the basket with snakes, and brought it back."

"Somebody could have seen him?"

"Or her!" Telamon added. "I didn't like the way Demerata was looking at me: those hate-filled eyes in that dark face of hers. She's as lecherous as a she-goat on heat and her husband knows it! Our chambers are open." He sighed. "If we had stayed with the king and come in here at night, a viper bite could have been deadly."

"So they want you dead?" Cassandra whispered. She sat opposite Telamon and leaned slightly forward. The physician tapped her on the tip of her nose.

"They were unlucky, weren't they? Whoever the murderer is now knows that I know that Pamenes's death was murder. We are all very knowledgeable, but it doesn't get us anywhere."

Telamon stared across at the bed. "A priest in Egypt once told me, if you have three encounters with snakes and survive, you'll never die by snake-bite."

"And is this your first?"

"No." Telamon laughed, getting to his feet. "My second. I count Olympias, Alexander's mother, as my first."

He went across to his bed and scrupulously searched the bolster, the heavy blanket and linen sheets. Sounds from below drifted up: shouts and cries, the clatter of pots, the neighs of horses from the courtyard.

"The king's returned!" Cassandra exclaimed. "And the drinking party has already been organized."

"I don't really care." Telamon lay down on the bed. "I am going to sleep."

Telamon lay there rigid for a while, eyes closed. He heard Cassandra moving round the room checking all was well, then his body jerked as he slipped into sleep. When he was roughly aroused, he opened his eyes, startled, on Cassandra crouched beside him.

"It's late." Her face looked ghostly in the light of the oil lamp she carried, and the villa lay strangely quiet. "You've been asleep for hours," she explained. "And I have been watching you. Don't worry, there are no more snakes."

"Any visitors?" Telamon opened his eyes and pulled himself up. "Why is it so quiet? I thought I'd wake to the clash of sword against shield, the Macedonian war chant."

"You've missed all that." Cassandra grinned. "The king wants you. He's summoned the scribes as well. Something's gone wrong."

Telamon groaned and got out of bed. He was still wearing his marching boots. He changed into sandals, splashed some water over his face and, recalling the snakes, made his way gingerly out of the chamber. They reached the andron, its corridors guarded by officers from the Shield-Bearers. Inside Telamon realized how frenetic the feasting must have been: cups and platters lay on the floor, scraps of food swam in pools of wine. The chamber glowed with light from torches and oil lamps. Alexander's commanders, lounging on couches, were strangely silent. They had stopped their drinking: the musicians and dancing girls sat huddled, frightened, in a corner. The small table before the king had been knocked aside. Alexander, a myrtle wreath on his head, his gold tunic wine-stained, was listening intently to the soldier kneeling in front of him.

Telamon heard a sound and turned. Solan, Bessus, Cherolos, Gentius and Demerata crowded into the room behind him. The king, annoyed, lifted his head. He glared at the late arrivals before tapping the man on the shoulder, ordering him to continue. The soldier was exhausted: a member of the Thracian light horse, he was dressed in a sweat-stained leather cuirass, the back of his kilt and the sides of his legs caked in mud. He mumbled and muttered: at one point Alexander made him drink from his own cup before telling him to continue. When the soldier was finished, Alexander thrust the cup into his hand and gestured at him to withdraw.

The scout brushed by Telamon and stumbled through the door, which closed behind him. A guards officer took up position, shield in one hand, drawn sword in the other. The chamber lay deathly silent. Alexander appeared to be in a reverie, staring down at the floor, lips moving wordlessly. His hand went in beneath the cushions, he drew out a dagger and drove this, time and time again, into the horse hair-filled couch, working himself up into a rage.

148

"Myndus!" he roared, naming the port to the west of Halicarnassus. "Myndus has closed its gates!"

This drew horrified gasps from his commanders.

"Do you know what that means, Ptolemy?"

"That we have to grow wings, sire, and fly over the walls of Halicarnassus! If we have no port we have no ships! And if we have no ships, no siege equipment! Perhaps we will grow wings!"

Ptolemy ducked as Alexander threw the knife, but it sailed well above his head, crashing against the wall. Alexander stared round at his commanders, then at the group huddled near the door.

"Nicanor commands my ships!" he bellowed. "His task was to bring them into Myndus, a Persian squadron of war triremes was waiting for them! Socrates was to strike south-west. Our partisans in Myndus were supposed to open the gates."

"Instead of which," Ptolemy, unabashed by Alexander's violence, broke in cheerily, "the gates were closed and they catapulted the severed heads of our friends at poor Socrates!"

"In a word, yes." Alexander fell silent, returning to stare at the floor.

Telamon caught something, a shift in Alexander's eyes as if he and Ptolemy were savouring a joke, some secret shared between them.

"Then what are your orders?" Parmenio the grizzled veteran spoke up. "We still have some light siege machinery."

"Oh, we'll encircle Halicarnassus," Alexander agreed. "Seal its gates and see what we can do with that bloody ditch. How Memnon and Ephialtes will be laughing! Parmenio, Hephaestion, Amyntas, Seleucus." Alexander went round his commanders. "Divide the army into four brigades, set up camp with a line between you. Camp on the edge of the grasslands but establish an advance line just beyond the range of their catapults."

"And me, sire?" Ptolemy spoke up.

"You, Ptolemy, will take the Old Guard." Alexander referred to the veterans who had fought for his father. "With some Cretan archers and Rhodian slingers." Alexander gestured at the maps heaped on a small stool beside him. "There's a place on the Halicarnassus peninsula, the rocks of Nyssa, a barren outcrop. I

149

want you to set up guard there. It gives a vantage point to east and west."

"And the siege weapons?" Hephaestion demanded.

"That's why I want you." Alexander pointed to the group at the door. "Solan, Bessus, Cherolos and Sarpedon."

The Spartan had slipped through the door; he was dressed in a simple tunic, one hand gloved, the other not: he stared sleepy-eyed at Telamon. "I was changing my bandages."

"I don't want you whispering!" Alexander bellowed. "Just come forward, all who served with Queen Ada!"

Solan led his group into the space between the tables. He almost slipped on a piece of roast meat lying on the floor, which provoked giggles from Ptolemy and Seleucus. Telamon watched Alexander. The rest of his commanders were drunk, faces flushed, eyes gleaming under the myrtle wreaths perched haphazardly on their heads, but Alexander was acting. Telamon wondered why.

"Right!" Alexander sat on the edge of the couch and held his hands up. "Both harbours at Halicarnassus and Myndus are held by the Persians. So where can I bring my ships in and unload my siege weapons?"

"There's no port." Bessus added quickly, "No deep water harbour where ships can unload."

"There's no harbour," Alexander mimicked back.

"There is one place." Sarpedon spoke up. "The cove of Hera, an inlet, only a few miles to the south. If beacon lights were lit, your admiral could bring his ships in."

"But the waters are treacherous," Solan pointed out. "The cove is rather narrow: you'd have to keep the triremes at sea. It could take days, even weeks to unload."

"No, no." Sarpedon shook his head. "My lord, when you landed at Troy . . . ?"

"I beached my ships." Alexander finished the sentence for him. "What are you saying, Spartan?"

"If you brought your ships in," Sarpedon replied, "they could be beached, dragged out of the water, allowing others in after them. The siege weapons could be unloaded, placed on carts, they could

150

be here" – he shrugged – "after no more than a day or a night's march."

Alexander was nodding in agreement. "But how do we get the message to Nicanor?" Parmenio asked. "He's paddling about like a duck on a pond."

"No, no, he has a second set of orders," Alexander replied. 'If he could find no berth in Myndus, he was to set out to sea, avoid the Persian squadron blocking Halicarnassus harbour and sail due east. He is then to move inland and look for a beacon, the sign that I wish to meet him: at night a roaring fire, columns of smoke during the day. He'll be past Halicarnassus by dawn. You know what he'll do. He'll go inshore looking for our signal, or water for his sailors and marines." Alexander rubbed his hands together. "Amyntas, send out some scouts. No, take them with you. Ride as fast as you can for the coast. You'll be safe, there are no Persians, they're all locked up in Halicarnassus." Alexander scratched his head. "Have the beacon fires lit. Take a team of scouts. Nicanor will send a boat in. Study the maps, take one with you. He's to search for the cove of Hera." He glanced at Sarpedon. "Why is it called that?"

"On the promontory,' the Spartan replied, "stands a disused temple to Hera. Once upon a time it was further inland, but the seas ate the land away, and the temple was abandoned."

"We'll have the fire there," Alexander replied. "Late this afternoon. Seleucus, take two squadrons of Shield-Bearers, Sarpedon can go with you. Nicanor will bring his ships in. Have the carts ready and, if fortune favours us" – Alexander squinted down the room – "within two days we'll be able to give Memnon and Ephialtes the fright of their lives."

Telamon caught his gaze and glimpsed the mischief in Alexander's eyes.

"Well, I've given enough orders." Alexander got to his feet brushing down his tunic. "The rest of you can eat and drink like pigs then go to bed. Me? I am going for a walk with my personal physician."

Alexander sauntered across. The Guards officer stood aside to open the door, and Telamon followed the king out. Alexander strode down the passageway clapping his hands, nodding at the

151

different soldiers on duty. Now and again he stopped to examine a piece of equipment, the insignia on a shield displaying the bull of Minos, or test the sharpness of a sword. He continued out through the entrance into the great cobbled yard. He went across and sat on the wall of the well and stared up at the stars.

"Are you in good health, my lord?" Telamon asked, warily coming across. "For whose benefit was all that?"

"Why," Alexander smiled through the darkness, "for all of us, Telamon. If we can't take Halicarnassus, what can we take? I want to get my hands on Memnon and Ephialtes, teach them a lesson they'll never forget. I want that harbour. I want to show all of Persia, all of Greece, that no city can withstand me! That's why I need the Pythian Manuscript translated so I know the weakest point in those soaring walls."

"Do you really?" Telamon came and sat beside him. "Swear to me, Alexander, you don't know what the Pythian Manuscript contains?"

"If I knew its message then I'd be a most fortunate man."

Something in the king's voice, an edge of sadness, alerted Telamon.

"There's more to it, isn't there, than just those walls?"

"That I do concede, but we'll have to wait, won't we?" Alexander teased. "Are you making progress?"

"Some," Telamon replied. "But we've been down this path before, haven't we, Alexander? Are you going to tell me that you didn't know about the cove of Hera? I've seen you poring over maps for hours. You must have suspected Ephialtes and Memnon would be waiting for you at Myndus? Even the rawest recruit realizes you must bring your ships in. You have your maps and your spies. You know this coastline like the back of your hand. You're playing games again. Why did you summon everyone into the andron? You realize there's a spy among us? You are misleading Memnon and Ephialtes."

Alexander gazed up at the starlit sky as if listening intently to the sounds of the night: the shouts of officers organizing the night watch, the ringing of the bell which was passed from guard to guard to show that they were all alert and the picket line unbroken.

152

"When Father taught me how to fight," Alexander replied slowly, "he said my first task was to mislead the enemy. I misled them at the Granicus. The Persians expected me to go wandering through the countryside, trying to take this city or that city, seize a port to bring my warships in. I did the opposite. After I captured Ephesus, they thought I would wallow in its riches."

"And instead, you struck swiftly for Miletus. So now it's the turn of Halicarnassus?"

"I won't tell you everything, Telamon, but you have the gist of it. However, I haven't invited you out on a starlit night to discuss strategy, but sickness of the mind. I have been talking to Hephaestion and Black Cleitus. One of these days, when there's a lull in the fighting, I want to recreate the very circumstances surrounding my father's death. I want to act out what I saw, the way I felt, what actually happened. Is that possible, Telamon? Will it help me?"

"It could hurt or it could heal."

Alexander got off the wall and walked back to the entrance. "No, no, it won't hurt, Telamon. Nothing can hurt me more than these hideous nightmares."

Alexander sauntered back through the doorway. Telamon heard him laughing and joking with one of the guards and wearily followed him inside. By the time he had returned to his chamber, Cassandra was all ready for bed.

"What did he want?" Her voice was low, sleepy. "You know, Telamon, I watched your face. If Alexander hadn't been a general, he should have joined Gentius on the stage."

"I agree." Telamon slipped off his sandals and lay down on his bed. "At least you know what play Gentius is acting. With Alexander you never know until the final lines. Now, I am tired and wish to sleep."

Telamon planned to rise late. He groaned when he felt himself being poked and prodded. He opened his eyes and stared straight up into the cold, lean face of Aristander, the Master of the King's Secrets.

"What are you doing in my bedchamber?" Telamon stared at the shutters: the light was still dull. He heard a sound and gazed at the door. "I see you've brought your Chorus with you."

"My lovely boys," Aristander simpered. "Look, Telamon, how pleased they are to see you!"

Telamon glared at the tall, burly Celtic warriors dressed in a motley collection of armour: they thronged in the doorway smiling appreciatively across.

"They see you as my friend," Aristander whispered, crouching by the bed, "so you are their friend. They know you as the Healer." His voice fell to a whisper. "They even think you have magical powers."

Telamon gazed quickly across at Cassandra's bed: it was empty.

"We passed her on the stairs," Aristander declared, following Telamon's gaze. "She looked as pleased as ever to see us."

"I am sure she was." Telamon pulled back the sheets. "I want to go to the latrines, I want to eat and drink. I certainly didn't expect you."

Aristander got to his feet and stepped back, his face still wreathed in smiles, though Telamon noticed that he was nursing his left ear.

"Is that still troubling you?"

"Oh, yes!"

Telamon groaned at his own weariness. In the poor light he studied this secretive man's sunken-cheeked face: his hollow eyes, the scrawny hairs, the prim lips and beak-like nose. Even from where he lay he could see mucus forming around the nostrils: Aristander obligingly sniffed.

"It does ache," he moaned.

"You've had a cold, a severe one?" Telamon asked. "And the rheums run thick and fast?"

Aristander nodded mournfully.

"I can cure it, but not now." Telamon lay back on the bed.

"That's why I came last," Aristander wailed. "The jogging of the carts just made it worse." His face lightened as he stepped forward. "But, I understand, the great Gentius is here. He's going to perform Sophocles's plays." He looked over his shoulder. "Sophocles," he whispered to the burly ruffians standing in the doorway. "How does it go, lads? The chorus of the Theban elders?"

"In Thebes, city of light," the leader spoke up, his Greek guttural and harsh, "From the Pythian house of gold . . ."

154

"I recognized the line from *Oedipus*," Telamon hastily broke in. "We have also been studying our Pythian Manuscript but, for the love of Apollo, Aristander, can't you leave me?"

"I know all about the Pythian Manuscript," Aristander retorted. "I wish I hadn't frightened that charlatan the Eunuch away, but, there again . . ."

Telamon closed his eyes. Aristander moved to the door, muttering, "Not even the great philosophers could break it . . ." He then added, in a hushed stage-whisper to his bodyguard, "Let the great physician sleep for a while, he must be tired after his labours . . ."

"Go to Hades!" Telamon whispered. "And stay there till I summon you!"

His eyes grew heavy again. He slept fitfully for a while, aware of Cassandra coming in and out. Aristander returned, so he rolled over pretending to be in a deep sleep.

"He's gone now," Cassandra called out.

Telamon looked over: the light round the shutters was brighter.

"Shall I open them?" Cassandra offered.

Telamon was about to reply when he heard a pounding on the stairs. Bessus burst into the room.

"You'd best come now, physician!"

"Why, is something wrong? Am I the only person?"

"Perdicles and the other physicians are with the army." Bessus blinked. "That's what the king said. You'd best come, sir. A kitchen wench, the Mageros's daughter, has been poisoned!"

Telamon hastily put on his sandals and went downstairs. He realized how late he had slept; the sun on the cobbled yard dazzled his eyes, and he raised his hand to shade them against the glare. Beyond the courtyard wall he heard a heart-rending wailing. He followed Bessus out across the grass to the same vine arbour he and Cassandra had used when they had dressed Sarpedon's wound.

The girl lay on the grass, body contorted. Alexander and Hephaestion stood nearby. They looked rather ridiculous, Hephaestion holding an Egyptian-style parasol above the king's head against the sun. Beside the girl knelt the Mageros. Every so often he would take his face out of his hands, throw his head back and howl up at the sky. Telamon glanced quickly around. On the seat was a

155

platter of bread, cheese, some grapes, and an earthenware cup of watered wine. He noticed the cheese was half gnawed.

"No one touch that!" he warned.

Telamon gently pushed the Mageros aside and pulled the corpse over so the girl lay on her back: her black, greasy hair framed a white face twisted in death. Her eyes were popping, the muscles of the face slightly rigid, a light purplish hue showing just beneath the cheekbone, white froth staining her mouth. Cassandra handed him a napkin.

"It's from our chamber," she explained.

Using the napkin Telamon forced open the girl's mouth: her jaw muscles were rigid. He poked around inside and turned her head to catch the light: her gums and palate had turned a strange purplish hue, her tongue was slightly swollen and covered in a dirty-looking mucus. He sniffed, caught the tang of goats' cheese and the sickly-sweet smell of almonds. He felt the rest of her corpse: her muscles were rigid and hard, her neck still slightly warm.

"Who found her?"

"I did," the Mageros wailed. "She brought out Sarpedon's meal." He gestured at the mercenary, who knelt on the grass some distance away, staring unbelievingly at the body. "I came across. I wondered where she'd gone. She loved cheese. I thought she was sitting with him."

"Hush now!" Telamon gestured at Sarpedon to come over. "What did happen?"

"I met the girl earlier," the Spartan muttered. "I told her I was leaving for the coast. I asked for some food, would she bring it out to the arbour. I gave her a coin – I needed something before I left. That's the last I saw of her. She went to the kitchen . . ."

"Did you expect her to be here when you returned?"

"No, no." Sarpedon shook his head. "She used to cover the food with a linen cloth and leave it in the arbour. I never saw her, nor did I go into the kitchen, did I?"

The Mageros, eyes swimming with tears, shook his head. "She prepared the food," her father explained, "put it on the platter, covered it with a linen cloth and took it out. She did love goats' cheese, but . . ."

Telamon glanced to where the king and Hephaestion watched like spectators at a play, cold and distant.

"So, the girl poisoned herself?" Hephaestion called out.

Sarpedon turned, his face twisted with anger. "No, my lord, she didn't poison herself, she was murdered. That food wasn't meant for her. The killer wanted to strike at me!"

Chapter 8

———∘∞∘———

"The Persian commanders Orontobates and Memnon
now met to discover the situation."

Arrian: *The Campaigns of Alexander*, Book I, Chapter 23

T he clash of sword against sword echoed round the exercise
yard. Orontobates and his officers watched the two Greeks,
dressed as for battle, circle, parry and feint. Each was dressed in the
full armour of a hoplite: large helmets hid their heads and faces
except for slits for eyes and mouth. Memnon's helmet carried a
black crest, Ephialtes's was blood-red. Both were dressed in bronze
cuirasses and leather kiltlets reinforced with bronze studs, and
greaves protected their legs. They fought barefoot in order to
maintain a better grip on the sandy ground. Each carried a great
oval shield, Memnon's decorated with the leaping lion of Rhodes,
Ephialtes's with the crested Red Griffin of Thebes. Both fighters
were drenched in sweat. They circled each other, Ephialtes a little
faster, more agile; Memnon more cunning, calm and poised.
Ephialtes came in shoving his shield forward, feinting with his
slightly curved sword. Memnon countered, bringing his own shield
further to the right while jabbing down with a shorter, blunter
sword. The blades locked. Ephialtes tried to unbalance Memnon
with a vicious shove of his shield. Memnon was faster. Breaking
free, he moved quickly to the right and brought the flat of his
sword down on the exposed part of Ephialtes's neck between
helmet and breastplate.

"A death wound!" Memnon shouted.

Ephialtes stepped back, dropping shield and sword to the
ground. He took off his helmet; Memnon did likewise. They

clasped hands and turned to accept the plaudits of the spectators. Page boys brought forward two beautifully fluted cups of iced sherbet.

"Drink slowly," Memnon warned. "Last time we had the cramps. Ephialtes, you are too impetuous!"

"I kept thinking you were Alexander!" the Theban replied.

They walked into the shade of the portico, where servants helped them strip, and padded along to the small Pool of Purity, down its marble steps. Each swam languidly for a while, turning and twisting, allowing the water to cool, cleanse and soothe their bodies. Orontobates joined them, sitting on a nearby marble bench. He watched these two Greeks, their tawny bodies criss-crossed with old scars, skim through the water. Orontobates didn't trust Greeks, he didn't like them, but these two were an exception – honourable men, brave warriors, cunning commanders. He had stood in the fortress above the great Triple Gate and watched Ephialtes fight the Macedonian cavalry, only to see Alexander slip through the trap Memnon and Ephialtes had set.

"You're thinking how close we were?" Ephialtes demanded, as he came back up the steps and plucked a towel from a waiting page. He dried himself quickly, wrapped a clean loincloth about him and slipped a linen tunic over his head, putting on his bracelets and rings from a tray carried by his body-servant.

"I am thinking how close," Orontobates agreed. "We nearly had him trapped."

Memnon joined them, shaking himself like a dog. He dressed quickly in a striped robe.

"The sun is too hot for me," Ephialtes said. They retreated into the shade of the portico, either end of which was guarded by soldiers dressed in the household colours of Orontobates. Members of Memnon's and Ephialtes's personal bodyguard crouched in the shade of trees, shields beside them, swords drawn. Orontobates licked his lips. He understood the nervousness of his companions: all was not well in the city. The atmosphere had changed: their spies reported that Macedonian sympathizers were stirring up discord, agitating, whispering. Attacks on Persian soldiers and sympathizers had become commonplace.

160

"Your spy was correct." Orontobates picked up a bowl of fruit and plucked at the grapes.

"I didn't need a spy to tell me that Alexander would come," Memnon replied. "He's like our friend Ephialtes here, far too impetuous for his own good."

"Well, he escaped," Ephialtes said, chewing a grape, cleaning his mouth with his tongue. "But we have greater problems: this unrest in the city."

"I know." Memnon felt the rage seethe within him. He had fortified Halicarnassus and hoped to trap Alexander outside its walls. Now, trouble within it threatened all this.

"More weapons have been found," Orontobates confessed. "I have a spy, a Theban merchant. I am not too sure whether he's drunk or sober, but he claims to have seen a Macedonian soldier."

"What?" Memnon spun round.

"That's what he said. A Macedonian soldier, dressed in their distinctive body armour with the shoulder flaps and bronze-studded kilts."

"Where was this?"

"In the tent-makers' quarter."

"Perhaps he was mistaken?" Ephialtes whispered. "An illusion? The people are fearful of the Macedonians."

"Alexander can't break through those walls," Orontobates reassured them. "His ships didn't gain entry to Myndus, and we beat his troops off."

"There's still the Pythian Manuscript," Ephialtes intervened.

"Captain!" Memnon summoned over one of his mercenaries. "Go down to the cells. Tell our gaoler Cerberus to bring up the Eunuch. He's to report on what progress has been made."

"Is there a traitor among us?" Ephialtes stared across the garden.

"In our council?" Orontobates shook his head. "I don't think so."

"Could the Eunuch be a spy?"

"What does he know? Where does he go?" Memnon scoffed. "He's kept in the cells, allowed to exercise in the garden. The only person he talks to is Cerberus."

161

They heard sounds and the captain returned; the Eunuch, carrying a leather satchel, loped behind like a dog. Cerberus the gaoler shuffled beside him, hands to his eyes, unaccustomed to the bright daylight. The Eunuch came across and, uninvited, squatted down, cross-legged.

"You may stand away." Memnon nodded at the gaoler and the captain of the guard, who walked off under the shade of a great overhanging date tree. Memnon pulled across a stool, almost touching the Eunuch, and sat down. The prisoner gazed sly-eyed back. "What progress have you made?"

The Eunuch opened the leather satchel and handed Orontobates, Ephialtes and Memnon a square of freshly scrubbed parchment each. "You will notice, my lords," he began, "how the alphabet is organized into five rows across, five down." Memnon studied his copy. "Beneath that, the first numbers from the Pythian Manuscript. I have also inscribed what we learnt from Pamenes: his mysterious reference to pente, the Greek for five, and the letter epsilon, the fifth letter of your alphabet."

"What progress?" Memnon demanded.

"Pamenes had established a very important principle. He quoted a line from Sophocles's play and ringed every E in that extract: he did the same with verses from the *Iliad*."

"And?" Memnon curbed his excitement.

"It is just a theory," the Eunuch blithely continued, "but, I suspect Pamenes realized that the letter E is the most commonly used in any document." He smiled ingratiatingly at Orontobates. "Of course this may not be true of the Persian tongue."

"But of Greek?" Ephialtes demanded leaning forward.

"It certainly is."

"So, if I understand you correctly –" Memnon ignored the heat. He was no longer aware of the scent of the flowers, the buzzing of the bees, the distant sounds of the palace or those from the city which drifted over the walls. He felt he was on the verge of a great secret, of discovering a weakness which Alexander would surely give a ransom for.

"If I may explain for you, my lord," the Eunuch flattered, "if E is

162

the commonest letter, then we must look for the commonest number in the Pythian Manuscript."

"Which is?"

"Fifty-four, perhaps, but I don't think that's the E."

"You're almost there, aren't you?" Memnon said. "Once you've found the number which stands for E, you'll be able to find the same for every other letter."

"Precisely." The Eunuch's smile faded. "But so far, I have been unable to do that."

"Why?"

"I don't know: that's what I am trying to work out. Pythias must have realized that, one day, someone would reach the same conclusion as myself. He therefore built a defence into his cipher to protect the letter E."

"Explain!"

"My lord, look at the manuscript. Its first numbers are as follows: 45 : 64 : 54 : 33 : 34 : 11 : 53 : 11 : 52 : 23 : 33 : 34 : 54 : □ : 23 : 54 : 54 : 44."

"Four 54s," Ephialtes murmured. "But if E, the most commonly used letter, isn't that, where is it?"

"Hidden away, well protected," the Eunuch replied.

"How?" Memnon demanded.

"Possibly by the square between 54 and 23?"

"And?"

"Did Pythias deliberately choose words, at the beginning of his manuscript, which omitted the letter E? Or . . ."

"Or," Memnon interrupted, "you are not so sure whether 54 does stand for E?"

"It could be 23," the Eunuch murmured. "Or that might be another diversion."

"How much longer do you need?"

The Eunuch spread his hands. "My lord, in a few days I am sure I will have a translation."

"If you give me that," Memnon smiled, "you will leave Halicarnassus wealthier than you came."

"And if you fail," Ephialtes broke in, "we'll sever your body into chunks of butcher's meat and catapult it into the Macedonian camp!"

* * *

163

"Is it murder?"

Alexander sat in the vine arbour, squatting on the ground, his back to the wooden seat. Telamon sat opposite, Sarpedon beside him. The Mageros, still sobbing, knelt to his left: Alexander had tried to soothe him but every attempt brought fresh bursts of weeping. Telamon glanced over his shoulder. Hephaestion and Cassandra were standing by the pool talking quietly. Somewhere in the house Gentius was rehearsing his lines. Aristander had apparently brought his Chorus to complement the great actor's work.

"It's murder," Telamon replied, looking back. "A deadly poison, the juice of almonds. It's not wholly that, it just smells and tastes like almonds. A distillation of deadly plants which can be purchased in any city. The real victim was supposed to be Sarpedon."

"It must have been," the Spartan insisted. "I am shortly to leave for the cove of Hera. Someone wished to stop me."

"My poor child!" The Mageros took his hand away from his face.

Alexander snapped his fingers at Telamon and rose to his feet. "I leave this to you." The king strode off the grass, calling for Hephaestion to join him. Telamon got up, sat on the wooden bench and stared down at his two companions.

"Sarpedon, where did you meet the girl?"

"I took some water from the well. She was there. You know I had a fancy for her. I told her I would be leaving soon." He shrugged one shoulder. "I admit I was flirting. I asked her to bring some bread, cheese and a cup of watered wine out here. Perhaps she would give me a kiss before I left? I then went to the stables to tend my horse."

"Mageros?" Telamon asked quietly. "Mageros, your daughter is dead. I am sorry. You can grieve over her corpse. But, surely, you want justice, vengeance?"

The Mageros took his hands away from his face again and fought to control his sobs.

"You were in the kitchen. You must have seen your daughter prepare the platter. The bread and cheese were fresh?"

164

The Mageros nodded. "She placed them on the table," he half-sobbed, "and covered them with a linen cloth. I asked her who it was for, she replied Sarpedon. I was busy baking fresh loaves."

"Who came into the kitchen?"

"Everyone did, even your red-haired friend!" the Mageros exclaimed.

"So it would have been easy for someone to lift that linen cloth, remove the cheese and replace it with a poisoned piece?"

The Mageros agreed. "Anyone could have done it," the man confessed. "Master, you know what it's like, people coming and going, demanding food? Soldiers, who are ever hungry, the king and his companions . . ."

"Did you go into the kitchen, Sarpedon?"

The Spartan shook his head. "No, I didn't. The first I knew of what had happened was when I heard the alarm being raised." Sarpedon shrugged. "She must have come back to see if I had arrived and decided to eat some of the cheese herself. If she hadn't —" the Spartan got to his feet "— my corpse would be lying under a sheet in the outhouse. Telamon, I must go."

The physician heard sounds from the stables, of horses being prepared.

"I must go too," the Mageros mumbled. He rose and stumbled across the grass like a man being led out to execution.

Telamon picked up the platter and removed the linen cloth. The wine and bread were untainted, but the cheese carried that blood-chilling, yet slightly fragrant aroma of almonds. Telamon called across a soldier, covered the tray and handed it to the man.

"Take this!" he ordered. "Get some kindling, don't touch whatever is on it and burn it!"

The Macedonian, a burly farm boy, took off his causia, the broad-brimmed hat, and scratched his cropped head. "It's not dangerous?" he protested.

"Do as I say," Telamon insisted. "Don't touch anything, just burn it!"

The soldier walked away. Telamon went across to the pool, where he washed his hands in the water and dried them on his tunic. A shadow fell across him.

165

"Don't be alarmed," Cassandra called out. "But there's been another death."

The physician whirled round. Cassandra pointed to the trees.

"Do you remember Pamenes's cat? Well, someone took it into the orchard and beat it to death with a club. I've just found its corpse. Your soldiers can burn that as well."

"Why should they kill a harmless cat?"

"I don't know," Cassandra murmured. "It might be unconnected. Don't some Macedonians regard the cat as unlucky? A creature of the night?"

Telamon got to his feet and walked back to the vine arbour. Cassandra sat beside him. They listened to Sarpedon and his party leave in the clatter of hooves and the blowing of horns.

"Will they bring the siege engines ashore?" she asked.

"Oh yes, what Alexander wants Alexander gets." Telamon narrowed his eyes and watched a butterfly hover above the grass. "They'll be ashore by nightfall. This time tomorrow Memnon will look over the walls of Helicarnassus and be surprised."

"I've just seen Ptolemy leave for the rocks of Nyssa."

"I wonder what Alexander intends?" Telamon mused. "His mind is a mosaic made up of small, exquisite different pieces. You have to collect them together and sort them out."

"Someone tried to stop Sarpedon."

"But who?" Telamon asked. "It would have been so easy to walk into that kitchen with a piece of cheese, take one piece away and replace it with another." He paused. "So, what do we have, Cassandra? Pamenes's mysterious fall from his window. Someone tried to kill me with those vipers. Now, that poor unfortunate who mistakenly ate a piece of cheese intended for Sarpedon."

"Why should they want to kill him?" Cassandra demanded. "I know he's leading the troops to the cove of Hera, but that's not any great secret."

"Perhaps he saw something untoward and doesn't realize it? We know Pamenes was alive early that morning. Bessus could have slipped into that chamber, or did the priest Cherolos return? Did Sarpedon see any of this?"

"And, of course, there's our great actor, I can hear him from here," Cassandra laughed. "With his secretive-faced wife."

"Yes," Telamon replied. "We have only their word that Demerata wasn't in Pamenes's chamber. I wonder where she did go for a walk? Do you remember that evening, Cassandra, we were out here, preferring the garden to that gloomy house? We never saw her. And that dead cat? Why should someone kill a poor animal?"

"Perhaps it was a sacrifice?" Cassandra murmured. "I still have doubts about Cherolos." She added, "He's shifty-eyed, secretive."

"It's all about a piece of manuscript."

"Do you think Alexander will ever uncover its secrets?"

"I am nearly there."

"What!" Cassandra exclaimed.

"I've been thinking. Pamenes was absorbed with the letter E, the fifth in the Greek alphabet. He circled it in lines taken from a Sophocles play. When I was in Egypt I used to study the hieroglyphics in the tombs: the most common was the one which stood for the pharaoh. Once you understood that, the rest was quite easy. Did you know the vowels E, A and I are the most commonly used letters? E certainly is. I am not too sure whether it's A next, or I. But if we can discover what stands for these three in the Pythian Manuscript, the rest will soon follow. I wager a jug of wine to a bowl of fruit that Solan and the others are following the same path."

They heard sounds from the courtyard: Alexander, Hephaestion and other commanders came out, followed by servants carrying camp stools, a wooden bench, even chairs from the loom room.

"Oh no!" Telamon murmured. "Gentius's great moment!"

He watched the chattering servants set up the makeshift theatre, arranging the chairs, stools and benches in a horseshoe pattern. Alexander glanced across: he raised his hand, beckoning them to join him.

"I suppose we have to."

Servants brought out small tables with cups and platters. A makeshift awning was set up, supported by four poles driven into the ground. Telamon and Cassandra took their places behind the king. Aristander, dressed fastidiously in a gaudy orange robe, came bustling through the gate, a laurel wreath on his balding head. He still nursed a sore ear.

"That reminds me," Telamon whispered. "When this is all over, go to my medicine chest, Cassandra; you'll find a small phial of camphor oil. Tell our noble Keeper of the King's Secrets to warm it and shake a few drops in his ear. It will weaken the wax and his discomfort will go."

"My Lord King." Aristander stood beneath the canopy, his loose sandal caught in the folds of the cloths strewn there, which brought shouts and exclamations from his audience: Alexander clapped his hands for silence. "My Lord King, fellow thespians, today we bring you the splendour of Sophocles's play *King Oedipus*."

"The what? The whole lot?" Black Cleitus shouted.

"Just extracts," Aristander retorted testily, "performed by Gentius in the role of Oedipus and my lovely boys as the Chorus."

Aristander disappeared back into the courtyard and brought out his bodyguard. Telamon found it hard to keep his face straight. The Celts had now removed their armour and were all dressed in long, flowing robes and sandals. Black Cleitus's head went down, shoulders shaking, even as the king jabbed him with his elbow. Aristander, however, had his own ideas about how the play was to be performed. He marshalled his bodyguard, the great oafs shuffling about, scratching heads and beards, hands falling to knife belts no longer there. Telamon had to pinch himself: Alexander's world was like a strange land between waking and dreaming. Here they were on the verge of laying siege to one of the great cities of the Persian empire, yet they were sitting in the gardens of a villa watching Sophocles's *Oedipus*. The Chorus was not a gaggle of Athenian youths but a band of Celtic cut-throats, taught by their master to recite some of the greatest lines ever written.

For a while there was shoving and pushing as Aristander arranged the group to his own liking. At last he was satisfied, turned, and bowed to the king. He shot a venomous glance at Cleitus, who now had his head in his hands. Even from where he stood, Telamon could see the tears coursing down the old rogue's scarred cheeks. Hephaestion was made of sterner stuff. Telamon thanked the gods that Ptolemy wasn't there. He hated Aristander and ridiculed him at every opportunity; Alexander's monkey-faced general, however, had disappeared, taking his elite contingent of troops to the rocky outcrop of Nyssa.

Servants, slaves, off-duty soldiers also drifted in. Cassandra was strangely quiet, as if unaware of the comedy around her. She sat, mouth half open, staring ahead. Telamon realized that the last time she had seen this play was in her native city of Thebes. Once the home of Oedipus, Antigone and Creon, Thebes was now a sea of cold, grey ash.

"We are ready." Aristander bowed at the king. "Right, lads, begin where I told you!"

"Beyond all telling, the city
Reeks with death . . ."

"No, not that!" Aristander slapped the leader of the Chorus with his hand. "Further down! Further down!"

The leader, a huge brute with blond hair and a thick, luxuriant moustache and beard, stood like a chastised schoolboy.

"Slay with thy golden bow!" Aristander hissed.

The Chorus began again.

"Slay with thy golden bow, Lycean. Slay him!
Artemis, over the Lycian hills resplendent!
Bacchus, our Name God, golden in the dance
Of Maenad revelry!
Thy fiery torch advance
To slay the God of Death, the grim enemy!
The god whom all other gods abhor to see . . ."

Gentius, dressed in a grey robe and wearing a tragic mask, came out of the courtyard and in under the canopy.

"You have prayed and your prayers shall be answered with help and release . . . !"

"Oh great King!" the Chorus replied, "listen to our prayer!"

Gentius took up the line. "If you obey me . . ."

Telamon watched, fascinated. Despite the humour, the awkwardness of the Chorus, Gentius had a presence, a powerful mourning voice which conveyed the soul-wrenching sadness of this play. As he spoke, Black Cleitus stopped laughing and pulled himself up, turning his twisted face to hear more clearly. Cassandra began to sob softly. The interplay between Chorus and Oedipus, the principal character, had a sombre music all of its own. Even the farmboys and servants gazed open-mouthed. Telamon recognized the true genius of Gentius: his posture, the way every movement counted, his voice which would bring words and phrases to vivid life. So engrossed in the play, Telamon wasn't really aware of the shrieks and screams until a greasy-faced pot boy came charging out of the courtyard.

"The Mageros is sick! The Mageros is sick!" he yelled. "Oh sirs, come quickly!"

Alexander turned and snapped his fingers at Telamon who, muttering apologies to Gentius, crossed the makeshift stage and hurried into the courtyard. Servants were clustered at the kitchen door. A girl was screaming, waving her hands. The baker, covered from head to toe in flour, was trying to placate her.

"What is it?" Telamon demanded.

The baker gestured vaguely into the steam-filled kitchen. Telamon stepped in warily. A flesh-cutter crouched behind a table, a bloody knife in one hand, eyes popping with fear. A spit boy sat cradling a small pot, rocking himself backwards and forwards. Telamon gazed around. A ham dangled from the rafters over one of the portable ovens. Onions and other vegetables hung from pegs driven into the grimy white walls. He heard a moan and stopped by the table. At the far end of the room was an open hearth under a gap in the roof. A great bronze cauldron filled with water was bubbling merrily on the charcoal, next to it a large earthenware jar; in between that and the pot lay the Mageros, body jerking.

Telamon hurried across as Cassandra also entered the kitchen. The heat from the charcoal and bubbling pot were intense. Telamon, taking the cook by the shoulder, pulled him away. The man was choking to death, his face had turned a livid hue, lips slightly purpled. It looked as if his cheeks and thick neck were enlarged: his flesh was clammy cold, eyelids fluttering.

170

"What is it, man?"

A white line of dribble spurted out through the Mageros's lips and down his chin. Telamon forced the man's mouth open, searching with his fingers, but he could find no blockage.

"Is it a seizure?" Cassandra asked. "Oh, for Apollo's sake, Telamon, look at his right arm!"

Telamon saw the huge raised welts, about four in number, on the inside of the arm just below the elbow. Telamon grasped the Mageros's wrist and felt for a pulse. It was weak, erratic like the wings of moth beating vainly for life: his right arm was already puffy. Telamon felt it carefully.

"The eels," the Mageros muttered. He began to shake, the death rattle loud in his throat.

Telamon got to his feet. Inside the tall earthenware jar coiled the shiny bodies of the eels, their black, scaly flesh still wet. He stepped away as the baker, a large, florid-faced man, came striding back into the kitchen.

"What happened?" Telamon demanded.

"He was preparing a delicacy for the king. Rock eels. You know, his speciality? He baked them in cups, with oregano and mulberries."

"Yes, yes. Continue!"

"He thrust his hand into the eels, withdrew it screaming and collapsed to the ground. It's a wonder he didn't hit the cauldron!"

Telamon grabbed a large pole with a linen cloth handle, used for stirring the pot.

"The Mageros!" the baker wailed, pointing at the prostrate cook.

"There's nothing I can do." Telamon already half-guessed what had happened. "He's been bitten at least four times. One bite can be cut, but not four." He gingerly shoved the pole into the pot of eels and stirred carefully.

"But they are dead!" the baker shouted, coming across.

For a moment Telamon glimpsed a yellow-black, scaly body moving across the eels.

"What is it?" Cleitus came swaggering into the kitchen.

The Mageros now lay still, mouth open, tongue slightly protuberant, eyes half closed.

"I love the smell of fish," Cleitus sniffed as he came across. "What's wrong with this greasy slob?"

"He's been murdered," Telamon whispered. "Cleitus, now is not the time for your drill-ground manner. Have the corpse removed. There is nothing I can do." He kicked the jar of eels. "Have this also taken out, by soldiers wearing marching boots. Empty the contents. Tell them to be wary, it contains vipers, their bite is venomous . . ."

"Two plays at the same time." Alexander, clapping his hands softly, came into the kitchen. "I heard you, Telamon. Cleitus, do as he says! Physician, I want a word with you."

He almost pushed Telamon out through a small door at the far side of the kitchen into the smelly yard where the rubbish was piled. The birds plundering the refuse rose and squawked, black wings beating.

"The Mageros's daughter was poisoned," Alexander began, "and now the Mageros himself. Why?"

"I don't know. If I did, we'd all know the truth. She was killed with a piece of cheese meant for Sarpedon. Now the eels are fresh, they were brought in this morning. Yes?"

Alexander shrugged. "I am a general," he grinned, "not a cook." He sighed. "So I won't be having rock eel for supper tonight."

"I suspect the eels were brought in wicker baskets," Telamon continued, "and emptied into that large jar. Someone placed the vipers in either the jar or the baskets."

"Of course," Alexander murmured. "And the Mageros put his hand in."

"He was bitten at least four times," Telamon explained, "by different snakes with different poisons. For some there are antidotes. One bite can be cut clean, but not so many."

"Snakes!" Alexander hissed the word. "I understand they are all over this farm. Who chose it?"

"From what I understand, Solan."

"I'll bring some Cretan archers in," Alexander declared. "They're used to clearing the ground of them. You aren't telling

172

me everything, are you, Telamon?" He stared out of the corner of his eye. "I understand something happened in your chamber yesterday?"

Telamon told him.

"So, whoever it is" − Alexander kicked at a pile of apple cores, squashing one under his sandalled foot − "killed the scribe, tried to murder my physician, and now strikes at the cook and his daughter. Now, Pamenes I can understand." Alexander scratched his chin and faced Telamon squarely. "The Persians would certainly pay for your head. But why a cook and his daughter?"

Alexander ran his fingers through his red-gold hair, his strange-coloured eyes staring fixedly at Telamon. He moved his head slightly to the right as if studying the physician for the first time.

"And why didn't you tell me about the attack on you?" He tapped Telamon gently under the chin. "You are precious, physician! An attack upon you is an attack upon me. You don't like snakes, neither do I. They always remind us of Mother. Next time, search your chamber. Be careful what you eat or drink. Do you have any suspicions?"

Telamon shook his head.

"Are you telling me the truth?" Alexander's head came forward.

"Are you?" Telamon mimicked the king, pushing his face forward only inches from Alexander's. "Are you telling me the truth, Alexander, about the Pythian Manuscript, or are you in your own play? What role now? The bluff general worried about the fortifications of a city? I know you, Alexander, I was raised with you. I have been marching with you, the great pretender, the man who misleads his enemies, who strikes as hard and as viciously as any serpent."

The king drew his head back: his harsh look gave way to a mock bashfulness. He fluttered his long eyelashes like a girl. "Why Telamon," he cooed, "I don't know what you are talking about. Now, I do have a play to watch."

The king re-entered the kitchen. He stopped to console some of the servants. Telamon heard the clink of coins on the floor and, when he entered, the king had gone. The servants, forgetful of the tragedy which had occurred, were scrabbling about searching for the coins. Telamon called the baker across. The fellow came over surly-faced, narrow eyes still searching the floor for coins.

"When were these eels brought in?"

"Just after dawn. A peasant and his son: he supplies the kitchens with produce. The eels were fresh, caught yesterday evening."

"And how were they brought in?"

"Baskets."

"And they were tipped into the jar?"

"That's right," the baker smirked.

Telamon grasped him by his floury tunic and pulled him closer. "A man has been brutally murdered," he whispered. "Within hours, his body will be ash and his soul wandering the cold fields of Hades. Now, do you want to join him?"

"The eels were brought in in baskets," the baker gabbled. "They were put into the jar and left there."

"Were you here at the time?"

"Yes . . ."

"But you saw nothing out of the ordinary?"

"Master," the man bleated, "someone may have put the vipers in, but it could have been an accident."

"I don't think so." Telamon pushed him away.

"At least five." Cassandra came into the kitchen. "Five vipers in all. The guards have killed them. Our noble king is now ordering Cretans to search the grounds to hunt and kill as many as they can. Cleitus claims he'll hire a mongoose . . ."

Telamon brushed by the baker and gestured at Cassandra to follow him out into the courtyard. "Is the play continuing?"

"Yes. Alexander, as you know," Cassandra smiled bleakly, "is single-minded in what he wants."

"Is Cherolos there? Go and get him," Telamon asked. "I will meet him outside his chamber. Or, if it's unlocked, inside."

"Why?"

"You'll find out."

Telamon went into the villa, up the stairs and along the passage-way. Someone had put out fresh flower baskets; the polished wood smelt of some fragrance Telamon couldn't place. He walked down the passage, past Bessus's chamber, and turned left into the small

174

alcove. He paused outside Pamenes's door and pushed it open. The chamber was still unused, much as he had left it when he and Cassandra had searched the dead scribe's possessions. Telamon walked across to the open window and stared down at the dark-red paving bricks. He heard Cassandra calling his name, so he went out and joined them. Cherolos's thin, sour face was all a-glower: the priest stood tapping his hands against his thigh.

"I was enjoying that play."

"Where's your chamber?"

Cherolos went across to the door beyond Bessus's, pushed down the latch and threw it open. Telamon stepped inside. The priest was very neat, his bed made up, hidden behind its white veils, clothes hung from a peg in the wall. The small desk had been turned into a makeshift altar. Telamon went and stared down at the carved head, a circlet round its forehead, which had the face of a striking cobra.

"Meretseger!" Telamon exclaimed. "The Scorpion or Snake Goddess! Her shrine overlooks the Necropolis in Thebes, doesn't it? Meretseger! She who always watches and waits!"

Cherolos agreed.

Telamon stretched out his hand and touched the blood-red marble headstone on its polished oaken base. He heard Cherolos's sharp intake of breath.

"Are you proficient with snakes?" Telamon turned to face him.

"I have some knowledge."

"Do you know how to handle them? How to pick them up?"

"A little!" The priest wiped his palms on the dark-blue tunic and pulled his mantle closer about his shoulders.

"You've travelled to Egypt?"

"I have been in the kingdom of the Two Crowns," he replied pompously. "I have worshipped at Meretseger's temple."

"So what are you doing at Queen Ada's court?"

"Misunderstandings along the path of life."

"Have you been hunting snakes here, Cherolos?"

The priest just smirked.

"Don't the devotees of Meretseger sacrifice cats to her?"

Cherolos's eyes remained flinty hard, and he made to turn away.

"Oh, one more question." Telamon laid a hand on his shoulder. The priest turned back, gazing at Telamon's hand as if it was polluted.

"The morning you went down to Pamenes's chamber?"

"It was locked."

"And did you go back? You were the last to join us in the andron."

The priest's head went down.

"I think you did," Telamon continued. "You returned to Pamenes's chamber: this time the door was open, and you went inside. You picked up his saddlebags and brought them here. You went through them – that's when you found that scrap of parchment, not the night before."

Cherolos swallowed hard.

"I do have a witness." Telamon smiled to hide the lie. "You were seen carrying saddlebags."

"But that's im –!"

"Impossible?" Telamon offered. "Because you hid the bags here and took them out in the dead of night, after you had searched them thoroughly?"

"I didn't kill Pamenes."

"No, but you did steal his possessions. What was in those saddlebags?"

"Clothing, sandals. I threw them into a small mere at the far side of the villa."

"Very good." Telamon stared across at Cassandra, who stood with her back to the door. "You found sandals, tunics, paltry possessions and a scrap of parchment, what else?" He looked down at the marble head of Meretseger.

"I am a stranger at Queen Ada's court," Cherolos confessed. "I wanted to make my name. I did go back to Pamenes's chamber. It was empty, the window was open, his saddlebags were there. His possessions, well –" he shrugged "– his table was clear of parchments, only the saddlebags remained. I thought I'd search them and put them back later. I heard the others calling for me, so I hid the saddlebags under my own bed and joined the meeting."

"And after Pamenes was found dead?"

"I had no choice but to get rid of them."

"And what else did you find?"

Cherolos picked up the marble head attached to the wooden base and took out a scroll, small, tightly bound with a piece of cord. He slipped it into Telamon's hand. "You may make more use of it than I. All it says is the usual 'Pente', 'Epsilon', and the number 10."

"The number 10?" Telamon queried.

"I couldn't understand that."

Telamon stared down at the parchment.

"But Pamenes's chamber was locked when we came up." Casandra asked. "How could you enter twice?"

Cherolos shrugged.

"I can answer that." Telamon put the piece of parchment away. "And Cherolos's confession proves my theory. The locked chamber was simply to confuse us. I believe Pamenes was dead, must have been dead, long before that chamber was locked."

There was a knock on the door; Cassandra opened it. A royal page almost fell into the room.

"A message from the king," he spluttered. "The play is finished, but the real one is about to begin. Everyone is to prepare to leave for the camp."

Chapter 9

━━━━◆○○◆━━━━

"On the following day Alexander brought up his siege
artillery to attack: and his move was promptly countered
by a party from the town."

Arrian: The Campaigns of Alexander, Book I, Chapter 22

T he heat was oppressive, the sun a fiery disc, heating up the
rocky peninsula round the city of Halicarnassus. Buzzards
floated on the faint breezes which the perspiring soldiers below
wished they could feel. Halicarnassus was now under all-out
assault. Alexander had deployed the entire Macedonian army,
phalanx after phalanx, reinforced by regiments of Shield-Bearers.
On each flank the Peltasts, mercenary hoplites, Cretan archers and
Rhodian slingers. Slightly behind each wing, squadron after squadron of cavalry clustered, a sea of angry colour as the men of war
prepared for the clash of combat. Trumpets and war horns brayed.
Horses neighed and shook their heads, the plumes between their
ears dancing like a sea of standards. Alexander was garbed in the
full-dress armour of a Macedonian general; golden cuirass, purple
cloak, snow-white leather kilt, silver greaves, while his feet were
encased in sandals, their thongs decorated with purple and silver
studs. As usual he occupied the place of honour on the right flank,
surrounded by his personal bodyguard. The rest of his Companions, the brigade commanders, had now assumed their commands.

Telamon sat on his horse in the second rank behind the king
along with other members of the royal household. An hour past
midday, and it was still fiercely hot. Telamon felt he was gazing into
a roaring fire rather than at the granite walls of Halicarnassus, which

179

soared one hundred and fifty feet into the air, their towers and battlements thronged with men, small dark shapes against the blue sky. He glimpsed the jutting props of the siege towers behind the walls, where Memnon would place his catapults, slings and mangonels, all the hideous engines of war.

Alexander had deployed the entire battle line so Memnon could see his might. Arranged in front of the Macedonian army were the precious siege machines. Amyntas had been successful. Nicanor and his second-in-command Nearchus had beached the Macedonian warships, line after line, on the white shingle in the cove of Hera. The siege weapons had been securely landed, placed in carts and hurried up into the main Macedonian camp. They had been hastily assembled and deployed opposite the Triple Gate just out of range of Memnon's engines of war behind the walls. Telamon smiled to himself: he and the rest, with the exception of Cassandra, had been almost force-marched from the villa. Alexander wanted them near him, but that had been a mistake. Over the last few days, Solan had done nothing but moan. The king had relented and muttered that they could return to the Villa of Cybele once his beloved siege weapons were in place.

Telamon gazed at these infernal machines, capable of wreaking such bloody carnage. As a boy he had watched Philip's principal military engineer Demades construct the most awesome engines of war. Alexander had now perfected these: siege towers built of wooden poles and wickerwork which soared almost as high as the walls of Halicarnassus, with a range of platforms and storeys inside. On the top, soldiers; on the second and third storeys, small siege weapons such as dart- and missile-throwers; at the bottom, heavy rams with metal heads slung on pulleys so the men could swing them backwards and forwards to crack the strongest walls. Yet these towers were nothing compared to the other terrifying weapons. Huge bows on square wooden frames reinforced with metal strips: these could loose darts, three yards long, and rake the walls of any besieged city with a devastating accuracy. Sling-shots which could hurl boulders or pots of fire; such deadly missiles were given extra propulsion by the new technique, introduced by Demades, of using twisted horsehair rather than rope, anchored on a wooden frame winched back by pulleys and levers then released with devastating effect.

Between the siege weapons were movable wooden mantlets, their roofs covered with animal skins soaked in water against fire arrows from the besieged. These could be wheeled up against the walls, their sloping roofs protecting the soldiers inside manning the rams. These machines now lay ominously silent, like predators waiting to spring. Telamon's gaze moved to the great ditch, and he wondered how Alexander was going to fill this in order to get both men and machines up against the walls. During the last few days the carpenters had been busy constructing dozens of flat-topped sheds, but the king had refused to say why he needed these.

Of course, Alexander wished to observe the niceties of the war. He wished the besieged to perceive his full might before the attack was launched. According to the rules of war, one last offer should be made for Memnon and his garrison to surrender. Alexander drew his sword and held it high as he galloped along the entire Macedonian front, to be greeted by the clatter of shields and the shrilling war cry of Macedon. "Eynalius! Eynalius! Eynalius!"

The sound roared up to the skies, to be greeted by cat-calls and jeers from those on the walls. The defenders were now unrolling great leather sheets, hanging them from the battlements, further protection against the rams and the fiery missiles soon to be released against them. The king reached the far left of the Macedonian battle line: he turned and rode back along the line, his black war horse Bucephalus thoroughly enjoying the attention and acclamation, tossing his head, the vivid star-burst in the centre very visible. Alexander had chosen his headstall and harness from the plunder of the Persian camp after his victory at the Granicus: black leather with precious jewels and studs, with a cloth of gold as a shabrague or saddlecloth. Alexander looked an awesome sight; as one of Telamon's companions whispered, "The very God of War incarnate." The sun dazzled on his brilliant armour, the horsehair plume of his helmet streaming out behind him, glinting sword held high, the usual gesture of a commander about to launch an all-out attack.

Once Alexander rejoined his staff officers, he doffed his helmet, face boyish, gleaming with sweat, those strange-coloured eyes full of mischief. He peered round the circle, caught Telamon's gaze and winked.

"Gentlemen, enjoy the calm," he declared. "For soon all the Furies will be released!"

"What about that bloody ditch?" someone bawled.

Alexander raised a finger to his lips and turned away. He rode slightly forward accompanied by two heralds and a trumpeter. At Alexander's signal the herald lifted the bronze salpinx and blew a braying blast before cantering forward almost to the edge of the ditch, his words carrying faintly on the breeze.

"Men of Halicarnassus, open your gates and surrender! Hand over to our king, the adopted heir of Queen Ada, rightful ruler of Halicarnassus, the men who have misled you: Orontobates, Memnon and Ephialtes!"

A chorus of derision greeted his words. An arrow smacked into the ground beside the herald, sending his horse skittering. The herald stooped down, picked up the arrow, broke it as a gesture of contempt and rode back to Alexander. Two further heralds went forward, carrying the accepted tokens of war. They reached the edge of the ditch. The man with the burning firebrand tossed it across while his fellow, armed with a spear stained with animal blood, hurled this as hard as he could across the ditch: it fell into its yawning blackness to the hoots of derision from the men on the battlements.

"Prepare to attack!"

Seleucus, who had been appointed second-in-command during Ptolemy's absence, issued his orders. Immediately the phalanxes and regiments of Shield-Bearers parted, allowing the engineers' carts to trundle up. The battle line retreated, breaking up into brigades. The engines of war were prepared, braziers carried forward to stand by carts full of stones, darts, bolts, boulders and missiles for the catapults and sling-shots. The line of siege engines were transformed, no longer huge wooden frames with levers, slings and horsehair torsion. The machines sprang to life as pulleys were made tight, winches turned, pots of burning fire placed in the leather slings, spears, darts and arrows lodged in the smooth grooves of the catapults and huge bows. Siege towers were prepared: lightly armed soldiers going in, up the staircase to the different storeys: archers and slingers on the top, javelin men below and, at the base, the men who would man the great battering rams. Mantlets and sheds were prepared. The air was rich with the creak of rope and pulleys, the screech of levers. Black smoke curled up from the braziers, and the air grew rank with the stench of oil.

The defenders of Halicarnassus let loose volleys of arrows and sling-shots, but these fell short. At last the Macedonian engines of war were ready, catapults winched back, sling-shot ready, huge bows primed: each machine was guarded by units of Cretan archers. The siege engines were pushed slightly forward, wheels creaking.

"Prepare!"

Seleucus's order was taken up by trumpeters, who gave three short blasts.

"Be ready!"

Again the trumpet blast, but only two.

"On my mark!"

One further trumpet blast.

"Prepare to loose!"

The salpinxes chorused again, accompanied by flautists and musicians from different brigades. Telamon felt as if the whole army were tensing itself. He was aware of the awesome walls of Halicarnassus, figures along the battlements, the sun-filled blue sky, the first traces of a late afternoon breeze. A moment of absolute silence.

"Loose!"

The silence was shattered by the curses and cries of the men operating the machines, the chilling sound of levers being released, pulleys springing forward, the creak and groan of wooden frames. The death-bearing missiles, boulders, pots of fire and darts soared into the air and fell with an awesome screeching against the walls or, in some cases, even over the battlements of Halicarnassus. Three figures slipped through the crenellations and fell, arms and legs flailing, into the yawning ditch. Spouts of fire and smoke flickered up as Macedonian missiles reached their targets and set fire to buildings, sheds, even bodies of defenders. The siege weapons possessed a dreadful music of their own. Once the missiles were released, levers were winched back to shouts and yells and the harsh creaking of pulleys. Fresh bolts, arrows, pots of fire and boulders were loaded. The chief engineer on each machine, having gauged their first shot, now ordered their equipment to be rolled further forward.

The defenders replied. Whirling boulders came soaring over the city walls, flights of fiery darts, pots of burning oil; most missed, but those which did hit a target created bloody carnage and havoc. One pot of oil burst against a catapult being loaded, engulfing the wooden frame and all around it in roaring sheets of fire.

"It looks good," someone whispered, "but we need to get closer. What's the use of all this with that bloody ditch in the way?"

Fresh instructions were issued. Trumpets and war horns brayed. The Macedonian army was ordered to retreat and, as they did so under the harsh discipline of their officers, the different units broke up. Telamon heard the rumble of wheels and stared round. The great wooden sheds Alexander had built and hidden behind his lines were now brought forward. They were nothing more than a platform on wheels, a wooden pillar in each corner supporting a flat wooden roof over which water-drenched animals skins had been stretched. Each shed, about nine yards long, stood on six fast-moving wheels. Cretan archers on each side carried small buckets of grease for the axles. The sheds were pushed through the ranks, up past the siege machinery. Telamon watched in amazement.

"Very clever!"

Telamon looked over his shoulder. Sarpedon, seated on a sorry-looking nag, shook his head in admiration.

"Watch this, Telamon" he urged, "and you'll learn something!"

Alexander's siege machinery stopped firing. They had loosed about four or five volleys, creating chaos and consternation along the battlements for a stretch of ten yards between two towers just near the Triple Gate: about thirty of the leather-covered sheds were aimed directly at the centre of this. Telamon realized what Alexander intended. The commanders on the battlements also understood what was happening: their catapults, sling-shots and bowmen tried to bring down the men pushing these mantlets forward. The sheds, however, served as shields for the soldiers, while the closer they drew, the more difficult a target they proved for those on the walls. Some damage was inflicted. A pot of fire went straight between the pillars of one shed, smashing against the wooden floor and engulfing it in flames. The Macedonians pushing it immediately ran away; two were caught by the spurting flame and turned into cavorting human torches, each of whom was brought down by an archer high on the walls. One burning man, crazed with pain, received an arrow in his chest and, instead of retreating to the Macedonian line, in his hysteria ran to the great ditch and toppled over its edge. Another shed was hit by a boulder which smashed its top, but still it moved forward.

The three lines of sheds edged closer. The first reached the ditch. The men behind, ignoring the arrows and sling-shots, the hideous cries of their wounded, pushed the shed into the ditch. The men behind withdrew. Archers on the battlements picked their targets and left their victims writhing on the ground. The more fortunate reached the second shed in each line, clambered through and helped their comrades push this one into the ditch even faster.

"He's building a bridge," Telamon whispered.

The defenders on the wall loosed everything they had at these advancing sheds, but Alexander's tactics proved successful. One shed toppled in, another followed; even from where he stood Telamon could see the makeshift bridge emerging from the ditch, one shed on top of another providing a clumsy pathway across. It didn't matter if the sheds toppled on their sides or moved slightly askew – the ditch was being spanned, allowing the Macedonians to bring their rams up against the walls.

The besiegers, because the ditch was so close, found it difficult to direct their fire: to do so they had to expose themselves more. Seleucus ordered up row after row of Cretan archers and Rhodian slingers, who kept up a sustained and well-directed attack of the defenders. The walls of Halicarnassus became drenched in blood, men screaming as they fell from the battlements, bouncing against the wall, hitting the ditch, or falling onto the bridge their attackers were building.

The Cretan archers crept closer, loosing devastating volleys to clear the walls of defenders. Alexander's catapults, ballistas and stone-throwers remained silent, lest they do damage to their makeshift bridge or the men still pushing sheds up towards it. Alexander had chosen his place, packing each area of the ditch so close that the stout wooden frames of the sheds provided adequate support. The air grew dense with smoke billowing backwards and forwards, while the area in front of the ditch was littered with corpses; some sprawled in pools of blood, those caught by the fire reduced to smouldering piles of flesh, bone and blackened armour.

The Macedonian army now retreated back to its camp: a few brigades of phalanx men, regiments of Shield-Bearers, lightly armed troops and hand-picked squadrons of cavalry remained in line of battle. Eventually the last shed was in the ditch. Telamon felt someone tugging at his arm, a signal to withdraw, but the physician was fascinated by what was happening. Already the walls of Halicarnassus were blackened by fire, stained with burning oil: its battlements dented and cracked, the leather coverings placed over the walls scorched and rent. The bridge across the ditch was now complete.

Now the pent-roofed mantlets were wheeled forward, each protected by a screen of archers. Two were hit by boulders, one set on fire, engulfed in a whoosh of flame. These, too, reached the edge of the ditch and were now pushed onto the flat-topped sheds. Some of the sheds were higher than the rest: makeshift ramps were made while engineers clambered down into the ditch to strengthen the sheds by lashing them together with ropes. The bridge was uneven, clumsy, but it held. Alexander had reached the walls, though the cost had been cruel: the wounded and dying stretched like a gory carpet across the hard white rock.

Telamon heard the first thuds as the great iron-tipped rams inside the mantlets were swung backwards and forwards against the wall. He peered up at the battlements. Figures still thronged there, archers were leaning over, arrows, boulders, pots of burning oil and scalding water were loosed onto the mantlets. These, however, were too well protected, while the Cretan archers posed a deadly threat to any defenders who exposed themselves for long.

"It goes well, Telamon."

Alexander was beside him, his ceremonial armour removed, seated on a common cavalry mount. The king chewed the corner of his lip. Now and again he'd turn to whisper an order to a page, one of the many who accompanied him at such times, to take messages to this commander or that. Telamon was about to excuse himself when he heard a roar from a group of Macedonians opposite a small postern gate in one of the towers.

This was now flung open. Persian footmen raced forward, carrying long wooden boards, which they shoved across the pit to form their own makeshift bridge. Alexander urged his horse forward as rank after rank of Greek mercenaries poured through the postern gate across the wooden ramp, moving quickly towards the mantlets. A squadron of Persian cavalry, in their gorgeous tunics and cloaks, also thundered out, aiming straight for the line of Cretan archers. Alexander would have ridden to meet these, but Black Cleitus grabbed at his reins. The king's personal bodyguard rode up and surrounded the royal party. Already a regiment of phalanx men, sarissas lowered, were hurrying back. Squadrons of Macedonian cavalry galloped in a charging mass at the Persian horsemen already doing bloody execution among the Cretans. The lightly armed archers had little chance. Some were simply bowled over like skittles. Others tried to run, to be cut down by spear or lance, or trampled by their own cavalry, eager to drive back this surprise attack.

Telamon, next to the king, was circled by a ring of Shield-Bearers; between bobbing heads, men turning and twisting in the saddle, he glimpsed what was happening. The line of Cretan archers had broken, and the Persians were now heavily engaged, trying to block the Macedonians desperate to break through to help their companions on the makeshift bridge. The sheer force of the Macedonian phalanx pushed the Persians back. They withdrew, retreating to the bray of a trumpet: as they did so the mercenaries they were protecting broke off their attack against the mantlets, though Telamon could see they'd wreaked havoc. Blood rushed out of one where the engineers inside had been slaughtered to a man. Alexander's men could not pursue the enemy, because the battlements over the gate were thronged with well-armed defenders. The Persian cavalry retreated across the ditch, protected by the Greek mercenaries. These, too, fell back, faces to the enemy, shields locked. They recrossed the makeshift bridge, which was immediately pulled away, the postern gate slamming behind them.

The Macedonian army began to mass again. Scurriers rushed forward to bring back the wounded, only to be cut down by archers on the walls. The ground around the Triple Gate turned into a slaughter yard. Horses struggled to get up. The dead sprawled silently in widening pools of blood. The cries of the wounded for help and water echoed piteously. Alexander was beside himself. His personal safety forgotten, he rode up and down. An elite corps of Shield-Bearers hastily formed a horseshoe round the king and his entourage, shields locked on all four sides. Others, in a similar formation, moved forward to protect the Cretans, as well as to allow more of the wounded to be dragged back. A regiment of phalanx men advanced right up to the makeshift bridge across the ditch: its officers entered the long line of penthouses. The dead and wounded were dragged out and reinforcements left. Despite the counter-attack from the city, the ominous sound of the rams busy against the walls continued. Alexander ordered forward four of the siege towers to clear the battlements from the Triple Gate to the corner tower. The garrison, however, believing they'd done what damage they could, now withdrew.

Order was reimposed. Despite heavy casualties, the Macedonians had filled in the ditch, brought up rams and kept their siege towers in place. These were now busy pouring missiles over the walls as well as affording protection to the catapults, mangonels and dart-throwers which, once again, began their dreadful music. Alexander had besieged the city with a horseshoe ring, a series of camps which stretched around the walls linked by a makeshift ditch, mound and palisade. The king gave further orders: the first flurry of the siege was over, the harsh business of waiting had begun.

Alexander, grim-faced, left the battlefield, riding along the rocky peninsula past his retreating men and line of hospital carts. They crossed the tawdry defences built on the edge of the grasslands, and rode into the principal camp. Eumenes, head of Alexander's secretariat, had organized the erection of tents and pavilions intersected by two broad avenues running north to south and east to west. The royal enclosure, defended by a palisade guarded by royal Shield-Bearers, lay at the centre, with its altar to Zeus the All Powerful. Alexander had placed at each end of this altar trophies and armour seized from the Persians after his victory at the Granicus.

Alexander and his staff officers dismounted, grooms and pages running up to take their mounts. Hephaestion, who had been left in charge of the camp, hurried up anxious-faced. Alexander pushed him aside, lifted the tent flap and almost threw himself inside. Telamon would have slipped away – a smaller pavilion had been set up near the royal enclosure, which he shared with Hephaestion – but the king came back to the mouth of the tent.

"Don't slink off, Telamon! And you, Hephaestion, Cleitus!"

All three joined the king in the tent to witness one of his royal rages. Alexander threw off his cloak, armour and tunic and walked up and down, sweat gleaming on his bare torso: in one hand a sword, in the other a shield. Now and again he paused to bang one against the other, muttering under his breath.

"You were successful." Cleitus, sitting cross-legged on the ground next to Telamon, tried to placate this ominous raging. "We've put rams up against the walls. We'll have more tomorrow. We'll keep pounding away till we break in."

Alexander paused in his pacing. "What do you know about sieges, Cleitus? When we knock that wall down we'll find Memnon's built another! How many men did we lose today, two hundred, three?"

"And they lost men too," Hephaestion declared. "Alexander, the use of the sheds to bridge the ditch was brilliant."

"Telamon, you're not a soldier," Alexander jibed. "Tell these thickheads why I am in a rage!"

"They were expecting us, weren't they?"

"Yes, they were expecting us," Alexander mimicked childishly. He threw the shield and sword away and crouched down before

Cleitus. "Sometimes," he snarled, "you can be as thick as you are ugly!"

The bodyguard didn't flinch: he was used to the king's insults.

"The Persians executed a well-plotted manoeuvre. That wasn't something done" – Alexander snapped his fingers – "in the twinkling of an eye. They knew which section of the wall would be attacked."

"Well, that was obvious!"

Alexander slapped Cleitus on the face. The bodyguard's hand dropped to his dagger.

"There's no need for this," Telamon said quietly. "If Cleitus was taken by surprise, so was I and so were you. I agree, my lord," he added drily, "a sally from the city gates takes time to organize: the Greek mercenaries, the way the Persian cavalry went to shield them while they destroyed the mantlets and the battering rams. But they weren't successful, were they?"

"No, they weren't." Alexander forced a smile. "They moved too slowly while we struck back faster than they thought. Ah well!" He got up, walked deeper into the tent and brought back a tray of goblets and a jug of chilled white wine. He served them himself, and pressed his own cup into Cleitus's hand.

"You can slap me back if you wish."

Cleitus did so, a stinging blow which turned the king's right cheek a glowing red.

"A Macedonian never strikes a Macedonian!" Cleitus growled. "Your father never did, and neither should you."

Alexander put his cup down, leaned forward and kissed Cleitus on both cheeks. "The drill master ever," he murmured, sat back and picked up a goblet. "To our glorious dead!"

He offered the toast and poured the libation onto the ground. They sat for a while drinking silently, listening to the sounds of the camp and the faint cries from the battlefield, where the siege weapons still pounded against the walls.

"They'll hit nothing," Alexander mused. "If I know Memnon and Ephialtes, they've burnt everything within a mile radius of the wall and stood down their troops: that's not the real issue." He tapped the side of the cup. "We have two problems. The first is the

190

Pythian Manuscript. Are we battering the right place? Perhaps tomorrow I'll move further to the north, keep Memnon on his toes."

"The second problem?" Cleitus asked.

"The second problem, my lovely man," Alexander replied, "is that Memnon knew what we were going to do." He gestured with a finger and thumb. "They were within an inch of success. If we hadn't broken that cavalry, the mantlets, the battering rams and the men inside would have been destroyed. They would also have set fire to our bridge."

"They could still do that."

"They can try." Alexander shook his head. "But we'll be ready for them. The penthouses are well protected, while anyone who leans over that wall will be killed by our archers, if not shattered by a boulder or dart."

"They might try another sally," Hephaestion persisted.

"It's possible," Alexander agreed, 'but it would have to be very well planned. Memnon's a cunning commander. He doesn't like to meet me in the open. If the Persians had followed his advice, there would have been no victory at the Granicus. True, Ephialtes is rash and impetuous. However, don't forget he was one of the commanders of Thebes. They sallied out from that city only to be defeated, and when they fled, left a gate open, which we exploited. No." Alexander slurped from his cup. "Sallies like that would be a very rare event. What I want to know is how and by whom Memnon was informed. Our camp is sealed, and so is their city."

"By arrow?" Hephaestion asked. "It's the only way."

"Impossible," Telamon declared. "I know little about soldiering or military matters, but if anyone had stolen forward during the night or this morning to loose an arrow, he would have been seen. Moreover, how would the garrison know it was a friend?"

"Go on!" Alexander urged.

"I agree Memnon soon realized which part of the wall we were going to attack. However, someone must have given him very detailed knowledge about the sheds being built to span that ditch." He grinned at Alexander. "No one has ever done that before?"

Alexander raised his eyebrows at this mock flattery. "True," he agreed. "Memnon would probably expect us to bring forward ladders or planks of wood, which can be easily destroyed by well-aimed boulders or pots of fire. Moreover, such bridges cannot bear the weight of a battering ram. Memnon didn't know about the sheds, but anyone with sharp eyesight in our camp would have soon realized what we were doing. Memnon's sudden sally was organized to destroy them: a well-planned strategy rather than a sudden, sharp counter-attack. That explains the use of cavalry to shield his mercenaries . . ." Alexander picked his cup up and toasted Telamon. "I agree with you. The information must have been lengthy and detailed. If it was attached to an arrow" – he pulled a face – "such an arrow would never reach the wall, never mind soar over it. So how? We know they have spies in our camp."

"As we do in theirs?" Telamon asked.

Alexander dabbed at the sweat on his chest with a rag. "We have spies and a surprise," he replied enigmatically.

"By the way, where is Ptolemy?" Hephaestion asked. "I thought he would have been with us today. He always likes to be in the front wearing that stupid plumed helmet."

Alexander got to his feet, muttering under his breath. "Hephaestion," he ordered, "make sure the camp is well ringed and guarded. The password for tonight is Apollo. Arrange a system of bells to be passed from hand to hand. Tell any sentry that if I find him asleep, I'll catapult his head over the walls. Telamon, you are going back to the villa. Your red-haired friend is there. Take the scribes with you. The sooner they translate the Pythian Manuscript," he added bitterly, "the better for all of us!"

He walked deeper into the tent, a sign the interview was over.

"I'm going to finish my wine," Cleitus declared sourly. He sat like a huge bear in his black furred cloak, nursing the bruise on his left cheek.

Hephaestion followed Alexander deeper into the tent. Telamon went outside, still slightly dazed by the battle. He recalled his father's words: "You never really know what happens in a battle. All that's left is images, pictures in your mind." Telamon looked up at the sky and realized how quickly the hours had passed; the sun was setting, a cool breeze curbing the heat. His mind still teemed with memories of the fighting: the screeching of the catapults, fire falling from the sky, the sheds being taken forward, archers dropping under a hail of arrows. Men jerking, panicking; black smoke billowing across. The thundering hooves and flashes of colour of the Persian cavalry; the Macedonian phalanx surging forward . . .

"It could have been a disaster," he breathed.

Telamon recalled the wounded, and felt guilty. He left the royal enclosure and went into the camp. The soldiers had forgotten the horrors of the day, busy round their camp fires. Horns and trumpets brayed for those who still had duties tending the horse lines or digging latrines. The rest were eager to open their ration baskets containing the standard issue of barley, meat, bread and onions, sprinkled with salt and thyme and wrapped in fig leaves to stay fresh. The wine cart had been pushed through, each unit taking their portion in great two-handled jugs. Telamon hurried by these. On the far side of the camp a makeshift hospital line had been set up. Three of the royal physicians, Perdicles, Cleon and Nicias, were already busy, aprons, hands and wrists caked in blood.

The wounded had been split into three sections: those who could be healed quickly, those who would take some time, and the desperate cases for whom there was nothing to be done but a cup of drugged wine and the mercy cut across the throat. The latter had already been dealt with: on a hillock overlooking the camp a makeshift funeral pyre had been erected, the corpses tossed on.

"The priests will say the prayer," Cleon shouted from where he crouched by a stretcher, "and once it's dark it will be lit."

"How many dead?" Telamon asked, taking a leather apron from an orderly.

"About four hundred in all."

Telamon stared at a fresh line of corpses laid out on the grass, each on its bed-roll. He could understand his father's revulsion: young men of different nations – Greeks, Cretans, Rhodians, a few Syrian mercenaries and Macedonians, naked except for their loin-cloths – all lay in the peace of death, hands by their sides, bodies witness to the terrible wounds they had received. A number of corpses were headless, others lacked arms or legs. Some were nothing more than blackened skeletons, charred strips of flesh hanging off like withered leaves on a tree. The stench was offensive. An orderly pushed a pomander into his hand, and Telamon sniffed the sweet smell of cassia. Nicias was shouting for help, so he went over to assist. Afterwards he moved down the line of casualties: bandaging wounds, setting splints, reassuring the wild-eyed, anxious-faced soldiers that all would be well. Darkness fell. Cresset torches were lit. Telamon was busy bandaging, smearing honey and salt on a leg wound, shouting at the orderly to keep the man still, when he heard the clamour, a great roar from the camp. He sprang to his feet. A page came scurrying across the grass, leaping like a deer.

"There's been another attack!" he shouted. "There's been another attack!"

Telamon told the orderly to tie the bandages and hurried back into the camp. All was confusion and chaos. Men were searching for shields and swords. Officers were screaming at units to reform. War horns brayed the alarm. Cavalry horses were being led out. Telamon entered the royal enclosure. The king, surrounded by his staff officers, was busy rearming.

"Why are you here?" Alexander glared at Telamon. "I thought you'd be with the rest in the secretariat tent. Oh well, come on! Come on!"

Telamon didn't know why he went. Cassandra would ask him the same question and the answer was simple: he was curious. Someone brought him a horse and he joined the king in his wild gallop through the camp, back along the trackways up the rocky peninsula now bathed in moonlight. Even as they arrived they could hear the war horn braying the call for retreat. The king and his party reined in. Officers carrying torches ran up. Beyond them, stretcher-bearers were bringing back more wounded.

"What happened?" Alexander demanded.

"Two men from Perdicles's regiment," an officer explained, "drank their wine too fast. They left the camp and challenged Memnon to personal combat, asking him to repeat the same trick he'd done today."

"And what happened?"

194

The officer took off his helmet. "The guards above the Triple Gate must have been as drunk as they were. A sally was made, fighting began and our picket guards joined in. It's all over, my lord, the enemy has retreated."

"And the two soldiers?" Alexander demanded.

"They are dead!"

"Good!" the king breathed. "If they weren't, I'd have crucified them for everyone to see. Officers, check your units. Tell the camp marshals to order the men to stand down. Give the order, no more fun and games. Oh, by the way," Alexander reined in. "The guards who let these two drunks through the perimeter?"

"Yes, my lord?"

"They can dig latrines for the rest of the night."

Alexander and his party now relaxed, and stared for a while at the walls of Halicarnassus. Torches and braziers blazed along the battlements. Alexander rode closer. The battering rams were still busy; they were now connected to the Macedonian front line by a long column of flat-topped sheds through which men would move up towards the walls. These were all covered with water-soaked leather awnings, protection against flaming missiles. On either side of the line of mantlets, sheltered ranks of Cretan archers watched the walls.

"Good!" Alexander murmured. "We are creeping forward slowly but surely. I want those battlements kept cleared and the rams to continue their music."

They rode back to the camp. As they dismounted Alexander grasped Telamon by the arm. "I want to show you something."

He led Telamon and Hephaestion through the royal enclosure to Aristander's pavilion. The lovely boys were sprawled outside. They'd ignored the recent tumult, busy feasting their faces. As the king approached, they scrambled to their knees, heads bowed, though their leader still gnawed on a chicken leg. Aristander's pavilion was small but elegant, smelling sweetly of musk and frankincense. The Master of the King's Secrets, as he always did to relax, wore a long blond wig and was dressed in the dark-blue gown of a woman. He was perched on his chair, carefully examining his painted fingernails.

195

"My lord," he sniffed as he got up, "how long must it stay here?"

Alexander pushed by him and crouched before a blanket roll. He pulled back the flaps, and Telamon looked down at the corpse: a young man, naked as he was born, with a gaunt, sunburnt face and shaven head. He noticed the blue tattoo on the left arm, the leaping bull of Minos. Telamon crouched and gingerly turned the corpse over: the back of the man's head was a bloody mess.

"He's a Cretan." Telamon lifted the dead man's fingers and felt the callouses, the mark of a master bowman. "But there were scores killed today, what's so special about this one?"

"Oh, can't it be taken away?" Aristander snapped. "Must it be kept here?"

"That man wasn't killed in the fighting," Hephaestion explained. "His corpse was found out on the grasslands."

The corpse felt cold, the belly distended; already the muscles were thickening and hardening. "Yes, you're right," Telamon agreed. "He's been dead for at least a day, a savage blow to the back of his head."

"A hunter found it," Aristander explained. "A Thracian looking for fresh meat for the pot. He noticed the buzzards hovering above a small bush and found the corpse about a mile from the camp."

"You do realize," Alexander whispered, "what this means?"

Telamon covered the corpse up and got to his feet. "Someone killed a Cretan archer and took his bow and arrows."

"That's right," Alexander agreed. "Aristander, tell your men to take the corpse back to the Captain of Archers. It's the work of our spy," Alexander continued. "What you've got to do, Telamon" – he poked him in the chest – "is discover his name! Go back to that villa and do it!"

Chapter 10

"Alexander himself, at the head of all, took command and made a stand against the enemy who had supposed that, because of their mass, they would be invincible."

Diodorus Siculus: *Library of History*, Book XVII, Chapter 26

"**S**ome Egyptians believe there is only one god and the sun is his physical manifestation. All I can say is" – Telamon chewed slowly on the grape and squinted up at the over hanging, interlaced branches of the sycamore – "nothing on earth's more pleasant than sitting under the sun in a beautiful garden with food and wine."

"We have no food and wine," Cassanda intervened.

"We soon will."

"With a beautiful woman," Cassandra added.

"Why, where is she?" Telamon flinched as Cassandra dug her elbow into his ribs.

"You were saying, master?"

"It's just so pleasant to sit here," Telamon mused. "I am glad to be away from the battlefield."

"Where the Great Killer is busy wading through corpses. He's a blood-supper," Cassandra continued fiercely. "He doesn't give a fig for other men's lives. It's all for the glory of the great Alexander."

"I am glad he's not here," Telamon replied.

"So am I," Cassandra retorted. "Why did he send you all back?"

"He wants the Pythian Manuscript translated urgently. The camp is getting crowded and rather fetid. Solan objected, so Alexander told Sarpedon to take a troop of lancers and archers and bring us all back here." Telamon shrugged. "Gentius and Demerata weren't pleased to see us," he continued. "And since the death of the Mageros and his daughter, the servants are surly-eyed."

Telamon leaned back against the trunk of the tree and stared across at the Pool of Purity glinting in the sunlight. The villa was very quiet, guarded by a small military escort camped beyond its walls. Solan and the rest, pleased to be back, were busy on the Pythian Manuscript, while Sarpedon had returned to his gardening. Telamon closed his eyes and smiled. Their stay in the camp had definitely affected the scribes: Bessus now shared Sarpedon's eagerness for the fragrance of the gardens, and even Solan worked outside more often. And where they went Cherolos always followed. They had been back two days. Telamon felt as if he were in a different world. Gentius had jokingly remarked that the gardens were safe now the snakes had been removed.

"You should have questioned Cherolos more closely."

Telamon opened his eyes. "My dear Cassandra, what more could I question him about? All he did wrong was filch scraps of parchment from Pamenes's chamber and decide to go through his saddlebags."

"Did you find them?"

"Yes, they were hidden in some reeds. Nothing but clothing, rolls of parchment, extra styli and inkpots, not enough to hang a man."

"Cherolos could have thrown him from that window."

"But if he did," Telamon argued, "he wouldn't have confessed so quickly."

"He is proficient in the handling of snakes."

"Anyone could do that with a sack and a rod."

Telamon plucked at the grass and rubbed it between his fingers. The confrontation with Cherolos seemed an age away, yet it was only seven days. After that Alexander had intervened, frenetically busy as the siege engines were brought up from the cove of Hera. Everything had come and gone in a hurry, thoughts and words speeding like birds across an open field. Telamon had little time to reflect. He had hastily packed with the rest, telling Cassandra to look after herself. The hurried march, the hurly-burly of camp life, the opening attack on Halicarnassus, tending the wounded and viewing that strange corpse.

"It's strange Alexander didn't send his necromancer back."

"Ah, you mean our good friend Aristander?" Telamon joked. "I am beginning to wonder why the king has kept his spider well away from our assembled notables. Apart from tending his ear, which is now better, I have hardly had time to reflect on Aristander's role, if any, in all this."

"Well, you're back now." Cassandra knelt beside him. She'd fashioned herself a wreath of wild flowers, which she took off and placed on Telamon's head. "There, you look like the god Pan. I shall bring you a flute, and perhaps I will dance."

"Can you dance?" Telamon asked.

"Like a camel with the itch."

Telamon sighed, and glanced at the pieces of parchment stacked on his right, a small rock placed on top to prevent them being blown away by the afternoon breeze.

"And our great king is sleeping well?"

"Yes, he is. I offered to recreate the circumstances of his father's death. He shook his head and said he was too busy. I am still intrigued" – Telamon pushed the flower wreath more firmly on his head – "why Halicarnassus had evoked such memories. I'm puzzled by the way Alexander keeps Aristander away from me, and about why Ptolemy, who is never far from the king, seems to have a life of his own."

"So our great king is plotting something?"

"He's always plotting." Telamon paused. "That's the great mistake people make with Alexander. At a banquet he can act the drunk and engage in bawdy talk. He has the profile of an athelete, the noble, well-formed face of an Athenian scholar. Some people even say his head could be taken for that of Apollo in human form." Telamon ignored Cassandra's chuckle. "But his mind is like a pit of writhing snakes. He's inherited all the subtlety and cunning of his parents. Alexander loves to mislead his enemies. I once heard of a fox who used to trail his leg so his quarry would think he was more concerned with his injury than he was with them. I don't know whether the story is apocryphal or not, but the fox always killed. In the fields of Mars outside Rome . . ."

"You've been there?"

"Oh yes," Telamon smiled. "The Romans organized combats between their heroes, with wooden swords and shields. I once saw a breathtaking display, a swordsman pretending to be injured luring his enemy into a trap."

"And Alexander's doing that now?"

"I think so. Before I left the camp, Hephaestion told me a strange story. I asked him the same question you did me, was the king sleeping well? Alexander is always in bed by the third watch. Hephaestion replied the king wasn't sleeping well at all. In fact, he was often wide awake and wouldn't go to bed until the third watch had finished. He would sit on a hillock where we tended the wounded. You can study the sky above Halicarnassus: Hephaestion thinks Alexander's waiting for something."

"A signal?"

"Something like that. A fire arrow, it must be."

"So there are traitors in Halicarnassus?"

"Cassandra, are there fleas on a dog?"

"But Halicarnassus is loyal to Darius," Cassandra objected. "Everyone knows that. There may be a few rabble-rousers, trouble-makers . . ."

"I know, I thought the same." Telamon paused at the clash of cymbals from the house. "Gentius and Demerata," he sighed, "are rehearsing again. Apparently the king may return for another display of our great actor's skill. Cassandra, it's your turn to get the food and wine."

"Can't a servant bring it?"

"I don't trust them. Check our chamber very carefully, I placed something just within the door, then fetch the food and wine. We'll eat out here and be asleep before the sun sets."

Cassandra got to her feet. "What about the Pythian Manuscript?"

Telamon grinned.

"You know something, don't you?" She crouched back down.

"I'm beginning to." Telamon raised a finger to his lips. "But I am going to do it slowly and thoroughly. Now, what about that wine?"

Cassandra flounced away. Telamon picked up the writing tray and laid it across his lap. He opened an inkpot, dipped the sharpened stylus in and began to write. He formed his letters carefully.

"Pamenes! Why did he die clutching bird seed?" Telamon paused. "Should he have still been clutching the seed?" he murmured. "Wouldn't that have fallen from his hand?"

Telamon recalled some of the corpses from the battlefields where swords and daggers had to be prised from dead, nerveless fingers. Why was one sandal loosened? Why did Cherolos go back? Telamon stared up at the branches. Undoubtedly the priest was ambitious. He would love to be the one who translated the Pythian Manuscript and won the affection of his queen. Was Cherolos the one who had removed the stylus and some other manuscripts from Pamenes's room? Did Cherolos know that Pamenes was really a Persian magus, a spy? Telamon paused and stared down at what he had written. And how was it Pamenes had made so much progress, with his constant reference to five and the letter epsilon? What was the significance of the quotations from Sophocles where the letter E was ringed? Pamenes had taken an extract from the *Iliad* for the same purpose. Why was the number ten important? Had Pamenes been murdered simply to steal all this knowledge? But no one had any guarantee that Solan, Bessus, even Cherolos, hadn't made their own successful but secret progress with that strange manuscript. And what had Aristander said about it? "Not even the great philosophers could understand it?" Telamon shook his head.

"That's strange," he murmured. "That's very strange!"

So, was Pamenes's death the work of a traitor? Or a fellow traitor, eager to silence him and steal what he had learnt? Telamon chewed the corner of his lip: that was a conundrum he still could not understand. Was Gentius the killer, the Persian spy? Did he believe Pamenes, a charming young man, had seduced his wife? Was Gentius settling a personal grievance as well as advancing the work of his masters in Halicarnassus? Telamon sighed and put the writing tray away. He folded his arms and closed his eyes. If Pamenes's death was a mystery, then the murders of the Mageros and his daughter were equally perplexing. True, the girl's killer may have been hunting Sarpedon, but why murder her father?

"Our chamber's safe." Cassandra stood over him. She placed the tray on the grass and rearranged the napkins.

"The bread's freshly baked," she explained, "and the cheese is safe." She smiled. "I cut it myself. I also poured the wine. You are right. The servants are surly, they don't like it here."

"You can't blame them," Telamon replied. "I was just wondering about the murders. Why should the Mageros and his daughter be killed? Oh, I know Sarpedon was the intended victim, not her." He scratched his face and wafted away a fly hovering over the bread. "But why the cook? What was so important about him? Had he seen something as well?"

They sat and ate in silence.

"Look." Telamon grasped Cassandra's arm. "I would like an audience with our colleagues. Ask Solan, Bessus, Cherolos and Sarpedon to come here."

"What for? They'll ask the reason. They'll claim they are busy."

"Just say Pamenes's death."

Cassandra left. A short while later she came back across the grass. Her companions, apart from Sarpedon, were far from happy. Solan strode, swinging his hands. Cherolos looked rather frightened, while Bessus was deep in thought. They sat in the shade of a tree. Sarpedon had now taken off his gloves and removed the bandages. Telamon quickly inspected his hands.

"Yes, the cuts have healed nicely: the skin's pink and fresh."

"Is that why we are here?" Solan jibed. "To discuss Sarpedon's hands?"

"No, Pamenes. How long had he worked at the court of Queen Ada?"

"About two years."

"And was he good at his post?"

"He was a skilful enough scribe." Bessus spoke up. "He was fluent in Greek, the Koine, Persian, Arabic and Egyptian."

202

"When did Queen Ada's interest in the Pythian Manuscript quicken?" Telamon asked.

"She was always interested in it," Solan replied. "As long as I served her. Some years ago, when Alexander first intended to cross the Hellespont, the manuscript was taken out and examined, but her scribes could never understand it so it was put back and forgotten. After the battle of the Granicus, Queen Ada provided us with our own special chamber in her palace. We had one task and one task only: to translate the Pythian Manuscript. Pamenes," Solan spat the name out, "was the person in charge, so he did most of the work."

"What do you mean?" Telamon asked.

"He read Herodotus's history, and other accounts of how different generals send secret messages but," Solan smiled falsely, "nothing really worked. He seemed as confused as we are."

"But you are the principal scribe of Queen Ada?"

"Oh yes." Solan's voice turned waspish.

"Now," Telamon brushed away crumbs from his tunic. "You are all intelligent men."

"Oh thank you."

Telamon ignored Solan's sarcasm. "We know that Pamenes was a spy, a Persian magus. No wonder he was so skilled. Did it ever occur to you that Pamenes knew more about the Pythian Manuscript than he ever told you?"

The smile faded from Solan's face. "You've said that before," he accused.

"Well, I say it again. What is more, how do we know that Pamenes didn't deliberately mislead you, obfuscate the issue, take you down paths which led nowhere?"

"You mean . . . ?" Bessus exclaimed.

"I mean that Pamenes was two people. In public the well-beloved and much trusted scribe of Queen Ada, confused as you are about this enigmatic manuscript. In private a Persian spy working hard to translate the cipher for his masters in Persepolis."

"That's possible," Sarpedon confessed.

"Did any of you become his friend?"

"He was likeable enough," Bessus replied. "He ate and drank with us, but he kept to himself."

"And we didn't think that strange," Sarpedon added. "Everyone in the palace knew Queen Ada would reward the person who translated that manuscript."

"How many copies were made of it?"

Solan picked at ink stains on his fingers. "Pythias wrote the manuscript describing how he built the walls of Halicarnassus. He gave it to Queen Ada. Of course, copies were made."

"Could one have been sent to Macedon?"

"It's possible. Only the gods know how many copies exist." Solan paused. "No one was really interested in it. Whoever dreamed that Halicarnassus would be besieged by a Macedonian army?"

"So people were more interested in the treasure?" Cassandra spoke up. Solan gave her a withering glance.

"I still think," Bessus said softly, "Pamenes's death may have been an accident."

"I don't," Telamon replied, getting to his feet.

"Can we go now?" Solan asked. "Alexander will be sending messengers to see what progress we are making."

"And are you?"

His question was received with blank stares. Telamon lifted his hand. "Then you had better be busy about your task."

He walked across the garden, past the entrance to the great cobbled yard, and down the track. The late afternoon was warm; birds swooped low, lizards basked on the rocky walls. Telamon paused as a snake slithered out across the grassy verge and disappeared into the thick undergrowth. He walked on. He stopped to examine some wild flowers, plucked a bunch and smelt their sweetness, and looked quickly back. No one was following him. He reached the entrance to the villa where the two Persians had been crucified. The ground was still stained from the funeral pyre, though in accordance with custom the ashes of those consumed had been scattered to the four winds. The camp of lancers and Cretan archers lay in an adjoining field: typical soldiers, they couldn't believe their luck at being withdrawn from the fighting to laze, eat and drink among lush green grass. They had set up their tents or ramshackle bothies using branches and bushes. The air smelt of horse dung, wood smoke, the bitter-sweet taste of dried meat being grilled. Soldiers lounged about dressed simply in tunics, eating, drinking or playing dice. An officer came hurrying up, apologizing for the chaos.

"I'm not here to inspect you," Telamon informed them. "But I would like to talk to one of your archers, the best you have."

The officer, trying to hide the wineskin he had been drinking from, was only too pleased to hurry away. He returned with a young man dressed in a short leather vest and linen kilt, a quiver of arrows hung from a strap over his shoulder: he carried the powerful, composite bow his people were famous for.

"Do you speak Greek?"

"Just as well as you." The Cretan's thin face broke into a smile. Telamon noticed how long and strong his arms were. His wrists were protected by leather guards, and small canvas pouches adorned the fingers of his left hand. The Cretan followed his gaze.

"It's the best way," he said. "Otherwise your callouses get worse. You want to ask me something?"

"Shall I leave you?" the officer asked.

Telamon nodded, opened his purse and took out a silver coin. "I don't assassinate people," the Cretan protested sullenly, though his close-set eyes fastened on the silver piece like a hawk would on some plump prey.

"I don't want you to assassinate anybody," Telamon replied. "I am the king's physician."

"I know who you are." The Cretan's gaze shifted to Telamon. "You have that red-haired wench, the one my friends and I drool over. You don't like men, so why are you offering a Cretan archer a silver piece?"

"I want to examine your bow."

"It's sacred."

"That's why I am offering you a silver piece."

The Cretan snatched the silver piece and handed his bow over. Telamon examined it curiously. It was composite, made of different strips of wood, the grip of hard, boiled twine.

"It's fashioned out of cornel and ash," the Cretan explained. "As are the arrows. They are tipped, or barbed, according to what you want. The bowstring is animal gut, though you can use twine. Vulture feathers are best for the arrow flight."

He handed one of these over. Telamon notched the arrow and turned the bow up as if firing into the air. He was clumsy, and recalled Cleitus bawling at him on the drill ground at Mieza.

"You're not very good, are you?" The Cretan took the bow and arrow from Telamon. "It's much harder than you think."

He notched the arrow and, using the two forefingers of his left hand, pulled the bow taut, the arrow's gleaming steel point aimed directly at Telamon's chest.

"At this range," the Cretan murmured, "I could put an arrow straight through you."

"And if I ran?"

"You'd have to run like the wind! On a good day with a clear view and no breeze," the archer continued, "I could bring you down at up to two hundred yards." He lowered the bow. "You've seen these used against the defenders of Halicarnassus?"

"That's what I must talk to you about. Meet me outside the camp." Telamon gestured over his shoulder. "At the entrance to the villa. I also want you to ask that officer for some strips of parchment."

The Cretan looked bemused.

"You've taken my silver piece," Telamon explained. "I want to send a message."

Telamon walked out of the camp and sat at the entrance to the villa, staring up the dusty track. He recalled the archers at the siege, lithe, quick-moving figures, bow strings pulled back, loosing one arrow after another, filling the air with a black heavy rain. He heard a sound. The Cretan had put on a pair of sandals, and he was carrying his bow and strips of greasy parchment.

"You were at the siege?" Telamon asked, getting to his feet.

"Oh yes, I was lucky to escape."

"It was possible for you to put an arrow over the walls?"

"Of course: there was very little wind, and the closer we crept, the easier it became. If you mass archers together," the Cretan declared, "and aim at any particular place, you are certain to hit something or someone."

206

Telamon recalled Alexander staring up at the night sky.

"And a fire arrow?"

"Easily done," the archer replied. He took an arrow from the quiver. "You daub the head here, near the point, with tar, notch it and dip it into a flame, then you loose it as quickly as possible."

"Won't the flame burn the wood?"

"Not immediately, it licks the tar and stays there. You'd probably choose a longer arrow."

"Show me."

The Cretan notched the arrow and bent the tip as if taking a flame. "The tip's now glowing." He brought the bow up smartly, pulled the cord taut, back towards his ear, and released the shaft. Telamon caught a blur as it disappeared up into the blue sky.

"On a dark night," the Cretan explained, "you would see it clearly enough. As the arrow begins to fall, the flame spreads."

"And a message?" Telamon asked.

The Cretan took another arrow from his quiver.

"Where would you put the strip of parchment?"

"Around either end of the arrow, but it would have to be small. I'll show you." He crouched down, picked up a strip of parchment and wound it round the arrow, plucked a piece of twine from his pouch and tied the strip tight. "Now, watch what happens."

Again he notched the arrow and shot the shaft into the direction of the trees. This time it dipped.

"You see what I mean?" The Cretan pulled another arrow from his quiver. "The shaft is finely balanced." He tapped the black vulture feathers. "There's this and the point. If you put a weight at either end, its flight will be hampered."

He must have seen the disappointment in Telamon's face. "This is about the archer who was murdered, isn't it?" He asked. "The one who had his skull crushed and his weapons taken? It's all over the camp."

"You knew the victim?"

"He came from the same village as I did, near the ancient palace of Knossos."

"Why should he be out on the grasslands by himself?"

"For the same reason I will be when you're finished. Don't you ever get tired of salted meat, dried fruit and stinking fish? He was hunting."

"Someone must have ambushed him."

"He was a notable drinker," the Cretan replied. "Maybe he fell asleep? It's not unheard-of, after a long march and a belly full of wine."

"I'll tell you." Telamon took another coin out of his purse and handed it over. "A traitor or a spy was hunting for a bow, the type only used by skilled archers like yourself. He couldn't very well take one from the quartermaster's store or ask your officers to borrow one: they are jealously guarded. He took those weapons and, in the fighting for a brief while, loosed a shaft carrying a message which went over the walls of Halicarnassus."

The Cretan's thin face broke into a grin. "I can understand your logic, sir. Yes, to loose a shaft over the walls of Halicarnassus, you would need one of these. But an arrow carrying a message?" He held up his fingers. "The message would have to be very small, the piece of parchment light, otherwise the arrow would never reach its destination."

Telamon sighed. "Ah well." He extended his hand. "I thought I would try."

The Cretan clasped his hand and strode away. Telamon leaned against the gatepost. Not so clever, he reflected. A spy tells the Persians that Alexander is at the Villa of Cybele, vulnerable to attack. How could he do that? Shoot an arrow from the villa, leave the message beneath a stone? He did the same when the Persians attacked, giving them advance warning that the king would probably visit Halicarnassus, ride up to see the fortifications. So how did he do that, as well as get a message over the walls of Halicarnassus about the sheds Alexander was building?

Telamon, lost in thought, walked back up the track. He passed the courtyard and stared round. The servants were washing clothes round the well. Gentius was shouting, "Demerata! Demerata! Where have you gone?"

Telamon walked on. The garden was empty: the cups and platters he and Cassandra had used still lay in the shade of the tree. He walked across, picked up the wine jug, sniffed and emptied it

208

out on the grass. He looked around; no one. The heat was oppressive, and the grass was becoming badly scorched: Telamon recalled Alexander's officers praying there would be rain. He considered returning to his chamber, but he was still fascinated by the problem of why the spy had killed that Cretan archer. He wandered across into the cool shade of the orchard. Telamon paused at a stain on the grass, illuminated by a sliver of sunlight through the overhanging branches.

"And that's another mystery," he whispered, staring down. "Why was that poor cat killed?"

Telamon walked on. He stopped to examine fungus on the bark of a tree. Stretching up, he picked at this carefully. Sometimes he regretted having to leave Egypt in such a hurry: he had made so many friends there, physicians and healers in the Houses of Life. Many claimed fungus such as this had magical healing properties; that if mixed with sour milk and ground into a powder, it could often cure deep-set infections of the lung and throat.

"I wonder if I should try?"

Telamon stretched up to take a piece, but his foot slipped, and his bare knee scraped the hard bark. He winced and crouched down. As he did so, the arrow struck deep into the tree above him.

Telamon whirled round, all tiredness forgotten, his throat dry. All he could see were trees, overhanging branches, patches of dappled sunlight. He stared at the arrow, long and slender like the one the Cretan had shown him. Telamon heard a sound. He moved behind the tree even as another arrow zipped through the air.

"Who's there?" he called out.

The orchard had fallen silent, as if every living thing realized death had arrived. Telamon quietly cursed. If he ran, the mysterious bowman would follow. If he stayed here, eventually the assassin would draw close and finish the task. Telamon picked up a fallen bough. He felt slightly ridiculous, with his only weapon a thick dry stick. He looked to his left and right: no sound or movement. Nothing but trees and undergrowth.

Telamon moved back. Beyond the orchard lay a meadow where Alexander had set up his tents. If the bowman drove him back there

. . . He heard the faint sound of shouting; Gentius was still calling for his wife. Telamon glimpsed a shadow, nothing but a black shape, move to his right. Using the trees as protection, he made his way back towards the garden.

His pursuer realized this. An arrow sliced through the air, a warning that the way back was watched and guarded. Telamon tried to control his breathing, the trembling in one of his legs. He was about to make another dash when a war horn brayed loud and clear. The alarm was being raised.

"Cassandra!" Telamon shouted. "Cassandra! Sarpedon! Cassandra! Cassandra!"

Again the war horn brayed. Telamon dashed forward. This time no arrow followed him. The trees began to thin, the edge of the garden was clear. He kept up his shouting.

"Cassandra! Sarpedon! Cassandra!"

"Telamon, what is it?"

He burst from the trees and collapsed to his knees. Cassandra hurried over.

"Telamon, what is it?"

He staggered to his feet and pointed at the trees. "An assassin, there!"

"Who?" Cassandra's lower lip jutted out.

"No, don't go back!" Telamon warned. "Whoever it was is armed with bow and arrow. I wish to Apollo I knew who!" The war horn brayed. "What is the matter?"

"I don't know," Cassandra replied. "I came looking for you, something's wrong in the villa."

Telamon forgot his own troubles and they made their way across the garden into the villa. Sarpedon was there, and he certainly looked as if he hadn't been out. Was that assassin still lurking in the orchard? Telamon wondered. The Spartan stood at the foot of the stairs staring up. A soldier clattered down.

"Where are the rest?" Telamon demanded.

The soldier looked as if he had been sleeping. "I don't know, sir."

Telamon grasped him by the shoulder and pointed to the horn slung on the baldric round his neck. "You raised the alarm. What's the matter?"

An eerie wailing echoed from the gallery above. Bessus, Solan and Cherolos came through the doorway, pieces of parchment clutched in their ink-stained fingers. "We were out in the gardens."

"Together or alone?" Telamon snapped.

"We always work by ourselves," Solan declared.

Telamon had already started to climb the stairs. The wailing was heart-rending. He reached the gallery and hurried along. The door to Pamenes's chamber was flung open. Gentius knelt on the floor beside the bed on which Demerata sprawled, the cord which had strangled her still tight about her neck. The actor was lost in his own grief and pain, head in hands, rocking backwards and forwards. Telamon studied the corpse: Demerata's face had almost turned a blueish-black, eyes popping out, tongue clenched between her teeth. He touched the corpse. It was already growing cold.

"What happened?" Telamon looked over his shoulder at the soldier.

"I'm the house guard, sir. I was standing at the top of the stairs."

Telamon studied him closely: he was dressed in a shabby leather tunic, marching boots on his feet, tousled hair framing a dark face. "Which regiment are you from?" Telamon asked.

"The fourth line of Agrianian foot," the fellow replied. "Our nickname is the Bulls. The rest of my unit is up the road in the fields."

Gentius was still moaning, unaware of others crowding into the chamber.

"Tell me what happened," Telamon demanded.

"He came upstairs looking for his wife," the soldier replied.

"How long had you been on duty there?"

"Not long. I wander round, sometimes upstairs, sometimes downstairs. He seemed all anxious so I came along with him. We first searched their room, but there was no one there." The soldier shrugged. "I went downstairs, he told me to keep an eye out. I did, then returned. He still hadn't found his wife. We searched other chambers, opened the door to this, and she was lying there, throat all twisted, so I raised the alarm."

211

"And the rest of you?" Telamon gazed bleakly round.

"Out in the garden," Sarpedon replied. He pointed to the soil on his tunic. "I came back some time ago, the others stayed out."

"Gentius, what happened?" Telamon gently peeled the man's hands away from his cheeks. Gentius gazed up, stricken-faced.

"I was rehearsing Creon's lines. She was to be Antigone. I went into the kitchen for some bread and honey." He tapped his lips. "My throat. When I came back . . ."

"Where were you?"

"In the andron. When I returned she was gone. I then began searching: as this soldier said, I couldn't find her anywhere. I came upstairs. At first I daren't open the other chambers, but the door to Pamenes's was open. I looked through, she wasn't here. I went downstairs and came back up. We searched the house again, we found her and he raised the alarm."

"And you came up here and looked in Pamenes's chamber twice?"

"Yes. The first time," the soldier replied, "it was empty, then we searched again, came back and discovered her corpse."

Gentius stared at his wife's corpse and burst into tears. Telamon gently pulled a sheet over the dead woman's face. "I think it's best if we leave," he declared. "Gentius, Cassandra will look after your wife's corpse. In this heat, the funeral pyre must be lit this evening, the offerings made then . . ."

Chapter 11

"Ephialtes advised them not to wait till the city was taken and they found themselves captive."

Diodorus Siculus: *Library of History*, Book XVII, Chapter 26

"You cannot alter this. The gods themselves
Cannot undo it. It follows, of necessity,
From what you have done. Even now the avenging Furies,
The hunters of hell which follow and destroy,
Are lying in wait for me and will have their prey!"

G entius, standing beside the funeral pyre, intoned the sombre speech of Tereisias the blind seer of Thebes in Sophocles's play *Antigone*. Telamon, Cassandra and the others stood behind him. The funeral pyre, built by the soldiers, rose over six feet high. Demerata's corpse lay on top: a coin between her lips to pay Charon the deathly boatman of the Underworld, as well as scraps of bread, clutched in each dead hand, to feed the dreaded watchdog of Hades. Gentius lifted the wine cup, drank, and scattered the dregs on the funeral pyre. Darkness was falling, that strange twilight between day and night when the sky turns an eerie blue. Telamon felt as if he were watching a play: Gentius sprinkled some oil, picked up a firebrand and threw it on top of the pyre. The flames caught the kindling, at first slowly but, wafted by the breeze, the flame reached the oil and the entire pyre became a tongue of fire roaring up to the darkening sky. Gentius, followed by the rest, sprinkled handfuls of incense. They stood for a while, as the rite demanded, until the flames began to subside, then made their way back through the gateway up to the villa.

Telamon caught Cassandra's arm. "Stay back! Wait a while!"

The rest walked on, grouped round Gentius, murmuring their condolences. Telamon walked over to the Cretan archer whom he had talked to earlier in the day, now on sentry duty guarding the funeral pyre until the flames died. In the light of the fire the Cretan's face looked leaner, hungry, more predatory: his glittering, greedy eyes studied Cassandra's ample bosom: stretching out his hand, he touched her red hair peeping out from beneath the mantle.

"That's enough!" she snapped.

The Cretan grinned and rested both hands on the long lance he carried. Behind him, his companions murmured and moved closer to get a better view of Cassandra.

"I have a further question for you," Telamon said.

"You paid well. Ask it."

Sparks from the fire drifted in as the kindling burst and snapped. They walked further away.

"What happens," Telamon asked, "if I take your bow and arrow and tie a strip of parchment to it like a streamer? Would that affect its weight or flight?"

The Cretan made a face and shrugged. "A piece of parchment?"

"Yes, about as long as the arrow or even longer. As I said, like a streamer or ribbon?"

The Cretan turned and jabbered in his own patois to his companions. A heated conversation took place. The Cretan lifted his hand for silence and glanced back to Telamon.

"It might affect the flight a little, but not much. We have archers here who have taken part in spectacles when coloured ribbons are tied to arrows and loosed into the air. They say it would make little difference."

"Thank you very much." Telamon opened his purse and slipped a silver coin into the man's hand. "Drink a libation to the dead woman's health. Oh," Telamon turned back. "This afternoon, after I left you, did any of your archers leave the camp and enter the villa?"

The Cretan shook his head. "Of course not. We much prefer to be out here in the open. Our orders are quite strict. There's a guard

214

on the house. The only reason we would go there," he grinned wolfishly and pointed at Cassandra, "would be to see her."

Telamon and Cassandra walked away, the archers chuckling behind them. One gave a loud wolf whistle.

"I don't think you should go for a walk," Telamon murmured. "Or leave the villa."

"I've met Cretans before!" Cassandra snapped. "In Thebes, along with the Thracians and Thessalians and the other dregs of humankind."

Telamon stopped and stared at the lights from the villa winking through the trees.

"What's the matter, great thinker?"

"Much and more," he replied evasively. "Danger sharpens the wits and stirs the memory, Cassandra. I am puzzled about a lot of things. Do you remember that strip of parchment we found in Pamenes's chamber with the strange symbols, as well as the round pole, about a yard long?"

"Yes, we thought it was rubbish."

"I don't think it was. After the attack in the orchard this afternoon, and Demerata's murder, I decided to stay in my own chamber."

"I know that," she snapped. "You wouldn't speak to me and tell me what happened."

"Never mind. Never mind." Telamon grasped her hand and rubbed her fingers. "You look as lovely as the night, Cassandra, in your dark-blue mantle."

"Why, master!" She fluttered her eyelids. "You haven't brought me out in the dark to have your evil way?"

"You should rub oil into your hands," Telamon replied. "Your fingers are slightly calloused. Perhaps it's the water round here?"

"Or the hard work I do for the master."

"I was thinking," Telamon continued. "About our friend Pamenes. He was a Persian spy and worked at Queen Ada's court. But what do spies do?"

"Betray secrets."

"But how would Pamenes be able to communicate with his masters? He couldn't very well leave the court and ride down to

Halicarnassus or anywhere else: that would be suspicious. Anyway, I recalled a story I read years ago in Herodotus. I asked Solan for his copy to study it again."

"I know, you kept mumbling to yourself."

"There used to be a system for secret messages." Telamon ignored her jibe. "Called scytale."

"What does that mean?"

"Scytale is an old word for staff: it was a system used by spies. Apparently it consists of two round pieces of wood, of exact length and thickness, so that each corresponds to the other in precise dimensions. The spy keeps one staff, his masters the other. Whenever the spy wishes to send a secret report or message, he takes a long, narrow scroll of parchment and winds it round the scytale: he leaves no vacant space but covers the staff with the parchment. After doing this, he writes what he wishes on the parchment, then takes it off the scytale . . ."

"Of course," Cassandra intervened. "And if they are using a cipher, all that appears is a piece of parchment with strange symbols on it."

"Precisely," Telamon agreed. "You can only make sense of it if you have a similar staff, identical in length and thickness, to wrap the piece of parchment round."

"And Pamenes did that? That's why we found the pole in his room, and the scraps of parchment?"

"I believe so." Telamon walked on. "We threw them away as rubbish. I suspect Pamenes's assassin found out about the scytale method, that's how he knew Pamenes was a spy. He killed him, but used the same method to correspond with his masters in Halicarnassus."

"And the Pythian Manuscript?"

"I don't think the Pythian Manuscript is what Alexander claims it to be," Telamon replied. "Tonight I am going to try and unlock its secrets. No." He raised a hand. "Don't mock me. I didn't fashion the key, we owe that to Pamenes."

"Is that why he was killed?"

"Perhaps."

"And his assassin is now telling everything to Memnon?"

"Definitely," Telamon murmured. "The spy, this assassin, used the scytale method to send the information to Memnon that Alexander would be lodging at the villa. It could easily be done – a piece of parchment left out under a rock or in the hollow of a tree, collected by some courier who wouldn't be able to read it."

"And he left similar messages with Pamenes's corpse, to be taken back to the Persians?"

"Yes, I think so."

"And Alexander's surprise attack?" Cassandra asked. "That's what you were talking about to the Cretan, wasn't it?"

"I was looking at the problem from the wrong angle," Telamon replied. "I kept thinking of a thick wadge of parchment tied to the end of an arrow. However, with the scytale method, the piece of parchment becomes a streamer. The spy tied it to the end of an arrow. He disguised himself, a slight risk, then he loosed it and the message was sent. I am talking of a strip of parchment no more than a yard long. In the thick of the fighting, who would notice except Memnon, who would be expecting it?"

"Of course he would, but your reasoning is slightly muddled, Telamon! The arrow was probably launched at night, the day before Alexander launched his attack."

Telamon agreed. They walked slowly on, pausing now and again as Telamon explained how the spy had killed the Cretan archer, taken his bow and arrow and used the same weapon against himself in the orchard.

"If I knew who it was," Cassandra hissed through the darkness, "I'd slit his throat or poison his food. It must be one of those scribes! I talked to that guard, the one who helped Gentius search for Demerata: he reported that Sarpedon was inside during the time you were being attacked. The scribes, however, were out in the garden. Such ingenuity," she continued. "Snakes, arrows, secret messages."

"It's not so surprising," Telamon replied. "All of Greece is talking about new inventions, the work of this engineer or that physician. Have you ever seen Aristophanes's comedy *The Clouds*?"

"Yes, I saw it once at the Oedipus festival in Thebes."

"Do you remember the part where Socrates is arguing with a friend about a court case?"

"Yes."

"His friend replies: 'He'd get a piece of glass, use it as a mirror to attract the fire of the sun and so melt the wax writing board which bore the summons.'"

"Oh yes," Cassandra replied. "When Alexander besieged Thebes, one of the city council suggested erecting huge mirrors along the walls to magnify the heat of the sun and set fire to his siege equipment."

"Why didn't they?"

"Someone asked what would happen if it was a cloudy day."

Telamon laughed and made to walk on but Cassandra caught his arm. "I know the assassin would want to kill you. You ask too many questions. But poor Demerata?"

"Ah yes, poor Demerata! I must see Gentius about that."

They walked into the courtyard. The rest of the guests had assembled in the andron, where Gentius had arranged a funeral supper. Telamon and Cassandra joined it for a while. Sarpedon sang a sad song. Gentius recited more lines: a beautiful poem by Sappho. Bessus intoned a funeral dirge from Homer. The wine was served. Telamon, remembering what he had to do, excused himself and returned to his chamber. He took the Pythian Manuscript and studied it, writing down his observations.

Cassandra came up and talked to him. Telamon replied in grunts and vague comments. She declared herself to be exasperated and flounced down on her bed. Talamon kept working. Now and again he paused, walked to the window and stared out. The sky was bright with stars: a breeze ruffled the trees. Telamon recalled the funeral pyre and Gentius's mournful words, and his heart skipped a beat. In a way, if it hadn't been for Demerata, his corpse might have been lying on that funeral pyre, being reduced to ash. He returned to his writing, but found he couldn't concentrate. He picked up the history by Herodotus that Solan had loaned him, a fair copy transcribed by some scholar.

I should have known about the scytale, Telamon reflected. Hadn't he seen a similar device in the temples of Egypt? He recalled his beautiful Anuala taking him round one of the great pillars in a Hall of Columns, translating the hieroglyphics of some decree or story, round and round until he almost felt dizzy. She had clapped her hands and laughed. Cassandra murmured in her sleep. Telamon smiled to himself. What would Anuala have made of Cassandra? In appearance they were so dissimilar, yet they shared the same bluntness of speech and dark sense of humour. Telamon sighed and returned to his studies.

"I know," he murmured, scratching his cheek with the end of the stylus, "that E is the most commonly used letter of the Greek alphabet, which explains why Pamenes talks of number 5; epsilon is the fifth letter. Pamenes was proving this with quotations from Sophocles, or counting how many Es were contained in a section of the *Iliad*. But why the ten?"

Telamon worked on. He looked at the alphabet arranged in five columns and rows and the different numbers of the first line of the Pythian Manuscript. The numbers he might understand, but why the small squares? Telamon ringed these on his copy. He returned to the alphabet and glanced back at the Pythian Manuscript. Could it be? he wondered. Was it possible? He wrote out the first line of the cipher. Slowly and laboriously, he began to use the alphabet to understand the numbers. At first he couldn't believe what he discovered. He went back and checked again, but it made sense. Telamon became so excited he sprang to his feet and kicked over a stool. Cassandra stirred.

"What is it?" she moaned.

Telamon lit more oil lamps and brought them over to the table.

"I believe this manuscript can be translated!"

Cassandra wrapped a blanket around herself and hurried across.

"Here's the alphabet arranged in five rows and five columns," Telamon explained.

	1	2	3	4	5
1	A	B	C	D	E
2	F	G	H	I/J	K
3	L	M	N	O	P
4	Q	R	S	T	U
5	V	W	X	Y	Z

"I understand that," she said.

"The fifth letter, E, is the most commonly used one. Now the code could be quite simple: A was 11: B was 12: C was 13: D was 14: and E 15. F becomes 21, G becomes 22, and so on. Pythias, however, was very cunning. What he did was remove the letter E and replace it with this small square. So if you are looking for a number for E, which is the vital one, you never find it. Sometimes, I suspect he just omitted the symbol for E. Pythias, as I shall prove, also opened this manuscript by using as many words as possible which did not contain the letter E. He then complicated matters further by introducing the following system. For the letter A he uses 11, which is simple enough the way the alphabet is arranged, but again this is misleading, because B should be 12. However, what Pythias did with every letter after A was add the number 10. So B is 22 rather than 12; C becomes 23 rather than 13; D is 24, while E is hidden. F becomes 31. Moreover, there are only 25 letters, so anyone who tried to break this code would only become more confused."

"And you applied this to the Pythian?" Cassandra asked.

"Yes, I have." Telamon lowered his voice. "I want it to be kept secret, because it will take some time to translate it fully. I have to be accurate."

"Is it about the walls of Halicarnassus?"

"I don't think so." Telamon picked up the piece of parchment and passed it across. "Here," he explained, "are the opening numbers of the Pythian Manuscript. I've put the letters below: remember to add ten, the number I found on the scrap of paper Cherolos handed to us."

45	64	54	33	34	11	53
P	Y	T	H	I	A	S
11	52	23	33	34	54	[ ]
A	R	C	H	I	T	E
23	54	54	44			
C	T	T	O			

Cassandra glanced up.

"Pythias, architect to . . . ?"

"Philip," Telamon replied. "That's the next word. What I think happened was this," he continued. "Pythias was corresponding with Philip. He sent a copy to Queen Ada. I doubt if it has much to do with the fortifications of Halicarnassus."

"But that's what people say it is."

"That's what people were meant to say it is. I wager a silver piece to a gold coin that this letter arrived, either just before or just after Philip's assassination. Alexander or Olympias could not understand it. Only Philip had the translation and kept it to himself, that's why our Alexander is so fascinated by it. I wonder what it truly does contain? Pythias, mischievous as a monkey, gives the impression, because he's disgruntled, that he's locked away a certain secret about the redoubtable walls of Halicarnassus. It's like a child's game, sending people running through a maze looking for something which isn't there."

"So there is no weakness in the walls?" Cassandra demanded.

"There might be. We know Alexander is moving his siege machinery; perhaps there is a flaw." Telamon tapped the parchment. "But there's more to this than meets the eye. You see, Cassandra, years ago, just before Philip was murdered, the king tried to marry his other son Arridhaeus to a princess of Halicarnassus. Alexander secretly offered himself. Philip got to know and this led to a serious breach between father and son. I have a deep suspicion that this letter had more to do with that than any military fortification. Which is why" – Telamon got to his feet and stretched – "Alexander is having more nightmares about his father. I look forward to discovering the truth."

"Will you continue?" Cassandra asked.

Telamon shook his head. "No. I have opened the door, I'll return to it more refreshed. Tomorrow I wish to have words with Gentius." He kissed Cassandra quickly on the brow. "I am going to wash and sleep." He glanced towards the window. "And hopefully dream."

"About what?"

Telamon nearly replied Egypt, but caught himself just in time.

"And the assassin?" Cassandra's voice sounded hollow in the dark.

"Slowly but surely." Telamon paused to splash water over his face. He grasped a napkin and dried himself. "I have always thought Pamenes is the key. I have my suspicions, but very little proof."

He took off his tunic and lay down on the bed, staring across the chamber, his mind teeming with possibilities. What had Aristander said? Not even the great philosophers could understand it. Of course, the Master of the King's Secrets must have tried to translate the Pythian Manuscript and failed. Telamon smiled to himself. Aristander would have been beside himself with fury! However, Aristander had not just been talking about himself. Had Alexander shown this to his former tutor Aristotle? Had the great philosopher tried to decipher it? Aristotle wouldn't have given it much time or concentration: he didn't like such riddles and puzzles, being more concerned with what he termed "real problems".

"What are you thinking?" Cassandra's voice sounded sleepy. "I can almost hear your mind, like the wheels of a cart, turning over and over and over."

"I'm beginning to understand why Alexander visited Queen Ada. He must have known the scribes were busy with the Pythian Manuscript. I suspect if Pamenes had lived a few more days . . . !" He abruptly sat up.

"Oh, what is it?" Cassandra demanded crossly.

"What if," Telamon exclaimed, "Pamenes had reached the same point as I have tonight, but had not put his thoughts into writing? Cassandra, think, you are a Persian spy. You've resolved a certain mystery, a secret your masters would dearly love to know. What would you do next?"

"I'd run," Cassandra replied crossly. "Run like the wind."

"That's what Pamenes was preparing to do. That's why he was murdered. Do you remember the saddlebags Cherolos stole? Pamenes had packed those ready to slip away. The killer knew this, and struck before he did."

The tawny eyes of the tame cheetah, a gold chain round its neck, stared glassily at Memnon, who looked away in distaste.

"I never did like the animal," he murmured. "I saw it bring

222

down a peacock in the gardens. Orontobates has owned it since it was a cub."

Ephialtes sprawled on a couch, staring up at the ceiling of the great banqueting hall of the palace; he lifted a sandalled foot and, once again, studied the scar just above the instep.

"You were fortunate," Memnon declared. "That arrow could have struck you instead of grazing you."

"Not as fortunate as Alexander," the Theban replied. "If we had managed to cut off those mantlets, we would have burnt that bridge and massacred the lot." He held up a hand. "Don't you hear it, Memnon? Listen to that pounding."

Memnon got to his feet and walked to the window embrasure overlooking the garden. The Governor's palace was not far from the walls. Memnon closed his eyes and listened. He heard it, like distant waves beating against rocks, the thud, thud, thud of the Macedonian rams battering the masonry, trying to force a way through. Memnon opened his eyes and savoured the fragrance of the garden.

"Do you think he's translated the Pythian Manuscript?" Ephialtes asked. "He moved his siege equipment to the north, now he's come back. He seems intent on that area between the Triple Gate and the tower."

"He'll break through. When he does, we'll have a surprise for him," Memnon replied. "Another great wall, concave in shape, so the defenders at each end can pour down whatever they want on Alexander's engineers. He might as well bay for the moon. Alexander," he added, "doesn't concern me at the moment."

"Nor me." Orontobates, dressed in a dark purple and gold tunic, soft buskins of silver on his feet, a Phrygian cap on his black oiled curls, leaned elegantly against the lintel of the doorway.

The cheetah got up and padded towards him, soundlessly like a ghost, muscles rippling under its satiny skin. Orontobates crouched down and fed it morsels taken from the table. He stroked the cheetah's face, scratching between its ears.

"As lovely as the dawn," he murmured. "I've had to keep it with me. The city is now unsafe. I am abandoning my private houses, bringing all my treasures here."

223

He spoke softly, but his words chilled Memnon. He had fortified this city, its walls were thick and impregnable. He had food supplies, munitions, arms, squadrons of cavalry, the best mercenary hoplites gold could buy as well as elite units from Darius's army. They had water and food to last them for ten years while the Persian war fleet lay in the harbour. Alexander should be camped on the rocky peninsula being burnt black by the sun, throwing himself futilely against the walls.

"We didn't count on that." Orontobates lifted his head, his jewelled fingers still caressing the cheetah's face. "We didn't think of that, my lord, did we?" he repeated. "Of traitors within?"

Orontobates got to his feet and sat on the couch next to Ephialtes. He gazed round the chamber: its walls were painted gold, decorated with silver-purple lozenges and bunches of grapes. The same motif decorated the round, squat columns, while the floor and ceiling were of marble and shone like glass, creating the impression of being between two pure pools: water above and water below. The chamber was brilliant with light: at least a hundred oil lamps glowed on ledges and niches. The furniture was of the best acacia and sandalwood, beautifully carved tables edged with gold and silver and richly quilted stools. The banqueting couches were a personal gift from Darius, covered in scarlet cloth and emblazoned with leaping golden lions.

Will I have to burn all this? Orontobates thought. He splaycd his fingers and glanced up under his eyebrows. Memnon was watching him curiously.

"You are nervous, my Lord Governor? Why?" Memnon stretched out his own hands, fingers splayed. "You always do that when you are anxious."

Orontobates smiled. The cheetah jumped on the couch beside him, turning and twisting so it could rest its head on his lap.

"I am nervous," the Persian replied. "Do you realize, Memnon, we have as many soldiers patrolling the city as we have manning the walls?"

"But why?" Memnon exclaimed. "Ten days ago the city was ours. Now you are talking of unrest, of weapons being found, our soldiers attacked."

"The potters' quarter is almost a garrison in itself," Orontobates replied. "And yet, when we send soldiers in, our opponents melt away with surly glances and dark mutterings."

"We should surround the place!" Ephialtes bawled. "Level it to the ground and kill everyone we find." He swung himself up and sat, feet apart. "But there's more, isn't there, Orontobates?"

"Our spies are busy," the Persian agreed, "in the wine booths and the markets. They listen to conversations. They are sure they have heard the Macedonian tongue."

"But there are Macedonians here," Memnon declared. "Every nation under the sun lives in Halicarnassus."

"Young men?" Orontobates raised his eyebrows. "Lean of body and face? Smelling of horse sweat?"

"Why aren't these men arrested?" Ephialtes demanded.

"I am merely repeating gossip and rumour," Orontobates smiled falsely. "It's possible," he continued, "that Alexander may have sent a secret column into the city before we sealed our gates."

"But that would be less than a hundred men," Memnon declared. "Anything else would be noticed."

Orontobates rubbed his hands together. "What if . . . ?"

"What if what?" Memnon snarled, coming back to sit beside Ephialtes.

"What if there are more than a hundred?" Orontobates replied. "Hasn't your spy told us anything?"

Memnon shook his head. "He despatched one arrow before Alexander launched the attack," he replied. "He told us about the flat-topped siege sheds and that the Pythian Manuscript was not yet translated. But –" Memnon shrugged "– after that, silence."

"Do you know who he is?"

"I wish I did. He's received his gold, and my promise that if the Pythian Manuscript is translated the hidden treasure is his. What I want to know is what Alexander will do next? Is there a weakness in the walls? Will he find it? And how do we . . . ?"

Memnon broke off at the sound of hurried footsteps. One of his staff officers, dressed in half-armour, burst into the chamber.

"My lord, you'd best come!"

"What is the matter?"

"Out in the gardens, my lord!"

All three followed the officer out through the colonnaded portico and down the steps. Even as they did so, the night breeze brought the smell of burning and, turning to their right, they saw the flames leaping up above the trees. Palace servants and soldiers were already carrying buckets; chamberlains shouted for help, horns blared and cymbals clashed as the alarm was raised.

"Stop the panic!" Memnon ordered.

"What is it?" Ephialtes murmured.

"It looks like one of my summer houses. There's a small cypress grove, a pleasaunce, a paradise," Orontobates explained, "just near the walls. We'd best . . ."

"We'll go nowhere!" Memnon retorted. "It might be an accident, or it might be something else!"

Palace guards from the barracks were now spilling out into the gardens, hastily dressing, being shoved into position by officers. Memnon's own personal bodyguard came hurrying through the doorway, armour clattering. Order was imposed. Two rings of armed men formed in a horseshoe pattern, Greeks and Persians, carrying sword, shield and javelin, guarded the main approaches to the palace.

A page came running across the grass, the cresset torch he carried flickering and dancing. The soldiers let him through. An officer took the torch and the boy staggered forward and fell to his knees before Orontobates. He chattered in Persian, pointing back towards the flames. He talked so quickly Memnon couldn't follow. Orontobates held his hand up for silence.

"My Lord Memnon." Orontobates's face was ashen. "That was no accident! We are under attack!"

The page was dismissed. Memnon's staff officer returned.

"The blaze is under control," he said, wiping black grime from his face.

"Are there intruders?"

The officer shook his head. "No, my lord, just fire arrows loosed from across the wall, and this."

He handed across a cylindrical leather case, the type used by messengers, battered and scuffed: the strap which the envoy would

226

use to hang it over his shoulder was frayed and discoloured. Memnon grabbed it, took off the stopper and plucked out the small scroll of parchment. He moved back to read it.

"It's not for me," he declared, handing it to Ephialtes.

The Theban snatched it, barking at the officer to bring the torch closer.

"I'll tell you what it says," Memnon murmured. "Alexander of Macedon to Ephialtes of Thebes, traitor: Ephialtes of Thebes be not so bold, for Memnon your master is both bought and sold!"

Ephialtes tore up the manuscript, throwing it onto the grass. He ground it under his heel, his face a mask of fury. "They bait us, Memnon: they are closer than we think. So what reply do we make?"

"Bought and sold," Orontobates murmured. "That means we have traitors closer than we think."

"My lord."

Memnon turned. A chamberlain stood on the steps beckoning him. "My lords, you'd best see this."

They followed him back into the portico, where smoke from the fire now curled. Memnon found it difficult to control his fear. The chamberlain's face did nothing to help: a thin-faced old man, eyes red-rimmed from lack of sleep.

"My lords, the prisoner, the Eunuch is dead!"

"What?" Orontobates exclaimed.

They followed the chamberlain through the palace, hurrying down the steps into the maze of mildewed tunnels leading to the dungeons. They turned a corner. A babble of voices greeted them. Guards and gaolers clustered at the door to the cell where the Eunuch had been imprisoned. Memnon pushed them aside and went inside. The room was comfortable, more a chamber than a cell. Apparently the Eunuch had climbed onto the table, taken the cord from round his waist, fastened one end round a hook in the beam, fashioned a noose for his neck and simply stepped off: his long body hung slack, swaying slightly like some broken doll, feet apart, arms hanging by his sides, neck and head strangely twisted. His ugly face had turned a mottled hue, eyes staring sightlessly, a drool of saliva running down his chin.

Memnon sniffed and stared across: tendrils of smoke still curled up from the water bowl.

"Cut him down!" he ordered.

A soldier held the corpse while another climbed on the table and sliced through the cord. The Eunuch's corpse was laid on the floor. Memnon knelt beside it. The flesh was still warm. He snapped his fingers. The soldier handed over a dagger and Memnon cut through the noose: the corpse gave a slight shudder as trapped air escaped from the dead man's lungs.

"He's only been dead a short while."

Memnon examined the Eunuch's head and neck. He could find no mark or bruise except for the dark purple welt around his throat.

"What happened?" he asked.

He got up and walked across to the smoking bronze bowl. The water had been poured out, and it was full of black smouldering ash. He stared round the cell. Everything was in order: the small cot bed, the cloak and belt hanging from a peg on the wall. One oil lamp was extinguished, but the other still glowed fiercely. On a bench near the wall stood a platter of half-eaten food, a cup and a wine jug.

"What happened?" he repeated. He pointed at the bulbous-faced gaoler. "You, Cerberus?"

"We made him comfortable." The gaoler refused to be cowed. He shuffled forward, hands spread beseechingly. "My lord, you told us to make him comfortable."

"I know that," Memnon retorted.

"He had his clothes, a belt, even a knife. We were eating at one end of the passageway, the guards at the other. We heard the alarm being raised."

Memnon looked at the soldiers. "That's true, sir. We left the passageway and went up the stairs. Cerberus and the turnkeys followed. We wondered what was happening. Someone said we were under attack, we smelt the smoke . . ."

"And then what?"

"I came back down to the cell," Cerberus replied. "I smelt smoke and thought it was from outside. When I looked through the grille the Eunuch was swinging by his neck, flames and smoke coming from the bowl. By the time I found my keys and opened the door . . ." The man shrugged. "It was too late. The Eunuch was dead."

Memnon studied the fat, crafty face, the slobbery lips and shifty eyes.

"My lords," the fellow whined, "I did talk to the Eunuch. He was frightened. He thought, once he had finished his task, he would be crucified. He believed there was no way out."

Memnon turned and stared down at the bowl.

"He's burnt everything?" Ephialtes asked.

Memnon nodded. "He burned his copy of the Pythian Manuscript and all the notes he made." Memnon closed his eyes to control his fury. "Have the corpse stripped!" He went to the door and turned. "No, on second thoughts we are past all that. You" – he pointed to the gaoler – "take it to the fire outside. Let's put that to some good use. Throw his corpse on the mess and let's be done with it!"

When they returned to the banqueting chamber the chamberlain was waiting for them, standing in the doorway. This time he fell to his knees.

"What is it?" Orontobates demanded.

The chamberlain raised a tear-wet face. "My lord, worse news after bad."

"Get to your feet!" Orontobates hissed.

The chamberlain refused. "My lords, you know I have been working hard both day and night." He spoke slowly so Memnon and Ephialtes could understand him. "I listen to the reports brought in by our spies from the city. Just before the alarm was raised, one of my best, a man sober and quick-witted . . ."

"Yes, yes?" Orontobates interrupted testily.

"This man" – the chamberlain raised his head – "this man would swear on his mother's soul he saw a file of Macedonian Shield-Bearers very close to the palace."

Orontobates grasped the man by the tunic. He pulled him to his feet and shook him. "You lie! Your spy's mistaken!"

The chamberlain, shaking with fear, shook his head. "My lord, I speak the truth!"

Ephialtes stormed away, kicking over a stool. Orontobates pushed the chamberlain out of the chamber and slammed the door behind him. The cheetah came padding across, but skittered away as Orontobates lashed out with his foot. The animal screeched and went to skulk in a corner.

"Could this be true?" Ephialtes hissed. "Shield-Bearers! From the Macedonian Guards Regiments, here? How?"

"The spy must be questioned," Memnon retorted. "He talked of a file, maybe twenty to thirty men. Now." Memnon tried to marshal his thoughts. "They could be a small group hidden away here before the siege began."

"But they were wearing armour!" Ephialtes shouted. "Why wear armour and attract attention to themselves? Don't you see, Memnon?" Ephialtes picked up a cup, drained it and dashed it to the floor. "They wanted us to see them. How do we know other files weren't seen elsewhere in the city? What if they brought in standards to incite the mob? Distributing gold and silver as bribes?"

"And the Eunuch's death?" Orontobates intervened. "Is it such a coincidence? The message to Ephialtes. Now Macedonians have been glimpsed inside the walls."

Memnon walked across and picked up a scroll, a detailed map of the city. He brought this back to a table, knocking off the cups and platters, and rolled it out.

"My lords." He used cups to hold the scroll flat and summoned the other two closer. "Now is not the time for tantrums and rages." He traced the horseshoe formation of the city walls. "This is where we have made our stand." He pointed to the centre of the horseshoe. "This is where Alexander and his army batter away at the walls. To face that we left only a token force elsewhere and concentrated our forces here. We had to let the Macedonians break through." He moved his finger. "Between the walls and the harbour lies the sprawling city of Halicarnassus. Now, I am going to describe something of a nightmare. What if there are Macedonians in the city?" He glanced warningly at Ephialtes to keep quiet. "Only the gods know how they came here or where they are! Let us say, while we are manning the walls, trying to throw Alexander back, the city rises behind us, armed and led by

Macedonians. We would then be caught either way. If we turn to face them, the Macedonians might break through and we would be trapped. If we ignore them, this mob may storm the gates and Alexander won't need his battering ram or siege towers."

"We could divide our forces," Ephialtes intervened.

"That would mean stripping the walls, there would be chaos. Ephialtes, you are a seasoned commander. One thing soldiers cannot tolerate is the realization that the enemy is no longer in front but behind them. There would be desertions, mutiny, some would surrender. We would either be murdered or captured and handed over to Alexander." He held Ephialtes's gaze. "He has given his solemn word, if we fall into his hands, he'll crucify us high against the sky."

Orontobates removed his Phrygian cap and flung it on the floor: he loosened the neck of the tunic beneath his gorgeous cloak of glory. "What can we do?" he murmured.

"You know what we have to do," Memnon replied. "Something I thought I would never agree to, but the sooner it's done, the better!"

Chapter 12

"Pixadorus, King of Caria, made an offer of his daughter in marriage to Arridhaeus."

Quintus Curtius Rufus: *The History of Alexander the Great*, Book I, Chapter IX

"**W**hy did you murder your wife?"

Gentius would have sprung to his feet but Telamon, sitting on a stool in front of him, forced him back down. The actor's mouth opened and shut, fingers fluttering, eyes blinking. He swallowed hard. "I don't know what you are saying," he stammered.

Telamon looked at Cassandra, leaning against the door of the chamber. He stifled a yawn and rubbed his face. He'd had very little sleep, but considered it best to grasp the nettle and confront this murderer.

"You murdered your wife," Telamon repeated. "You took a cord and strangled Demerata."

"I didn't."

"Then who did?"

Gentius's head twitched. Telamon noticed the muscle spasm high in his cheek. "You are not a very good liar," he added quietly. "If you didn't murder your wife, who did?"

"Why, one of the others. It could even have been you!"

"Why should I murder your wife? I hardly knew her. The same could be said for Solan, Bessus or Sarpedon. Gentius, you are a killer. You are full of guilt and remorse. You didn't really plan to murder her. You just lost your temper and it happened. You went looking for your wife and found her in Pamenes's chamber, grieving over

233

her former lover. Your patience snapped. You couldn't take any more of the baiting or teasing. You had some cord and you wrapped it round her throat with your powerful hands. She would have died quickly, like some farmer wringing a chicken's neck."

Gentius tried to speak but his voice croaked.

"And then you began that charade, not a very good performance, Gentius, of searching for your wife. You brought that guard upstairs, moving from chamber to chamber. What he didn't know was that you had already murdered Demerata and concealed her body in Pamenes's chamber, under the bed or behind the door. You would open that, look quickly in, to all intents and purposes it was empty. You then directed the search elsewhere. While the guard did that you slipped back, picked up your wife's corpse and laid it out on the bed. The guard took up his position at the top of the stairs while you continued your fictitious search. You returned, asked him to accompany you and, lo and behold, your wife's corpse is found sprawled in Pamenes's chamber, a garrotte round her throat. The guard was your witness. You'd been searching frantically. You had already entered Pamenes's room and found nothing. The murder, therefore, must have occurred while you and he were elsewhere. That's all nonsense, a poorly plotted play."

"What, what do you mean?" Gentius croaked.

"No one was seen climbing the stairs or talking to Demerata," Telamon replied. "There was no sign of any struggle. She may have been slight and fragile, but Demerata would have struck out at anyone she didn't know who drew too close. No." Telamon tapped Gentius gently on the shoulder. "You killed your wife. You strangled her, hid her body, organized that fictitious search and arranged for the guard to be present when you decided your play had come to an end."

"What proof do you have of this?"

"More than I need. I'll ask the guard, who came up those stairs? Who brought Demerata to that chamber? Why should she go there?" Telamon paused. "There's other proof. You are full of guilt and remorse. When I was examining the corpse you appeared to be lost in your grief, almost witless. However, after the guard had told his story, you answered logically. You must have been listening to his every word."

Gentius's face relaxed, his shoulders drooped.

"Why did you kill her?" Cassandra asked quietly.

"Because I loved her. Demerata was my audience, my inspiration. Every soul has its song, and she was mine." Gentius's eyes filled with tears. "We met in Athens at the Festival of Flowers some sixteen years ago. She was a wine merchant's daughter, small and dark. She came to watch my nightly performances. I fell in love with her immediately. We had no children, but she joined me when I travelled from city to city to receive the plaudits of the great and the good." The tears rolled down his cheeks. "Women accosted me, but I ignored them. Demerata also had her admirers. At first I tolerated them. I thought there was no harm, but then, like great gaps in a script, I knew something was wrong. This young soldier, that young poet. Soon I had cuckold's horns, but I loved her even more. I tolerated her. She always swore she would never do it again, that she would be faithful and that she really loved only me. I considered myself to be a great actor, physician, but on reflection" – he laughed sharply – "Demerata was even better. She became upset when she broke her word. I was grief-stricken because she broke my heart. But, Pamenes." Gentius sighed. "When we heard how Macedon had won the great battle of the Granicus, we decided it was safer to leave the roads to the marching armies, and shelter for a while in Queen Ada's court at her fortress of Alinde. It was cool, away from the heat and dust: that plump old queen welcomed us with open arms."

"And Demerata met Pamenes?"

"Demerata met Pamenes. This time it was different, not some casual affair." Gentius fought back the sob. "Demerata really liked him. By then the court was all agog with chatter and gossip: of how Alexander was marching south: how we would have to lay siege to the great city of Halicarnassus. How it had weaknesses. Well, the Pythian Manuscript became the centre of Queen Ada's life. Solan, Bessus." Gentius waved a hand. "I met them all."

"And Demerata and Pamenes became lovers?"

"Yes, they became lovers. By then I was the compliant husband.

I was terrified of Demerata leaving me. I decided to look the other way. Eventually I left Alinde. Demerata was cut to the heart, but what did I care about her pain? I'd won the patronage of Alexander." He spread his hands. "The rest you know."

"Did you have words with Demerata about Pamenes?"

"She swore she would be faithful to me and avoid him, but he was a handsome fellow, with his dark liquid eyes and secretive face. I knew she was lying," he added bitterly. "She returned to him like a dog to its vomit."

"And the night before Pamenes died, you went looking for Demerata?"

"I was looking for her, physician, and I found her late at night in Pamenes's chamber. They were both sitting on the bed. Oh, I never caught them in the act, but you could just tell. If I have any gift, I can distinguish between reality and role. They sat there, faces flushed, clothes dishevelled, a cup of wine on the floor."

"Did you have words?"

"I just glared at them, closed the door and walked quietly away. I pretended to be asleep when Demerata joined me. I decided to continue as if nothing had happened, rehearsing my lines while she played the role of the dutifuly perfect wife, prompting me when I forgot." He smiled thinly. "Introducing me with a clash of cymbals." He wiped his cheeks with the back of his hand. "When Pamenes was found dead, I acted the part. I kept my face solemn and acted concerned."

"Did you kill him?" Cassandra asked, ignoring Telamon's warning glance.

"I never went near the adulterer's chamber," he retorted. "I didn't kill him, but I was delighted he was dead. I went for a walk in the orchard. I was so pleased, I danced like a maenad."

"Did you suspect anyone?" Telamon asked.

Gentius snorted with laughter and turned away. "I've watched you, physician. You study symptoms, don't you? Always searching, always studying. I don't know! Solan, Bessus, Sarpedon and Pamenes! Like the four corners of a room joined together. A close, secretive group."

"And Cherolos?"

"Oh, he joined them rather late. I'm not too sure about Cherolos, with his love of snakes and that strange cult. Do you believe in the gods, Telamon? I don't. Cherolos is what he pretends to be, a priest, possibly Queen Ada's spy on the rest." The actor shook his head. "I don't really know, I don't really care."

"And yesterday?" Telamon asked.

"Oh, it started well. Alexander had said that when he took Halicarnassus . . ."

"I beg your pardon?" Telamon interrupted.

"That's what he told me. That he would take it like Agamemnon took Troy, but he didn't explain. Anyway" – Gentius rubbed his hands together – "when Halicarnassus falls, I am supposed to act in the great theatre there. I was very excited. If I secured the patronage of Alexander of Macedon . . ."

"But Demerata spoilt all that?"

"Yes, she went missing. The guard was asleep downstairs, the rest were out in the garden, I saw Sarpedon in the kitchens. I found Demerata in Pamenes's chamber. She was kneeling on the floor crying, reciting a love poem. She didn't hear me come in. I stood behind her. It was the love poem which cut my heart. Pamenes was dead, but she'd still come to visit his shade and whisper sweet endearments. I had a cord in my pouch, the sort you use to slip through the eyelets of a tunic. One moment I was standing behind her, the next it was round her throat. I was tightening it fast. She hardly resisted, fluttering like a little bird caught in your hand. Then she was dead. I hid the body behind the door." He made a face. "Demerata was small. I gave that performance – not very convincing, was it?"

Telamon shook his head.

"I knew it would only be a matter of time," Gentius mused. "But I thought you'd be distracted by the other business. Demerata's death could be one more mystery in the strange killings which have taken place here." He held Telamon's gaze. "You are much sharper than I thought. You would have made a fine actor, physician. I would have cast you in the role, perhaps, of Creon in *Antigone*, or even Oedipus himself."

"That was your other mistake." Telamon smiled thinly. "At the funeral pyre you quoted a speech from *Antigone*. If I remember the lines correctly, you said 'The hunters of hell which follow and destroy are lying in wait for me'. But that's not accurate. In the play Tereisias is speaking to King Creon, and the line should read: 'The hunters of hell which follow and destroy are lying in wait for you!' You virtually admitted your own guilt."

"Did I?" Gentius pushed back the stool. "Did I make a mistake like that?" He rubbed his face in his hands. "And what is my fate, physician?"

"That is not for me to decide: it will have to be held over until the king is informed." Telamon's heart softened at the grief in Gentius's eyes. "If you speak the truth, you were much provoked. A period of madness which the gods can send."

"Or the demons of Hades!" Gentius retorted.

"You will be held here," Telamon continued. "But there is a way of softening the king's heart."

Gentius narrowed his eyes.

"Do you remember the night you went to Pamenes's chamber? It was dark?"

Gentius nodded.

"But his chamber had oil lamps?"

"Yes, yes, they were lit: three of four, if I remember correctly."

"If you can," Telamon urged, "try and remember what else you saw. I know about Pamenes and Demerata, but what else? Please, Gentius, think!"

The actor folded his arms and sat, head down. Telamon heard the clatter of hooves from the courtyard below, shouts and cries, but he ignored them.

"How was Pamenes's chamber, Gentius? Can you remember? You are an actor, you have a very good memory. Imagine yourself standing in the doorway: the darkness, the pools of light from the oil lamps."

"It was very tidy," Gentius replied. "Yes, that was my impression. The desk was clear, not littered with manuscripts."

"You are sure of that?"

"Oh yes, and something else."

Telamon curbed his impatience: he did not wish to suggest anything.

"Pamenes's saddlebags were leaning against the wall, unstrapped; they were full of clothing."

"Did you get the impression he was going to leave?"

Gentius looked up sharply. "Why do you say that?"

"Just a suspicion. Why did Demerata," Telamon persisted, "visit him that particular night? Did she say anything?"

"She later grieved for him. I did have words with her, and she turned on me. She claimed Pamenes's death made no difference. If he had lived, she wouldn't have seen him again."

"So, he was leaving . . ."

Telamon paused at the clatter of footsteps outside, a knock on the door: it swung open and Hephaestion, dressed in the armour of a cavalryman, came swaggering in. He carried a war helmet in one hand, a small riding crop in the other.

"Hail to the new Patroclus!" Cassandra hissed. "Sent hotfoot by the beloved Achilles!"

Hephaestion, used to such teasing, winked at her. He stared at Telamon, then at Gentius. "Trouble, physician?"

"Trouble," Telamon agreed. "Even more, with your arrival."

"Our master wants us," Cassandra murmured.

Hephaestion gestured. "I've been sent to bring you. The king needs your advice. He wants to have you close by."

Telamon got to his feet. "Guard!" he shouted.

The soldier outside entered. Telamon pointed at Gentius.

"This man is to be confined to his own chamber: food and drink are to be brought up. You will accompany him wherever he goes."

The soldier straightened up, hand falling to the hilt of his sword. "And if he tries to escape, sir?"

"I won't escape," Gentius declared wearily, getting to his feet. "I won't escape at all. I'll never escape from what I have done."

Hephaestion glanced, puzzled, at Telamon, who shook his head in reply.

"Is there anything else you can recall?" Telamon asked.

Gentius turned in the doorway. "Yes. My wife's last gasps." His hands went to his ears. "Everywhere I go I hear them." The soldier led him away.

"No, don't ask me." Telamon stretched to ease the cramp in his back. "We are to leave now?"

"I've brought horses," Hephaestion replied. "The king will want to know about the Pythian Manuscript."

Telamon stared back.

"We'd best go now," Hephaestion urged. "The king needs every soldier. I'm to leave two guards here and collect those lazy buggers sunning themselves in the fields outside."

"Why, what has happened?" Telamon demanded.

"I'll tell you as we ride."

A short while later, their bags packed, Telamon and Cassandra, surrounded by Hephaestion's unit, left the Villa of Cybele. Two officers stayed behind to organize the men camped in the field. At first Cassandra had to put up with the gentle badinage of her companions. One drew his horse too close and tugged at her red hair. Cassandra screamed an obscenity back. Hephaestion growled over his shoulder and the cavalrymen left her alone.

"What was that all about?" Hephaestion demanded.

"I'll tell you when I've told the king."

"And the Pythian Manuscript?"

"I'll tell the king." Telamon smiled. "And he can tell you."

Hephaestion put his helmet on and squinted up at the sky. "We had great excitement last night," he declared. "Something was happening in the city. Alexander saw his fire arrows."

"Fire arrows?" Telamon queried.

"Oh yes, five or six up into the night sky. Only the gods know what they mean. Alexander was beside himself with joy."

They cantered on. The road became busier: carts taking up provisions, outlying pickets and units falling back to the main camp. They breasted the hill, and the Macedonian camp sprawled in front of them. The contrast was so sharp. The rolling grasslands seemed to disappear under a sea of tents and pavilions, haphazard bothies, herds of horses, picket lines, ditches and, everywhere, the dark smoke of the camp rising against the sunlit blue sky. The smell of the countryside faded, giving way to acrid wood smoke, the stench of burning meat, horse dung, leather, sweat: the odour of wax, of tens of thousands of men camping in the fields waiting for the carnage of battle.

Hephaestion led his group through the main gate of the camp, up the broad avenue which the camp marshal kept clear. Telamon gazed around. "All the world," he murmured, "follows an army."

The local peasants had flocked in with handcarts and barrows piled high with produce: hard-baked bread, overripe fruit, leather buckets full of water from some spring. The air was rich with cooking spices, the pervasive smell of fish-oil and figs. Travelling troupes had also arrived to entertain the soldiers. A group of Syrian dancing girls, faces painted, black hair flowing down their backs, sinuous bodies oiled and gleaming, whirled in a clatter of bracelets to the heart-catching sound of lute and drum: they danced, a sea of moving colour, clapping their hands while soldiers clapped with them and cheered them on. A fortune-teller claimed to have the gift of discerning who would do well in battle and who would not.

"I'd wager a silver piece," Hephaestion said, "that he tells no one they are going to die."

Barbers and leeches had set up their makeshift stalls. Tinkers and pedlars offered cheap bracelets and rings. Scorpion men sold amulets and charms to ward off any evil. Now and again Telamon caught a face he knew, and raised his hand in greeting.

"The hospital tents are at the far side, where there is some shade," Hephaestion explained. "But I don't think Alexander needs you for that."

They reached the royal enclosure guarded by a regiment of Silver Shield-Bearers. Grooms took their horses. Hephaestion led Telamon round the great altar surrounded by its trophies. Cassandra was told to wait while Telamon was led into the royal tent. Telamon paused, surprised: he thought Alexander would be here, surrounded by his commanders, poring over maps, but the tent was dark, no oil lamps lit. A heap of clothing on a couch moved. Alexander pushed these aside and sat up, rubbing a face heavy with sleep. He got up and came forward. His hair was neatly cut, his face shaven, his tunic clean. He smelt fragrantly of oil.

"I have been sleeping."

"Dreaming?"

Alexander rubbed his eyes. "No, no more nightmares. That physician from Corinth, Nicias. He gave me a sleeping draught."

"Use such things prudently," Telamon warned. "You might slip into a sleep and never awake."

"Sleep is the brother of Death," Alexander quoted the famous line. He grabbed a cloak from a peg driven into one of the poles and, leaning on Telamon, walked back to the tent flap. "The Pythian Manuscript," he murmured.

"You know it's a letter from the architect Pythias to your father?"

"I suspected as much." Alexander's face didn't change. "It arrived in Pella five days before he died. You know Father, he was busy courting all his guests. So he never fully translated it. Now" – Alexander waved his hand – "don't badger me, Telamon, just wait and see. Hephaestion!" he shouted. "A squadron of Shield-Bearers. I am going to show Telamon how busy we have been."

Pages ran forward with the king's armour. He took his war helmet and shooed them away; horses were brought and they mounted. Alexander led them out of the enclosure across the ditch. The stench was offensive: human ordure mixed with the vile cooking fat the soldiers used and the acrid smoke wafting from the funeral pyre beyond the camp palisade. They left the heathland and came onto the seething hot promontory, where the white rocks threw back the glare and heat of the sun.

Alexander had now returned to his original point of attack, battering the walls near the great Triple Gate. Telamon had never seen such devastation. The walls of Halicarnassus now looked as if they had been burnt by some giant fire, blackened and cracked from base to battlements. The yawning ditch was slowly being filled in with earth, in other places with more flat-topped sheds: there was even a bridge leading up to the main gate of the city. The dart-throwers, catapults, ballistas and other siege machinery had all been pushed closer, now defended by soaring wooden shields protected by leather padding. The fighting ground between the siege weapons and the ditch was littered with corpses. Alexander followed Telamon's gaze.

"I have had to send out heralds," he murmured, "to seek permission to retrieve our dead."

"And Memnon has honoured that?"

"He has to," Alexander replied grimly. "He's a Greek. One day he may have to ask the same favour."

Telamon stared up at the battlements: the gaps in the crenellations had now been filled with wooden shields, but he could see the glint of armour. Now and again one of the wooden shields was abruptly withdrawn: archers, clustered together, released a volley and then retreated before the Cretans, prowling like wolves below, could retaliate.

"There's no weakness in the wall, is there?" Telamon asked, staring at a black oil stain which seemed to cover the entire wall beneath one of the city towers.

"Why, have you translated the manuscript completely?"

"No, I have only begun."

"There's no weakness," Alexander whispered. "I wager this part of the wall is as good and strong as any other section."

He paused as a horn brayed. The catapults and ballistas were winched back creaking and groaning, the pulleys slipping, men shouting as they were loaded and primed. Again the war horn brayed, a long, blasting echo.

"Loose!" an officer shouted.

The engines were released in a whoosh of air and screech of levers. The deadly darts, rocks and pots of fire either crashed against the walls or soared over the battlements to create chaos beyond. The battering rams along the wall now took this as a sign to recommence their thudding, echoing like the beat of a drum. Lines of Cretan archers in their red war kilts crept forward, arrows notched. On the battlements the shields were removed, pots of fire and boulders rained down onto the thick leather coverings of the roofs protecting the rams. Alexander's engineers responded. One pot of fire, hurled by a catapult, hit a group of enemy archers clustered between the crenellations. The figures were transformed into living torches. One body, a human firebrand, tipped slowly over the wall to bounce on the top of the sheds before sliding into the ditch.

"So it goes on," Alexander murmured. "Day in, day out, though I have been promised a surprise."

243

Alexander edged his horse forward, ignoring Hephaestion's warnings. Telamon sensed something was about to happen. He saw fire break out near the walls where one of the battering rams was working. Suddenly the men inside left the long line of mantlets, running for the safety of the archers. Telamon watched in amazement.

"See!" Alexander cried. "There!"

A crack had appeared in the wall just above the battering ram which the Macedonians had now deserted. The fissure widened and the masonry tore as if it were a piece of parchment, there was a rumble of falling masonry, and the section above the battering rams collapsed in billowing clouds of white dust. This in turn was followed by falls from either side. The top section of the wall, supporting the battlements, looked as if it was going to stay poised like a bridge in the air. Further showers of dust followed by small bricks, pieces of mortar, and that section, too, collapsed in a resounding crash. Alexander's face, no longer sleepy, was wreathed in smiles. The siege engines ceased their fire and a resounding cheer broke out along the Macedonian line.

For a while all was confusion. The ruined section lay in a great heap of jagged rocks and boulders. Clouds of dust still fanned out. The walls on either side of the great gap were now deserted. The dust cleared, and the Macedonian cheer died.

"I thought as much!" Hephaestion shouted. "They've built a demi-lune." He made a shape with his fingers. "Like a crescent moon: a wall behind the wall."

Telamon glimpsed what Hephaestion had described: a wall, very similar to the one which defended the city, had been erected. A soaring concave shield of stone, not as high as the main wall, but still battlemented and fortified. Enemy soldiers and archers already manned it. The fallen wall had crushed the mantlet below, but Hephaestion explained that the battering ram had been withdrawn.

"Now the fun really begins," he whispered. "If we attack the demi-lune, Memnon, using that new wall and the old one, will be able to pour volleys down into our flanks."

Alexander, however, seemed unperturbed, indicating to his captains that the battering rams should be taken forward.

"Hit the new wall!" he declared. "It cannot, must not, be as strong as the old."

And, turning his horse, Alexander signalled to Telamon and the rest to follow him back to the camp. They left the battlefield to the roar of soldiers, the screech and thud of the catapults and ballistas, as the furious onslaught was renewed.

Once they returned to the royal enclosure, Alexander allowed Telamon to visit Cassandra: she had been taken to an adjoining pavilion which they would have to share with the other royal physicians. Once he had done this, Telamon was summoned back to the king's tent.

"I want you to work on the Pythian Manuscript." Alexander pointed to a table, already prepared, with oil lamps glowing against the gloom.

"Why now?" Telamon asked. "What's so urgent?"

"I want to know what it says. I'd like to know before I take Halicarnassus."

"Why were the others left in the Villa of Cybele?"

"Because I don't trust them. One of them's a spy and a murderer. Hephaestion mentioned something about Demerata being killed?"

"Gentius did that," Telamon replied, "in a fit of jealousy. He is being held under guard."

"Oh, I'll release him," Alexander muttered. He gestured at Telamon to sit at the table.

"If you don't trust them," Telamon replied, opening his saddle-bag and taking out writing instruments, "why were they entrusted with the Pythian Manuscript?"

"I had to accept Queen Ada's offer of help."

"And you need all the help you can get," Telamon replied, opening the inkpot. "You've tried to translate this before, haven't you?"

"Of course! Aristander tried, failed miserably, and lost his temper. I gave it to Aristotle, but he declared it was beneath him." The king narrowed his eyes. "I don't know whether he found it difficult or just couldn't be bothered. You're quite remarkable, Telamon."

"No, I'm not," the physician replied. "Pamenes the dead scribe was. He virtually handed me the key: it was just a matter of fitting it into the lock."

He explained to Alexander what Pamenes had discovered. The king, seated on the edge of his bed, listened carefully, nodding now and again, interrupting with the occasional question. Once Telamon was finished, Alexander lay on the bed, one arm over his eyes, muttering to himself.

Telamon returned to his translation. There were constant interruptions: messengers came and went, commanders reported in hushed whispers. The day wore on. Telamon translated line after line. He left on two occasions to take some air and to see Cassandra, but returned to his task. At first it had been slow, but now he was past the defences Pythias had set up he began to work faster: he soon realized why Alexander was so eager to discover the secret of this manuscript. He translated one line and glanced up.

"The Villa of Cybele," he declared. "Did you know it was once owned by Pythias himself?"

Alexander now slouched in a camp chair, a map across his lap, glanced up quickly. "Are you sure?" He studied Telamon's face. "You are sure," he smiled. "And what else?"

"Pythias didn't bury his treasure in the city. He buried it in that villa."

Telamon cursed and closed his eyes. Images came and went. Solan and Bessus out in the gardens, never in one place. Sarpedon tending plants and digging as if the land were his. Pamenes sprawled beneath that window, a pool of dark blood like a nimbus round his shattered head. Solan's strict instructions to the maids and scullions not to wander about the house.

"What's the matter?" Alexander was studying him curiously.

"I think I know who the spy is and how Pamenes was killed. We've been misled."

"We always are," Alexander retorted.

"Did you know?"

The king shook his head. "Telamon, I only know three things. First, Pythias sent that letter to my father: a copy was kept by Queen Ada. Some spy at her court then translated it and gave it to the Persians. Secondly, Pythias, when he heard about my father's death, as well as to wreak his own revenge on the rulers of Halicarnassus, must have spread the story that the manuscript contained secrets about the weakness of Halicarnassus's walls." Alexander sighed. "And that, before he fled the city, he buried his treasure there. I didn't know the Villa of Cybele belonged to him!"

"And the third secret?"

Alexander rolled up the map, put it on the table and walked to the tent flap. He told the guards to stand away and, bringing across a stool, sat next to Telamon.

"Shall I tell you the third secret, Telamon? Pythias sent a messenger to my father with that manuscript. He told him something extraordinary – that the weakness of Halicarnassus lay in the rocks of Nyssa."

"Nyssa!" Telamon exclaimed.

"Yes, the rocky outcrop to the east of the city: a warren of caves. One of those caves, according to Pythias, contained a secret passage from ancient times which ran under the peninsula and up into the city. Pythias told my father that he had been through that tunnel: that in places it was narrow, no more than a yard across, sometimes blocked, but a redoubtable soldier would still break through. Now, you know my father had ambitions to invade Persia. Halicarnassus is the greatest seaport on the Aegean. Sooner or later it has to be taken. Philip sent spies into Halicarnassus and they searched the rocks of Nyssa. Many of them did not return, but one did: the messenger sent by Pythias, a cunning man who called himself the songster of Ephesus."

"The songster of Ephesus!" Telamon exclaimed.

"Sharp-eyed and sharp-witted. The songster found both the entrance and the way into the city. I sent him back to spy, but he never returned: he was probably captured and executed. Now, he had left me a rough map. When I arrived before Halicarnassus, Ptolemy hand-picked certain heroes from the Silver Shield-Bearers regiment under trusted officers . . ."

"So that's where Ptolemy has been?"

"Ptolemy has been very, very busy," Alexander replied. "Like a tailor threading a needle, Ptolemy has been sending men down that passageway into the city: they were to join others I'd sent before. From what I can gather, the men emerge from a dry well in the potters' quarter. Members of the anti-Persian party within the city gave them refuge. Anyway, we now have enough men in the city to pose a real threat to Memnon."

"How?" Telamon asked.

"I asked for a signal to be given once the officers believed they had sufficient men in Halicarnassus to create a diversion or provoke an uprising. Last night that signal was given: three fire arrows up into the night sky. Ptolemy is under strict orders. Once there are enough men within the city, they are to arm and dress like Macedonians and show themselves, be seen by Memnon's spies."

Telamon laughed.

"What is it?" Alexander asked.

"You said you'd take Halicarnassus like Agamemnon took Troy. Ptolemy is your Trojan horse?"

"Yes, he is!"

"Memnon must be terrified."

"Memnon will be. If he suspects there is a hostile force behind him or, even worse, that an uprising in the city could cut him off from his troops in the harbour and the Persian fleet, he'll think again." Alexander turned and stared at the tent flap. "Good, the light's already fading," he murmured.

"Why didn't you tell anyone of this?"

"Ptolemy was sworn to secrecy. No one knew except me. None of those men who went to the rocks of Nyssa will be allowed to return before the city is taken."

"Does Aristander know?"

Alexander shook his head. "Now, Telamon, you are a physician not a soldier, but put yourself in Memnon's position. Your men are all gathered on the walls around the Triple Gate. My siege engines could batter away at those walls until the fires in Hades burn out . . ."

"But if Memnon fears an uprising," Telamon interrupted, "he'd be constantly looking over his shoulder. He could turn to deal with the threat from the city?"

Alexander shook his head. "Too dangerous. Memnon would be

lashing out. He might provoke the very problem he is trying to avoid. Think, Telamon!"

"He'll launch an attack," the physician replied. "He'll try to create a breathing space, an all-out attack on your siege weapons, even your camp."

Alexander tapped Telamon gently on the cheek, imitating Aristotle's famous gesture when he was rewarding a pupil.

"Very good, learned physician. Memnon never dreamed he would have to leave those city walls for an all-out assault, Ephialtes also, but they have no choice. It's what I would do if I was in their place – a fierce bloody offensive: create carnage among the archers, burn the siege machinery, attack the camp, then retreat back into the city to deal with the problem."

"Is Ptolemy within the city?"

Alexander shook his head. "No, he's too valuable. He's under strict orders to stay at the rocks of Nyssa and see those men go in." The king pulled a face. "As you can appreciate, Telamon, I couldn't breathe a word of this to anyone else. I had to discover if the passageway could be used, if I could get enough men into the city. Can you imagine what would happen if Memnon discovered it? He'd tear that city apart. Pythias was the only person who knew all about that tunnel. He discovered it when he supervised the building of the city walls."

"And the songster of Ephesus?"

"Oh, he had family in Macedon. My mother looks after them." Alexander smiled thinly. "He was well rewarded."

"But if he was taken prisoner by the Persians?"

Alexander shrugged. "By then it was too late. He wouldn't betray me, whilst the Persians would show no mercy." Alexander pushed back the stool. "Moreover, I have friends in Halicarnassus who would take care of him. Don't worry about the songster."

Telamon studied Alexander's face. "Now you'll reap the glory, won't you, my lord?" he said quietly. "The great city of Halicarnassus, falling like a ripe apple into the hands of the brilliant general from Macedon, the besieger of cities, the stormer of gates. Your star will rise even higher. 'Can any city withstand this man?' they'll ask. 'Is he not favoured, chosen by the gods?'"

"The news will shake all of Persia and Greece." Alexander lifted his hands. "A victory just as great as the Granicus."

"Did your father tell you about Nyssa?"

"No, he didn't. He told his new wife Eurydice. When Father was murdered, Mother, of course, captured Eurydice and threatened to kill her and her newborn son unless Eurydice told her everything Philip had said. The poor girl believed the threats. She confessed all: Philip's lovers, his secrets. How, in his cups on their wedding bed, he boasted he could seize the great city of Halicarnassus."

"And Olympias told you?"

"Of course." Alexander got to his feet. "Just after she killed Eurydice and her baby son." Alexander played with the rings on his fingers. "That was not my doing. You know Mother. She never could stand a rival. She told me about the rocks of Nyssa. She said she didn't fully understand it, but I did. I knew my father's mind. When he besieged Byzantium, Philip sent a message to the citizens that he would have taken their city peacably, only their leading citizens had demanded too high a bribe."

"And what did they do?"

Alexander laughed. "They believed my father. They killed their leading citizen, and those who supported him, opened the gates, and my father took the city."

"And you'll take Halicarnassus?"

"If the gods are favourable: Memnon will strike tonight and I shall be waiting!" Alexander resumed his seat. "This time tomorrow, we may well be celebrating in the Governor's palace. Now, Telamon, continue with your studies, but before you do, tell me what else has been happening out at the Villa of Cybele."

Chapter 13

"They succeeded in slaying Ephialtes and many others,
and finally forced the rest to take refuge in the city."
    Diodorus Siculus: *Library of History*, Book XVII, Chapter 27

"Pythias, architect, to Philip, King of Macedon, health and
greetings. I thank you for your recent letters sent in our
mutual cipher. I have read and destroyed them. I urge you to
do likewise, to protect my own personal interests. Pixadorus
has now seized power in Halicarnassus and exiled Queen Ada.
He has not paid me for work I have done, he has defrauded
me in a false and vile way . . .."

T elamon stopped reading and glanced up. Darkness had fallen.
Outside, the royal pavilion was ringed by an elite unit of Foot
Companions. Only Alexander was present, seated in a throne-like
chair looted from the Persian camp after the seizure of Miletus. He
was dressed in half-armour, his gold-embossed cuirass leaning
against the leg of the chair, his ornate war helmet, with its plume
dyed red and black, on a stool: his oval shield, bearing the leaping
lion of Macedon, lay on the ground between himself and Telamon.
"A bitter man," the physician declared.
"Continue reading!" Alexander ordered.

"You ask about the fortifications of Halicarnassus." Telamon
coughed to clear his throat. "The outer walls are strong and
reinforced by towers, while the postern doors and the great
Triple Gate can easily be fortified. In the event of a siege, a huge,

251

yawning ditch would be built around the circumference of the walls in the shape of a horseshoe to impede siege machinery, battering rams and the work of any miners to burrow beneath and so weaken the foundations. Inside the walls, houses and tenements can easily be levelled to provide a military camp for the defenders, while the two citadels on either side of the harbour would be reinforced and defended by the Persian Imperial Fleet. The grasslands and countryside beyond the promontory of Halicarnassus are fruitful and lush, rich in trees, crops and flowers. It will provide good fodder for horses. There is an abundance of small streams running to the sea and a number of spring wells; such fertile countryside would support an invading army. The harbours of Halicarnassus and Myndus are held by the Persian fleet, but war triremes could be brought into the cove of Hera, a small bay some miles to the south. My own residence, the Villa of Cybele, lies on the road leading to it. It is from here that I write. I will tarry one more day before joining Queen Ada in her fortress at Alinde. I have buried my wealth here, not left it in the city."

Telamon broke off reading. "I have spoken to you, sire," he said formally, "about what I believe is the truth at the Villa of Cybele and the strange deaths which have occurred there."

Just for a few seconds Alexander allowed the fury to show in his face: he leaned forward, lower lip jutting, sandalled foot tapping the footstool as if he wished to kick it away.

"I beg you, sire . . ."

"Alexander, my name is Alexander to you, Telamon, who have done such good service."

"A company of lancers should be despatched," Telamon persisted, "to the villa immediately."

"I can't afford that." The king's hand flailed the air. "I want no disturbance in the camp tonight. The Persians may have spies out on the road: that matter will have to wait. You began the hunt, Telamon, and you can finish it. I want to know about Pythias. Continue!"

"The real weakness of Halicarnassus" – Telamon picked up the letter – "lies not in its walls, fortifications, defences or gates, but a needle-thin passage which can be found in the rocks of Nyssa, an outcrop to the west of the city, the abode of jackals, snakes and reptiles. If my deductions are correct, this needle-thin file will allow a besieger to thread men into the city. If those within discovered the passageway, it could soon be sealed. I discovered this flaw while searching for quarries, and used it myself to flee the city, well away from Pixadorus's officers."

"Stop!" Alexander scratched his chin. "Pythias's letter arrived in the spring my father was murdered." Alexander leaned back in the chair. "I can just imagine Father, belly full of wine, jumping like a goat on heat." He glanced from under his eyebrows at Telamon. "He used to dance in his bedchamber like a boy: that's probably where he told his second wife Eurydice about the rocks of Nyssa. How Philip must have dreamed of being hailed as the great besieger of cities, the general who sacked Halicarnassus. All so secretive, just like the scytale method." Alexander bit his lip. "I had also read about that, but forgot it. A piece of manuscript wrapped round a pole! How curious, how sly!"

Telamon watched him. "Do you know what Pythias says next?"

Alexander nodded. "I suspect. Continue!"

"It is my belief –" Telamon wetted his lips and throat with a goblet of wine. "It is my belief," he continued, echoing the dead Pythias's words, "that the fortifications at Halicarnassus can only be taken by stealth: without the rocks of Nyssa it would mean a siege lasting as long as that of Troy. The city can be supplied from the sea, it has an abundance of wells. Greeks figure prominently among the city population, but many have accepted Persian rule and see themselves as the natural subjects of the Great King. Now to other matters." Telamon cleared his throat nervously. "You may recall that you wished to create an alliance between the royal house of Macedon and Pixadorus, ruler of Halicarnassus. You offered your son Arridhaeus as a possible husband for Pixadorus's kinswoman: unbeknown to you, Pixadorus also received an offer of a marriage

253

alliance from your other son Alexander, the offspring of Olympias. I communicated this news to you only to find that no less a person than Olympias had already informed you."

"What?"

Alexander sprang to his feet, kicking over the footstool. He advanced on Telamon, hand going to the Egyptian dagger pushed into the cord on his belt.

"Alexander, I am not Olympias, I am Telamon!"

Alexander raised a clenched fist, arm quivering, a muscle high in his cheek twitching. Alexander wasn't staring at Telamon but at a point above his head, lips moving, uttering a litany of silent curses.

"So that's how Father got to know!" Alexander returned to his chair. "I have always wondered that, Telamon." He was in one of his most dangerous moods, not a dramatic, hot rage but that cold, silent fury so reminiscent of Olympias.

"Philip had divorced Olympias," Alexander explained. "He ignored me, and hoped to marry the poor half-wit Arridhaeus to a princess of Halicarnassus." Alexander threw his dagger to the floor. "I thought my days in Macedon were over. I sent one of my best agents, an actor called Thessalus, to negotiate with Pixadorus."

"Why?" Telamon asked.

"I thought I'd have to flee Macedon," Alexander replied. "If I wished to conquer my own empire, what better place to have than Halicarnassus? Father discovered my secret embassy. Thessalus fled to Corinth. Ptolemy, Hephaestion and the rest were exiled and my father gave me a lecture, cruel and cold, in which he threatened that if I ever crossed him again, I would be sent to a place where I could no longer trouble him. I told Mother all about it."

"And a few weeks later Philip was killed?"

Alexander stared back.

"You mustn't blame Olympias," Telamon tried to soothe the king.

"Why not?"

"Can't you see?" Telamon declared. "She had plans of her own for Philip. She did not want you to become some minor princeling of a Greek city in Persia. Macedon was your strength, so in Macedon you had to stay. Olympias had her own plans for Philip, Eurydice and their

254

baby son." Telamon tapped the letter. "As you say, Philip didn't have time to translate this before Olympias struck."

"Oh, yes," Alexander replied, as if speaking to himself. "Mother struck fast and furious like one of her snakes. She had Eurydice and her child executed and their bodies burnt. Every day she mixes a little of their ashes with her wine, the product of the most fragrant vineyards of Greece. No wonder Mother always claimed that, if you wait long enough by the riverside, you will see the corpses of your enemies float by. In her eyes, revenge is sweetest when it is full, long and lasting." He gestured angrily. "And the rest of the letter?"

"These startling developments," Telamon continued, "were much discussed by Pixadorus and his council. The question was posed: did Philip object to offering his own son Alexander because of rumours that Alexander was not his true offspring but an illegitimate by-blow?"

Telamon heard the king's sharp intake of breath. "Your envoy replied by saying that Alexander was your own true son and the offspring of a god." He glanced up. "That's what you wanted, wasn't it? That's what you were searching for all along? At a time when Philip had divorced your mother, when you were no longer considered the legitimate king-in-waiting, when he had taken another wife and begotten another son, Philip still confesses you are his true son."

"But what does he mean by an offspring of a god?"

Telamon, knowing how dangerous this path was, remained silent.

"What did Father mean?" Alexander sat straight up in the chair, his eerie-coloured eyes showed myriad emotions: pleasure, pride, relief, satisfaction, curiosity.

"Did you suspect all this?" Telamon asked.

"Philip's messenger died in the bloodbath following his murder, Olympias saw to that. I didn't know what to believe."

"And this," Telamon picked up Pythias's letter, "began to provoke those nightmares. You expected it to be translated for the whole world to read that Alexander was not the true son of Philip."

"The rest of the letter?" Alexander demanded sharply.

"I intend to despatch this letter to you" – Telamon returned to the Pythian Manuscript – "and flee to Queen Ada's court. The Villa of Cybele will lie empty. My servants have already gone. My arguments with Pixadorus are now public knowledge. I cannot wait to become his forced guest. All now lies quiet as I write to you: I have more trust in Philip of Macedon than those whom I have served so well. Health and greetings. Farewell."

Telamon put the manuscript down. "Everything else," he said, "is just a fiction: stories put out by Pythias that his letter could tell you which part of the fortifications were weak, when in fact it contained even greater mischief, a more deadly secret. Apparently he must have made a copy and taken it with him to Queen Ada's court. Pamenes discovered it and transcribed a version for his masters."

Alexander lifted his hand as a sign for silence. "Philip is dead! Pythias is dead!" the king murmured. "And Halicarnassus is betrayed. Tonight, or tomorrow night, Memnon must make his move. He will be urged on by Ephialtes, who is hot-headed and impetuous. In truth, they have no choice: they must come out and fight." He walked over, hand outstretched for Telamon to clasp. "You did well, physician."

"I'll pay homage to Pamenes's shade."

"Aye." Alexander waved his hand. "And I'll seize Halicarnassus and tell Mother what I know. You'd best get some sleep, Telamon, but not too deeply."

The physician had hardly returned to his own quarters when he heard the war horns braying, raising the alarm, the shouts of officers, the sounds of running feet. Cassandra groaned and rolled over in her sleep. Telamon seized his weapons, a battered helmet, cuirass, shield and sword. He looped the belt over his shoulder, ignoring Cassandra's muffled calls to be careful. Telamon knew he had no choice but to go. He was a member of the royal household: where the king went, particularly into danger, Telamon had to follow.

Alexander was already busy arming, Hephaestion and Seleucus likewise. Other commanders were gathering, most of them prepared, as Alexander had issued secret orders for the camp to go on a war footing. Staff officers milled about. More torches were lit. Horses neighed and skittered, catching their riders' excitement. War horns and trumpets bellowed through the night. The whole camp was being aroused.

Telamon mounted his own horse, and circled by the royal bodyguard, they left the enclosure. The Macedonian units, shield-bearers, phalanx men, companies of archers, the lightly armed peltasts, the mercenaries, all being shoved and pushed by their officers, streamed across the camp defences, trampling down the palisade, using it to cross the makeshift ditch, heading like a great arrow to where the fighting already raged. Alexander and his household, roughly clearing a path, left the grasslands and rode onto the rocky peninsula. The night air was rent by the hideous clash of battle, the bray of trumpets, the clatter of weapons. Fire scorched the night sky, the pungent smell of smoke curled every-where. The walls of Halicarnassus came into view, battlements lighted; the area around the Triple Gate had become the battle-ground. Siege engines, mantlets and pent sheds were all ablaze, their flames turning the night into day.

Alexander reined in. The battle had swung on its axis. The Persians had broken out of a side gate, both horse and foot, and were busy trying to cut the Macedonians off, pin them up against the ditch and slaughter them. They had already driven Alexander's troops back, setting fire to the machinery while a fresh Persian force, both foot and cavalry, Greek and Persian, had emerged from another gate further down the wall to complete the encirclement.

"How many men?" Alexander cried. "How many men did we have here?"

"About three thousand!" an officer shouted back.

The Persians, so intent on annilihating the trapped Macedonians, were unaware of the king's arrival from the grasslands. Alexander had gambled, and was now hostage to Tyche, the Goddess of Fortune.

The enemy force were pressing in on either side, doing their best to complete the encirclement. Alexander sat like a statue, watching his men being slaughtered, his siege weapons totally destroyed. In the darkness Telamon could hear the rest of the Macedonian army marching into battle. He looked over his shoulder; the troops seemed like ghosts thronging through the darkness, the Macedonian battle line spreading out like a crescent, the usual formation – cavalry on either wing, the lightly armed foot, mercenaries, regiments of Shield-Bearers and, at its heart, the great Macedonian phalanx, foot soldiers armed with their small shields and eighteen-foot sarissas. Trumpets called, but the Persians, locked in battle, seemed unaware of the force now assembling in the darkness behind. No one had escaped through their ring of steel, no officer or engineer to take news back to the Macedonian camp.

"If we hadn't expected these," Alexander turned to speak to Hephaestion, "they would have massacred everyone here and attacked our camp." He drew his sword and held it up. "Eynalius for Macedon!"

The war cry was repeated across the rocky peninsula to cheering and the blasting of trumpets. Telamon, seated on his horse, pushed and shoved by those around, felt a trickle of fear. Still the Persians were unaware.

"Eynalius for Macedon!"

The war cry was again repeated. Alexander's own trumpeters had been summoned up. These now proclaimed the order for the general advance, long, heart-chilling calls. The night was transformed: no longer cool breezes, a starlit sky, a moon riding like a ship at anchor, but hard ground littered with corpses, great fires raging, consuming Alexander's dreadful machines of war, the press of bodies, the shrieks and cries of the wounded. Telamon expected the Persian line to turn to face this new threat, or even break off and retreat. However, even as the Macedonian line advanced, the Triple Gates of the city were thrown open, a harsh, grating sound which brought the Macedonian line to a halt. Through the gateway poured squadron after squadron of Persian cavalry, riding to intervene between the Macedonians and the fierce fighting taking place under the walls. Behind these, advancing at a run, a mass of armed foot, Memnon's Greek mercenaries, easy to distinguish with their rounded shields and plumed helmets. Alexander had no choice but to pause at this new threat. The Persian horse galloped across the rocky ground, dividing into two, allowing the centre between them to be rapidly filled with phalanx after phalanx of Greek mercenaries.

The attack had been well plotted. There would now be two battles. To win, Alexander had to break through this new force: his officers were muttering why had he delayed, giving Memnon time to deploy. Telamon knew the reason: Black Cleitus had drilled it into them time and time again. Philip had come down to the Groves of Mieza and described all the intricacies and subtleties of such a battle. Alexander had to be sure that this sally from the city walls was the last.

Memnon's manoeuvre was hardly completed when the king raised his sword, bright and flashing in the roaring firelight. The trumpeters took up the signal, a long bray of defiance. The Macedonian line advanced. The intervening ground between themselves and Memnon's force was too narrow for a full gallop, but the Macedonians, led by Alexander, hit it in the centre. The king, surrounded by his companions, Black Cleitus his bodyguard as usual on his right, Hephaestion to his left, began their bloody work. Telamon felt as if he were rushing through a nightmare. Screams and yells, horses and riders crashing down. Javelins and spears being flung through the air. Here and there a rider received a direct hit, or a horse, stung to fury by some barb, bucked and reared, throwing its rider.

Telamon didn't know how the battle was proceeding on either flank. He could hear the roar, the clatter of battle, the clash of arms. Alexander and the royal party in front, like an arrowhead, bit deeper and deeper into the enemy. Telamon, trapped inside the royal circle, had no choice but to follow. He had experienced the same before and, as he had confessed to Cassandra, did little fighting. If that circle was broken, Alexander's power and legend were shattered.

The Macedonian army was moving forward, in front of Telamon flashing steel, the clash of sword against shield, the bloody push and shove of hand-to-hand fighting. Alexander and his party were now attacking the elite corps of Memnon's forces, Greek against Greek, their fighting fury fed not only by the prospect of money or glory, but in settling blood feuds and grievances. At one point the royal line did break. Four Greek hoplites, armour glistening with blood, broke through, only to be surrounded and cut down by the royal bodyguard.

Telamon could understand Alexander's tactics. He must break this Persian threat and drive back those slaughtering his men near the ditch. The walls of Halicarnassus drew closer. Telamon, looking up from under the rim of his helmet, could glimpse small figures on the battlements, silhouetted by the firelight. He was distracted by a clamour to his right. They were no longer flanked by Macedonians but Memnon's mercenaries! A section of Alexander's army had now given way in the face of such fury. The king himself was being forced to retreat, falling back lest he be cut off. Alexander was helmetless, his blond-red hair matted with sweat, legs and arms splattered with blood. He was screaming at Hephaestion, who extricated himself from the fighting. For a while the Macedonian line was on the defensive, being slowly inched back. Telamon lost all sense of what was happening. He was trapped in a dense crush which swayed backwards and forwards. Now and again he would look down and glimpse the unseeing eyes of a corpse, a severed arm still clutching a sword. Men writhed in agony, only to be crushed as Alexander's cavalry was driven back. The din of battle sounded like a drum, staring faces, stricken eyes. Men wrapped up in the frenzy of killing and blood-letting. The Macedonians' arrowhead was being thrown back, buckling in on itself. Here and there a Persian broke through, or a cluster of Memnon's mercenaries. It was hack and cut, swords slashing, biting deep. Telamon fought to remain mounted; his horse, sure-footed, did not panic. The press was so intense, in some places soldiers were unable to lift their arms. Trumpets brayed. A great roar went up.

"Eynalius! Eynalius! Eynalius for Macedon!"

For a few seconds the whole battle was frozen; men turned to stone, like a frieze of a battle on a temple wall. Again the roar. The intense pressure began to give, like a river breaking its dam. Men were moving away. Alexander was leading the advance. Telamon felt as if a huge wall had crumbled. The space between himself and his companions grew. They were going forward and then stopped, the Macedonians turning to the left and right. Telamon's heart sank at the line of men, bloody and battered, staring at him, but they weren't the enemy; they were what was left of Alexander's besieging force trapped by the Persians. They had broken through! The Persians and Memnon's Greeks were shattered and were fighting their way back, desperate to reach the gates and gain the security of the city.

Telamon stared to his right and caught his breath at the awesome beauty of an entire phalanx of Macedonian pikemen, sarissas down like the quills of a porcupine. He recognized their colours and the armour. They were the veterans, the Old Guard, the heart of Alexander's army, Philip's old soldiers, who always served as the rearguard. They must have seen the chaos and advanced, brushing aside their own men. Telamon found he couldn't stop trembling. He felt sick. He was aware of the soaring walls of Halicarnassus, the fires still burning fiercely, the crack of timber and the heat from the flames, the billowing wood smoke swirling like a mist to cover the iron stench of blood.

The battle had now divided. The Macedonians were pursuing the Persian army, involved in fierce hand-to-hand fighting before the Triple Gate. Memnon's mercenaries were making a brave stand, but the rest of the Persian force poured across the makeshift bridge under the soaring gatehouse into the safety of the city. Telamon pulled his horse away. An arrow whipped his face. He rode back to where the Macedonian battle line had originally stood.

Telamon gazed up at the orange glow in the night sky: fires had started beyond the walls. The clatter and screech of battle was all around. To the right, the Persians had been able to clear the postern gate and close it securely behind them, but the Triple Gate proved a more difficult task. Memnon's rearguard was now on the bridge. Telamon watched in horror as the great gates, black against the night sky, edged closer and closer together. They were almost shut when a hideous crack sounded. The gates closed, trapping those outside even as the bridge on which they were fighting gave way beneath them. Telamon closed his eyes. Memnon's rearguard fell into the ditch, trapped like wolves in a pit.

The Macedonian pikemen retreated. The Cretan archers ran

261

forward, rank upon rank. They knelt on the rim of the ditch and poured in volley after volley of arrows. The nightmare screams drifted across. Some of the more resolute defenders now manned the tower and walls on either side of the Triple Gate, but the hundreds of men lost in the ditch were a gory sacrifice for the failure of Memnon's plan. More Cretan archers were running up. Javelin men joined in. Telamon stared around the battlefield. The dead lay in heaps on the rocky ground which stretched in front of the walls. Here and there a man moaned and groaned. Fear-crazed horses tried to rise, legs kicking, heads twisting, like monsters trying to emerge from the ground. The Macedonian battle line was already falling back, men stopping to slit the throat of a comrade or a fallen enemy. Orderlies were running forward with stretchers. Telamon dismounted swiftly. He staggered across the battlefield, slipping and slithering on pools of blood. A hand touched his ankle. A Persian lay there, eyes staring, body trembling. Telamon crouched down and loosened the man's grip even as the Persian gave one last shudder and his head lay still, eyes glassy and unseeing. Other men were crying out. Telamon stopped by a young Cretan archer crouching on all fours, and helped him to his feet. He put his arm round the man and helped him over to a group of stretcher-bearers. As he did so he recalled his father's words: "Always remember, Telamon – in the end, for the wounded, there is really no difference between a battle lost and a battle won."

Telamon gave the man over to the orderlies and staggered back, searching the mounds of bodies for signs of life. The cries now dinned in his ears. Men with hideous wounds to belly and chest, cried desperately for water. A babble of voices, different tongues, and all around the shattered panoply of battle: helmets and shields, greaves, shattered swords and daggers, broken bows and lances. Pinpricks of torchlight appeared. Macedonians were looking for comrades or for plunder. Now and again a scream would ring out as some unfortunate was found and dealt with. Telamon found two Persians shivering beside the corpse of a horse. He helped them to their feet, pushing them towards the Macedonian lines, gesturing that they hold their hands forward as a sign of surrender. The two men had hardly walked a few paces when there was a whistle of arrows and both crumpled down. They had hardly hit the ground when the Cretan archers came loping out of the darkness, like wolves searching the corpses for plunder. Telamon could take no more. He sat down on the ground and put his face in his hands.

"What's the matter, Telamon? Soft as ever?"

The physician took his hands away and glared up at Black Cleitus, seated on his great war horse next to Alexander.

"And I suppose you've had your day, blood-supper!" Telamon shouted back.

Cleitus laughed, hawked and spat in Telamon's direction. Alexander urged his horse forward, his armour dented, splattered with mud and blood, his face bruised and blackened by the smoke. "Come on, Telamon. What on earth are you doing there? Get up, man!"

Telamon seized the king's outstretched hand and got to his feet. Alexander gathered his reins in one hand and, gently holding Telamon's with the other, led his party off the battlefield into a circle of torches where makeshift headquarters had been set up. The king dismounted, shouting for wine. Pages ran up with earthenware beakers and bulging wineskins. Telamon still felt unsteady so he sat back on the ground. Alexander left him alone as his commanders reported in: Seleucus, Amyntas, Hephaestion. Even Ptolemy made an appearance, his face brown as a nut, cheeky as a monkey, eyes glittering. He gently cuffed Telamon on the back of the head.

"The battle is ours, the city is ours, physician!"

Telamon swore about the gates still being closed. Ptolemy whispered that he should wait and see. Hephaestion brought across a beaker of wine and helped Telamon to his feet. The horses were led away and Alexander, one hand resting on the shoulder of a page, was staring hungrily across at the Triple Gate.

"I want the keenest scouts deployed!" he ordered. "They are to watch the battlements!"

"Why?" Cleitus demanded.

"Because in a short while they are going to be deserted." Alexander gulped at the wine. He was about to continue when there was a shout, and a group of Foot Companions came hurrying across carrying a bloody bundle between them. They laid this down at Alexander's feet and threw open the flaps of the cloak. Alexander and his companions gathered round. The corpse was battered; a deep sword cut had sliced the left side of the man's face, removing teeth and mouth, and part of the jaw was missing.

"Ephialtes!" Alexander exclaimed. He knelt down and touched the man's blood-soaked hair. "Where was he found?"

"Near the bridge."

"A warrior's death," Alexander murmured, getting to his feet. "I wish I had a man like that with me. But, because of Thebes, a blood feud existed, life for life."

Ephialtes was dressed in a tunic. His cuirass, greaves and kilt had apparently been plundered, along with his helmet, shield and sandals.

"Dress him in the armour of a warrior!" Alexander looked at the fingers of the dirty, soiled corpse. "Have his body washed in oil. Give him a hero's funeral!"

The guards picked up their grisly burden and carried him off into the night. Alexander returned to stare at the fortifications. "You see." He pointed.

They followed his direction. Already the lights were disappearing. A strange, silent emptiness had descended, shattered now and again by the cries of the wounded or the neighs of a stricken horse.

"Hephaestion! Cleitus! Order the battle line to be assembled!" He turned and caught Telamon's arm. "You, physician, go back to the camp. Drink some wine and have some sleep. Tomorrow, just after dawn, take a company of scouts, go back to the Villa of Cybele, and do what you have to."

Telamon murmured his thanks: he staggered off into the darkness even as Alexander began to shout for his heralds and trumpeters.

Memnon sat at the foot of an acacia tree in the gardens of the Governor of Halicarnassus, his bloody, dented armour piled beside him. The Rhodian, busy with a sponge, was wiping the sweat and dirt from his face and body. Now and again he would clutch a cup proffered by a staff officer, drink carefully and thrust it back. Orontobates, squatting near him, had already changed. He had dispensed with all the finery of a Persian commander and was dressed in a simple quilted jacket and leggings; his shield, sword and a Persian cap lay on the ground beside him. The Governor's palace was a blaze of light. Scribes and clerks were already burning precious manuscripts, records, journals, anything they couldn't carry.

"Ephialtes is dead." Memnon tried to keep his voice level. "He was retreating with me back towards the bridge when he and his officers were surrounded by a group of Shield-Bearers."

He glared across at Orontobates. The Persian seemed to have aged in a matter of hours: his fine, fleshy sheen had disappeared, his cheeks were furrowed, his eyes wild and staring. He, too, had fought bitterly.

"All is lost," the Persian whispered.

"We could still man the walls," Memnon retorted. "Hold fast."

But, even as he spoke, a messenger came loping across the grass, squatted down and whispered in Orontobates's ear. The Governor got to his feet, hands splayed. Memnon watched as he strode up and down beating his fist against his thigh. All across the parkland men were recovering from that bloody onslaught near the Triple Gate. Already some of them were slipping away into the night, and Memnon couldn't blame them. If the Macedonians broke through the Persians could ask for terms, but Alexander had issued a proclamation that any Greek found in arms against him should expect little mercy.

"How many men do we have left?" He turned to the staff officer.

"A few hundred, sir."

The man hadn't bothered to clean himself, his face still caked in dried mud and blood. Memnon felt guilty, and offered him his cup. "Drink," Memnon urged, and gestured towards the food baskets. "Renew your strength. Do you wish to go as well?"

The man shook his head. "I'll stay with you, sir, life or death. None of your officers will leave the standard of Memnon of Rhodes." The man sighed wearily. "We gambled and we lost. Next time we gamble, we might win!"

Memnon patted him on the shoulder. "Fill your belly," he urged.

265

"Tell the men to do likewise and gather their arms, take whatever plunder they can find." He knew what Orontobates had been told: the Persian still walked up and down muttering to himself.

"Macedonians are in the city, aren't they?" Memnon demanded, his voice cracked.

Orontobates nodded. "At least a regiment of Shield-Bearers."

"Will they block our passage if we come on?" Memnon demanded.

"I don't think so." Orontobates shook his head. "Their officers will be hosted and dined by the leading democrats, the leaders of the mob. They'll try and seize the most important buildings: the treasury, the temples, anything the Macedonian will need."

Memnon felt a surge of rage within him. "How?" he demanded, getting to his feet, snapping his fingers at his officers to help him arm. The cold night air bit at his sweaty skin. Memnon struggled to put his tunic over his head, then raised his arms to allow the cuirass and backplate to be fastened on.

"I don't know." Orontobates spread his hands and stared up at the sky. "That damnable Pythian Manuscript. There is no weakness in the walls, but there must be a secret passageway into the city." He threw out a hand. "Probably out there in the peninsula, an underground river which had dried up."

"The Pythian Manuscript!" Memnon snarled. "Our Trojan horse! We were tricked, my Lord Orontobates, well and truly deceived!" He glared towards the palace and recalled the corpse of the songster of Ephesus and the Eunuch's body hanging from its noose.

"Well, if the Macedonian wants the city, let him have it!" he rasped.

"Will you sue for terms?" Orontobates walked over and stretched out his hands. "My Lord Memnon, I am with you life or death. What are we to do?"

"Fire the city!" Memnon ordered. "Let's burn it as we go. Orontobates, some of your men can act as incendiaries. Let them disguise themselves as citizens. They must do as much damage as they can." He scratched an unshaven cheek.

"Fires have already started," Orontobates declared. "The work of the Macedonians."

266

"Well, let's finish what they've begun." Memnon called his heralds over. War horns and trumpets shrilled. The entire garden came to life: men gathering their arms, searching out officers, assembling in their units. Orontobates issued an order for the cavalry to create a path before them.

"We'll fall back on the harbour!" Orontobates shouted. "Fortify its two citadels and, the gods willing, hold out till the Great King sends more troops!"

His words sounded hollow. He turned in alarm as Memnon drew his sword from its scabbard.

"My Lord?"

Memnon gestured at the palace. "I have unfinished business."

The Rhodian strode across the grass surrounded by his officers; they ran up the steps into the hallway. Already servants were fleeing, arms full of whatever loot they had pillaged. Orontobates also followed, escorted by his officers. Memnon walked along the marble passages, fury boiling within him at the splendour he would have to leave.

"Burn it!" he shouted. "Don't let the Macedonians sleep in our beds!"

His companions obeyed: oil lamps were overturned, cresset torches pulled from the walls and thrown into chambers. At the end of one passageway Memnon stopped and stared sadly at the Governor's cheetah lying in a pool of blood, its throat cut.

"Who did that?" Orontobates pushed himself forward. "By the Lord of Light!" He knelt down and gently stroked the paw of his favourite pet. "He did no harm to anyone. They have even taken his chain."

They hurried on. Memnon reached the steps leading down to the dungeon and clattered down. The guards were all gone, the cell doors open, the passageway empty, but the gaoler Cerberus and four of his turnkeys sat sprawled on stools in the torture chamber at the far end. They had drunk deeply, and didn't even bother to rise as Memnon entered.

"My lord." Cerberus leaned against the wall. "I understand a great disaster has befallen us."

Memnon seethed at the impudence in the man's fat, slobbery

face. Behind him his officers gathered, puzzled why their master had brought them here.

"Look at his neck," Orontobates whispered. "My cheetah's chain!"

Memnon noticed the silver circlet round Cerberus's neck, the rest of the chain hidden beneath his sweat-stained tunic. The turnkey followed his gaze. "I found the cheetah myself," he slurred. "It was dead, so I took this."

"The songster of Ephesus." Memnon took a step forward. "He could have told us so much. You silenced his tongue lest he confess everything. In truth he was dead before Lord Mithra arrived here. You are in the pay of the rebels in the city, aren't you?"

Cerberus staggered to his feet, face all alarmed. One of his companions reached out, searching for his sword lying on the floor beside him.

"You are in the pay of the rebels," Memnon repeated. "You fired the Governor's summerhouse and, while everyone was distracted, you and your companions hanged the Eunuch and burnt his manuscripts."

"That's ridiculous!"

"No, it's the truth."

Memnon stepped forward. Cerberus went for his sword even as his companions sprang to their feet. One lunged at Memnon with a dagger. Memnon knocked him aside with a fist: he lunged across the table and thrust his sword deep into Cerberus's chest. The turnkey gagged and clutched at the blade, eyes popping, mouth wide in fear and pain. Memnon thrust again and stood back. Cerberus staggered forward then collapsed. The rest of his companions stood frozen with terror. Memnon clicked his fingers.

"Kill them all!" he ordered.

Turning on his heel, he strode out of the chamber. Behind him he could hear the screams and groans of the turnkeys as they were seized by his officers and summarily executed. Memnon didn't care. He had lost another battle, and tomorrow would be another day.

EPILOGUE

―――――◦◦◦―――――

"Memnon . . . assembled his generals . . . held a meeting and decided to abandon the city."
Diodorus Siculus: *Library of History*, Book XVII, Chapter 27

The slaughter at the Villa of Cybele began just after dawn. The
cooks and scullions were the first to die. A girl out at the well,
drawing up the leather bucket, heard a sound and stared in horror: a
masked figure, dressed in a mantle, its hood pulled up, stood in the
portico, a cruel barbed arrow notched to his bow. She let the rope
slither and turned to run, but the arrow pierced her throat. She
crashed to the cobbles, hands slightly shuddering, then lay still, her
blood mixing with the dirt. The cooks and scullions in the
kitchens, four in all, were heavy-eyed with sleep, yawning and
stretching as they tried to fire the coals and begin the day's tasks.
They were glad the villa was now deserted, fewer mouths to feed.
The killer struck as fast as a plunging kestrel. One minute the
doorway was open, allowing in the grey light of dawn; the next it
was blocked by the archer, who loosed two arrows; each found its
deadly mark before the rest realized what horrors were upon them.
The baker died stretching for a cleaver on a table. The young spit
boy tried to open the rear door and was pinned there by the force
of the arrow. The killer stared round, eyes gleaming behind his
mask. He inspected each of the corpses before counting the
remaining arrows in the well-packed quiver. He crossed the room,
picked up a wine jug, sipped from it and poured the rest over the
smouldering charcoal.

Cherolos was in his chamber, kneeling on a cushion, hands
extended, eyes fixed on his Serpent Goddess. He found it difficult

to pray. He dearly wished to be back at the court of Queen Ada. What did he have to do with manuscripts which held secrets he couldn't understand? Those scribes who kept to themselves, muttering and talking, whose whispered conversations he found so difficult to eavesdrop on? Cherolos's task was to spy on them, and he had to admit ruefully that he had been a failure. He had been clumsy. That sharp-eyed physician, with his red-haired bitch who followed him everywhere, had soon discovered that he had entered Pamenes's chamber and taken those saddlebags. Ah well, Cherolos sighed to himself, the physician had gone to join the fighting men. Perhaps he would never return. Perhaps none of them would, and Cherolos would steal back to Alinde to resume his very boring but comfortable life in its gloomy halls and galleries.

He heard a sound in the passage outside, and wondered who was stirring so early. One of the scullions had been sent to the Macedonian camp in the early hours. There were rumours of a great Macedonian victory; that the defenders of Halicarnassus had tried to break out, only to be repulsed. The scribes had been very mournful at the news. They had failed to translate the Pythian Manuscript, and now it seemed their labours would no longer be necessary. Solan, in fact, had been furious: he suspected that the physician had learnt Pamenes's secrets and had already won the race to unlock the mysteries of the Pythian cipher. Bessus, too, had acted disappointed, long-faced and mournful. Sarpedon had just laughed. The mercenary was eager to leave the villa and enjoy the rich pickings when the Macedonians entered the city.

Again the creak in the passageway outside. Cherolos peevishly got to his feet and opened the door. The arrow struck him hard in the chest and sent him crashing back. His killer followed quickly in, kicking the door shut behind him with his heel. He leaned down. Cherolos stared up, fighting for breath, trying to understand the hideous pains in his chest and neck. The sudden swiftness of the attack, the blood bubbling in his throat, those eyes watching him curiously as if they wanted to catch the last glow of life in him. Cherolos shuddered and lay still.

The killer moved on, slipping down the stairs into the andron where the two Macedonian guards, who had drunk deeply from the wine jugs given to them the previous evening, still lay sprawled on the floor, lost in their wine-sodden dreams. The assassin drew his dagger and quickly cut both their throats. A killing blow, like a farmer would slit a lamb's gullet: knife slicing through skin, windpipe and artery, blood bubbling out. The men jerked in their death throes. The killer watched and waited till they lay still.

"Is there anyone there?"

He smiled behind his mask at the sound of Solan's peevish voice.

"Is there anyone there? Guards! Why is the house so silent?"

The killer stepped out of the andron. Solan stood at the end of the passage, his back to him. The bow was slung, an arrow notched. The killer braced himself. Solan heard and turned, but it was too late. The arrow caught him in the chest, sending him skittering back against the wall. The killer strode down the passageway, stared down at the old man's face, the look of surprise frozen there. He kicked the corpse and turned towards the door. The daylight was strengthening. He had done what he could.

The sun had risen by the time Telamon reached the Villa of Cybele. He and Cassandra had snatched a few hours' sleep before being rudely awoken by the captain of the Prodomoi, the lightly armed troops who acted as the skirmishers, advance guard and scouts for Alexander's army.

"We have to go now, sir," the officer insisted, staring appreciatively at Cassandra, also struggling awake. Telamon had told him to wait outside while both of them hastily dressed and ate the hard bread and rather wizened fruit left in their ration baskets by the quartermasters. The captain of scouts was elated by what had happened during the night: he was impatient to take Telamon to the villa and return to join the rest of the army. Alexander had now entered the city of Halicarnassus, and was desperately trying to save much of it from the fires Memnon and Orontobates had started.

When Telamon and Cassandra emerged from their quarters they found most of the camp deserted. Many of the tents and pavilions had been taken down, including those in the royal enclosure. The altar had been dismantled, and the palisade which separated the king's tent from the rest of the camp had been flattened.

"Oh yes, sir, they're all in the city now," the captain had observed. "Couldn't believe our eyes. One minute the battlements were defended, the next we were pounding at the gates with our rams and no one resisted." He coughed as a gust of smoke swept by them.

"And the fire?" Cassandra asked.

"Burning merrily," the captain replied. "They fired the Governor's palace and every building they passed."

"And Memnon?"

"He and the Persian Governor have retreated to a fortress in the harbour. Rumour has it they'll be allowed to sit there and rot."

Telamon fastened his cloak and nodded. Cassandra went back into their tent, packing her bag to "protect", as she put it, her precious possessions from thieving Macedonians.

"They won't stay in the citadel long," the captain chattered on. "Now we have the city, the Persians will have to leave the harbour."

"And the citizens?" Telamon asked.

"Oh, the city was taken safely. The king ordered no looting, or harm against anyone. The only people who were to be attacked were those carrying arms against us, but they've all disappeared. But come on, sir, the sun is strengthening. Oh, sir, the king left you this."

Telamon unrolled the scroll. Its message was short and terse.

"Alexander, King, to Telamon the Physician, health and greetings. You are to return to the Villa of Cybele and do what you have to. Take whatever action is necessary but bring me the traitor's head."

The bottom of the scroll was stamped with the royal purple seal bearing Alexander's personal insignia.

The captain offered his wineskin. "Do you want a drink, sir? Or your woman?"

"I am not his woman!" Cassandra snapped, coming out of the tent. "What shall we do with our saddlebags?"

The captain sighed, went in, and returned carrying both. Telamon offered to help.

"No, sir. The king told me to look after you."

272

They left the battered enclosure. A squadron of scouts was waiting; they had taken a leading part in the invasion of the city, and their faces and arms were still blackened by fire and smoke. Some wore expensive jewellery round their necks and wrists: Telamon suspected they had honoured the king's order not to pillage more in the breach than in the observance. Cat-calls and whistles greeted Cassandra's appearance. The captain drew his sword and yelled for silence. The men turned away sheepishly, as if interested in the harness of their horses. A pack mule was brought and loaded with their baggage. Telamon's horse from the night before was ready.

"You look better than I feel," Telamon whispered to it.

Cassandra was given a small pony, one of the shaggy, sure-footed breeds. Different scouts offered to lead it by the reins, but Cassandra snatched these up and glowered back at them. They left the camp and made good time. Telamon slouched in the saddle, Cassandra trotting behind. The captain chattered like a monkey about the glories of Halicarnassus, how pleased the king had been that the great Mausoleum had been saved. He was still talking when they entered the villa courtyard and saw the corpse lying by the well.

The captain fell silent and reined in. The scouts immediately formed a defensive ring around Telamon, while others ran into the house and began a thorough search. Telamon heard shouts and yells. One of the scouts emerged.

"No danger, sir!" he shouted. "You'd best come in!"

Inside, the grisly finds were everywhere: corpses slumped in the kitchens, the fire doused, the two guards with their throats cut. Cherolos lying twisted in his chamber. Solan, his hands still clutching the arrow which had pierced his chest. Telamon felt the corpses: they were cold, the blood congealing, already attracting flies and ants. Cassandra, white-faced, sat down at the foot of the stairs.

"Corpses and blood," she muttered.

"What happened, sir?" the captain demanded.

"I don't know."

"Persians?"

Telamon shook his head. "I doubt it. I think . . ." He broke off as he heard shouts in the gallery above. The scout returned, pushing Gentius before him. The actor was dishevelled, dirty and unshaven, his eyes heavy with sleep. Telamon could smell the wine on his breath, and noticed the stains on the grey tunic he wore. Gentius took one look at Solan's corpse, the thick pool of blood, and slumped to his knees.

"And another one, sir."

Sarpedon came downstairs, his face all bloody. He was nursing his wrists, his hand went to his scalp: his cropped hair, just above his left ear, was stiff with dried blood. He had a cut to his face and a blow to the side of his mouth.

"Bring them to the loom room!" Telamon ordered.

Once there, he ordered wine to be brought, and whatever food could be found in the kitchen. Sarpedon and Gentius sat slumped at the table. When the food and wine was served Gentius ate greedily. Sarpedon, as if in a daze, sipped at his cup and gnawed at a piece of bread.

"They are all dead," Telamon began. He paused as Cassandra came into the room, followed by the captain of the guard, who went to the far end of the table and sat between Sarpedon and Gentius.

"My men are outside, sir. I understand one of the scribes is missing."

"Bessus." Sarpedon looked up blearily. "Bessus has fled, hasn't he?"

"The only people remaining, sir" – the captain gestured to either side – "are these two. The rest are all dead, killed by an arrow or had their throats cut."

"What happened?" Telamon asked.

"Life as usual," Sarpedon replied. "We knew you had left a guard on him – " he gestured at Gentius. "Solan became curious about what was happening in the city. We heard rumours and despatched one of the kitchen boys. He came back with the news that a great battle had taken place and the city had fallen, so we decided to celebrate. Everyone, even Gentius, drank and ate." Sarpedon shrugged, his hand going to the knock on his head. "And then we went to bed."

"What hour was this?"

"Oh, it must have been about the third watch. I'm a light sleeper. I drank almost as much as everyone else did. I got up to relieve myself. The next moment, someone struck me on the back of the head. I turned." Sarpedon gestured at the bruise on the corner of his mouth. "He hit me again. I remember falling. When I regained consciousness, I was in the corner of my room, hands and feet tied. I kept losing consciousness. I heard screams. When my mind cleared, the scouts were cutting my bonds and dragging me to my feet."

"And you, Gentius?"

"Is everybody dead?" The actor gazed mournfully down the table. "Has everyone died, like Demerata?"

"They have been murdered!" Telamon snapped. "I wonder why they didn't kill you?"

"I was frightened," Gentius slurred. "Solan said not to worry about you and your orders, that I could join the celebrations, but I am worried, I see things. I am frightened of Pamenes and Demerata visiting me." His fingers went to his lips, and he gazed up at the ceiling.

"He's losing his wits," Cassandra whispered.

"But why weren't you killed?"

"I drew the bolt on my door. I drew the bolt," he repeated, "and fell asleep. I woke this morning. I went out onto the gallery, but I felt cold so I went back to bed."

"That's where we found him, snoring like a pig," the captain declared. "Oh, by the way, sir, a horse has been taken from the stables."

"Bessus!" Sarpedon grated. "He must have realized the city had fallen and fled back to his Persian masters."

"Could Bessus have killed all these?" Cassandra asked.

"Why not?" Sarpedon picked up his wine cup and winced as he made to drink.

Telamon beckoned to the captain of the scouts. They left the loom room. Once they were in the courtyard, Telamon seized the man's arm. "Captain, you found Gentius asleep in the bed?"

"He's the witless one? Oh yes, as I said, snoring like a pig."

"And the other one?"

"Bound hand and foot, his door half open, cords tight around his wrists and ankles."

Telamon stared across at the corpse of the kitchen girl, still lying in a pool of blood. He closed his eyes and breathed in deeply. He hadn't expected this. He had thought he would find the villa as he had left it, with the miscreants fled. But this? He turned back to the captain.

"Have the corpses collected. You'll find wood. The day will soon become hot. They must be burnt. Oh" – he gestured at him to come closer – "you are a captain of scouts, yes?"

"Best in the army, sir."

"You have men who can pick up tracks? The man who fled, Bessus, would not use the roads, but ride out across the grasslands. Could your men find his tracks, follow him?"

"Can a bird fly?" The captain grinned. "Two of my lads will tell you if a snail has left this place, never mind a horse and rider."

"Tell them," Telamon said, "that if they discover something surprising – do you understand that? Something surprising – they'll have a silver piece each."

"I'd best go with them, then, sir."

"In which case, it will be three silver pieces," Telamon replied.

He returned to the loom room. Gentius had crossed his arms, head down, muttering to himself. Sarpedon was eating. Every so often he'd shake his head, as if trying to free himself from the pain.

"You can rest here for a while," Telamon announced. "More food will be brought once we have the kitchens ready. If you have to relieve yourself, the guards outside will accompany you." He gestured at Cassandra to join him.

"What's happened?" she asked, once they were outside the door.

"I don't know." Telamon slipped the ring off his finger and studied the insignia of Aesculapius. He winked at Cassandra. "You've seen the symptoms. Let's find the cause!"

Telamon began a search of the villa: the gallery, the chambers, the cellars, the storerooms and the gardens outside. The morning passed. The scouts collected the corpses together, and some wood, kindling and oil. Telamon watched as men and women he had lived with were consumed in sheets of flame.

"This place stinks of death!" Cassandra declared. "I am not going back into that house!"

Telamon joined her in the small flowery arbour. Now and again the scouts came over to see that all was well, or share out the food and wine they had found. The day drew on. The sun became too strong, so they moved to sit in the shade of a sycamore tree: they were resting there when the captain of the scouts returned. He crouched before Telamon and told him what he had found.

"Very strange, isn't it, sir?"

"Go back out again." Telamon opened his purse and dropped three silver coins into the man's calloused hand. "Go back and see if you can find him. There'll be three more of these to share out."

Once the captain had left, Cassandra began to question him. Telamon shook his head, finger to his lips. "Let's wait and see," he murmured, leaning back on the grass. "There's no hurry, and I am so weary."

Telamon forced himself to relax, letting his legs and arms jerk, his mind drift. Thoughts came and went. The hideous battle before the walls of Halicarnassus; the blood and horror in that place of slaughter; the silent corpses; Gentius acting witless; Sarpedon nursing his injuries. He was shaken awake by the captain of the guard.

"We've found him, sir."

"The rest don't know?" Telamon asked, sitting up. "You're sure no one knows?"

"Only me, you, and two of my lads."

"Good!" Telamon breathed. "Captain, when this is all over, I will tell you the full story, but now I am going to tell someone else the truth."

Sarpedon and Gentius were sunning themselves in the court-yard. Telamon ordered them to return to the loom room. Both men seemed stronger, more alert. Telamon waited until they took their seats. The captain of the scouts sat between them while some of his men, at Telamon's orders, lounged against the walls, curious at what was about to happen: they'd chattered among themselves about this mysterious villa with its silent corpses, and this physician so interested in the rider who had fled.

"Why are we here?" Sarpedon demanded. Cassandra noticed that he had become more alert, anxious.

"I am going to tell you a story," Telamon replied, "about the city of Halicarnassus. Its old ruler Pixadorus drove out his sister, Queen Ada, who went to shelter in the fortress of Alinde high in the mountains. She became an exile. No one really bothered about her. Nothing interesting happened to her except that the famous architect, the one responsible for the fortifications of Halicarnassus, gave her a strange document which later became known as the Pythian Manuscript. Pythias was mischievous, and all sorts of wonderful stories began to grow up around his manuscript. That it contained a detailed report on a serious weakness in the fortifications he had constructed, as well as where he had buried his considerable treasure. In truth, the Pythian Manuscript was merely a copy of a letter sent to Philip of Macedon."

Sarpedon moved to face Telamon squarely, playing with his leather wrist-guard.

"Now everyone became interested in the Pythian Manuscript, particularly the rulers of Persia when they came to realize that Macedon was about to invade their western provinces. Halicarnassus is the greatest harbour in the Aegean . . ."

"So they obtained copies of the Pythian Manuscript?" Sarpedon finished the sentence. "What has that to do with me?"

"After the battle of the Granicus" – Telamon held Sarpedon's gaze – "Queen Ada decided it was time to have the manuscript translated. She'd gathered about herself a number of adventurers, wanderers, men like yourself, Sarpedon, mercenaries who had sold their skills or their swords. What Queen Ada didn't know was that one of these hired scribes, Pamenes, was in fact a high-ranking Persian spy, a magus, a priest, who probably worked for the Lord Mithra himself: a scribe of great skill, versed in translating secret codes and ciphers. Pamenes began his work with Solan, Bessus and their guardian, you, Sarpedon, the Spartan mercenary. Queen Ada may have had her suspicions, but decided to keep an eye on this select group by putting in her own spy, the priest Cherolos."

"I know that," Sarpedon smirked. "Cherolos was a snooper."

"Yes, and not a very good one," Telamon retorted. "What Queen Ada didn't realize was that you, Sarpedon, had inveigled the rest into your own secret conspiracy. You weren't really concerned about the defences of Halicarnassus. What did it matter to you, Solan, or Bessus, who ruled that city?"

"Me?" Sarpedon broke in. "Are you accusing me?"

"No, I am proving it," Telamon retorted. "Your real concern was old Pythias's treasure: to be more precise, this house, the Villa of Cybele where Pythias once lived. Solan would know that, and that the villa had been sold, and would deduce that if Pythias buried his treasure anywhere, it would be here, not in the city of Halicarnassus." Telamon shrugged. "Solan must have moved heaven and earth to make sure this villa became the headquarters where he and his scribes could work. All of you would have persuaded Queen Ada that it was essential for you to follow the Macedonian army. She, of course, would have gladly agreed, as would our king. After all, Queen Ada was going to get her city back, and you would be watched by the Macedonians, not to mention her own spy Cherolos. I am right, am I not?"

Sarpedon, not a whit disturbed, nodded slowly.

"I could send messengers to Queen Ada," Telamon continued. "I am sure she will have copies of the warrants authorizing Solan to seize this house." He paused.

Gentius was also listening intently. Now and again he would raise his head or look at the ceiling, as if these sharp words were dispelling the fog of grief which clouded his soul.

"Anyway, you all arrived in the Villa of Cybele," Telamon continued. "A happy little company, but there was a fly in the ointment. Pamenes! He kept to himself, but Solan, Bessus and you, Sarpedon, realized he was making excellent progress. I also suspect that, by then, you recognized Pamenes to be what he really was, a Persian spy. You also discovered how he communicated with his masters in Halicarnassus and elsewhere, the scytale method."

"The what?" Sarpedon demanded.

"Oh come, come," Telamon smiled. "The scytale method, used by Spartan commanders to send messages to each other. You use a

279

pole about a yard long, wrap a parchment round it, write your message on it then unroll it. Unless you know exactly what's happening and have an identical pole, all you see is a parchment with strange markings on it."

Sarpedon's hand strayed to a platter and the knife resting on it, but the captain of scouts leaned forward and snatched this up. Sarpedon smiled to himself.

"You must have watched Pamenes," Telamon continued, "like a cat does a mousehole. Sooner or later he would translate the Pythian Manuscript and flee. You couldn't have that. You had to stay here to continue your search for the old architect's treasure. Moreover, Pamenes might have found something interesting to help you in your searches. Now, on the evening before he was killed" – Telamon pointed to Gentius – "I know, through him, that Pamenes was about to flee. More importantly, so did you. Early that morning, while you were supposedly busy in the garden, Solan and Bessus visited Pamenes in his chamber. They lured him to the window, or perhaps he was already there with his bird seed, looking for his friends the pigeons. Pamenes was arrogant. He had the measure of Solan and Bessus. He had nothing to fear. He had found the key to the Pythian Manuscript, and would flee before Alexander and the Macedonian army arrived. So, he's standing at that window. You, Sarpedon, are in the garden below keeping watch: Solan and Bessus, who've quietly bolted the door behind them, push him out. They will later claim they heard no noise, no shout, no scream. Of course Gentius, rehearsing his lines to the clash of cymbals, provided further protection. You then ran over very quickly to make sure he was dead and give your fellow conspirators the signal that all was well. In the meantime, they ransacked Pamenes's chamber and took away any interesting documents . . ."

"But the chamber was locked!" Gentius interrupted. "I remember, the chamber was locked!"

"No, it remained open," Telamon replied. "Bessus would later fabricate the story that he heard someone moving inside: that was to heighten suspicion. He also knew Cherolos had tried to meet Pamenes, so he mentioned footsteps to turn this suspicion into blame."

"And it was true." Cassandra spoke up. "Cherolos *did* go looking for Pamenes, but on the two occasions he visited that chamber, the scribe was already dead, his body sprawled beneath the window."

"Cherolos couldn't really care less about Pamenes," Telamon continued. "He was just trying to gather information for his royal mistress. He seized the packed saddlebags and took them out, quietly promising himself to return them at an appropriate time. Of course" – Telamon spread his hands – "when Pamenes's corpse was discovered, Cherolos decided to hide the bags out in the garden: he found very little in them. Solan and Bessus had taken what was important."

Sarpedon gave a big sigh and made to rise, but the captain of the scouts quickly drew his sword and pressed the flat against the Spartan's neck. The other scouts shifted, hands falling to the hilts of their swords.

"I would sit still if I were you," Telamon murmured. "Sarpedon, you are going nowhere except back to that fateful morning. You now had Pamenes's secret journal, which, I suspect, Solan threw down to you from the window. You hid that in the garden, that's how your hands were cut. You wrapped it in a cloth and buried it beneath a prickly rose bush. You then came running across to me and Cassandra to have these cuts tended. We would certainly remember that when Pamenes was killed, Sarpedon was either busy gardening or having his hands bandaged, a small price to pay for what you had achieved."

"You have no proof!" Sarpedon's face had turned ugly. As if to remind Telamon of his own injury, he nursed the side of his head.

"I now know Pamenes was leaving." Telamon used his fingers to emphasize each point. "That was why he was wearing his sandals – he usually stayed barefooted in his chamber. His saddlebags were packed. He'd also had a love tryst with the lady Demerata. She sensed he was going."

The mention of his wife sent Gentius into another bout of weeping.

"Solan and Bessus would have looked through Pamenes's manuscripts very quickly, and made a fair copy. Or it could have been done by you, Sarpedon. You are not the illiterate you pretend to be. You know poetry. You know that your namesake was the son of Zeus and fought at Troy. But now we come to the interesting part . . ."

Telamon rose and went to a side table: he poured himself and Cassandra goblets of water from the pitcher and brought the cups back.

"If Pamenes worked for the Persians, you, Sarpedon, worked for Memnon the Rhodian renegade, Commander-in-Chief at Halicarnassus. Did you meet him? I suspect you did." Telamon didn't wait for an answer. "You had offered to be his spy."

"But according to you," Sarpedon shouted, "the Persians already had one, Pamenes!"

"I know Greeks and Persians," Telamon replied. "Pamenes would work for the Lord Mithra. Orontobates may have known about him, but Memnon wouldn't resist the opportunity of having his own spy: someone who might be able to deliver Alexander the King into his hands. You really don't care about Memnon or Halicarnassus. You wanted gold and silver, and Memnon would pay. Now" – Telamon ran his finger round the rim of the goblet – "thanks to you and Pamenes, the Villa of Cybele is closely watched. Indeed, we all knew it was, and how Pamenes sent his messages into the city – a roll of parchment left beneath this tree, rock or bush. You followed the same method. Early on the day Pamenes died, you informed your new masters of the news that Pamenes's manuscripts would be found on his corpse, while Alexander would be arriving at the Villa of Cybele protected only by a light force."

"Why should I do that?" Sarpedon sneered.

"Oh, you had to: Solan and Bessus would agree with you." Telamon sipped from his cup. "You had to reassure your masters in Halicarnassus that, despite Pamenes's death, his good work would continue."

"But," Gentius scratched his head, "wouldn't they be angry that their spy had been killed? A sacred priest, a magus?"

"Of course. Sarpedon knows the Persians: if possible, they'd recover Pamenes's corpse. That's why he left the manuscript with it

282

after it was laid out under its sheet in the outhouse. I don't know how Sarpedon portrayed Pamenes's death – possibly an accident, or murder by Alexander's agents. That could be Cherolos, me, or even you, Gentius. A very clever, subtle ploy. Solan, Bessus and Sarpedon have removed a rival and stolen his knowledge. At the same time, Pamenes is out of the way but you, Sarpedon, have the full attention of his masters in Halicarnassus. Solan and Bessus concentrate on translating the Pythian Manuscript while you, pretending to be a gardener, search the grounds of the villa looking for Pythias's treasure. The others eventually joined you. I noticed how, as the days passed, Solan and Bessus continued their studies not so much in their chambers as outside. Why was that, Sarpedon? Had Solan already searched the house from top to bottom and found nothing? Is that why he hired the servants and gave them clear instructions not to wander upstairs? He didn't want some quick-witted, sharp-eyed scullion or kitchen maid to realize what was happening."

"But you said Cherolos was watching them?" Gentius asked.

"I suppose, like me," Telamon smiled back, "Cherolos wasn't a very good spy. You can walk around the house pretending to admire it, be lost, or looking for something. Our conspirators soon reached one conclusion. If Pythias had hidden his treasure, it certainly wasn't in the villa itself, but somewhere in the grounds."

"You haven't answered Gentius's question!" Sarpedon declared hotly. "When we tried to enter Pamenes's chamber, the door was bolted, and there was no ladder . . ." He bit his lip.

"What were you going to add?" Telamon asked. "There was no ladder for you to climb up and bolt the door and so deepen the mystery? No." Telamon put out a hand. "After Solan and Bessus left, Cherolos came along. Bessus heard him, and he mentioned that to me to divert suspicion to the priest. After your hands had been bandaged, Sarpedon, you were wearing gloves. You took one of those vine poles – they are long enough to reach Pamenes's chamber. You are a skilled soldier, a resourceful fighter. You climbed that pole as nimbly as a monkey, entered Pamenes's chamber, checked all was well, locked and bolted the door and came down again."

"I could have been seen," Sarpedon replied.

"I doubt it. I recall Bessus coming out to the garden to summon us in for the meeting. He'd first go and stand guard while you climbed up and down." Telamon shrugged. "The shortest span possible. You throw the pole into the bushes. Bessus enters the house, and you join us, acting the innocent. After that meeting, you and your conspirators went through Pamenes's manuscript to discover what you could. Using the scytale method, you left a message for the courier, some peasant or a wandering tinker. Pamenes's death was made to look like a possible accident. You had what you wanted, enough to keep your masters in Halicarnassus happy. You told them about the king's imminent arrival here, the token force he would bring with him. Memnon would probably know about that from his own spies. You really wanted him to attack the villa and collect the information you had furnished." Telamon tapped the table top. "I suppose they left their reward somewhere?"

"What reward?" Sarpedon blustered.

"Gold, left in the agreed place, for you to share out with the rest. Everything was arranged. Of course you didn't want the attack to be too successful. You, or one of your conspirators, lit a lantern and placed it in the window to guide the Persians in. To prove how innocent you were, you decided to take the night air with that kitchen girl. Once again you were defending your own position. If you were outside, then it couldn't be Sarpedon holding a lantern at the window. You arranged for the girl to notice it as well. You also acted the hero, being the first to raise the alarm. You wanted to make sure that the Persians were successful, but not too much so: a night attack which could be driven off while you depicted yourself as the ever-faithful guard. The Persians came. They knew where to find Pamenes's corpse. They removed it and the documents hidden on him. They would also leave the agreed payment. You should have been pleased, Sarpedon, but you are too clever. The kitchen girl? She wasn't as dull-witted as you thought. Did she begin to reflect and ask why you took her out on that particular evening? Did she really see the lantern, or did you have to point it out to her?"

Sarpedon's face had lost its air of surly defiance: his courage began to ebb, his nervousness appear. Gentius abruptly stood up.

"I don't feel well." He clutched his stomach. "I had no part in this."

Telamon gestured at one of the scouts, who grasped the actor by the arm and pushed him out of the room.

"Stay guard over him!" Telamon called. He gazed around at the other scouts. Most of them were Macedonians, intrigued by this war of words. The captain had taken an obvious dislike to Sarpedon, while the rest of his men now understood they were dealing with a man who had tried to betray, even kill, their precious king.

"You murdered that poor girl," Telamon declared. "You may not have been in the kitchen, but Bessus or Solan exchanged a good piece of cheese with a tainted one. You told her to bring it into the garden for you. You knew she liked cheese, she wouldn't be able to resist it. Once again you diverted suspicion – you went nowhere near the kitchen, and the poison was apparently meant for you. She had to die to stop her questioning, and her father suffered a similar fate, just in case she'd confided in him. You work in the garden. You could gather snakes into a sack and put them in a jar of eels." He paused. "Or my chamber."

Sarpedon laced his fingers together: he had a hunted look. His eyes strayed to the door.

"I had to die, didn't I?" Telamon persisted. "Whose idea was it? Solan, Bessus, yourself? Fearful that I might be picking up the loose threads Pamenes had dropped?" Telamon sipped at his cup. "You tried again in the orchard, you or one of your fellow conspirators, only to be frustrated by Demerata's mysterious death. You hoped Cherolos would be blamed: he worshipped the goddess Meretseger and was skilled in dealing with snakes. You killed that helpless cat so we'd think it was part of some macabre sacrifice by Cherolos to his Egyptian goddess. You had to continue your chosen role of being the faithful guard . . ."

"I helped the king at the cove of Hera!" Sarpedon shouted.

"I suspect Alexander already knew what to do with his ships. It was in your interests to help him. You wanted the siege to continue until you had finished your search here. You did a similar favour for your own master Memnon and the Persians at Halicarnassus. You lured that Cretan archer out onto the heathlands. What with, food or wine, or were you just waiting for him? A swift blow to the back of the head: you stripped his corpse and took his bow and quiver. That night, using the scytale method, you fastened a piece of parchment to one of those long arrows. You are an archer, Sarpedon. You crept near the walls and loosed your message telling Memnon about those flat-topped sheds Alexander was going to use to fill the ditch." Telamon shrugged. "Memnon would welcome such news. Afterwards you returned with me to the villa. You tried to kill me, failed, but you must have been delighted when I left with Hephaestion. That's when you found the treasure. You sent the kitchen boy up to the camp to discover that Halicarnassus was about to fall. You and your fellow conspirators had your plunder, so it was time to celebrate and leave. Only you'd planned differently." Telamon rose to his feet and walked around the table. "I've met men like you, Sarpedon, brave as panthers, ruthless, tough and hard, enduring as the desert sun. You enjoy danger and love the excitement of battle. You weren't going to share the plunder of your victory, so you murdered everybody here."

"I had a blow to my head. I was bound. Your own captain said this."

Telamon leaned over, his face only a few inches from Sarpedon. "A self-inflicted blow, cuts and bruises. For a hardy man like yourself, Sarpedon, what a small price to pay for a treasure trove! You tied your ankles yourself, and wrapped the ropes around your wrists. Anyone would think they were tied securely, especially when the cords were slit in a darkened chamber. I would like to examine those cords, though I am sure you've thrown them away. There wouldn't be any trace of a knot."

"And if there was another killer?" the captain now intervened. "Why didn't he slay you like he did the rest?"

"A good question," Telamon replied. "Bessus was to be portrayed as the assassin. Sarpedon could explain it away. Perhaps Bessus panicked? Perhaps he felt friendship for Sarpedon, as he did

286

for Gentius – that's why the actor was also left alive: it was to divert and dull suspicion. Gentius, of course, was in a wine-drenched sleep."

Sarpedon tried to jump to his feet, only to be restrained by the captain of the scouts. "And where is Bessus?" he yelled.

"Oh, we found his corpse."

"You couldn't . . ." Sarpedon closed his eyes.

"Oh, but we did," the captain intervened. "I and my men can track snails. We can tell you what birds have pecked the soil. We found the tracks of a horse which had recently left by a rear gate. We thought it was surprising, the tracks weren't as deep as they should have been if a rider had been on its back. We found the horse grazing miles away. We also discovered the tracks of a man walking, carrying a heavy burden. We dug Bessus out of his shallow grave: he had his throat cut from ear to ear, mouth and eyes filled with dirt."

"So you see." Telamon sat on the bench vacated by Gentius. "Who else is there, Sarpedon? Not the actor? He's so witless and full of stale wine he'd find it difficult to climb stairs, never mind pull a bow. That leaves Sarpedon the Spartan, the traitor, spy and assassin. The cunning man who hoped to bide his time and slip away."

Sarpedon's face remained immobile. Only a flicker of the eye and a bead of sweat coursing down his cheek betrayed his agitation.

"The king will crucify you," Telamon murmured. "You might take days, even weeks, to die."

"No mercy?" Sarpedon croaked.

"One mercy," Telamon replied, steeling himself against this assassin who had slain and slain again without a moment's thought. "You will not need Pythias's treasure. Where is it?"

Sarpedon put his hands over his eyes. "We found it in the well." He took his hands away. "You'll find footholds down the side, iron rungs. Just above the waterline there's a ledge. It holds a bronze-embossed coffer full of golden darics from Persia, and freshly minted silver from Macedon."

"And my allegations?" Telamon asked.

"Pamenes's death is as you describe. We thought it would be

287

taken as an accident. I knew he was a spy. I entered Halicarnassus and offered my services to Memnon. He said he would pay, once I had proved my good faith. But what does it matter?" Sarpedon sighed, eyes crinkling in amusement. "A game of chance, isn't it, physician? Everything is as you say. I gambled and I lost. I broke the first rule. I became greedy. You'll grant me a quick death?"

Telamon gestured at the captain of the scouts. "Bring up the treasure!"

The captain ordered two of his men to go to the well. Telamon returned to his seat beside Cassandra. Outside in the corridor Gentius let out a gentle wail. A short time later, the soldiers returned and placed the dirt-encrusted coffer on the table. Telamon tipped back the lid. Cassandra gasped at the gold and silver winking in the light. Telamon nodded at the captain.

"Make it quick!"

Orders were shouted. Sarpedon, unresisting, was bundled from the room. Telamon heard a piece of wood being thrown down onto the cobbles in the courtyard outside. A man shouted. Sarpedon replied, then there was silence broken by a dull thud. Telamon closed his eyes. The captain of the scouts swaggered back in, the edge of his sword laced with blood.

"Take the corpse!" Telamon ordered. "Have it burnt with the rest. Put the head in a basket and send it to the king. Cassandra, find me some sealing wax and pieces of strong twine." He tapped the coffer. "The king will be pleased."

The loom room emptied. Telamon put his arms on the table and stared around this chamber, now so quiet and calm. Would the ghosts throng here from the gates of Hell? Would they follow the army? Would Alexander's march be flanked by a growing horde of those who had died, been killed, caught up in the bloody mayhem of his conquests?

288

Author's Note

—————◦◦◦◦—————

Alexander's siege of Halicarnassus in the late summer of
334 BC is as described in this novel. Some historians claim
the city fell in days rather than weeks, and that the fighting on
both sides was ferocious and bloodthirsty. Memnon, Ephialtes and
Orontobates were wily, cunning commanders: they truly hoped
Alexander would shatter his armies against the soaring walls of
Halicarnassus, that he would never take the city or seize its deep-
water port. Alexander did ride out to view the fortifications and
had to retreat hurriedly. He fully expected to seize the port of
Myndus and was cleverly frustrated. Apparently he kept looking
for a weakness in the defences of Halicarnassus, and regularly
moved his siege equipment from place to place. He also had to
face sudden sorties by Memnon, who inflicted considerable losses
on the Macedonian army. The last great fight before the walls at
night is vividly described by the primary sources. When Alexander did force an entry, he found the city had been put to the
torch.

Alexander's relationship with Queen Ada is faithfully reflected
here, so I doubt if he was responsible for the fire which
devastated her city. I suspect this started when the Persians
withdrew to the citadels in the harbour. Indeed, the way the
siege was brought to an abrupt end, the sudden sorties by
Memnon, as well as the fire which broke out just before
Alexander entered the city, are the sources for my story. Memnon and Ephialtes knew better than to attack Alexander out in
the open, yet they both broke their own sacred rule at Halicarnassus and Ephialtes paid for it with his life. On a number of
occasions, if it hadn't been for Alexander's Old Guard, the

Macedonian force would have been massacred. The only explanation for Memnon's tactics, the sudden fall of the city and the consequent fire, is that Alexander had some sort of "fifth column" in Halicarnassus which Memnon and Ephialtes found impossible to control. They had to deal with the external enemy before they could resolve the problem of the enemy within. According to all military theories, Memnon and Ephialtes should never have opened the gates of Halicarnassus and launched such a desperate counter-attack. The most suitable modern analogy is a tank crew leaving their vehicle to fight on foot with side-arms: the only explanation for such a move would be that something had gone terribly wrong in the tank. The siege was as ferocious as I have described, while the exploits of the two drunken Macedonians who began a night battle out of sheer bravado, as well as the effects of alcohol, is faithfully recorded by Arrian and others.

The medical theories and treatment mentioned in this novel are based on extracts from Hippocrates of Cos's notebooks, as well as other primary sources. Greek physicians may not have understood the full complexity of the human body, but they were keen observers of it. Physicians such as Telamon did travel the known world acquiring knowledge from different sources: Telamon, in fact, is based on one of Alexander's physicians, Philip.

Of course the political axiom that where there's a power struggle, intrigue flourishes, spies and assassins move from camp to camp, and the use of ciphers and secret messages proliferates is well attested by primary sources. The scytale method is described by Thucydides, Plutarch and Xenephon, whilst in his, *On the Defence Of Fortified Places* Aeneas the Tactician devotes an entire chapter to cryptology. The arrangement of the alphabet in a square, 5 down 5 across, is a basis for modern cryptology. However, it is important to recognize that this "chequerboard" system is called the Polybius Square, after the Greek writer Polybius who mentions it in Chapter 10 of his *Histories*.

Alexander is a chameleon-like figure. He was a consummate actor who deliberately misled both his own court and the enemy. He did this at the Granicus, and again in his brilliant siege of

Halicarnassus. One of Hegel's great figures of history, Alexander was a shooting star whose life and exploits still fascinate us thousands of years after his death. He was deeply influenced by his parents: his filial relationship can be succinctly described as one of love and hate. He adored both Philip and Olympias, but their constant feuding wreaked its psychological effects on him. For most of his life, Alexander tried to escape from the shadow of his father and the brooding presence of his mother. Philip's attempt to marry off the weak-minded Arridhaeus, and Alexander's interference in such a scheme, is based on fact. It led to a violent altercation between Philip and Alexander, and fuelled Olympias's schemes to remove her former husband.

Alexander was a Greek who wanted to be a Persian, a man who believed in democracy but could be as autocratic as any emperor. He could be generous to a fault, forgiving and compassionate, but when his mood changed, could strike with a savage ruthlessness. The utter destruction of Thebes and Memnon's mercenaries at the Granicus illustrate Alexander's darker side. Sometimes he could be child-like, trusting and innocent, regarding life as one great adventure and military problems as puzzles to be resolved.

Alexander was a loyal friend and companion. Once he gave his word, he kept it. He had a passion for poetry and drama, particularly Homer's *Iliad* and, thanks to his tutor Aristotle, a deep interest in the natural world. He could be superstitious to the point of being neurotic but, as at Halicarnassus, could display a personal courage which is breathtaking. His genius as a general and leader have perhaps not been surpassed, yet he also had a vein of self-mockery, even humility. His drinking has been the subject of much debate. Some authorities, such as Curtius Rufus, claim he was a drunkard given to homicidal rages. Aristobulus, his close friend, quoted by Arrian, claims that Alexander's long drinking sessions arose not so much because of his love of wine, but out of comradeship for his friends. Alexander was certainly a consummate actor: he delighted in misleading both friend and foe, and often used his banquets to convey whatever message he wanted. He did suffer panic attacks, but these were probably the fears of childhood, for his personal courage is breathtaking. He loved to tease and sometimes went too far, particularly with Ptolemy and Cleitus. Whatever, Alexander had his faults and failings, and wine brought these out! Perhaps that explains his continued fascination for us – not just his great victories and exploits, but his personality, which, at times, could sum up the best and worst in humanity.

Paul C. Doherty